DARK
HARVEST

DARK HARVEST

Cat Sparks

NewCon Press
England

First edition, published in the UK July 2020
by NewCon Press

NCP 241 (hardback)
NCP 242 (softback)

10 9 8 7 6 5 4 3 2 1

ISBN:
(hardback) 978-1-912950-66-9
(softback) 978-1-912950-67-6

Cover photograph and design by Cat Sparks; graffiti artist unknown.
Back cover layout by Ian Whates

Minor editorial meddling by Ian Whates
Interior layout by Ian Whates

CONTENTS

AUTHOR'S ACKNOWLEDGEMENTS

Ian & Helen Whates for publishing my stories and being, generally, damn fine company;

The Diogenes Club's Islington 'Petit Aubergine' chapter (they know who they are) for making me feel so welcome in their shadowy corner of the UK literary scene;

Isobelle, Jan & Adelaide for sharing their secret Santorini lair;

Charline & Dave for the Hong Kong back alley wall safari that resulted in this collection's cover image;

Tehani Croft for taking a chance on 'No Fat Chicks';

Dr Helen Merrick for encouraging me into the PhD which resulted in four of the stories in this book;

Dr Matt Chrulew for guiding me through & out the far end of the PhD wilderness;

Dr Sean Williams for decades of friendship and never being wrong about anything important;

And, as always, Robert Hood for putting up with all the things.

This book is dedicated to all those people fighting for better futures than the ones we are currently inflicting upon our world.

– Cat Sparks
Canberra, Australia,
February 2020

HOT RODS

The winds blow pretty regular across the dried-up lake. Traction's good — when luck's on your side, you can reach three hundred KPH or faster. Harper watches the hot rods race on thick white salt so pure and bright, the satellites use it for colour calibration.

Harper doesn't care about souped-up hot rods. Throwdowns, throwbacks, who can go the longest, fastest, hardest. But there's not much else to do in Terina Flat. She used to want to be a journalist, back when such professions still existed. Back when the paper that employed you didn't own you. Back when paper still meant paper. Back before the world clocked up past three degrees and warming. Back when everybody clamoured for Aussie coal and wheat and sheep. The sheep all died when the topsoil blew away in a dust cloud stretching almost five hundred K. Ships still come for the uranium. Other countries bring their own land with them. Embassies, fenced off and private, no one in or out without a pass. Cross the wire and they get to shoot you dead.

Harper thinks about her boyfriend Lachie Groom as the racers pick up speed. The future plans they've made. How they're gonna get the hell out of Terina, score work permits for Sydney or Melbourne. They say white maids and pool boys are in high demand in the walled suburban enclaves. Only, Lachie couldn't wait. Said they needed the money now, not later.

The racers purpose-build their dry lake cars from whatever they can scavenge. Racers used to care about the look; these days, it's all about the speed. There's nothing new, no paint to tart things up. No juice to run on except for home-strained bio-D. You need the real stuff for startup and shutdown. The racers pool their meagre cash, score black market diesel from a guy who hauls it in by camel train.

She can hear them coming before she sees them kicking up thick clouds of salty dust. The pitch drops dramatically as they pass; she takes a good long look as the cars smudge the horizon. Hot rods, classics and jalopies, streamliners and old belly tankers, all the side windows and gaps taped firm against the salt. It gets into everything: your clothes, your hair, your skin. Nothing lives or grows upon it. No plants, no insects, not a single blade of grass.

The short racecourse is five K long, the long one near to twelve. King of the short run is Cracker Jack, Lachie's cousin — plain Cracker to his mates. Obsessed with Dodges. Today's pride and joy is a 1968 Dodge Charger, manual, gauges still intact. Purpose-built for the super speedway, veteran of Daytona and Darlington.

He loves those cars like nothing else alive. Spends everything he has on keeping them moving. Harper has come to envy the racing regulars: Bing Reh, Lucas Clayton, Scarlett Ottico. Others. There's enough on the salt flats to keep them focused. Enough to get them out of bed in the morning.

Cracker nods at Harper; she throws him half a smile. Checks out his sweat-slicked, salt-encrusted arms. "I'll take you out there," he says, wiping his forehead. No need to specify *where* out there. She knows he's talking about the American Base – and Lachie.

She doesn't say no but he gauges her expression. "After sundown. The others don't have to know."

Unfortunately, in towns like Terina Flat, everyone knows everybody else's business.

"Was a stupid plan," she tells him. "We never should have…"

Cracker dusts salt flecks off his arms. "It was a fuckn' *awesome* plan. 'Bout time we got a look behind that wire. Found out what all the bullshit is about."

She shrugs. Her and Lachie's 'plan' had sounded simple. Just two people trying to keep in touch. Inching around a Base commandment that seems much harsher than it ought to be.

Cracker tried to talk Lachie out of taking the job at all. Too late. By then, Base medics had tested his blood, piss, and spit. He'd signed away his rights on the dotted line.

Lachie's been gone almost a week – the full week if you're counting Sunday, which Harper is because she's counting days, hours, minutes, seconds. Segregating Sundays is for the churchy folks. Whole town's riddled with true believers since the heavens clammed and the good soil blew away.

"'Sno trouble," says Cracker.

Harper shakes her head. Her eyes are focused on the middle distance. On Janny Christofides and that beat up 1968 Ford Mk 2 Cortina she loves more than most girls love their boyfriends. Janny's boyfriend's been on Base six months. She never wins a race but she keeps on trying.

Lachie's not so far away, just over the wire on newly foreign soil – American, although it could just as easily have been China or India or Russia.

Once past that wire, you don't come back until your contract's through. Money comes out, sometimes with a message. Stuff like *I miss you honey* and *I love you* and *tell grandma not to worry* and *its okay in here, the food is pretty good.*

The whole town knows about that food. They watch it trucking in by convoy, trucks long enough to fit houses in them. Refrigerated, loaded up with ice cream. Bananas from the Philippines, prime beef barely off the hoof. They stand there salivating in the hot red dust. Whole town's been on starvation rations since before the last town council meeting proper, the one where Mr Bryce got shot in the leg.

Crude jokes about Lachie circulate, not quite out of earshot. Somehow everyone found out about their ribbon secret. Voices carping on about how he's probably too distracted. Too busy shagging those hot chick Growler pilots. Boeing EA-18Gs — sleek and fast — have been burning across the blanched blue sky all week.

She ignores them, watches as a flecked and rusted 1936 Plymouth sedan tailgates a '58 Chevrolet Apache that once used to be red, apple rosy.

Cracker tries to shift the subject. Says those 18Gs were manufactured in Missouri — what's left of it. Mumbles something about future threats across the electromagnetic spectrum.

Harper recalls peculiar ads on free-to-air: The smiling lady saying shit like *Stealth is perishable; only a Growler provides full-spectrum protection.* Making *stealth* sound like a brand of sunscreen. What use could there be for *stealth* in Terina Flat? Nothing but more sky than anyone can handle laced with impotent wisps of cloud.

The racers pass, wave, whoop, and holler, some of the vehicles disintegrating in motion, belching smoke and farting acrid fumes. People used to think that only topless roadsters could hit top speeds. Back when Lake Gairdner was the only lake to race on. Back before the Bases and the droughts. Back before a lot of things that changed this country into someplace you'd barely recognise.

Harper turns her back on them all and starts walking toward home.

Cracker runs to catch up with her. "Those guys don't mean nothing by it. Half of 'em's gonna be taking Base contracts themselves."

She keeps walking.

"Wanna ride?"

"Nope."

"You really gonna hoof it all the way?"

She nods. Walking gives her time to think. Time to run through all the reasons she's not going back to the Base. Not tonight — or any other night.

Not even with Cracker, who she trusts more than she's ever trusted anyone aside from Lachie.

Eventually, the salty crunch gives way to russet dirt. Her boots disturb the road's powdery dust. No salt here, just brown on brown. Crooked fence posts, barbed wire curling in the sun.

Not everything is dead or dying. She admires the millet, still holding its own, but the sorghum fields have seen far better days. There used to be rice, but rice needs irrigation, and for irrigation, you need rain. No decent rainfall three years running, which is how come council got desperate enough to call in a priest-of-the-air. Prayer vigils week in, week out have altered nothing.

Apparently, a flying priest worked miracles in Trundle, scoring them forty millimetres three days in a row. Not just hearsay; plenty of Terina locals were present when the heavens opened. Plastic buckets clutched against their chests, praising Jesus and the man in the yellow Cessna.

When the downpour ceased, a flock of black-and-white banded birds descended. Whole sky was thick with them. Stilts, reportedly confused, as if they had been expecting something other than Trundle mud at the end of their epic journey.

A year on now and prayer vigils have all dried up. Terina passed the hat around, everybody kicking in what they can scrounge.

Harper's toes are blistered and her shirt is soaked with sweat. Things come in threes – or so folks say. Three days of rain for Trundle in a row. Three nights was how long Lachie managed to tie a bit of ribbon to the fence. Low so the Hellfighter spotlights wouldn't catch it. Nothing fancy. No messages attached. But from the fourth night onwards, there was no ribbon. Nothing.

Lachie is as close to family as she has. Dad's long gone; there's only her and Mum. Mum was all for him taking that contract job.

Dusk is falling by time she makes it back. Still hot but tempered by gentle breaths of wind. A warm glow pulsing from the big revival tent. She knows her mother will be in there alongside all the other mothers. She knows she ought to go inside and grab a bite to eat if nothing else.

Beyond the fraying canvas flap lies a warm enveloping glow; a mix of lantern light and tallow candle. Town still has plenty of functioning generators but they made a lot of smoke and noise.

The overpowering tang of sweat mixed in with cloying, cheap perfume. Still hot long after the sun's gone down, women fanning their necks with outdated mail order catalogues. Out of their farming duds and all frocked up, like Sunday church, not plain old Thursday evening. Scones and sticky Anzac biscuits piled high on trestle tables. Offerings. Harper's stomach grumbles at the sight.

Reg Clayton has the microphone. He's telling some story she's sure she's heard before about nitrogen and ploughing rotted legumes.

Her mother claps and cheers from second row. Dry dirt has got inside her head. Made her barking mad as all the others. Farmers with their fallow stony fields, rusted-up tractors, and heat-split butyl tires. All praying for the rains to come.

The big tent puts some hope back in the air – Harper gives it that much credit even if she doesn't buy their Jesus bullshit. Jesus isn't coming and he isn't bringing rain. Jesus and his pantheon of angels have snubbed their town before moving on to bigger, better things.

She lets the tent flap fall again before anyone catches sight of her. Not everyone in the tent is old, but most of them are. Old enough to believe in miracles. To believe that flying in some Jesus freak from Parkes might make it rain.

When the singing starts, it's sudden as a thunderclap.

When peace like a river,
attendeth my way,
When sorrows like sea billows roll...

Three years have passed since any of them clapped eyes on the dirty trickle that was once the proud Killara river. Sea billows – whatever the hell they are, seem more than a million miles from Terina Flat.

Harper jumps when a firm hand presses upon her shoulder. It's only Cracker and he jumps back in response.

"Didn't mean to startle ya. Coming out to Base with me or what?"

She shies away from the tent flap, away from the candied light. He lopes after her like a giant puppy.

"Not going back out there again," she stops and says at last. "What would be the point of it? There's nothing to see but wire and towers – and what if we get caught? You know what they say happens to trespassers. Those two guys from Griffith that –"

"Those two bastards buggered off to Sydney."

"Cracker, nobody knows what happened to those guys."

The swell of hymns gets louder, the voices enunciating clearly.

He sends the snow in winter,

The warmth to swell the grain,
The breezes and the sunshine,
And soft, refreshing rain.

Cracker grunts at the mention of snow. "Not bloody lately, he doesn't."

Harper almost smiles.

The two of them bolt when the tent flap flies open, taking cover behind the shadowy row of trucks and cars that reek of sour corn pulp and rancid vegetable oil. Cracker barely spares the cars a glance. He has no interest in vehicles whose sole purpose is to ferry occupants from A to B.

"Yer mum in with that lot?" he asks.

"Yup."

"Mine too."

She nods. All the mums and dads are in the tent, banging tambourines and clapping hands. All the folks who yell at the younger ones for frittering their time and cash on hot rods.

They wait until the coast is clear, then climb the tufty knob of ground that offers a clear view across the dried-up river. All the way to the American Base. Harper can't see that riverbed without picturing Lachie, boasting about the time he and his brother dug a rust-red 1936 Ford Model 48 up out of the silt. How they had to scrape out twenty-six inches of dirt from firewall to tailpan.

The Base has a glow to it, a greeny-ochre luminescence. The kind of colour mostly seen in long-exposure borealis photos.

Behind that wire and the machine gun–guarded towers lies a big rectangular grid: a forty-eight-element high-frequency antenna array. Beyond it stands a power generation building, imaging riometer, and a flat-roofed operations centre built of cinder blocks. They all know this; it's no kind of secret. Base PR admits to investigating the potential for developing ionospheric enhancement technology for radio communications and surveillance. It supports a cluster of ELF wave transmitters slamming 3.6 million watts up at the ionosphere. There have been whispers of other things such as successful moon-bounce experiments – whatever that means. New kinds of weapons for new kinds of war, still in experimental phases. What weapons and what war are never specified.

The tent hymns fade, absorbed by other forms of background noise. Cracker stuffs his hands into his pockets, closes his eyes, as if feeling the warm breeze on his face. Harper stops noticing him, her attention drawn to the Base. She points, wordlessly.

Above it, the sky has shifted burgundy, like dried blood. Lightning bolts, ramrod straight – not jagged, strike the ground, then thicken, changing colour, and slowly fade.

"What the…"

"Did you just see that?"

She's fidgeting, running her thumb along the friendship bracelet knotted on her right wrist. Three blue ribbons tightly braided. Three wishes for bringing her Lachie safe back home.

The plane appears like a lonesome dove, winging its way to Terina Flat, bringing with it salvation in the form of a priest decked out like Elvis Presley. Elvises aren't unusual in these parts, what with Terina being so close to Parkes and its famous Elvis festival. Back in January, fifty thousand tourists flooded in to celebrate the King's hundredth birthday.

Harper has never seen one of them up close. The Elvis who lands on the blistered tarmac is dusty and kind of faded. Paunchy, but not in the proper Elvis way. A golden cross hangs around his neck. A knife tucked into his boot if he's smart. A pistol hooked through his belt if he's even smarter.

Town folk skip right past the rhinestones and move straight to calling him Father. Press around him like bleating sheep. Harper doesn't plan on making contact. She cringes as the shrivelled biddies primp and fuss and preen. Flirting with the sly old dog, promising him pumpkin scones and carrot cake – all chokos with artificial flavour added, if truth be known, although you won't catch any of them admitting such a thing. Lamington cakes run soft and gooey from the broiling sun. Local piss-weak beer to wash it down with.

The Elvis plane, though, that's something else. An ancient Beech A60 Duke, knocked up and turbocharged – Cracker had been mouthing off about that plane before the sunlight hit its yellow sides, planes being the one thing capable of distracting him from Dodges.

Harper waits until the fuss dies down. Elvis shoos his flock away from the landing strip towards the revival tent. Promises to be joining them just as soon as he's checked his luggage. Once the parents and grandparents have moved off, small children run to place their grubby palms on the fuselage.

"Piss off, you little buggers," spits Darryl Quiggen, charged with checking the battered old bird over, hand-rolled cigarette dangling from his pinched white lips. Used to be some kind of expert once. The tang of avgas hangs in the air – the good stuff, not the crap distilled from corn.

Quiggen pays Harper no attention. He's never had much luck with women, seems to find it preferable to pretend they don't exist. She makes sure she's out of his line of sight, inching as close as she can get away with to examine the peculiar assortment of religious symbols painted across the plane's canary yellow casing.

Jesus – rendered clear as day, hands pressed together in prayer. Surrounding his head, a thick halo of icons: an egg with a cross, a flaming heart with barbed wire wrapped across its middle. A snake and an anchor. Some poorly rendered birds. A hand with an eye set into its palm. A star made of two triangles. A crescent moon and a tiny little star. Some writing that looks like it might be Hindu – not that she'd know a Hindu from a Sikh.

There's something strange underneath the wings. Bulging clusters of attachments reminiscent of wasp nests. She steps up closer but she isn't game to touch. Up closer still, she can see the welds and other bodged repairs beneath paint blisters. Paint costs a fortune. There must be something well worth hiding under there.

She peers in through the grimy windows until Quiggen shoos her off. The rear cabin's stuffed with all kinds of junk. Maybe Elvis sleeps in it.

The plane serves well as a distraction. She's trying not to think about the Base's empty wire, the thick red lightning, and the sickly green light rippling over everything the night before. The Base is locked down, nothing unauthorised in or out – not even bits of ribbon tied to wire. 'Earn good money' was what they said, money they were all in need of. They were desperate or curious, all the ones that took up contract offers. Three months on. No worries. She'll be right. But how often three months extended to six or twelve? How often at the end of it, they climbed into one of those Blackhawks and disappeared?

She's sheltering beneath the concrete shade of what remains of a Shell service station. Hard to believe people used to drive right up and pump petrol into their tanks.

Dusty Elvis saunters over, his jaw working over a wad of gum. "Like the look of my equipment, now, do ya? Give you a private tour if you come back later." He winks.

Harper straightens up and inches back. "You oughta be ashamed of yourself," she says. "These people don't have much to spare. Drought's taken everything the wheat rust missed the first time through."

"Mind your own goddamned business," he spits, forcing her back with the bulk of his rhinestoned jumpsuited bulk, fiddling with a bunch of keys attached to his belt. Reaches into his pocket for mirror shades, the kind with wire frames. He somehow looks bigger – meaner – with them on. He leans his shoulder against the crumbling concrete wall, looks her up and down until she itches. Tugs a packet of cigarettes from another pocket. Tailor-mades – they cost a bloody fortune too. Sticks one on his lower lip, lights it with a scratched and battered Zippo.

"Girl like you oughta be thinking of her future," he says. Rhinestones sparkle in the stark midmorning light. The scent of tobacco curls inside her nose. "I was you, I'd be fucking my way up and out of this dustbowl shithouse." He jams the cigarette between fat lips and smiles.

"Lucky you're not me, then," she says drily. Waiting. Not wanting to give him the satisfaction. He keeps on smoking, smiling, leering, his BO permeating the plumes of tobacco smoke. She turns on her heel and walks away, angry but keeping it bottled up as she's learned to do with guys who stare at her like hungry dogs.

"Don't wait too long," he calls after her. "Yer not that far off yer use-by date, you know."

Harper avoids the revival tent and its excited, anticipatory believers. She heads for the crowd amassing in Whitlam Park, which still boasts two functioning wooden picnic tables not too warped and cracked from years of exposure. Young people cluster around a battered laptop, taking turns to log on through the Base's web page portal.

Janny looks up when she sees Harper coming. "There's one for you," she calls across their heads.

Harper almost doesn't want to read it. She already fears what it isn't going to say. Four simple words: *pet Cooper for me*. There isn't any dog called Cooper. Lachie created the imaginary pooch when he filled in his application form. Cooper is their private code meaning everything's okay. No mention of Cooper means everything isn't.

The message on screen supposedly from Lachie is bland and cold. Words that could have been written from anybody to anybody.

"They still eating like kings in there?" calls someone from behind.

She nods in silence and hits the delete key.

By sundown, everyone is drunk. Rain is the only topic of conversation. Anecdotes stretching from Lightning Ridge all the way down to the Eden coast.

Outside the tent, it's hard to tell at what point prayer vigil descends into full-bore hootenanny. Night wears on and the music gets louder. Clapping and shouting and stomping for rain, fuelled by Ray Clayton's palm-heart toddy, which is what they drink when they're out of everything else. Songs for Jesus, dancing for him too, work boots and sun-cracked plastic sandals thumping hard on the warped and weathered dance boards.

With a blast of laughter, a couple of Country Women's Association stalwarts burst their way out through the tent flaps. "Just as hot out here as 'tis inside," says one, fanning her bright pink face – frowning when she notices Harper, a look that screams, *Girl, you oughta be throwing your lot in with the righteous.*

Because everyone who's anyone in Terina Flat is stomping and shrieking and hollering, both inside and outside the revival tent – social niceties be damned. Priest-Elvis has prepared his song list well: 'Kentucky Rain' for openers, following on with 'How Great Thou Art.' Short-verse speeches in between, paving the way to 'I Shall Not Be Moved.'

In the pauses between numbers, conversational buzz drones like the chittering of cicadas. A few stray blasts of it swim towards Harper through the heat. Nothing she doesn't already know: that entrance to the revival tent is by gold-coin donation; that the way-past-their-bedtimes children scampering underfoot have been encouraged to write to God on precious scraps of multicoloured paper (the remaining dregs of the school's once-vibrant art department). At the crack of dawn tomorrow, smoke-lipped Elvis is going to hit the skies. Fly up high as close as he dares to deliver God their messages, extra personal.

Yeah, right.

As 'It's Now or Never' starts up, Harper's surprised to catch old Doc Chilby slipping out through the tent flap. The women exchange suspicious glances. Doc Chilby nods, so Harper returns the favour. Doc Chilby delivered her into this world. She deserves respect even if she's thrown her lot in with the Bible-thumpers.

Up on the knoll, the racers admire the Base lit up like Christmas squared, same as every other night, but this night, there's something extra in the air. The town itself emits barely a glow. Night skies dark enough to drown the Milky Way in all its glory.

There's talk of cars and trade in missing parts. Who needs what and what they're going to barter for it. How the camel guy is late again. How someone's cousin's investigating other sources.

Janny Christofides saunters over, sipping on a can of something warm and flat. "Saw you checking out that Jesus plane. A cloud-seeder for sure."

"Didya get a look at it up close?" says Harper.

Janny shakes her head. "Didn't have to."

Harper continues. "It's got these bulges under the wings like wasp nests."

Janny nods, enthusiasm causing her to spill a couple of splashes from her can. "Dispensers holding fifty-two units apiece. Flares built into the wings themselves. Avoids resistance. As little drag as possible." Her eyes are shining.

"How'd ya know all this?"

"Old man used to do crop-dusting, don't forget."

"But dusting's different. Seeding's illegal –"

"Dusting's illegal – there's nothing left to dust. Everything's illegal, unless you're frackers or big foreign money or those massive fuckoff land barges dumping toxic shit deep into cracks."

"We oughta report him," Harper says bitterly, remembering Elvis grinding his cigarette butt into Terina dirt.

"Like anybody's gonna give two shits." Janny cocks her head back in the direction of the revival tent. The singing has long since become incoherent. Songs mashing into one another, Presley numbers indistinguishable from hymns. "How much you reckon we're paying that –"

She doesn't get to finish her sentence. Somebody calls out, "Lightning!"

Janny looks up, startled, points to the empty airspace above the Base. Racers stand there frozen, jam jars of fermented melon hooch clutched in their hands.

"I don't see any –"

"Wait – there it is again!"

This time, they see and hear it too, a cracking split. Like thunder but not. Thick spikes stabbing at the fallow dirt. Aftershocks of colour, green and red.

There's a scrabble for phones as a volley of sharp, thick beams shoot upwards from the Base. High-pitched whining that fades, then swells, then fades. A sonic boom followed by overbearing silence. The town dogs start barking and howling all at once. Nothing to see now. No more laser lights. The racers stuff their phones into pockets and head for their cars.

Cracker's already seated behind the wheel of his precious Dodge Charger. Harper runs up to cadge a lift.

"Stay here," he warns as he's revving up his engine.

"Are you shitting me?"

But he's got this serious look on his face and he's not going to give her a ride. No matter. She waits till he takes off, then climbs in beside Bing Reh in his 1951 Ford Five-Star pickup. The racers are heading to the salt, their vehicles overloaded. Everyone's in a hurry to get out there.

17

The Base has fallen still and silent. No more lasers. No more lightshow. No Blackhawks either, which seems odd, considering.

There's more light than there ought to be, all coming from a suspicious patch of sky above the salt.

More lightning strikes drown out the growl of engines.

"Looks dangerous!" says Harper. Bing nods, eyes on the road. Half drunk or not, they have to go check it out.

Her heart pounds, thinking, *Lachie, please stay under cover; whatever you do, stay away from that chain link fence.*

Things are not as they had seemed when viewed from the edge of town. The lightning's localised, not spread across the sky – they got that right, but it isn't striking anywhere close to Base. The salt flats are soaking up the brunt of it. Singed salt particles fling themselves at Harper's nose. She sneezes, half expecting blood. Too dark to tell what she wipes across her jeans.

There's no stopping Cracker. He aims his Dodge straight out into the thick of it. Looks like he's deciding to play chicken with the lightning. Bing slows down. Harper knows what that means; he's giving her the opportunity to get out. And she *should* get out, because not doing so is crazy, but instead, she nods and the pickup's engine roars and surges.

She can smell that smell no one ever smells any more, that heady, moody tang just before a thunderhead lets rip. Plant oil sucked from dry rocks and soil mixed up with ozone and spores. Chemical explanations half remembered from biology class, never dreaming back then how rare the experience of rain would become in future times.

They gather, staring at the crazy lights.

"Red sprite lightning," says Bing, "Or something like it."

Nobody argues. They've all seen strange stuff above and around the Base. Clouds that didn't look like clouds when no clouds hung in any other patch of sky. Lenticular shapes like UFOs, only insubstantial. Ephemeral, like ghost residue of clouds. Not made of metal like anything you'd expect.

"Check it out!"

Sharp intakes of breath all round as a thick red lightning bolt travels horizontally from one cloud to another. Hits the second hard, like there's something solid at its core, then shatters into separate fragments which coagulate into orbs.

Balls of crackling light drift down, hover, pause, pink neon glow emanating from their centre mass. Pulsing. Like the crackling orbs are breathing.

"Man, I don't like the –"

"Shhh."

More crackling, louder, like automatic weapons fire. They cover their ears and duck, only it's not ammo. It's coming from the glowing orbs, close to the ground now, pulsing with red and light. A high-to-low-pitched whistle, almost musical.

A blood-red cloudshape jellyfish emerges, dangles tentacles of pure blue light. Drags across the surface of the salt. Almost moves like a living, breathing creature.

The air hangs thick with acrid ozone stench. Some of those lightning stabs are getting close.

Beneath the cloudshape, thick swirling coils writhe like a nest of snakes. Pale clouds forming angry faces, elongated skulls, animals with jagged teeth.

Somehow, some way, they lose track of time. Dawn is so insipid by comparison, they almost miss it when it finally arrives. Their eyes are dazed from the flash and flare. Colours dancing across their inner vision.

Harper isn't the one who first spots Lachie. She's staring in the opposite direction. Up into a pink-and-orange sky at the dark gnat wobbling across its luminescent swathe. Elvis in his patched-up plane, heaven-bound with a hangover, she hopes, of Biblical proportions. A plane packed tight with cigarette-size sticks of silver iodide if Janny's right. Cold rain. Pyrotechnic flares. At best it's alchemy; at worst, yet another hick-town scam. Perhaps he will coax moisture from the wispy cirrus. Not enough to make a difference. Just enough to make sure he gets paid.

"Harper!"

Cracker's voice. She turns around as, dazed and moaning, three figures stagger across the salt. Somebody's got binoculars. They shout the names out: Lachie, Danno, Jason. Staggering like zombies, only this isn't some kind of joke. They get back in their vehicles and race out to intercept the scarecrow men. Clothing torn up, singed, and smoking. Eyes wide and shit-scared sightless.

Harper's screaming, *Lachie Lachie Lachie*, when she comprehends the state he's in. He doesn't react. Doesn't even look at her. Doesn't stare at anything. Just ahead.

All three are hurt bad. Jason is the worst.

Everybody's shouting at everybody else. Eventually, Lachie cocks his head at the sound of Harper's voice. She goes to fling her arms around his neck but Janny grabs her wrist and holds on tight. "Needs Doc Chilby," she says grimly. Harper slaps her hand away but she doesn't dare touch Lachie, because Janny's right.

"Base's got a hospital," says Lucas Clayton, son of Reg. "State of the art."

Nobody else says anything, but everybody's thinking it. If they take the injured boys back to the Base, they'll never be seen again. That lightning was not the natural kind. Whatever just happened here is Base-related.

A siren wails in the far off distance. The sound makes everybody jump.

"Doc Chilby will know what to do," says Bing.

Lachie and Danno get loaded into the back of Bing's pickup. Harper spreads down a blanket first, a ratty old thing balled up and wedged beside the tool kit. She tries not to wince at the sight of those burns. Keeps saying, "Everything's gonna be okay," although it isn't.

The third guy, Jason, is laid gently across the back seats of a Holden Torana. Softly moaning like an animal.

They don't notice the Blackhawks until too late. The cars split up – a reflex action – fanning in all directions, two vehicles heading for Doc Chilby's by different routes, the others planning to drive decoy all over until they're apprehended or run out of juice.

Harper presses her back against the cabin, crouches, hanging on with one hand to the pickup's battered side. The ride is reasonably smooth until they reach the limits of the salt. Each bump and pothole sets the injured men off moaning.

By time they reach the town's outskirts, Lachie is delirious and screaming. Impossible to keep the salt out of their wounds. He tries to sit up but the passage is too ragged. Harper holds her breath, heart thumping painfully against her ribs. *Hang on, Lachie. Hang on till we get there.*

The sky is streaked with morning glow, the Jesus plane now the size of a lonely bird. A few clouds scudding, clumping stickily together. More than usual.

Any minute now the pickup will get intercepted by soldiers in full combat gear. Or a hazmat team in an unmarked van – they've all seen that in movies on TV.

But the streets are empty. Everyone's still clustered around the revival tent or passed out on the ground. All necks are craned, all eyes on the Jesus plane looping and threading its way through a puff of clouds like a drunken gnat. Rosaries muttered, beads looped tightly around arms and wrists. Clutched in hands, pressed against hearts and lips. Holy Mary, Mother of – Jesus, is that rain?

Thick, fat drops smack the dusty ground.

Proper rain for the first time in three long years. Rain coaxed from clouds not even in sight when the plane began its journey.

Looks like Elvis is no charlatan after all. Elvis is the real deal. Elvis can talk to Jesus and make it pour.

And then they're dancing, arms flung into the air. Laughing and shrieking and praising the heavenly host. "Ave Maria" as bloated splats drill down upon their heads, soaking their shirts and floral print dresses, muddying up the packed-dirt hospital car park. Mud-splattered boots and trouser legs.

There'll be time for Jesus later. Harper stays by Lachie's side as the injured men are unloaded off the pickup. Straight through to Emergency; lucky such an option still exists. Terina Community Hospital once boasted fifty beds; now only ten of them are still in operation. The place was supposed to have closed a year ago. They're all supposed to drive to Parkes if an accident takes place. Supposed to use the Base if it's life or death.

One of the racers must have thought to phone ahead. Two nurses stand tentatively inside the sterile operating theatre. Waiting for Doc Chilby to scrub up. Waiting for something. Harper doesn't find out what – she's hustled into another room and made to fill out forms. Their Medicare numbers – how the fuck is she supposed to know? Didn't they have their wallets in their pants?

"Don't call the Base," she says, but it's too late. That helicopter stopped chasing them for a reason – there's only one place in town they can go for help.

An hour of waiting before a nurse brings her a cup of tea. Two biscuits wrapped in cellophane and a magazine with blonde models on the cover. The magazine's two years old, its recipes ripped roughly out of the back.

"Is Lachie gonna be okay?" she asks.

The nurse is about her age or maybe a few years older. Nobody Harper knows or went to school with. The hospital has trouble keeping staff. They rotate young ones from the bigger towns, but they never stay for more than a couple of months.

"That other boy died," the nurse says eventually. "I'm not supposed to tell you."

Harper knows the nurse means Jason even though she didn't say his name.

"Were they all from the Base?"

"Yeah, reckon." The nurse doesn't seem to think anything of the fact. Definitely not a local, then. To her, the Base is nothing more than it seems.

The nurse chews on her bottom lip. "Never seen anything like it. Multiple lightning strikes each one, poor things. Left its mark on them, it did. Tattoos like blood-red trees." She points to the base of her own neck by way of demonstration. "What were they doing out there on the salt in the middle of the night?"

Harper doesn't have an answer. The nurse is not expecting one, not even wild speculation. She wanders over to the window and lifts the faded blue and purple blind. "Still raining, I see. "Least that's something."

Still raining. Words that take a while to sink in. Harper unfolds her legs from underneath her, heaves up out of the sagging beige settee.

The nurse's heels *clip-clop* against linoleum as she leaves.

The opened blind reveals a world awash with mud and gloom. Water surges along the gutters like a river. Slow-moving cars plough through, their wheels three-quarters covered. More water than Harper has seen in a long, long time.

"When can I see Lachie?" she calls after the nurse. Too late. The corridor is empty.

Harper slips the crinkly biscuit packet into her pocket, hops down the fire escape two steps at a time.

The water in the car park is brown and up to her knees already. A couple of men in anoraks wade out in an attempt to rescue their cars.

The rain keeps falling, too hard, too fast. Main Street is barely recognisable. Whole families clamber up onto roofs, clinging to spindly umbrella stems – and each other. Half drenched dogs bark up a storm. Nobody's singing songs of praise to Jesus.

She pictures the revival tent swept away in a tsunami of soggy scones and lamingtons, trampled as panic sets in, random and furious as the rain itself.

The deluge is too much, too quick for the ground to cope with. Hard-baked far too many months to soak it up. There's nowhere for the surge to slosh but up and down the streets. Vehicles bob along like corks and bottles.

She doesn't want to think about the cattle in the fields. Dogs chained up in unattended backyards. Children caught in playgrounds.

She's wading waist-deep in filthy swell when a wave breaks over her head. A wave on Main Street, of all unlikely things. Next thing she knows, she's going under, mouth full of mud and silt. Scrabbling for a slippery purchase, bangs her shins on something hard, unseen. This can't be happening. The rain keeps falling, mushing everything to brown and grey.

Her leg hurts but she keeps on moving, half swimming, half wading, crawling her way to higher ground. To the knoll. She doesn't recognise it at first. Not until she stands and checks the view. A line of lights snaking out from the Base and heading in her direction.

She's shaking, either from the cold or shock. Bit by bit, the sky is clearing, bright blue peering through grey rents and tears. Clouds the colour of dirty cotton wool break up. Voices shout from rooftop to rooftop. A sound that might be a car backfiring – or a gunshot.

She wipes grit from her eyes with the heel of her palm. Hugs her shoulders, slick hair plastered against her face.

"Leg's bleeding."

It's Janny. She glances down at red rivulets streaking her muddy calf.

"It's nothing."

"Can you walk?"

She nods.

"Better get you up to the hospital, then."

Steam rises from the rapidly warming sludge. A cloying smell like rotting leaves and sewage. Damp human shapes mill about, disorientated. Unanchored.

She watches three men in anoraks attempt to right a car. Others stand staring stupidly at the mess. Like they don't know where to start or what to do.

She limps back up to the hospital with Janny by her side. Only two army trucks are parked out the front of it. Doc Chilby stands her ground in a sodden coat, arms folded across her chest. Four soldiers briskly unload boxes, stacking them up on the verandah out of the mud.

Doc Chilby argues with another soldier. "We didn't ask for anything. You're not taking anyone out of here – that's final."

The soldier has his back to Harper; she can't hear what he's saying. Only that the doc is getting flustered, flinching every time a Blackhawk thunders close. She repeats herself but the soldier isn't listening.

The nurse who told Harper that Jason had died stands smoking on the verandah.

Loud voices emanate from inside the building, then a sudden surge of soldiers swarm. That nurse starts shouting, Doc Chilby too. Three stretchers are borne swiftly down wooden stairs. Weapons raised. Threats issued. The steady thrum of Blackhawk blades drowning out all attempts at negotiation.

The Base has come for its wounded contract workers. Wounded doing what, exactly? Harper has been watching without comprehending. Now wide awake, she adds her own voice to the shouting. Ignores the nurse signalling frantically from the verandah, the ache in her leg and the Blackhawk's thudding blades. She runs after one of the trucks – too late, it's out of reach. Picks up a rock and throws it. The rock bounces harmlessly off the taut khaki canvas. She almost trips as she reaches for something else to throw. The road's sticky and slippery from rain.

The convoy lumbers like a herd of beasts. A minute later and she's standing helpless in the middle of the road, a chunk of rock gripped tightly in her hand.

Her bleeding leg gets sprayed with mud as a car pulls up beside her. Cracker in a rattling old army Dodge from his collection. The M37 convertible minted 1953. Same colour as the green-grey mud. Dented. Spotted with rust and a couple of bullet holes. Thick treads built to handle difficult terrain.

Neither of them says anything. The crazed glint in his eyes fills her with hope. She climbs into the passenger seat. He floors it, following close behind the trucks at first, then lagging. The old Dodge putters and chokes, but it holds its own.

A bright new day. Sun and daylight are banishing the nighttime landscape's sinister cast. Red-and-blue jellyfish lightning seems like another world ago.

Cracker races, slams his palm down on the horn. The convoy of army trucks ignores him. He keeps his foot pressed to the accelerator. Harper keeps her gaze fixed on the Base.

They can't get in. They'll be turned back at the front gate. Threatened with whatever trespassers get threatened with. Whatever happens, she's ready for it. So is Cracker.

The Base's electronic gates do not slide open. The truck convoy halts. Cracker stops too but keeps the engine purring. Just in case.

A soldier gets out of the truck ahead and slams the cabin door. He's armed but he hasn't drawn his weapon. She's still gripping that rock chunk in her hand.

"Get out of the vehicle," booms a megaphone voice.

"Not fuckn' likely," says Cracker.

"I repeat: Get out of the vehicle."

Nothing happens. Nobody moves. The Dodge keeps grunting and grumbling like a big old dog.

Harper turns the door handle, slides out of the passenger seat. "You can't just do whatever you like," she shouts. She's shaking hard and she knows she'd better drop the rock, not give them any reason. She's waiting

24

for that soldier to draw his gun. "You've got no right," she repeats, softer this time.

He approaches, one arm raised. "Ma'am, this country is at war." The walkie-talkie on his shoulder crackles but he doesn't touch it.

"Which country?" she says, squinting through harsh sunlight. "Which war?"

He gives her a half-arsed smirk but doesn't answer. Mumbles into the electronic device. Turns his back, gets back in the truck.

She lets the rock fall to the dusty road. *Dusty.* It appears the rain didn't reach this far. Not the strangest thing she's seen in recent times. "Lachie," she says, but it's too late. Too late for Lachie, too late for her and Cracker. The gates slide open with electronic precision. Trucks pass through, one by one, Cracker's Dodge amongst them – too late for turning back. A voice behind commands her to keep moving. Not to turn. Not to pick up any rocks. Not to make any sudden movements.

She looks up just in time to catch a speck in the wide blue sky. A wedge-tailed eagle, coasting on the updraft, its diamond-shaped tail unmistakable. Those birds partner up for life – something else she learned in school. They fly together, perform acrobatics, but she cannot spot the other one, its mate. When she cranes her neck and shades her eyes, a soldier twists her arm behind her back. Pushes her forwards through the steel Base gates. Metal grates as they snap and lock behind her.

In the '50s and '60s, the British Government, with the agreement and support of our own, carried out secret nuclear tests on Australian soil, the most well-known of them being Maralinga in South Australia. The indigenous Pitjantjatjara and Yankunytjatjara people were forced off their land and suffered health issues as a result of radiation, as did participating Australian service personnel. No reason to believe such manoeuvres might not happen here again in a resource depleted, asset strapped future.

CASSINI FALLING

The woman seated across the dining table insists she is not a tourist. She and Filippe are *international travellers*. They sip heinously overpriced Sauv Blanc and peruse the photocopied list of day trips. She wrinkles her nose and declares the ice hotel and midnight choral performance in the old wooden church are likely 'twee'.

She tells you all about the time in Svalbard where rifle-toting men stood guard on craggy points just in case of bear attack, and then about the local boys who hacked a path through Rwandan jungle to take a group of six to meet gorillas. Such *authentic experiences*, darling. You sip twelve-dollar beer and nod politely.

The travellers tuck into venison. They are good with facts, like the name of the farm where they bought that brilliant Riesling, or the time they tangoed on the Tallinn-Helsinki ferry. They chew through mouthfuls of Machu Picchu and Kokoda Trail, while you mention countries you have visited, cities you liked and didn't like, places you are planning to travel next. You will be forgotten long before the ship hits Trondheim, your features being unremarkable, an important trait that landed you this job and all the jobs that came before it, leading to this voyage, place and time.

After lunch, you retire to the Vesteralstuen lounge, and its assortment of scattered, mismatched chairs. On the farthest wall, a blue impressionistic triptych depicts some long-forgotten colonial event: boats and houses, men in fancy hats. In front of it, a parquetry dance floor, too small to permit even a modest tango.

A bald man slouches, paperback in hand, oblivious to passing scenery and the midnight-hulled patrol boat bathed in gorgeous afternoon light, attended by a flock of hopeful seagulls.

Thus far, Vardo, Hammerfest and Oxfjord have passed without incident. You expect the same from Skervoy and Risoyhamn and consider selecting a book from the library cabinet. Not much to choose from: obligatory Cornwalls; Ken Follett's *Winter of the World*. Bypassing a couple of unfathomable Japanese tracts, you settle on Lynda La Plante's *Cold Shoulder*.

On each assignment, you pit yourself against the algorithm, trying to ID your target before the Lance kicks in. Your track record is roughly

60:40, running in your favour. The Lance exists to ensure you follow through.

When the seas get choppy, glass buoys nestled in the window space start rolling. Cerulean sky triggers a memory fragment, brief and unsatisfying. A seaside pier with striped umbrellas. Screaming gulls *and you can't remember where.*

Childhood memories were forsaken when you had the Lance upgraded, a necessary condition of promotion. *Small price to pay*, you had thought back then. You have come to regret such rash decisions.

You while away an hour skimming pages, systematically ticking passengers off your list: the paunchy cluster of white-haired Germans; the girl twirling and untwirling a lock of nutmeg hair; the woman in a scarlet jumper and ridiculous high heels, knitting with three needles, wool trailing out of a plastic bag. Any of them could be Cassini, your shipboard target's official designation.

Constant rattling and shuddering of the ship, rolling and sliding, dipping and plunging. Announcements come in four languages, preceded by three chimes. Occasionally a fifth attempted, but Robin, the tour manager, does not have more than a smattering of Arabic. His Italian is also poor – at dinner, Phillipe's wife shared rumours of how he lied about Italian on his application. *Of course he lied… everybody always lies.* On occasion, you have taken credit for results you didn't action. On serious matters, you have fooled them only once.

Your gut floods with momentary panic at the sight of a small abandoned camera haphazardly positioned on a table. You may yourself be a target on the *Vesteralen*. One of these innocent-looking passengers might have you marked as a target of their own, an officially sanctioned response to Cairo, or, perhaps, a further consequence of Mumbai.

You relax a little as a fat old woman claims the camera and attempts to take a photo. Muttering to herself in German, something's going haywire with the settings. She seems dissatisfied with the swiftly passing scenery. The light has changed and it's no longer worth the effort.

A bug crawls up the porthole glass as the ship is moving past Gjerdoya. Red and white and yellow houses. Bright green grass surrounds each dwelling. Rows of strategic windbreak trees.

You've said it many times before, that this assignment is to be your last, that you are getting too long in the tooth, that you deserve a different kind of life. You stare at the claret-coloured armchairs, then across to large windows rimmed with rivets, burnt orange curtains threaded through with diagonal curves of red. Such hues remind you of burning buildings. Other decades, other lives and places.

The scruffy, bearded man at breakfast appears to be praying before his bowl of oatmeal. Turns out he is staring at the phone down on his lap, concentration eventually broken by a squirming child in a Star Wars T-shirt.

There is a killer on this ship, most likely decommissioned. You will be cleaning someone else's mess. You have done this gig too many times.

Your list is based on days of observation. Imaginary bets against the algorithm: the silver haired man, dark glasses, business shirt, binoculars he never seems to use. Or camo pants and camo cap, with lurid lime-green trainers. The way he paces in between the islands and does not check his phone often like others. Or perhaps the taut and wiry man who vaguely resembles Putin? That, at least, would give someone a laugh.

For certain, it's neither of the couple who are always kissing. Nor the windblown twenty-something flirting on the deck above the prow. Nor that one, heavily pregnant in a bright pink lacy top, tatty bra strap falling off her shoulder, children's faces tattooed on each bicep. You dismiss the pink-haired girl in the all-black denim. Jeans ripped neatly at the knees, impractical with all these icy winds. Only the old and serious rug up on deck.

The young ignite such jealousy, with their freedom and comfortable good looks. Things were different back in your day – and with that thought, you are suddenly transported. Designation: Anaconda, the Egyptian coup barely five weeks past, embedded amongst ten thousand supporters of deposed Morsi, impersonating an American journalist amongst the wound-tight, jittering young Muslim Brotherhood. In Raaba, at the peak of summer, drafting their wills and bidding their families farewell. Those Egyptian boys knew they would die, even though the killing of 800 at Midan Rabaa al-Adawiyya was still a week away and you still believed in the potentiality and space for alternative outcomes, so many ancient hatreds amidst the loudest calls for bread and freedom.

Another memory. Designation: Baskerville, and you are driving through a filthy, trash-strewn maze of narrow streets. 'El Sijn' – 'the prison' – a baby-shit brown cement compound. Clandestine locations around Cairo, changing your residence every other week, forever waiting for calls from unknown numbers. You cannot shake the violent memories, one hundred lingering Algerian ghosts. You have forgotten when your faith in the illusory notions of neutrality, western democratising pressures and the line between inaction and complicity died. The raging dissonance between ideology and practice has left you weary of so-called 'stability paradigms' and externally driven shifts in the cost of suppression.

Three chimes swiftly followed by Robin's tour manager prattle bring you back on deck, into the moment. 'We see the Globus! The Polar Circle is not far away."

Everybody cheers and an old man in knee-length shorts and sailboat-patterned shirt hobbles across the deck with his sturdy cane. Stops to converse with a smoking woman wearing a ridiculous floppy hat. Wind snatches at their conversation. "No gubbins," she seems to be saying, going into some detail, explaining *gubbins* as things you do not want on your plate, yet you have to have them in America. Whatever's listed on the menu, that is what you get, she says, smoke from her cigarette wafting in your direction.

Robin and his microphone intrude. "You might feel some vibrations so hold on to something… Maybe a glass of champagne, that will make you steady. A very nice lady called Ingrid, she is selling champagne here. Very nice."

A blast of ship's horn raises whoops and cheers as the *Vesteralen* crosses over.

"Can you feel the vibrations? What an amazing experience for us all!"

Robin's vibrations linger longer than they should and you know that *the process* has begun. The Lance in activation mode, insisting on redundant calibration and diagnostics. The Lance will be fully operational an hour or two past sunset. You need to stay on your guard until that point. You are, in fact, guarding the Lance. You are not required for measurement, evaluation or deduction. You are a bullet, a rough shove over the side later at night in ferocious, obfuscating winds. You are the anvil, not the hammer. An instrument, a weapon wielded. You play this game on every mission, trying to guess your target's form. There is no need. The Lance is implanted for this purpose.

This job is almost certainly a payback – Cassini, some retired operative twenty years out from the game. Embedded comfortably in an ordinary life.

Your ears prick up at the couple behind you speaking in secret code. You don't look, and you hold your paper steady.

"A gala? Birthday party you mean?"

"Was there a railroad?"

The ocean sparkles when the sun comes out and you comprehend they are doing crossword puzzles.

"What you got?"

"Forty-two down... Mystery times."

"This was W Somerset Maugham."

"Now this... World War II"

"He got killed just off the highland during the invasion..."

You smile and put the paper down to watch a trawler scudding by bleak rocks, and then, on deck, a man carrying tea in waxy cardboard cups, tea bag tags flapping wild, like little kites. A young girl, her hair in neat French braids, skips up and down the stairs clutching an ipad.

"Let's just keep moving along..."

"But this is how you spell it!"

"It is not! It's got a T. Like trident!"

"Mickey somebody..."

"I'll go across."

"Is that the home? Or is that the away team?"

You have been away too long. In the distance, snow-iced craggy peaks run through with mossy veins, soaring gulls, foam licked rocks. The sea enraged, desperate for purchase. The passengers begin to stagger like drunks across the deck. You remain in the top deck Plexiglas enclosure, seated near the crossword stalwarts, wrapped up tight against the weather, staring at the choppy, foamy grey. Catching glimpses of misty, descriptionless rock islands, like the backs of deeply sleeping beasts.

"... So the muse would be who..."

"I dunno... it says name..."

"No, we got 222 and 223..."

"That's gotta be Joe Lewis – he's a fighter."

You're a fighter too. Unexpected flashbacks to Black Friday, March 12, '93. Designation: Candyfloss. Bombay bloodied, charred and chastened by its first taste of international urban terrorism. RDX strapped onto scooters, left in suitcases, crammed deep into cars. Explosions tearing south to north, the death toll high, with countless literally vaporised. The double decker bus reduced to the size of a mangled Maruti, the suburbs filled with shattered window panes.

The woman you pulled from the burning building... her name... what was her name? The AI kicking in and over, separating you from memories you would have liked to keep. So precious, such small acts of rebellion.

No matter. You have done your bit for international diplomacy. The hour is long, and you have had enough.

Cassini is certain to be one of the smokers, up on deck at random hours. Nobody ever pays them any mind. You retire to *Trollfjorden Salong,* the up-front lounge with sea green leather armchairs. Royal blue curtains, brass fittings, blue and gold carpet.

A broad oil painting: *Der Gamletid*, 1949, depicting many kinds of ocean vessel. A selection of wall mounted crests: 'Komune', 'Bronoy', 'Batsfjord', 'Nesna', 'Bodo', 'Vagan', 'Hadsel'.

The *Vesteralen* passes an indistinct land mass. "Horse Mountain, because it looks like a horse," says Robin helpfully through the intercom. You see nothing even vaguely horse-like. Pattern recognition fading is another sign, that you will soon be shuffled down, along and sideways into some tedious office. You will miss the broad Atlantic Ocean and your desk will glimpse a patch of sky. Blue sky, blue water, blue reflections in bulletproof glass. For you, water has always symbolised freedom.

You are contemplating bourbon when an elderly man with bright green zippers surprises you by climbing out of his scooter. The machine had appeared to be a medical device. Back in the day, you did not make such mistakes and you have definitely sailed through better days.

You are fifty-five years old and Cassini is your swan song. You are pleased to have arrived at this decision. The AI does not know of it, or else it would have kept you in home waters.

Smoking woman selects a deckchair nestled between trios of white life raft capsules. Breaks against the bitter wind, rugged up bright in jellybean yellow. Passing long, low stretches of green land bejeweled sparsely with coloured dwellings, occasional churches and a slim lighthouse.

Placid gulls bob on the water. Two chunky, fortysomething men in T-shirts, blue jeans, plus binoculars, pore over maps and landmarks with extreme, almost childlike enthusiasm.

The tubercular purr of the ship's engines provides a comfortable baseline, as do occasional sailing or fishing vessels and windborne snatches of conversation in multiple European tongues.

The smoker carries two cups: one for tea and one to hold her ash. Behind her, neon mauve fluorescents wall-mounted like sleepy shuttered eyes.

Your bets continue – Cassini cannot be a member of the crew, the ones who scatter safety equipment across the middle deck, nor the tattooed girls who clean the cabins, then later change into more elegant attire to wait on tables in the dining room.

In a wash of sentiment, you hope Cassini is anyone but the cheerful English woman with her incessant smoking and her faded floppy hat. Her voice rising in pitch and tone, banging on about the obesity of Americans.

The time she watched one in a food court 'work through' an entire *litre* of frozen yoghurt. You suspect there has been someone like her within your distant past. You can't remember. *Why can't you remember?*

Blowing smoke as she criticises, oblivious to all irony. Too obvious. Too easy to be Cassini. If anything, she will be a plant, with her row of crooked teeth, placed on board to ensure you do your job. Trying a bit too hard to catch you out, the data from the Lance too inconclusive.

An old man oofing along on his three-wheeled walker, crash lands into a vacant deck chair. "A pretty bit of countryside we seem to be going through," he says as he flips through a book with yellowed pages.

Robin interjects via the crackly intercom. "Ladies and gentlemen, on the left you can see some very nice sailing boats and you can see as many as you would like."

There are times when Robin's English doesn't seem much better than his Italian.

"Little boats all racing about, eighty to a fleet... Flying their spinnakers... Very nice."

This ship is old, its passengers for the most part sober. Not like on the big American liners, with their 24-hour casinos and shopping malls.

You can't help wishing the bearded, oofing Brit a comfortable dotage. You no longer wish to be a weapon. Yet more evidence of your own deterioration.

Not many lights pepper this rugged stretch of coastline. Damp squalls have driven passengers upstairs to the Panorama Lounge, where they can drink, protected from the rough Norwegian weather.

Stage Two Lance activation kicks in with nausea, then a sharp pain running down your spine. A polypeptide flush slams you awake, heart sinking when you see the smoking woman in her stupid hat and puffy jacket. Pacing – too disappointing and too easy in the way this awful work should never be.

Smoking woman has not seen you. She stares out into the aching night, legs braced firm against the rocking.

You step, then pause. Something about this set up isn't right. The repetitious engine grumbling, the taint of smoke, the deep blue of the night, damp spray and the ever-pulsing deck.

You should run a diagnostic. You should do a dozen other things, but instead you step under the stairs and wait. At least, that's what you try to do, but your body stiffens in rebellion. Spine tingling, you can't stop your legs from marching briskly to an empty stretch of rail, not visible from the Panorama Lounge.

The truth slams home as you grip the side, your bowels turning to water. You are Designation: Cassini, now unstoppably compelled to throw yourself over, into the shadowed, freezing water, where you will not survive twenty minutes. The ship will never find you in the dark even if somebody noticed when you jumped.

You fight the Lance for control of your arms and legs – of course you do – but the AI has the upper hand. As you hoist your body up and over, grunting and grappling for purchase, smoking woman is shouting at you – *ahoy there – what do you think you're doing?* – then screaming for help in her irritating high-pitched voice once she finally comprehends.

But she's wrong. It isn't suicide. It's murder. The Lance, cleaning up after itself. No corner office, no window with a blue-sky view. Designation: Cassini. Permanent retirement.

You wonder if you might have had a mother or grandmother or perhaps a maiden aunt like smoking woman, with lank, thinning hair and a row of crooked teeth as the cold slams home and the waves take over and your mind is wiped by a white and blinding light.

Everything in this story is true to life, from the snippets of shipboard dialogue to the passing Norwegian ports – right down to the titles available in the Vesteralen's library cabinet. Except for the sci fi spy stuff. I made all that up.

HACKING SANTORINI

I collect dirty postcards – the dirtier the better. The faded ones with folds and creases, coffee stains and greasy donut smears. My cards have seen a lot of love and can fetch a pretty poem. Pennies and other fiscal residue make great exchange for embroidered lace, cupcakes and mechanical know-how.

Sometimes know-how is handier than poetry. I know how to sail the boat my Gramma crashed into Heraklion not too long after the 88-minute war. Crash landed and stranded as things turned out. Not so bad a place to wind up as many. Not that I've ever been anywhere else, but I've read much of other places, scrawled on postcards sent from Pasadena, Macao and Istanbul. Postcards salvaged from around the globe before the Exclusion Zones started excluding and Heraklion got roughed up and heritage listed.

You name it, reckon I got a card. Evidence exotic places once existed. Best of all are the cards from Santorini, the ones with beautiful blue domes. Sixty-five nautical miles afar says Gramma's stash of rolled and folded maps, only Santorini's own heritage listing means nobody has been near it in living memory.

Except for, that's a dirty lie. My Gramma's boat tossed upon its waves. Close enough to see the gleaming whitewash. But she couldn't land so she took the name of the island for her boat and I see no point in changing that boat's name now. Santorini speaks to excellence and names are things that get you noticed. Stories too, when you've got to make the best of seventh or eighth hand artefacts and promises. For instance, Maurice's brass hound dog head mounted coat hook – not much use for coats in these surrounds. Or Genevieve's darling 1940's folk art ice skates – brush painted with a centre medallion windmill. And Guadalupe's unforgettable chicken ranch bar spinner brass necklace bottle opener – spin to see who pays for all the drinks! Says she'd trade it for a chicken if such things still existed.

I could go on but a phalanx of Byrons, Plaths and Allendes fast approaches. Fancy folks are my bread and ouzo, aside from *cartes postales*, of course. Postcards always come foremost and first – folks share them when they want to hire my boat and why shouldn't they, being that there's not much else to do on Heraklion between sunup and down?

Seems at first a parade of poets, what with them being so numerous, a mix of tall and short and in between, all dressed in white and cream and ivory. Daisy, eggshell, snow and frost, chiffon, porcelain and pearl. Parchment, linen, bone and cream, all frou-froued up and past the nines.

Their couture should have given me a clue: guys and dolls in rosebuds, lace and taffeta. Fussing and flaunting, all tittery and jittery. But me, I'm playing it old school frosty, slouching against the concrete sea wall, waiting for whispered secret codes like *Turkmenistan*, *Nagasaki* or *Rotorua*, name dropping so I know they know about namesakes, keepsakes and significance and whatnot.

Finally, the one with sapphire hair separates from the whole. "We want to get married on Santorini," she tells me, pausing to draw breath. "Marriage is —"

"I know what marriage is." I cut her bridesplaining off because I know everything there is to know about brides and grooms, flower girls and mothers-of. Priests and celebrants, pageboys and designer cakes, groomsmen, candle lighters and *Vratimi*. The kinds of stupid folks did back in the days of connectivity to incite competitiveness and unnecessary complexity.

"Sailboat captains can do the ceremony, yeah?" She looks so young — fourteen or fifteen, born decades after the 88-minute war. Her stare is hard. Aegean blue and glassy. Like folks reckon the ocean used to be.

"Sure thing," I shrug. "Who's marrying whom?"

She grins. "We're all marrying each other." Hands me a faded, crumpled shape that had clearly once been proper postcard shiny.

Young sapphire hair informs me that her name is Rhizanthella. The one beside her is Goldeneye. I don't ask names for all the others — Captain's all they're going to get from me — but they know all about my Gramma's *Santorini* — and my doggo, Daisychain, who will be coming too — that part is non-negotiable.

The Winedark Soup is what we call the watery smear between Heraklion and Exclusion. Was once called something else, but weren't most things?

I get why kids like Rhiz and Goldie feel so urged to push the barriers, seeing past times as elegant and romantic. Getting married was what everybody did back when. Even folks who had never met before. My Gramma told me all about it. She'd been married loads of times and outlived every one of those long-lost brides.

But *these* brides are the serious kind and will not be trading ceremonials for poetics. They have dug their research deep. The one with the thick moustache hands me a six-pack of religious postcards still sealed in brittle, yellowed plastic with a faded sticker stating *Vatican 60 lira*.

Trying not to look too keen, but I've always been lousy with the bluff. Moustachio knows he has me snared. "Plenty more where they came from," he says with a wink.

Truth is, I've married folks before, only generally one to one or sometimes two. Got myself this little book with all the proper words in. Vilest words to ever splutter, but marrying types always insist on going through the motions.

Shrugging, I say, "Plenty more of what?"

He gives me the knowingest of looks, dips his hand, pulls out his stash and reels me in, with *Travel by Trans Australian Railway; Ireland, land of romance; Michie Tavern, Charlottesville; Fasco Mexico Panoramic Hillside View* and *1964 New York World's Fair Expo Postcard Souvenir Swedenborgian exhibit*.

Excitement sets my heart aflame, but he's not finished yet. Next up reveals an original *Philips' Comparative Wall Atlas South America Climate Summer Map* from 1921.

Seriously now, where did these brides unearth such precious treasures?

Rhizanthella of the sapphire hair pouts, signalling they know they've won me over.

"Genesis or Ecclesiastes?" I mumble, coughing sharp to clear my throat.

She shrugs, so I'm going for E over G, being that those words are kind of filthy when you get under their skin: All about God creating man in his own image, all male, female and blessed and lah-de-dah. Instructing them to get shagging and subdue the Earth, with dominion over everything that moves. Which is, of course, exactly how things played out, long term, unchecked dominion being what landed us all in this heritage listed, excluded and confined predicament.

No point arguing over spilled histories. I snatch the Vatican cards for my collection – can you believe there's a whole new city I never previously knew existed?

And then we're off as locals meandering the waterfront drop half-mended nets and basket traps, leave racks of drying fishy things and line along the concrete pier to clap and wave and wish us *bon voyage* and *happy trails*, with sun and breeze and wine and songs and the brides do look completely and utterly amazing. A lurid, groaning trifle of structured fashion-forward beaded bodices with restricted boning, clean lines managing to be classic, yet sensual and unique, delicate and romantic with renaissance lace and all the trimmings.

And yeah, it's definitely going to be a job for Ecclesiastes: *Two are better than one, because they have a good return for their labour. If either of them falls down, one can help the other up. But pity anyone who falls and has no one to help them...* Numbers in need of upgrading as it goes without saying that if seven lie down together, they will keep very much warmer than only two, reinforcing the that one cannot keep properly warm alone.

And the day *is* warm and the sun so lovely, waters calm and smooth and lazy, wind tousling my salty beard and I know I'm one of the lucky ones because although heritage listing is dull and slow and we live off algae pressed and shaped like fish, and nothing ever happens in this fragment of the world, it's a better life than we actually deserve.

Daisychain is the best of doggos, acquired from army surplus. Not the prettiest of pooches – a slightly rusty, dynamically stable quadruped military unit shelved (too loud for combat and too picky for reconnaissance), refitted, recalibrated and reclassified as a medical care device before washing upon these shores. Daisychain may well be dented, but he loves me best and that's what matters most.

Air stirs thick with pheromone pot-pourri as we're casting off from shore, with brides ever elegant and seductive in pastel ombres of buttons, beads, sequins and ribbon; mermaid tulle overlay with ruffles offering a playful commentary, a splash of colour infusion tiers and a touch of old-style Hollywood glamour, not to mention those iridescent vintage (obviously) blue-green embroidered Sternocera beetle wings.

They're waiting for me to do my thing. The Winedark Soup lies still so close to shore where safety is assured in shallows. Cloud banks brood along distant horizons, layered dark on dark, a moody, shifting mass of heaving coal from which forked lightning illuminates cracking, fizzing underbellies laced with spidery threads of forked electric sun.

Moustachio offers to take the wheel while I nip below to fetch my admiral's jacket, the one with the bullion embroidery and rank insignia anchor-embossed brass buttons, ribbon bar and breast eagle. The jacket hangs in a slim wooden robe alongside my deep and darkest treasures: a scrimshaw jagging wheel complete with mermaid breasts and tail; a love heart carved from Whitby jet and the assortment of strange pornography I keep in a *Hoyo de Monterrey Jose Gener Excalibur #11* wooden cigar box.

Within the box sit secret postcard remnants of a frightening domain. Dogs and cats stuffed into baskets captioned with *wish you were here*; the dolphin jumping through a flaming hoop; the woman in dotty bathers posing with a giant bear against a red curtains embellished with brassy handguns. Florida - Drop in anytime — says the reptile head with enormous spiky teeth, while WILDLIFE OF THE DESERT boasts improbably named gamble quail, horned toad, kangaroo rat, kiss bug, centipede, spotted skunk, ring tailed cat, elf owl, coral snake, side winder, bob cat and others you would never even believe.

Then there's Cove Haven Resort in the Pocono Mountains with a heart-shaped tub in every room; Ghost Riders in The Sky, the gone-but-not-forgotten 20 Mule Wagon team across a spectacular Death Valley sunset with the Devil's Golf Course in the foreground.

So many cards with old men posing alongside murdered animals, like they were somehow proud of what they'd done. The past is another country is what my Gramma used to say, but I reckon it must have been much, much worse than that.

A sudden lurch slams me hard against the companionway, the rise and fall bow into breaking waves creates a powerful sensation of forward surge. Somehow, against all odds, the wind has found us.

I stuff the porn back in the box and emerge on deck to a blur of brides grasping tight and pulling ropes, fighting gravity and wind, as waves slam fierce against the sides. Wicked gusts spitting mist into our faces, astonished as Goldeneye jumps up to the main mast to reef the sail, rigging singing as water rushes along the hull, sails popping and pulling taut as my *Santorini* heads straight for the belly of the beast.

"Oh hey," waves Rhiz through the foaming spittle.

"What the hell do you crazy brides think you're doing?" I bellow.

"We want to get married on Santorini," she shouts over the ocean roar. "As in, on the actual island, not the boat."

"Over my dead and destitute corpse! Nobody returns from the isle of Santorini!"

"We know that, oh excellent of Admirals. We want to find out why."

My startled, damp stare shifts from face to face. The brides are drenched and enjoying every minute. "Santorini is a smoking crater!" I shout out through my creaking lungs. "The 88-minute war. Everybody knows about these things!"

"Of course we know about the war, dear, lovely Admiral. But you've got a boat and we've got a collective insatiable urge to learn the ever-loving truth."

"The truth of what? What truth is there to learn? The Exclusion Zone…"

"… excludes exactly *what?*"

Thing is, I'm not an idiot. I've looked up *exclusion* many times, firstly in the *Collins English Dictionary Fourth Australian Edition Better by Definition*, with its shiny cover of black and gold. It states exclusion is an act or an instance of excluding or the state of being excluded. Not much help in the grander scheme of things.

"Question is," she continues in a loud and nauseatingly knowing tone, "is the state of being excluded keeping something *out* or keeping something *in*?"

"Santorini is radioactive," I shout back at her, adding a steely glint for emphasis. Which is quite a trick with Winedark spume spraying everywhere.

The fat one with the sideburns rolls her eyes. "No it isn't! No nukes were deployed during the 88-Minute war. That's why the damn thing went on for so long. Surely you've read the *Chronicles of Whatnot and Wherefore…*" Pudgy fingers attempt explanatory curlicues in fizzing, salt wracked air.

Above us, dramatic energy discharges flare in shredded indigo sky. "The volcano then. Nea Kameni must have blown its top again."

Sideburns nods wetly. "Plausible." She then leans in close and personal. "But don't you want to find out for yourself?"

"No I don't!" Words blurting far more forcefully than intended, surprising everyone including me. Even Daisychain cocks an ear and tilts his head.

"Just close enough to see if there's smoke," she adds. "If Nea Kameni's belching, we'll get out of there."

"I'm not going," I inform them, crossing sodden Admiral arms, "And you can all get off my Gramma's boat now, thank you."

None of them budge. They stare me down while steering the *Santorini* out into forgotten waters. Like they've done such things before. Like somebody has taught them all about it – which is more than anyone ever taught me.

Truth is, I have not the skills to sail this boat across the Exclusion Zone to Santorini. I've never been further than a couple of Ks from Heraklion's rocky shoreline. I am no more a sea captain than this lot are bona fide brides. Gramma's *Santorini* is heaving with impostors.

My Gramma taught me lightning strikes are five times hotter than the surface of the sun. With this in mind we navigate by sextant, compass, paper maps and stars through an exclusion zone as wifi sterilised as every other. We tug and grasp at hardy ropes, fighting fierce wind, gravity and rigging, sails popping and pulling taut. Reefing like our lives are depending on it. Needn't have panicked. These brides know all about the double play of sail and rudder, forward surge and running down the face of waves.

And as winedark soup slops over the deck, it all starts coming back to me in strobing shards and spits and slivers. A voyage under dead of night, ocean waves like thick and blackened blood. Tossed and pitched and rocked and roiled, Gramma's tanned arms straining against the wheel. Thunderous rumbles, random flashes. The slick and oily surface of the deep. Everything so much bigger than I'd ever dreamed of; the boat, the sky, the waves. Rapid dog-leg bolts firing from the base of vast formations, with me a bumbling, clumsy little boy bundled tight in orange polymer; lashed to the mast to stop me sliding overboard while Gramma's shouting words I can barely hear.

Well of course my memory can't catch her words – I was never on the *Santorini* – or any boat during exclusion years. I wasn't even born. I never got to meet my Gramma. But stories, they get under your skin, they sidle up and seep on through and before you know it, you're claiming whole great swathes of half remembered fancies. Heraklion boasts three Cleopatras, one small gay Napoleon and enough self-righteous Kennedys to inhabit their own island if we could spare one.

Memories are not to be trusted. Nor are digital remains. The 88-minute war messed with our hearts and heads. These days we put our faith in stain on paper. Our library-museum contains so many precious treasures, our paper made from seaweed and driftwood pulp. Ink from bottled squids, charcoal and boot black.

Remembering's what turned us into a nation of poet-gardeners, exclusion zoned and heritage listed, yet here we are on my trusty *Santorini*, slipping in under stealth of day. Crusty old salts back on land are certain old war drones see better in the darkness. Best we can hope for now is obsolescence.

My admiral's jacket's graphite thread count refracts sunlight and radiation. My doggo doesn't need protection – he runs on 100 percent bio-D. The brides have come prepared for anything. A corset bodice is a gorgeous vintage look, pretty bows or knots, cutouts, extremely flattering and the extra exposed skin adds alluring touches, pearls being the ultimate classic feminine detail – subtle yet beautiful embellishments evoking romantic sentiments.

Neither Rhiz nor Goldie listen when I explain exactly what we're going to find on Santorini isle. Bleached donkey bones and crumbling ruins and perhaps a mangled mash of cable cars. Feral cats in disintegrating doorways – haunted beasts, all matt and bone and sinew. The caldera harbour choked with cruise ship skeletons, all sunk and drunk and listing on their sides. A reef comprised of smashed remains of hulls and hulks and fallen Boeing carcasses.

Daisychain's barking up a frenzy and I cling on tight with both hands as memory intrudes of fire raining, people screaming, running with hair aflame. Gramma grips me, won't let go, crushed and mangled by a giant wave. Not my memories. How could anything like that belong to me? Might be my Gramma's boat but I never met her. All I've seen of anywhere is pretty postcards.

Eyes wide open and I can't believe it – no wonder Daisychain can't keep hushed. Laid out ahead is a real-life picture postcard. Skala Pier as good as old, nestled at the feet of impressive cliffs, the curve of donkey steps cut clear. Little boats of red and blue and white. I'm bobbing in a little boat myself, jammed between two bulky brides who don't seem the slightest bit impressed that we are literally entering a postcard, entering memories that can't possibly exist.

"But the 88-minute…"

Nobody cares about those minutes in this moment. Brides tumble from the shore boat in a confectionary of white chiffon and lace, dripping water and sloughing rosebuds and sequins.

Faint music wafts from a bistro embedded higher up in the volcano's side. Unfamiliar music that is neither old nor new. Murmuring voices and the clink of knives and forks on china plates. *Nice to meet you. Thank you. Bye bye.*

Santorini, ripped straight from the bluest blue of postcards. A wafting blend of seasoned, grilling fare distracts me from figures in dim corners, hovering.

The donkey trek is beckoning – not taking chances on the clack and shudder of a potentially figmentary cable car fighting gravity up grim volcanic rock the colour of sun blasted lichen.

I sweat up pathways lined with spiky cactus, eucalypts and oleanders, perfect as those pre-war era dirty postcards. White on white and blue on blue and the sun begins to sink as church bells peal. Hot young things pause, bating breaths and posed for tanned and tattooed boyfriends fumbling with large, expensive cameras. A miserable child throws its regular sunset tantrum as swarthy men heft luggage down the winding, pale grey stairs, white edged, the solid slap of sandals, passing locals sweeping and fixing and fetching and ferrying, pushing carts and weeding potted gardens.

A welcome splash of bougainvillea as drinks are stolen from passing trays and we merge with random wedding parties, pretty girls attached like limpets to my Admiral arms as fading sunlight dapples cheeks.

Daisychain barks and the girls let go as something emerges from the crowd, at first shapeless, shifting and coalescing, then hardening into solid and unmistakable bride. Not one of mine, this is something new, or perhaps much older as well as blue and borrowed. Brighter than a supernova, entangling me with its searing diamond glare. A being birthed during 88 minutes when humankind let go and dropped the ball.

No words from me. Nor from the bride. Daisychain does all the talking, barking and barking until the moment passes and the entity glides off about its business to the accompaniment of bouzouki, clarinet, lute and mandolin, santur, toubeleki and a flurry of enthusiastic stomping.

And I realise I've been waiting for this moment all my life, suspended in a thousand damaged windows to the past, in garish scenes frozen and manipulated, trapped in laminate, glossed and falsified and static. Whitewashed, airbrushed, Photoshopped, grand slammed and Instagramed, rose tinted, sunset squinted.

Familiar and comforting sounds envelop: the violent flap and rattle of sun umbrella canvas in stroppy winds and, somewhere in the distance, yelping. Eyes wide open – now what has that damn doggo got himself into this time? Over my shoulder, beyond the flat-roofed houses pressed into volcanic cliffs. Beyond misty blue deceptive Aegean remnants, dotted with white triangle sailboats leaning as bright pink petals scatter on gentle vespers.

Two wedding guests, lithe girls in livid blue, already drunk and separated from their pack. Above their tight-pinned fascinators bob blue and white balloons expelled into the wild, destined for the intestines of sea turtles and whales if only such elaborate creatures still existed.

Tears of laughter, tears of joy and hello, what is happening over there? One blue dome per church or maybe two, three at a pinch and I'm pretty sure that's law – but that one there, by the holy slippers of Saint Spyridon of Tremithus, that church appears to be *encrusted* with blue domes, pulsing and blooming like pustules of far cast cerulean pollen. Whitewashed walls butting against each other, doors and windows merging into tunnels.

And Rhizanthella, she's starting to resemble a tank with human legs and filigree, the bio-ordnance still configuring to her pearl-encrusted form, tugging and stretching, snapping and shifting, folding in upon itself, then outward along new lines.

Furrows ridging deep between my eyebrows. "They're gonna know you're not one of them. That outfit will not fool an artificial mind."

A familiar huffy pout distorts her face. "Who's trying to fool anyone or anything? My repurposed ordnance frock is an expression of solidarity, connectivity and haute couture." She winces as something unseen beneath a polymer chitin layer pinches. Tugs at it till the irritation passes. "Them. It. We are unsure of the correct applicable pronoun, greeting or salutation. Not sure of their status or their numerical identity. Their personhood, so to speak."

Not sure what I'm supposed to say to that, so I keep quiet as she continues. "We just want to talk is all. We –" and she gestures to the brides "– have come to join them."

"Join whom? Who is *them* exactly?"

"The collective entity now known as Santorini, Admiral dearest!"

"Can't be a person and an island both."

"Says who – you? Who made you the boss of regenerating land masses?"

I puff my chest up like one of those birds on the postcard advertising California iceberg lettuce, but she's already turning away as the wedding party ripples at its centre mass and an old bird emerges, swaggering into view like one of those vintage cigarette packet cowboys inviting you to come to where the flavour is. She is wire thin with hair like Alpine frost. Thin lips stained flamingo pink.

Daisychain yips and barks and does a mid-air backflip. Then another and another till he is nothing but a whirring hot metal blur. And I should have been yipping and flipping alongside, because there before us stands, impossibly...

"Gramma!" And not a day older than however old she was back when we fought our way across the post war soup. Except that...

"But Gramma – no way... How can you be here? And how come I can't remember... or maybe I can? I am molecules away from doing backflips of my own. Not the joyous type – the meltdown kind.

"Long story, kid. Turns out I'm older than I look – and so are you. Santorini, however, well now, this island is as young as a spring chicken. Great to see you've taken good care of my dog."

"*Your* dog?"

But by all that is almost holy I can see this fact is true – the doggo and Gramma, well now, they're a team. Daisychain dances around her in a smoosh of figure eights before rolling on her back in a wriggling frenzy.

Gramma bends and crouches down to scratch his tin can belly. "There's a good boy, best boy ever. Thanks for keeping an eye on my precious grandchild."

And I want to ask so many things, but they all get tangled in my throat before the moment slips away entirely.

"This island achieved sentience during the 88-minute war," said Gramma – as if that fact was anywhere near the top of my desperate-to-ask- list. "Must have been well shielded for this spittle-lick of salt and rock to avoid full spectrum wifi sterilisation."

As I watch our doggo wriggling in the dirt, it all clicks like it's never clicked before. Santorini has regenerated based on a million momentary fragments, postcards all, one form or another. Once a bridal theme park, now a living beast with shifting moods, beyond the captured, trapped and static. Imprisoned memories catapulted, free range to multiply and seed. Pollinating and embedding into pocked volcanic cliffs; gnawed and pushed and jabbed and punctured, flowed like lava, stabbed like steel. Surged and spilled like cactus flowers after a once-in-a century splash of rain.

And how well the shipboard brides are blending, some more dramatically than others, but that's brides for you, so the legends tell us, some being practitioners of stealth rather than flourish. No dress code regulations or traditions exist for interfacing with sentient islands – but looking like you belong here is a start.

And no one wore modular, load bearing tac force haute couture better than Rhyzonthella, who was always safe rather than sorry and looked amazing, blue hair blowing in the wind. But I soon lost her amongst the bustling, narrow streets, amidst manifesting holographic tourists and real-life flesh and blood descendant Greeks who'd never left, despite the manic changes. Who kept on playing, low and quiet, tricks learned withstanding decades of bridal entourage assault in summer months. AI governance seems a trifle in comparison. If governance is the appropriate word (it isn't). For all I know the Greeks are AI too. Never one to quibble over details – and I'm still not.

At the day's end, lurid sunset splashes fuchsia across vague Aegean dregs, when knowhow is all very well, but not much good until paired with targeted *know why*. And as for knowing wherefore, well now, that's a different story. Come back and check on that one next millennium.

Because I'm in love with this picture postcard, its vistas swift and inconsistent on the shift, and I can no longer tell my brides from ones with artificial hearts. Boatloads of tourists pull up at the groaning pier and wait for donkeys to take them up the side. Emissaries from other islands, joyous at heritage listing's feisty abolition.

My brides have seen a lot of love and can sing you all about their great escape with the Admiral who braved the Winedark Soup for connectivity with a future not yet written.

A couple of years ago friends invited us to stay with them in a holiday home on Santorini. I've never been anywhere that seemed so overwhelmingly like a living postcard. Slick locals work very hard to extract summer revenue whilst maintaining the quality of the surrounds. The volcanic clifftops are completely infested with bridal parties – my friend revealed she had once spotted 27 brides in a single day and I reckon if I had peered far enough over the rim I'd have discovered a pile of them on the rocks below, broken brides who had fallen off their shoes.

DRAGON GIRL

I fell in love with a dragon boy when I was seventeen. The dragon train –
five creatures long – camped near Grimpiper in the days before it crossed
the Great Divide. Beyond the stones lay the Dead Red Heart. Our 'stead
nestled in amongst the shadow dunes. Close enough to the Sand Road, not
too close to its bandits and its warlords.

We'd been pushing our water wheels across miles of stone when the
kite went up. Blue tail flags might mean many things but this time blue
meant dragons. We dropped the wheels and ran up Puckers Ridge. Right to
the top and there they were, five dragons chewing through wild melon
fields below. Thick-set creatures, bellies low to the ground.

We risked a whipping, abandoning our wheels like that, but dragons
were too tempting to pass up. Nothing ever happened out Grimpiper way.
We could not know then that the train would camp for three full days, and
when it left, I would be leaving too.

The youngest of his tribe, he was. His beast trod last in line. His
dragon smaller than the others by a head. Broad, flat teeth ripping through
dune melon stems.

"Does it bite?" I asked.

Iago (I didn't know his name back then) shot me a playful grin. Tossed
me one of the loose dune melons. I held it coyly, watching him stand so
close to that chomping mouth. Close enough to make the other girls
shriek. He tossed the melon. The dragon snapped it up. "You try," he said
and so I did, dallying with the beast for hours, until Carlina and her
Noahan witches came streaming down the dunesides, waggling their palm
frond shades, weighted down with baskets of throwing stones. Chanting
lists of animals that had been rescued by the boat and how no dragons
were written on that list. Dragons were abominations, made by human
hands. The same dab hands that brought the Ruin down. All misborn
beasts must be driven across the Great Divide, was what they preached.
That, and a host of other, darker things.

I didn't care about what Noahan witches said. Their praying and their
whining never rose the water table or brought the rain or caused the crops
to grow.

Iago's people were tall and dark, dressed in sand cloaks, deep blue like
the night. Merchentmen – or so I thought – with ancient rifles slung across

47

their shoulders. For show, they were, not fighting guns, but you never could be sure with Heartland folks.

Carlina stared with big wide eyes when she saw that thunderstick, all chipped and grey and mounted on spindle legs. A fearsome thing, even with its fire drained.

"For serpente hunting," Iago told me.

Iago's uncle never said a word. He stared me down as the Noahan's chanting drove the other girls away. I ignored them all, keeping up the melon game, watching lithe, brown-skinned Iago unwrap his turban and shake his long hair free.

Couldn't keep my eyes off him. We fucked in the shade of a withered copse of palms. Didn't care who saw us. Didn't even wait for night to fall.

"I'm not afraid of your uncle," I told him.

"You should be," his reply. Later, he told me how the dragons were not really dragons. Lizards, more like. Creatures bred in glass. True dragons were supposed to have had wings, their bones turned hard and trapped in stone for centuries.

I knew then that I would leave Grimpiper and the shadow dunes. The Noahans and the farmers, goat herders and beekeepers, fighting over water rights to the last uncontaminated wells. Mother shrieking after me to look out for my brother. Flint, who had hit the pilgrim trail, one year gone, his name not spoken since.

I remember laughing, warm wind blowing in my face. Getting sweaty with Iago, shirking chores and hanging at the dragon's feet. Telling no one of my plan to leave, except Iago who had known it from the first.

We were five days out when I learned the truth of it. The dragon train sought not new wells as Iago's uncle claimed. They followed the pilgrim trail themselves in search of Ankahmada. The same cursed city that enticed my brother to his doom. A city carved from a living sapphire, rumoured to be blooming in the Dead Red Heart. A pilgrim trail grown cold and strewn with bones. My brother's most likely lain amongst them.

The Dead Red Heart, land of stonewhales, skates and serpentes. The most we had glimpsed so far were ruins and the bones of creatures long dead. Maps by day and stars by night. Lands so repetitious they could barely be endured. We travelled under the sun's full glare, protected by flimsy canopies. Each beast flanked by point riders on camelback.

Dogs ran at the dragons' feet. They never tired or weakened. Dogs kept other predators at bay. Other dogs, mostly, and other things that looked a bit like dogs. Our beasts were fed and watered well, even when the rest of us were parched.

Iago's uncle never spoke a word to me. Few of the drovers were much for speaking words. They spoke in sign, signalling back and forth across the sand, that thunderstick remaining in plain view, attached to Iago's uncle's camel's saddle.

Wedged behind Iago, travelling last in line. Scanning horizons for serpente sign, chewing on leathery roo jerky and ember bread. Talking about the people we had lost: him two sisters stricken by the sweating fever. Me my one and only brother, leaving home without saying goodbye. The heat of the sun and the chill of the night. Sleeping upright in the saddle, sliding in and out of dreams, awakening under a different hue of sky, sometimes on an entirely different day.

The dragon people thought the sapphire city real. They carried tiny chips and shards of it in battered leather pouches. Held them up against the light, comparing them for purity. Poring over faded maps so creased and crushed they barely held a mark.

My mother collected Dead Red maps. She had close on to forty, every one a clever fake. The cheapest kinds you could score at any Sand Road trading post. Some were inked on ancient crumbling paper, others on treated hide, fabric or faded plastic.

I believed in many things: the Obsidian Sea and the giant ships that slid across its surface, borne on massive old-world butyl rollers, thick sails bulging with wild winds. Travellers claimed to have seen such craft push out from Fallow Heel. Souvenirs slung around their necks, wards and sigils carved from the slick black glass. But Ankahmada, a city carved from jewel? Not even a Noahan witch would fall for that one.

Fifteen days beyond Grimpiper's wells, I awoke to the sound of human voices. Iago, conferring with one of the camel riders – a man with his face obscured beneath a striped khafiya – both of them pointing to a dusty smudge that might have been no more than a pile of rocks. No kites hanging in the listless sky. If it was an outpost or a 'stead, its people did not wish to draw attention.

Iago's uncle rode his camel ahead, spyglass at the ready. Dragons plodding in a firm and steady line.

"Watch," said Iago.

"Watch what?" And then I saw it, a sliver-glint of sun. A flashing signal, patterned. No accidental reflection. Someone was trying to speak to us. I braced myself to swerve towards the light but we did not.

Iago's uncle appeared as disinterested as his camel. Iago, however, kept a keen eye on that flashing. More handsign passed between him and his cousins, swivelled in their saddles as the dragons took us closer. The glint and smudge took shape and form – a row of columns protruding from the sand. The dark, squat shapes of scattered tents and pens.

Three small boys burst from behind a low dune crest, running towards us, waving hands, shouting words of greeting in a mix of tongues.

Iago was not pleased to see them. The boys kept up their loud distractions. Iago's uncle regarded them with distaste. Iago tightened the grip on his dragon's reigns. The boys whooped and cheered, racing back the way they'd come, tripping and tumbling over their own feet. Four bells gave the dragons' signal. They pulled up to a slow stop, one by one.

Iago's uncle had apparently changed his mind.

I wrapped my arms around Iago's waist. "What is happening? What is this place?"

"Trading post," he answered grimly. He handed me the precious spyglass he wore around his neck on a strip of leather.

Grimpiper 'steads were parched and sparse, but even the meanest and driest of them was a grand bazaar compared to this sorry array. A handful of scrawny goats bleated miserably in ramshackle pens of unevenly-hammered stakes. The way was strewn with camel bones. Three mangy, fly-blown dogs growled at our own dogs and at the dragons. Catching their scent, but without the energy to jump and bark. So utterly malnourished, they might have been the undead demon dogs those Noahans swore ran rampant through the Red.

Our own dogs kept a wary distance. Dogs that had never before shown a lick of fear.

We were as close as we were going to get. Movement stirred at the base of the columns. Just the wind, or so I thought at first.

I sat up, straight and saddlesore, straining for a clearer view.

Iago's uncle wasn't getting off his mount. He stared at the trading post a lengthy while before sending two point riders to investigate. Neither man looked happy with the task.

"What do you reckon he's after?" I whispered.

Iago and I shared the glass between us, watching our riders approach the men who sat gambling around a coarse and tattered mat. Coins glinted sharply against the weave. Weapons placed within easy reach. Now and then, a glance would be thrown in the direction of the tents.

Tents that were thin and patched and faded. Through an open flap, a group of people peered. Women and children, they ranged in age from elderly down to a babe in arms. Their clothes were old, their faces tanned and lined.

The women whispered amongst themselves until one of the men called out, demanding silence. Abruptly, the women shushed, then the tent flap fell.

At seventeen, I knew little of the world's true pain, but this was plain as day. A slave market. The captives miserable wisps of skin and bone, huddled around the columns, weighted down with chains. The men on the mat were cowardly dogs, each one hung with the totems, tools and trophies of his trade. Men whose stench I could smell from the dragon's back. I would have spat except they weren't worth the water.

The condition of their animals spoke to many truths. Animals are everything, from Grimpiper all the way to Sammarynda, so often meaning the difference between life and death. Only the very stupid treat them like they do not matter.

The men got up from their gambling mat. All teeth and smiles with pudgy, waterfat flesh, greeting the point riders with open arms, clasping their hands as if they were old friends.

No need to hear the words that left their lips. Their smiles weren't fooling anyone. The 'merchandise,' still chained, was paraded before the riders single file.

Merchandise. My brother Flint. Had fate deposited him in this terrible place? I peered and squinted in the sun but could make out nothing. The scrawny captives had been too ill used. Too far away to make out better detail.

I lowered the glass. Iago stared intently at my face. Somehow he knew what I was thinking. He placed his hand upon my cheek. "The pilgrim trail ends sooner for some than others," he said.

Our people did not linger. The pitiful slaves begged our riders with outstretched arms, pleading for the turbaned desert men to take them. They knew they were done for if the men left them behind. Skinny and sick, no longer worth the waste of food and water.

"What if Flint is one of them?"

Iago grabbed my wrist and held it tight. "You can do nothing. Those men are dead already."

"Let me go!"

"It is not wise to annoy my uncle."

"Not wise? Is that all you can say?" Wrenching my wrist free, I jumped down to the sand. Further than it looked, I landed badly. Iago shouted words I didn't hear.

All I cared about was Flint as I hobbled through the loose-packed sand, particles clinging to my sweaty legs. Feeling the weight of Iago's uncle's eyes upon my back.

The two point riders offered me stony stares. The slavers, whose grimy odour filled my nose at twenty paces, observed me with amusement. Perhaps they thought me property for sale.

"Flint!" I scanned the row of suffering wretches, most barely well enough to stand. Walked from man to man to check their thirst-pinched faces. None were his. Relief came first, then disappointment. If he were here then I could save him. We would know what had become of him, what might become of him still.

"My brother Flint walked the pilgrim trail. Have you seen him?" I asked each man in turn. Some said nothing, others answered me with jumbled, rasping gasps of prayer.

It was hopeless. The slaves were close to death. I moved to stand behind the two point riders. One of them said something to the men who had been gambling. Words foreign to my ears but not theirs. Harsh, sharp words that left their mark. As we turned to leave, the leader of the slavers started cursing.

Tempers barely contained in the brittle heat. Anger that posturing and false cheer couldn't bury. Blades were drawn. The half-starved dogs skulking around the trading post perimeter started barking up a storm. Through all this, Iago's uncle watched in silence.

The three young boys edged close to the action, raising stones to throw just like the Noahans back in 'Piper. Fearful mothers called their names but dared not leave the safety of the tent.

We stood our ground against the gambling men. They outnumbered us and could have cut us down, but the pressure of five dragons kept them practical. Turned out they'd hoped we might buy the men for sport, or drink with them long enough to wind up drugged and robbed. Such was the way they made their coin, but Iago's uncle never got down from his mount.

Threats were shouted across the sand and then we parted ways. "What will happen to those slaves?" I asked. Neither rider answered. We all knew what would happen to the wretches – or at least I thought we did.

I turned back just in time to see a slaver draw his sword. Snatches of angry bickering bounced upon the wind. The tongue was foreign but its nuances were not. Somebody would end up punished for this day.

Iago's uncle stiffened in the saddle. His cloak billowed suddenly as if filled by wind only there was no wind to fill it. None at all. He reached both hands along the camel's side to heft the thunderstick.

Bells signalled that the dragon train was lumbering into motion. A single drum setting pace for the mighty beasts.

Iago waved his hands in a flurry, anxious for me to climb atop the beast where it was safe.

But before I could move, a sound like a mighty dragon's roar. What happened next was way too fast to see: one minute there had been a shiny row of columns. The next, all that remained was belching smoke. Exclamations of surprise, but the dragons did not miss a beat.

The thunderstick rested high upon Iago's uncle's shoulder. The air around him sparked with flickering embers, raining to the sand like firecracker dust.

Iago shouted out my name. He fought to still his beast but the dragons were expertly trained and the bells were ringing loud and clear and true.

"Hurry – you must hurry!"

I ran to his dragon, last in line. Raised my arms and he hauled me up the saddle's side. The thunderstick was fired again, aimed this time at the tents. Smoke cleared revealing nothing but flames and splinters.

The tent completely gone.

Slavers stumbled blindly through the sand, tripping over goats, dogs and each other. Too stunned to even curse or raise their fists.

"Your uncle planned to kill them all along," I whispered. "You knew what was going to happen."

Iago didn't answer.

Dragon drovers and camel riders stared blankly at the smoke, mesmerised by its ferocity. Gaping at the pale blue sky as black roils dissolved upon the wind.

"That tent was full of women and children."

The horror of it slowly sinking in. Suddenly it was all too much. The stench of singed flesh blended with gunpowder. The relentless ache of endless sun. The row of columns once shiny-white reduced to blackened rubble.

Iago's dragon was on the move, but all 'Piper brats knew how to jump and roll. Someone cried out as I hit the sand. Iago, perhaps. By then it hardly mattered.

The sand was soft. This time I landed well and scrambled up to standing. Hurried to chase down Iago's uncle, quickly before anyone could raise a hand. Most eyes remained on the burning mess that marked where the trading post had stood.

"You got no right!" I shrieked up at his back.

Uncle's cloak twitched like a living skin. At last I saw it for what it was. Old tech. Pre-Ruin. Forbidden. Dangerous. Marking Iago's uncle as a sorcerer. But it was way too late for backing down. What was started had to be completed.

"That tent was full of *innocents*," I screamed.

Uncle kept his back to me. I dodged my way around his camel's side. "You're a coward, hiding behind that ancient reliquary. Get down off that camel now and face me." My heart was pounding as the words flew out of me. Words that could do nothing but get me killed.

A curl of amusement touched the tall man's lips. The intense blue of his eyes pressed down like a weight against my chest.

"They were marked for death already. All of them," he said, his voice the deepest sound I had ever heard.

He urged his mount forward, our talking at an end. I held my ground as the dragons lumbered onwards, animals and people giving me a wide berth. Two dogs lingered, eyeing me with keen and hungry interest.

I wanted no part of any of it. The dragon train. The pilgrim trail. The sapphire city. Iago and his soft brown skin. They were all bad men and I would stand my ground until the desert claimed me – or the sun, or the sandskates, or my heart.

I didn't get the chance. One of the point riders pulled his camel up close beside me. The beast bared its crooked teeth, leered at me with annoyance.

"Get on," said the rider, voice muffled by a striped khafiya, his arm extended down towards my own. Iago's friend – I had heard them talking together often enough.

I stood proud. "What if I don't?"

"Then the vultures will eat well tonight." He glanced at the sky, then down at the dogs. "Your bones will be picked clean before too long."

"You cannot make me."

What was I saying? What had I just done?

I held my ground even though my legs were shaking. So did the man in the striped khafiya. Eventually, the last of the dragons passed.

Silence lingered, heavy and complete. Dark shapes flew across the sun. Vultures, real or imaginary.

"Please," he said. "Die before your time, if you so choose, but do not waste your death on this cursed place. Your brother, if he lives, will not thank you for it."

There was something familiar about his eyes. Rich and brown like fresh-tilled soil. He waited past the point of mere politeness. The man was right. Pride like mine was worse than useless. Reluctantly, I gripped his arm and allowed him to haul me up into his saddle.

A blast of singed flesh and hair enveloped us as his camel galloped to catch up with the dragons. I stared at the horizon and the future that lay beyond it. Grimpiper was now as lost to me as it was to my crazy brother. I could not go back; I did not know the way. There was only forward to a city that most likely did not exist.

The sun hung heavy overhead. No shadows. No perspective. Nothing but blinding glare and burning thirst. I didn't glance back at the ruined trading post. I couldn't.

The rider pulled his camel alongside the smallest dragon. When my eyes met Iago's, I saw what I had earlier failed to see. *Eyes the hue of fresh-tilled soil.* Iago and the camel-man were brothers.

A full day passed before Iago allowed me back up to ride behind him. Two before I was granted full forgiveness, my transgression evaporated like condensation on a bulging waterskin.

On the third day we passed a message scrawled upon a sun-bleached slab of stone. No words, just a diamond etched in blue. An arrow pointing to the far horizon.

Ankahmada, Ankahmada, whispered like a ward, snatched from cracked and bleeding lips, vaporised by canny, skittish winds. Beyond the rise, or the next one after that, or the next one.

We were almost out of water when a cry went up to stir my fitful saddle slumber. My eyes wide open, expecting the blue of jewels. In their place, something altogether stranger.

Jammed and scattered amongst the dunes the hulls of giant ships protruded: bows and masts, some of iron, others warped and rotted wood, swamped and choked in tides of shifting sand. I counted fifty before my numbers left me. What would Carlina have made of this strange sight – what could anyone ever make of such a thing?

Iago's brother had taken to riding his camel alongside Iago's dragon. Now and then he'd smile at me when Iago wasn't looking. One of the dogs had been bitten by a sandskate. The brother had refused to leave it, carried it tight against his chest wrapped up in the striped khafiya. He reminded me of my own brother in his courage and determination. I did not believe in Ankahmada but I was beginning to believe in Iago's brother.

The dragons wound their way through the sand-drowned ships in single file and silence. Late afternoon brought with it the welcome half moons of shadowed dune crests, clear of wood and weld. Once more we could see where we were headed, even if we had no knowledge of where the fabled city lay. The wind grew stronger, waterskins flapping empty. We shielded our eyes and stared out across the repetitive curve and undulation of the dunes, straining for a glimpse of kite, or the speck and shadow of a lonely bird, but there was nothing, neither human nor animal, larger than the skeletal bugs that I imagined clinging to the spindly thorn bush stems.

Set in the far future Australia of my novel, *Lotus Blue*, 'Dragon Girl' provides a bit of backstory for one of the novel's characters, Iago.

YOU WILL REMEMBER WHO YOU WERE

Amaryllis Storm-petrel, performance poet, essayist and famed orator of classical fantastika, had barely stepped upon the stage (where *Banksy himself* had grand debuted) when terrorists hit Solstice Arc with a data bomb. Barely whispered the opening to *The Inspiration of Botanical Forms on Twentieth Century Lithography* when screaming drowned out everything and shiny auditorium surfaces bloomed with liquid graffiti montage; a maelstrom of harried images and sounds, ugly footage of war and deprivation successfully penetrating the barrier fields.

Solstice Arc Security took several minutes to sanitize and flush offending contaminants. Handheld, implanted and wearable devices were proving trickier to purge than walls and surfaces. Data shrapnel, although crude, could be exceptionally sticky.

Zoo animals were the only exhibits to survive digital assault, with their impervious surfaces of follicle, hide and fur. The Siberian tiger, proboscis monkey, African elephant, brother lions, proud-horned buffalo, Tibetan mastiff and one slightly moth-eaten zebra watched over proceedings with glassy eyed indifference.

Not even the auditorium's magnificent rose window had been spared the gross indignity. Amaryllis screamed upon the dais beneath its pastel splendour, makeup streaming down her face, her elegant recitation trampled beneath the soles of a thousand panicked feet. Within hours, no one would remember the intricacies of her hand-stitched gown, incremental gradations of progressive blush, blonde dreadlocks embedded with ceramic and heat-set resin protuberances reflecting the patterned work of Axel Salto.

Injuries sustained in the crush and panic amounted to nothing worse than broken ankles. Better to be safe than sorry – Amaryllis's functionary Simpkins whisked her retinue back to the safety of the Pomegranate Suite while the scrubbers were still sanitizing the tiles.

Nobody said anything as Simpkins busied itself with making tea. Amaryllis, rendered temporarily speechless, presided over an unnatural blanket of strained and debilitating silence. Until her pulse returned to normal, no one would dare speak. Terrorist attacks were becoming more frequent. What was SolASec doing to make them safe? Edwina Yukatan's prose performance *The Symbology of Peacocks in Anglo-Japanese Aesthetic*

Interiors and the 24-hour live tattooing of Mori Yuzan's wonderful *Ha Bun Shu* had both been ruined by weaponised broadcasts from outside. "Those vile animals!" Flecks of spittle sprayed as Amaryllis clenched her fists, doubling over in mock intestinal discomfort. "Thoughtless, brainless, marauding beasts. Months of work and all of it ruined in seconds!" She kicked off her heels and began to pace the antique Persian Tabriz Tree of Life, a sign to all those gathered in commiseration that drinking was now permissible and in order. That a respectable pause had occurred between the tragedy and the first signs of recovery. That everything was going to be okay.

The entire Arc had apparently been infected. Various items tailored to the Pomegranate Suite's unique architecture still hissed and fizzed with electronic taint. Each one would have to be hand scrubbed, flushed and recalibrated. Stray code worked its way down deep, the same repeated images over and over. Muddied by pattern degeneration and interference, hard to make out the terrorist's original intent – if indeed there had been one beyond the simple, brutal plan of disruption and distress. And who knew what embedded stealth might lie within? Codes eroding structural integrity intended to endure unnoticed over time.

Simpkins proceeded to serve Bai Hao White Tip oolong tea in fine bone china cups to three seated Temperance League Angels. Everyone else got Scofflaws and El Presidentes. Matching appropriate drinks to unfortunate events was one of Simpkins' noted specialities.

SolASec would eventually send an emissary to check on everybody's health and wellbeing. All would be interviewed, invited to give statements outlining their discomfort and dissonance. Nothing could be done to stop the sporadic assaults – but such gestures were important and respected. Citizens were entitled to feel safe in the Arcology cluster 1500 metres off the ground. The sky forest endured perpetual bombardment. More and more strikes were getting through, sometimes even shorting out the storm shields or damaging the vital solar canopy.

As Amaryllis continued to recover incrementally, a trio of her closest confidantes clustered tightly side-by-side, heads bent forward examining the glossy surface of a lamp. Blurred terrorist faces stared up and back at them. Men with beards and ruddy sunburnt cheeks, babbling in unfathomable tongues. Amaryllis stormed across the open space to slap the lamp right out of the girl's hands.

"My private sanctum," Amaryllis spat.

All three flinched as pearlescent shards danced across the floor. They stared at her with glassy, unfocused vision.

"My heartbeat has been interrupted!" she informed them all.

Simpkins circled, fussed and fretted until every fragment had been collected, sucked up inside its compact polymer casing, whisked away to where the shards could do no harm.

Amaryllis resumed her pacing, which was evolving into an off-the-cuff solo performance. Glanced up as a stray image slid like liquid across the pale peach feature wall. More terrorists, with their wind-chapped cheeks, scrappy beards, beady eyes and pained expressions. The wall glitched and the bearded men were banished.

"This is beyond intolerable." She gestured wildly to the place where they had been. "Like we're supposed to believe *such people* could be capable of a full-on Arc assault."

The gradual murmuring that had been building across the minutes ceased. New tangents were often accompanied by hush.

"Computer generated," she continued now that she had everyone's attention. "Such shoddy work – those *men* don't even look real! This manifestation smacks of subterfuge, a contemporary rendition of the Sufi poet Rumi's 'Embroidery on Water' – with digital trickery in place of marbled paper." She nodded, agreeing wholeheartedly with herself, oblivious to the surrounding blank expressions. "Notice how the scrubbers always kick right in before we get a chance at a closer look. Those 'faces' crawling across my wall could be anything at all. And I'll bet that's just what they are – *anything at all.*"

She stopped pacing, started gnawing on a thumbnail. "No, not anything or anyone. Shhh. Somebody clever is behind all this disruption. Somebody who wishes to target me specifically. I sense an enemy hand. Vindictiveness and spite. One of my archest rivals." Her eyes narrowed. "Archangeline Nolde, perhaps, with her boring obsession with Eighteenth-century German chinoiserie and all brocade papers in general. Or Perron Ashlar? Yes, of course, Ashlar, that flake. He seems a viable contender."

She spun around to see which of her gathered coterie were in agreement. Continued once the drinks were poised midair.

"Remember that time Ashlar claimed to have an *actual* ninth century Su-I-chien sprinkled paper sample amongst his *so-called* private collection? How we laughed and laughed and nobody believed him? How he made such a big fucking deal over my minuscule slip up, when I confused 'bouquet' and 'peacock'? As if there is anybody alive who truly comprehends the intricacy of marbling. Anybody in here? I didn't think so."

That they did not, she already knew. Eighteenth-century German brocade papers were an utter bore. Which was why she concentrated her own work entirely in the Nineteenth-century, shining a spotlight on Scheele's Green and its associated 'Witch fever'. Arsenic paper – what was not to love?

The revelation, when it hit her, nearly toppled her off her feet. "Oh my god," she said, with heat-flushed cheeks, "It's Banksy!"

She had to repeat herself two times over, first for the ones who had not been listening, then again for the ones who couldn't quite wrap their heads around the *raw implication.*

She spoke slowly as though explaining a matter of life and death. "This recent spate of terrorist attacks bears every one of Banksy's signature hallmarks. The media-age guerrilla mystique, the visible poverty and degradation. The lack of a signature within the form – not to mention ambiguity. The absolute simplification, revealing its entirety in a moment. All so textbook, so antiquated, so phoney. Are we actually supposed to believe these bearded muftis are real people down there living on the ground?"

The murmuring started up again in earnest. Today belonged to Amaryllis – rules were, after all, rules – but now with the excitement over, her allotted performance time was draining fast, losing ground to new moments and new possibilities.

Glasses were raised, liquid was supped. The feature wall sat still and flat and featureless.

"Yeah, but you're forgetting one small thing," said Eevee, the girl who had been holding the shattered lamp and had now budded off from the main group. Gorgeous, young, and less than formally rehearsed. Her party trick was to ration words for added, weaponised impact. "Banksy's been dead for three whole years," she announced with a subtle twist of smirk. As if she was the only one who had ever noticed.

Girls like Eevee turned up often, cycling through the social streams, reinventing the wheel with monotonous regularity.

"So true, my dear, so very true," said Amaryllis, "but can you think of a better media stunt than being dead and returning from the grave?"

Footage of his body falling had appeared so nondescript. That body could have belonged to anyone and most likely did belong to anyone except the infamous artist known as 'Banksy'. And yet… Amaryllis played the footage on a loop, over and over from multiple angles, just to make sure she wasn't missing anything. The concept, now that it had manifested, would not release her.

"How certain are you that this footage is authentic?" she asked the room. "Absolutely – check out the sigstamp." Georgieau, well-known *hackstrordinaire*, waved his hand gracefully at the bottom corner of the wall.

Amaryllis flicked her gaze. "Would have thought he'd have dressed a little more appropriately for the occasion," she said.

Georgieau sniffed. "Equinox Arc, my dear – you know what *they're* like."

Only she didn't know. Nobody from Solstice Arc knew anything more about Equinox than what got screened on HiBeam and Toupe. Cryptic pseudonarratives intended to inflame and outrage. In Equinox, apparently, citizenry *lived* rather than *performed* their art. Nobody could sit through more than an hour or two of those imported tedious expressions. Not since the Vernal Biennale, in its own way the catalyst for a series of changes to inter-Arc immigration policies. It was almost impossible to get a visa these days. Not something many Solsticians cared about.

"But they never recovered Banksy's body, did they?"

Georgieau rolled his eyes theatrically. "Of course *they* didn't, darling – and who, by the way, might *they* actually be? Did you forget we're 1500 metres off the ground? Whatever's scuttling about down there below… Well, I don't think *they* would be up to the task of retrieving splattered broken human corpses."

"Unless they were hungry," added Absinthe – generally such a quiet boy – who had slunk in late and therefore missed both the attack and the follow up dramatics.

"No way there is anybody left alive down on the ground," chimed in Eevee. "I saw this documentary on how clusters of supercell tornadoes formed this cleansing breath and blew the people and animals all away." She held her hands out, palms up, fingers stretched, leaned forward and made to blow through puckered lips.

Georgieau and Amaryllis exchanged knowing glances. "Why don't I ask the wall…?"

"No, don't bother – I don't give a shit about what's crawling about on the ground. All I need to know is – is that *genuine* footage of Banksy's body falling through the clouds? Because it all seems so convenient, him just throwing himself out of a handy window. A recording becoming mysteriously available three years later."

"It's been available for ages. Nobody thought to look for it, is all," said Absinthe.

Amaryllis wanted to ask him how he could know one way or the other, but he'd come in late and was probably just being deliberately annoying.

"Well, honey, if anybody knows anything, it'll be in the wall there somewhere…" As Georgieau – good old reliable Georgieau – checked and checked again, Simpkins moved about between the seated guests, picking up discarded clothing and other items, clearing a space upon which to set the all-important drinks tray. Dodging Amaryllis whenever she veered too close as she paced awhile before spinning on her heels.

"Archive, play back last night's terrorist attack. Just the clip itself, not the security response."

At first nothing happened, and then, instead of the anticipated replay of those fuzzy, bearded men, the wall illuminated with the Solstice safety logo: two hands interlocked, one pale skinned, one dark, thumbs forming a cross.

"Damnit!" Amaryllis shrieked. She took off her shoe and threw it at the wall, where it bounced harmlessly off the safety logo. Simpkins ceased its fussing over the tea and moved immediately to retrieve the shoe. It placed it neatly near the door where it wouldn't be in anybody's way.

"But somebody must have kept a clip!"

Georgieau was already initiating a fresh search utilising those shortcut commands he was so good at. "You'd think," he said, "but apparently, this time, no. SolASec scrubbed the lot – can you believe it? I can't figure why you're so interested."

"Because I'm looking for proof, that's why. If Banksy's responsible – and I'm sure he is – clues will be embedded in that fake footage."

Eevee let loose a small volley of coughs. The artificial kind most commonly uttered to pave the way for some kind of overblown, showstopping statement. "Well, if that's true," she said, standing up to stretch her long white arms and legs, "he's likely to strike again, don't you think?" She finished her stretch and sat back down to find both Amaryllis and Georgieau staring at her hard. Waiting for the punchline, the payoff, the point to the boring girl's entire existence. Even Absinthe was paying close attention. Or seemed to be – it was hard to tell through that obscura he always wore. Obscuras and other forms of masque seemed to be the latest fad in pointless, decorative triennial accessory.

"Like, why wouldn't he?" Eevee added, comprehending slowly that her companions were expecting something more. "No point in making art if nobody sees, is there?"

"No point at all," conceded Amaryllis, "but I still need to get my hands on that clip. I need to know if that man intentionally ruined my presentation. If he intends to go on hounding my career."

"Acts of disruption as actual performance art? I get it!" Her face lit up.

"Soul graffiti," Amaryllis replied, nodding vigorously. "Drawing energy directly from my suffering."

"Yeah, well best of luck with that," said Georgieau, slumping backwards into the couch's heavily embroidered depths. "There's no trace remaining of that last attack – I've checked and checked the wall. And checked again."

"Fuck it." Amaryllis kicked off her other shoe, stood tall and combed her fingers through her thick blonde dreads. "I'm going over to Equinox. Somebody must have been there when he jumped. If he jumped, which is seeming less and less likely by the minute."

As Simpkins dutifully set out to retrieve the second shoe, both Georgieau and Eevee shifted uncomfortably in their seats.

"You know you can't do that, Amaryllis, my dove. You know that tower-to-tower immigration is restricted. You remember that time we borrowed that teeny-weeny cloud hopper and buzzed around that stained glass atrium, and how those arseholes in black mozzies actually tried to shoot us out of the sky! Like we were criminal freeloaders, or land crabs crawling up the flipping sides!" The distressing memory had Georgieau visibly flustered.

Amaryllis flopped down on the lounger beside him. "There simply has to be a way."

"Oh, there is," said Georgieau, dabbing at his tears, "but it's dangerous." He inched closer and lowered his voice. "You gotta go down below and under." He made a snakelike motion with his hand.

"Down below and under where?" she said, leaning in.

"Solstice Arc base, sweetie. Do keep up. Everything's connected. Everything is part of the greater whole."

He reached across to place his index finger on her lip just as she was about to ask the wall to clarify. "Don't be an idiot," he whispered harshly. "No one's supposed to ask about shit like this."

"But I honestly have no idea what you're trying to tell me."

"Second wave," he whispered in her ear, before getting up and brushing specs of imaginary dust from his jewelled slacks.

Amaryllis leaned back and closed her eyes. She had work to do. Important work. Today's aborted performance would not be a total waste if she could manage to recalibrate and rebadge her infamous installation

One Hundred Million Square Miles: Green Rooms On Trend. But she knew she was looking at months and months of work on top of bribes for a prime spot back in the queue.

Second wave. How very interesting. But could she dare? That was the important question.

By the time she opened her eyes again, Absinthe had moved to a corner space and was running through a sequence of yoga poses: Balancing The Cat, Bird of Paradise, King Pigeon, Hero Supine, while Georgieau had become absorbed within a game, one of those retro shoot-em-ups that had become incredibly popular in the months following on from that solar flare. She'd tired of the damn thing weeks ago, just like she'd never stuck with *Gangnam Posse* or *Weeping Angel.* Games so rarely held her attention these days.

She stood up. Simpkins swivelled, poised and attentive in the manner of an old-world dog, only a hundred times more irritating. "So I guess that's where I'm going – down and under, as you say, Georgie dear. Any of you got the balls to accompany me?"

Silence. Much more of it than expected, under the circumstances.

Absinthe held the downward facing dog with his eyes tightly closed.

She had to throw her cup at Georgieau just to get his head out of the game. Plenty of folks lost weeks or months in there. She had no idea where they found the time, or, more particularly, the inclination.

Eevee stared at her uncomfortably, chewing on a stray coil of blue hair. An irritating habit she'd picked up from old anime. One she thought made her look exceptionally young and vulnerable.

"Anyone?"

Eevee shook her head, letting loose a tousling mess of springy curls.

"Fine, then I'll be going on my own."

"It's not safe!" chimed in Georgieau, blowing imaginary smoke from the barrel of the weapon only he could see.

"What are you talking about – of course it's safe. There's nothing in the Arc bases but big machines and service functionaries. Unattractive things, but hardly dangerous. So long as one doesn't trip and fall into an air reconditioner." She laughed gaily at her own joke.

Georgieau shook his head dramatically. "I can't even…' He focused his attention back on the game. "Don't go telling me I didn't warn you.'

She shot a sly and subtle glance at Absinthe, with his eyes closed, still in the downwards facing dog, a pose he'd been holding much longer than anybody ought to. She smiled. God damn that Georgieau, but he was good.

She clicked her fingers until Absinthe opened his eyes and straightened up.

"How about you then, Absinthe? Got some secret *tips* that might come in handy?'

The room was suddenly quiet. Eevee squirmed uncomfortably. Georgieau increased the vigour of his shooting.

Absinthe offered her a stony gaze. "People don't go down there if they don't have to. That's the way of things.'

Amaryllis stepped closer to him, glaring back with full force. "I have to go. I have to know the truth, no matter the terrible danger or the risk."

"I've been expecting you,' said Absinthe when the doors to Annapurna Lodge swished open with a sound resembling a bubbling cascade. Amaryllis stepped across the threshold, eyeing the waterfall-themed, blue tinted interior. The rain symbols etched into the walls, the semi-transparent raindrop patterned curtains.

Amaryllis Storm-petrel was not known for making house calls. Of late, she barely left Pomegranate unless absolutely necessary. Common spaces seemed so overwhelming, with their floor-to-ceiling metal trellis grids, vivid organic atriums with phenotypical plasticity intended to evoke a sense of permanent garden party.

She waited for him to elaborate, but Absinthe didn't say anything. Nor did he put down the book he had been reading – *The Truth of Rebirth and Why it Matters*.

Absinthe was not alone amidst the waterfalls, but none of the other Annapurna residents gave her more than a casual glance. One in flowing saffron robes was painting a delicate landscape, the other two were absorbed in private games.

She stepped closer so she didn't have to raise her voice.

"I'll get straight to the point,' she said softly. "They tell me there is no way down to the base of Solstice Arc, but that isn't true, is it? After all, there must have been a way *up*." She paused, hoping he was going to make things easy. When he didn't say anything, she continued. "I wanted to come to you in private. Not to make a scene. You know what I'm saying."

"Yes – and here you are."

"Indeed. Here I am. And I'm certain you understand what I am referring to."

She expected at the very least a sharp stab at denial, for him to sling her a volley of questions such as who had brokered his deplorable secret and if this knowledge was in common circulation. So many precarities that could get him into trouble. He flicked his gaze to the two ensconced in gaming. Amaryllis nudged him towards the raindrop patterned curtains and the susurrus of water they emitted.

Second wave. Those plucky souls who had managed to fight their way into the Arcs long after the bases had been sealed. The ones who had managed to acquire false identities and voluminous currency. All had stories even if they didn't choose to share them.

"Absinthe – or whatever your real name might have been. You can't have been very old when you and possibly your parents… did whatever had to be done. I'm not judging. I just want to find a way below. You know how important this mission is to me."

"It is not safe, going down below."

"But it is possible – yes? There is a staircase or some kind of secret shaft?"

"There is."

Silence filled the space between them. She became aware of the suite's medley of deep-hued blues and the calming force they encouraged.

"Guide me down and you can name your price." She made an expansive feature. "Anything. I'll use my influence to get you a solo exhibition space in Musée d'art Moderne."

Absinthe's expression remained grim. "I'm not going with you."

She smiled broadly. "Oh yes you are. I require a native guide in order to descend. You are my best and only option."

"You have no proof that I was *second wave.*" He spat the words out, as if they filled his mouth with poison.

"No, you're right. I don't. But I can use my influence to ensure *everybody* is talking about the *possibility* for as long as it takes. Looking for evidence. Going through your things." She started pacing across the hand-woven azure rug, gesturing at individual items that may or may not have belonged to him. The saffron-robed painter of indeterminate gender looked up from their work, then looked away.

"There'll be a souvenir in here somewhere. Something small. A token. A family memento, ugly pendant, or perhaps a nasty little toy. A faded photo of a brother or sister who –"

"Stop it!"

She stopped.

The saffron-robed painter pretended not to have noticed the outburst.

"Good," said Amaryllis, "then the matter is settled. You will tell me where to meet you and I will make no more mentions of *second wave.*"

The giant brushed steel elevator was taking the longest time. Simpkins had explained to Amaryllis with extreme and practiced patience how the descent had to be slow because of issues of vortex and velocity, balance and counter pressure, things peculiarly to do with the design of such a fearsome and towering construction.

Whatever. Amaryllis had not wanted to bring Simpkins along, but somebody had to carry their supplies and Absinthe was far too skinny and distracted. Enough to do a runner at any given moment. Not that there'd be many places to run to.

Amaryllis had prepared herself completely, fabricated an accurate historical reproduction of the explorer's outfit worn by Mary Kingsley in the 1890s, including a replica moleskin hat, the original of which had been sadly lost to the rising surge when the Royal Geographical Society went under. A damn shame that. So many treasures had been struck from the Earth, including the one so dear to her own heart, The Olga Hirsch collection, lost forever with the terrorist bombing of the British Library. Only digital images remained, along with downloads of Haemmerle's *Buntpapier*. Three thousand, five hundred irreplaceable treasures incinerated – with so few left to truly comprehend the tragedy.

"I apologise for the earlier unpleasantness."

Absinthe offered nothing in reply.

She longed to ask him how he had known about the secret elevator hidden behind the trellises. So many questions and details about the systems in place, just how far underground movements went to facilitate travel up and down the tall Arc stems. But the boy was keeping all his secrets to himself.

They travelled in silence for a while.

"You must have been so very young," she said.

He shrugged, eyes staring ahead at the blur of white visible beyond the glass. "Can't remember much."

"You must have seen –"

"I said I can't remember." He sniffed. "Got a block or two in place."

"Ah. Well, I guess you would have, wouldn't you?"

An hour passed as slow as dripping resin and still she knew virtually nothing about the boy and his past history. She tried to recall the time he'd first come to her attention, perhaps in Agnella Ferragamo's production of *Equus*, or Parinaaz Cusseta's overblown opera *Loufoque*? So many performances, so few of them worth committing to one's soul. Eventually, as the silence between them began to verge upon the stifling, Simpkins kicked in, playing music just to fill the void. Nothing recognisable, although Amaryllis could recall reading about how elevators in the time Before used to offer a selection of jaunty, popular tunes. To pass the time and make people happy – two things nobody worried about any more.

"Was there just you or were there other family members?"

His lack of response grated raw against her nerves. "The terrorist attacks are becoming more frequent," she said bitterly. "I don't know what Arc Security have got to say for themselves. We pay good money – a lot of good money – but how is one supposed to feel secure with ugly faces crawling across the walls? I think I had more sympathy when they used to blow things up. That was some mighty powerful aggression, but this? This – whatever they call it – is just graffiti."

"Guilt bombs," said Absinthe.

"Guilt? What has guilt got to do with anything? It wasn't Solstice Arc who broke the world. It wasn't me – I wasn't even born when the West Antarctic Ice Sheet slid into the sea.

"But your people managed to get out and up."

"Yes, they were the lucky ones."

"Lucky and rich. More rich than lucky."

"There wasn't room for everyone. You know that. You've seen histories."

"What I've seen is floors and floors of plundered art."

"Plundered!" She turned to give him a good, hard stare. "Are you saying they should have abandoned it all to the bottom of the rising seas? The point of the Arcs was to preserve the very best."

"And keep the richest handful safe from harm."

"To preserve the human race. For posterity," she added. "And beyond." The elevator continued its descent through swirling, storm bruised skies.

"The storms are pretty this far down, I have to say," she said. "So horribly ferocious, and yet… so mesmerising. Like wild animals cavorting in churning seas. Not that I've seen an ocean with my own eyes. Have you?" She paused, staring out through the thick protective window. When he didn't answer, she continued. "I've half a mind to write an epic poem about this whole experience. A retelling of Ishtar's journey to the underworld." She snuck him a sly glance. "Perhaps I could write a role for you? The part of Ishtar's lucky lover, Thomas."

Absinthe turned his face away. "Suit yourself," she sniffed.

More uncomfortable silence hung between them as Simpkins switched from Shostakovich to a medley of XTC songs: *Senses Working Overtime*, *Plans for Nigel* and *Wrapped in Grey* with no pauses in-between.

Beyond the window, now and then, gaps and cracks in the cloud cover revealed splashes of dirty blue.

"Perhaps guilt is the only weapon they have left," said Absinthe. "Perhaps *they* are trying to tell us something."

Amaryllis, brightened by the fact that he had finally decided to engage in conversation, shook her head. "But what stories could there possibly be left to tell out there? It's all so sad. So very, very sad. I feel for them, the ones still clinging, what it must be like, the ones not quick enough to scramble through the cracks, but we have such an important role. We are custodians of the future. The future, Absinthe, think of what that means. Our art, not just our bodies and our souls. There's a reason second wave is so taboo. Let even a few strays in and all hell breaks loose. An avalanche of human misery – that is what would follow, without doubt."

"Rather than a lapping tide, you mean?"

"Excuse me?" She turned her attention from the blue and angled her body around to face him. "There was not enough room for everyone – you know that. Everyone would have starved within a month. Who would take care of the art collections then? Who would protect our culture for the future?"

Evidently Absinthe did not have an answer to that. They travelled the next few hundred feet in silence, watching swirls and eddies through the vista window.

"I thought there would be more to see, the closer we got to ground," she said eventually.

Both of them stared out through the massive wraparound window, hoping for a break in the repetitive cloud cover. Perhaps even a bird if they got lucky. Plenty of people believed that birds had somehow found a way, but Amaryllis herself had never seen one.

"Look, I know you're less than thrilled at being coerced into accompanying me, Absinthe, but I'm positive I'm right about this recent spate of hideous attacks. You'll be entering into history when I expose that wicked fraud for all he's done. I would bet good gold that the attacks cease as soon as we examine the raw broadcast footage. Banksy's signature will be embedded. The man won't be able to help himself – trust me.

She raised her hands, making circles in the air. "All of this is a marketing stunt aimed at bringing back the Banksy brand. It's all a game to folks like him. Killing himself was really quite insightful."

Absinthe continued to stare at passing clouds lit up by occasional forks of lightning.

"I'll bet he's sitting up there in Equinox right now, sipping champagne and laughing at the rest of us."

"And if he isn't?"

"Then there's no harm done. Such adventure is almost an art form in itself."

She had thought the cathedral ceilings of the Odeon Auditorium and Royale Crystal Ballroom high enough – certainly the highest interiors in all Solstice, but this... Amaryllis gasped in involuntary wonder as the sturdy elevator doors grated open to reveal more open space than she'd thought possible. Neither Odeon Auditorium nor the Royale Crystal Ballroom could compare – three or four such chambers of magnificence could have huddled in here side by side.

Her heart expanded with joy and wonder as she stepped out, arms outstretched, fingers splayed, eyes closed at first, then opened brightly. She started spinning, swirling, dancing, making broad, dramatic gestures, taking up as much space as she could. Simpkins paused, emitting cautious meeps as it awaited fresh instructions.

"But what could all this space be for?" she sang out. "What's it doing here? Why has nobody told me?"

"We should hurry," said Absinthe quietly. "They probably have all kinds of surveillance."

She spun around a few more times. "The obscuras we wear serve to block digital intrusions. That's what everybody says." She brought herself to a dizzy standstill. "Now you're going to tell me they were lying?"

"Not lying, but down here it's different."

"Different in what way?"

Simpkins issued a polite robotic cough. The kind it generally emitted whenever it encountered people in a suite doing things they were not supposed to be doing.

"Base has a different set of rules," said Absinthe. "The shafts leading to Equinox –"

"Rules? What rules? You really do talk a lot of nonsense. My goodness – look over there – functionaries!"

Absinthe was already looking, being hyper-tuned to snatches of movement in his peripheral vision. Shapes emerging from and vanishing into shadowy spaces around thick column bases. Functionaries, perhaps. Perhaps something else. Difficult to make out in such dim light.

"We should go," he said, nodding to a narrow path that hemmed the wall. "We should not stay here out in the open."

"But out in the open is positively exhilarating!" said Amaryllis, who had bored of squinting at potential functionaries in muddy light and had resumed her arms-out spinning and laughing. "Out in the open. The obscura –"

"Cannot protect against line of sight," he warned.

She wasn't listening. So much fun and a secret chamber, vast and wide, her own private place; so much room, so far away from the crush and steam of everybody else. Proto-poems were gestating in her inner vision. One could burst forth at any moment. She must be ready for it when it landed. A work as powerfully inspired as this one could not be ignored or delayed.

Simpkins was becoming agitated, emitting a soft yet persistent alarm long before the strangers stepped out into view. Amaryllis had chosen to ignore the machine's vast array of irritating noises. The promise of the poem wholly occupied her senses and the machine was prone to overexcited outbursts.

The strangers – men and women, when she could actually see their faces – came as quite a shock. Their dull garb was akin to shadow, the expressions on their faces grim and cold.

The fabric of their clothes was coarse and their faces shadowed with subtle grime. She opened her mouth, prepared to launch into a myriad of questions, when one of them interrupted, cutting her off. A large man who nodded in Absinthe's direction.

Absinthe nodded back. "Don't say anything – I'll handle this," he said calmly.

The men shook hands and exchanged words that she could barely follow. What sounded like a name. A name that, apparently, belonged to Absinthe.

"Samih? What a dull, dull thing. I'm not at all surprised you changed it. Who are these people and what are they doing down here?"

The large man stared at her coldly.

Amaryllis had so many things she wanted to discuss, but she didn't like the way he eyed her outfit, as if her clothes did not meet with his approval.

"Absinthe, I don't think –"

"Shhh... it'll be all right. Come on."

In the end she followed rather than get left behind, especially when Simpkins wheeled itself dutifully after the group. Their footsteps echoed on the hard, ceramic tiles. Now and then she thought she heard the flutter of wings and pigeon coos, but surely such a thing could not be possible?

71

The installation occupying the grotto was retro of the purest stripe, some kind of bizarre studio-style set up, with its lopsided array of digital banks and screens. Thick cables coiling like polymer snakes; circuit breakers, panel boards, thermo units, switches, relays and solenoids. Equipment that had been superseded decades before sat stacked and gaffered in rough-cast assemblages and nobody seemed very bothered by the fact.

All attention was on the terrorist footage, to Amaryllis's relief. Finally, somebody was doing something about that. SolASec had fallen into lazy habits, behaving as if terrorism were just a part of the regular landscape. At least these scruffy people were taking it seriously.

She stared at mismatched mangled snatches of footage, some of it in black and white, other sequences in lurid colour, still other snippets bleached and singed with clever effects designed to make it seem antiquated. Some of it was genuinely old – *historical* footage from the time *Before*. There had been so much of it back then, so much more imagery than anyone had any clue how to deal with.

Simpkins had returned to emitting noises indicative of distress, bullet blasts of urgent data, strobing notifications of higher-than-tolerable pheromone discrepancies, air woven with unidentifiable chemical signatures, sounds below the range of human hearing. Hilarious, ridiculous little automaton, always worried about things it couldn't see. Or sense, or feel, or dream or extrapolate.

Amaryllis gave the machine a hefty kick.

She watched the screens over a squat man's shoulder. He didn't seem to notice she was there. Now and then she'd check something familiar: drone footage of overflowing refugee camps, flood-scarred farmlands, rotting carcasses of bloated animals, fire ravaging through blighted crops. Soldiers fighting to contain aggressive crowds. Burning office towers and cathedrals. Supercells uprooting mighty trees and flinging them in all directions. A massive ocean liner on its side, high and dry across a twelve-lane freeway. That last one – the beached liner – was something she had never seen before. The terrorists were obviously getting creative.

"Makes you think, doesn't it?" said another guy, one wearing camo pants, which, she considered, was designer overkill.

"Not really," replied Amaryllis. "I'm so bored of retro. All retro ever says to me is I got nothing so I'm sticking to the cycle."

She raised her eyebrow knowingly as camo pants guy turned to face her, slowly and theatrically.

"The cycle?" she repeated, "as in recycling? Get it? Yes, of course you do."

He stared at her for the longest pause, then turned back to his screens, which, being none too contemporary themselves, might have been more than half the point, she noted. Intentional, of course. Retro was always a statement in itself, a comment on consumer culture, but it was lazy, oh so lazy and she was sick and tired of it.

All of the people surrounding her seemed to be part of a single fashion movement. She glanced around in search of Absinthe, it being high time he explained all this rather than just dragging her through it like some kind of common and easily entertained tourist. Perhaps he hoped she'd become so overwhelmingly distracted as to let the matter of Banksy drop?

Amaryllis pursed her lips. If that were the case, he was sadly misinformed. She was a professional. She hadn't made it to the top of Artistes of Note and Consequence without digging in her heels when toughness was required.

"Simpkins!"

A stab of panic flushed her chest when she realised the functionary was nowhere to be seen. Just more and more of these drab toned people swarming in from dark recesses, rodent-like, smelling like they only washed once a week. What kind of fashion was that supposed to be?

"Simpkins!"

Instead of Simpkins she attracted the attention of men who might have been terrorists themselves, with their unkempt beards and shifty-browed expressions. They seemed to have noticed her for the very first time. They seemed to think they had something to say to her.

"What have you done with my functionary?"

Beyond the beards, some female faces, only not a single one would catch her eye. How very rude and she would definitely be lodging a stern complaint, but not before she'd located her functionary. She pushed and squeezed through the thronging crowd, trying to see over bulky, padded shoulders. Nobody would get out of her way. She did not have time for this – somebody had abducted Simpkins. The functionary had been programmed to defend itself and yet it had apparently not done a thing to stop them. She would be having words with its manufacturer. In fact, she'd be getting herself a whole new functionary. That one had always caused her trouble.

Finally she managed to catch sight of Absinthe, but something about him had changed. She couldn't put her finger on it. Body language – the way he slouched instead of standing tall. She had always appreciated his willowy countenance, his aloofness and nonchalance. Suddenly all the best things about him were gone. He appeared as ordinary as all the others –

73

whatever the hell these people called themselves. Illegals – that fact seemed beyond all doubt.

"It's time to go," he whispered when she finally crossed the floor to stand beside him. "Let me take you –"

"I'm not going anywhere until I've retrieved my functionary and solved the mystery of Banksy!"

"Keep your voice down low," he snapped. "You have no idea what you're dealing with."

"Oh come on… There aren't really any terrorists. Everybody knows it's true.

Somebody's cooking all this shit up, screaming for attention, same as always."

She snuck a look across her shoulder, then high overhead in search of bugs – both the electronic and the crawling kind.

Camo pants guy was staring at her hard. When Absinthe took her arm, she shrugged him off. For all she knew he was in on the whole Banksy scam. All of them down here were probably in on it.

"What the fuck are you staring at? What have you done with my functionary? That was private property. I can have you sued. My lawyers – "

Camo pants guy shook his head incredulously. "Lady, these broadcasts are coming from outside." He punched a sequence of command codes into an ancient keyboard.

"Outside of Solstice, definitely, I quite agree," she said. "One of the other Arcs is responsible. I'm thinking Equinox, but I suppose it could so easily be Midsummer or Midwinter…"

Camo pants guy cleared his throat and spoke with a slow drawl, like he was imitating an old-world farmer, someone who'd hauled around backloads of manure and got his hands dirty on a daily basis before the advent of vertical, soil free farming.

"I mean outside, as in *outside*," he told her. He raised his hand and pointed to the floor.

She looked to where he was indicating, as if there could possibly be anything to see in a spot of scuffed and dirtied ceramic tile.

There was more to be said and she was getting all fired up to say it when the hunching, gathered crowd split down the middle amidst a tide of murmuring, allowing a newcomer to shuffle his way toward them and the bank of screens. An old man wearing wide trousers, a blue checked shirt and a straw hat. Amaryllis had seen such hats in archived catalogues, but she couldn't remember what they were called.

Everyone else had gathered close in an effort to make sense of the intermittent broadcasts. The rough wide faces and the out-of-synch words being offered through parched, dry wind-chapped lips. Women wearing headscarfs, their well-padded arms wrapped protectively around small children. All seemed to be standing in a very windy place.

Silence crept over the gathering, everyone telling everyone else to shush. The old man's clothes stank of tobacco, perspiration and some kind of animal. Amaryllis wrinkled her nose in disgust. She had never smelled such taints beyond an installation's borders and she didn't want to be smelling them now, only nobody else seemed to care.

Everybody waited for the old man to do his thing. He spat out the toothpick he'd been chewing, cocked his head to one side. Listened hard as everybody watched, dividing their attention between him and the movement on the screens.

Amaryllis lost interest after a minute had passed. She turned her attention to the pools of darkness just beyond the stacks of old digital junk. Surprised herself by what she could make out: crates and sacks and tyres – Jesus – what possible use could all that rubbish be? A couple of manky-looking cats curled up on a dusty rug. What the hell was going on down here?

Somebody cranked the speakers way up loud, unleashing a torrent of foreign language gibberish. The old man nodded and almost smiled. Offered a string of words equally foreign.

"They are Druze," somebody said. "Druze? What the fuck is Druze?"

"They are people," the old man said in perfect, flawless English. "They are trying to deliver us a warning."

Just when things were beginning to get interesting, a hand pressed down on Amaryllis' arm. Absinthe, tugging her gently but urgently in the direction of the elevator. Nobody else was paying them any mind. A fresh attack was crawling its way across multiple glass fronts. This time, a climate ravaged wasteland. Not much growing. Skinny goats and children with bare feet, torn clothing and wild hair. This broadcast had sound, crackled and intermittent. Looming storm clouds threatened to dash the lot of them off the rocks on which they stood.

"Absinthe, you don't belong down here with all these dreadful people. We have to get to Equinox. We have to prove I'm right about Banksy."

"Don't make any sudden moves," he advised.

She let him lead her, but as soon as they were out of earshot, she whispered harshly, "Who are those Druze people? What the hell is all this business about?"

"They are really angry," Absinthe explained. "They say the world is coming to an end. That the cycles are all sped up. Messed up and broken… That they are coming back too fast. They are trying to warn us, up here in the Arcs."

"Warn us of what? There couldn't possibly be much left that could go wrong with what remains of the world."

"You'd think."

But she could tell that he was genuinely troubled. "I'm not sure I understand."

"Me neither. But you need to go. I can't protect you."

"But my functionary is missing!"

"I'm sorry. Simpkins was the price of admission."

"What? You can't be serious?"

He laughed. "What's it to you? You'll just get yourself another one. She's going to be much happier down here."

"She?"

Absinthe hurried Amaryllis onwards. "I'll take you back up top to Solstice," he said when they reached the elevator.

"No. Take me to Equinox, as planned."

"You don't want to go up there."

"You don't get to tell me what I want. I'm right about Banksy being alive and I can prove it."

Absinthe shook his head sadly. "You don't know anything. You don't even understand what you've just seen."

"I know you're not who you pretend to be – that's for sure, *Samih* – or whatever your real name is. Who are these people? How come they're living here against the law?" She stepped closer. "Do you think I can't find answers to these questions? Do you think no one will come looking for me?"

Samih took a small step back.

"Take me to Equinox and we'll call it quits," she said firmly. He nodded, just as she knew he would.

"Did you know there was another Banksy, back in the old days? His identity was a desperate secret."

Samih didn't say anything. They walked along a gradually inclining path, a corridor that gently curved in an upward spiral reminiscent of a shell. The hubbub of the crowd had faded and now there was nothing to hear but their own footsteps.

Amaryllis's long and heavy skirt was causing her great difficulty. "Why don't you take that off," he suggested.

"My outfit is a hand stitched reproduction of famed explorer Delia Akeley's. Her skirts saved her life, you know, when she fell into a spear pit dug out by the hostile natives. Thick fabric protected her flesh. Not that I'm expecting to encounter spear pits up in Equinox Arc."

"Equinox is not like Solstice."

She stared at him with a lifted brow. "So I've heard. But you have to understand that nothing you can say will stop me doing what I have to do. It's my art. My calling in this life. I don't expect you people to understand."

"You people?"

"Yes, Samih. I think we both know what you are. How much more there is to second wave. How second was not the last of it. All those people sponging off the system."

He had nothing to reply to that as they travelled along the corridor. Suddenly he stopped and she stopped too.

"This is it?" She had thought the rectangular wrought iron panels set into the wall to be designs, not elevator doors.

"One of them," he said.

"And I should press the button?"

"Yes, you should."

She did so with a flick of her gloved wrist. A ruby light began to glow and machinery behind the wrought facade groaned and clanked.

When she'd convinced herself that there was nothing yet to see, she turned her face back to Samih. Froze when she realised he had removed his obscura.

"Absinthe – your data. Anyone will be able to read your signature."

"I no longer answer to that name," he replied. "You'll be travelling to Equinox – if that's still where you want to go – alone."

"But I don't know where I'm going!"

He smiled. "Do any of us?"

She frowned, agitated. "No, that's not... what I meant is... when I get there..." "You're the one who believes in Banksy. Ask the poets when you get up top."

An ominous, yet distant-sounding clanking emitted from the mechanisms embedded invisibly within the wall.

Absinthe/Samih – or whoever he thought he was now – gave her a polite nod, turned his back on her and headed back the way they had come.

"Hey – wait!"

She had the strongest feeling she would never see him again. She wished she could feel more clarity about the elevator and where it might be taking her.

When it eventually arrived and the wrought iron doors jerked open, she stepped across the threshold boldly, letting go a small sigh of relief. A part of her had half expected the carriage to be strewn with bones. Georgiou would definitely have approved. Never mind poor Simpkins, she could always get another functionary. She was an explorer true – what poet could conceivably stand in her way?

She stepped out of the elevator into bold visions of an alchemist's garden, a purple fantasia in the royal shade, heart and kidney-shaped ceramic pools snug below rock waterfalls surrounded by thousands of waving *maneki neko*. Faces formed from grizzled clay suspended from the ceiling amidst gargantuan arachnid limbs that lurched and stabbed and shuddered. Not a single surface had been spared from cyber-faery bling and immersive installations – a nexus of haute couture fashion, technology, art and science.

Amaryllis took a deep breath, trying desperately to look everywhere at once. At marvellous fabrics seemingly fashioned by manipulating iron filings in resin. Pseudo-organic fabric forms pulled tautly into ligaments. Growing, coiling things for which there were simply no words. Tubes and flurries, hewn blocks, strewn boulders, parts that might have once belonged to animals. Chainmail kimonos and gratified Japanese parasols. A gown that appeared to be made of bubbles, another of geodesic metal lace.

Enchanting, mesmeric intensity fuelled such dynamic and path-breaking displays. Things looking fake but actually being real and vice versa. Abrasive, and yet calming, the textures, volumes, and techniques varied from graphic to graphic but were fluid, from apparently almost two-dimensional garments to wildly impractical exoskeletons. Awash with vintage, yet wholly futuristic references… a term not often used in Solstice Arc.

When she got back, she would write a sequence of gritty performance poems and perhaps an essay trying to capture the experience.

She pushed on past no fewer than four Abraham Lincolns amidst a watery tide of suicide Plaths, through to a maze-like structure with a pyramid at the centre, where heroes, gods and monsters wrought from marble, gold and bronze fought a giant dragon with three heads, surrounded by palm leaves and fern fronds emitting sounds simulating antique technologies.

Flesh and mecha organisms; Reiki-infused prehistoric plants rendered from plexiglass, synthetic coral, furry pink chairs, seedy neon signs all jutted out amidst the chaos. Chiselled skulls, bicycle bones, furniture made out of knives and teeth. A mixing of symbolic colour codes signalling a montage of unique creative processes. Two conjoined Audrey Hepburns flicking cigarette ash. People were allowed to smoke in here! How very Twentieth Century, so repulsive and invigorating. Everything was bright within – a region of extremes. How fascinating. Aside from the Lincolns, Plaths and Hepburns, no two people looked alike, yet all were possessed of a cross- wired and reckless swagger, resonating outsize personalities and self-accessorising style philosophy: stoned, nihilistic and celebratory combined with ostentatious flaunt.

Dreadlocked dandies in clashing printed fabrics, often richly-hued and ornately embellished, strolled through a massive indoor jungle where shrubs and vines did battle with Greek statues. Floral spores floated cloud-like around bodies in motion, effecting an elevation of the wearers, making them seem almost beyond human. Fantastical illustrations come to life.

They spoke in fabricated percussive dialect, from deep gurgles to high-pitched squeals, cooing, breathless come-ons and raspy, unintelligible mutterings.

It would be so easy to forget the reasons for her being here. Absinthe – Samih – it was getting hard to think amidst such overpowering, heady florals… that boy had brought her here for reasons of his own. Something he had wanted her to see, or touch or feel or experience in other ways. He seemed to think it would freak her out; she, Amaryllis Storm-petrel; performance poet, essayist and orator of classical fantastika. What did he know about her at all? Nothing. None of them knew anything, those scruffy second and third wavers, skulking around in the Arc's great roots like nuke-resistant cockroaches, praying no one ever flushed them out.

She would see about that, but not today. Today each open, crowded, colourful space presented its own delights and comforts. Bombarded her with sensory overload, made sticking to her original plan impossible. That, she understood at last, must have been the point, and she had fallen for it: hook, line, and sinker. She had let these people dazzle and excite her, with their loud and lewd, lavish displays and the knowledge that in Equinox, art was something inhabited, not performed. You lived it, breathed it, shat it, screamed it. What would one man plummeting to certain death signify to these people? Nothing!

Less than nothing. Barely even an incident.

Here she was, stumbling through a massive indoor jungle where technology and nature had become so entwined she felt her senses feeding back on themselves… hidden sensors triggered fake birdsong and blasts of pheromone-laced perfume, onomatopoeic lullaby propelling her across a jaded, has-been universe.

That fantasy from childhood – she'd had it so many times – awakening on a carpet of soft leaves in the warm and gentle sunlight of a secret forest. Impossible to realise, and yet… Child Amaryllis had been brought to Solstice long past the drowning of the last viable forest. She'd experienced nothing of the old, forgotten world. Impossible, and yet it was happening right now.

She dragged herself to sitting, clutching at the exposed tree roots that clung to mossy boulders all around her. Admired the threaded loops of gnarly vine, the fallen branches, pale as slender limbs.

All real then, not holographic. Dappled light falling on scattered leaves. Almost no sound. No animals. No birds. A sense of heaviness hung about this place, a dampness seeping through her weary bones.

Most definitely a forest – impossible but true. A marvel of environmental engineering, yet another example of their art. That boy had expected her to experience feelings of inferiority in Equinox. That made about as much sense as anything else. How wrong he was – how completely wrong! Every passing moment served as enhancement to the one before. So much beauty and serenity. All her thoughts were poems now, infused with graphic meaning and significance.

She trod lightly, step by step. The path wound upwards, as before, encouraging a teasing smile. So Equinox remained an Arc, despite such lavish illusory effects. The higher she climbed, the thinner the trees. Leaves blurred into trunks cancelling out what was probably artificial daylight, dampening the caw of distant crows.

Yet another installation. Best she'd ever seen. She would tell them all when she returned to Solstice, making good use of words like *authenticity*, *authoritative* and *convincing*. She believed in the substance of this forest, its sea of trees and foggy, filtered light. Her belief carried her on past turning, twisting, thrusting limbs and the chill damp that permeated the air.

No sound but the tread of her own feet on brittle, crunching leaves. The resonance of nausea – faint and fading. Perhaps she had drunk more than she could remember? Memories of the previous night and day hovered tantalisingly out of reach. A party; bacchanalia; phantasmagoria.

She remembered fleshy shadows sliding down white walls. Filaments of bright sugar-spun light.

More footsteps – and the sense that she was being watched. Of course she was. All art was ultimately for the viewer's benefit, the experiencer, the participant. She moved through somebody's installation. Somebody's *pièce de résistance*. Somebody's memories hammered into form.

A glitch in her peripheral vision: indistinct white figures drifting between trees. She tripped on undergrowth entangled with abandoned shoes. Leant her weight against a tree trunk encrusted with not fungus, but weathered plastic dolls. Hair and clothing rotted filthy by the damp. Parchment curses hammered in with nails.

She snatched her hand away just as a piercing scream cut through the tainted light. A suicide forest. She had read about such things, about the ghosts, vengeful and lingering. About the empty tents and crude stone altars.

She pressed onwards, heading for the light, ears filled with the sound of her own ragged breathing, feeling the pressing weight of centuries of despair and just when she could bear no more, she saw it, high above – the old stone chapel.

Amaryllis entered, stepping carefully, on the lookout, for what, she couldn't say. Only that she would know it when she saw it. Only that this was what she had come to see. The apex of her grand adventure. The moment that would weave the threads into a satisfying and coherent whole. The moment she would be remembered for. Everyone was going to know her name.

The inside of the ancient ruin was plastered with paper-printed faces. Images roughly tacked to crumbling walls. That someone should have such disregard for something as precious as paper filled her with a surge of blinding rage. Each ragged rectangle bore the image of a face, each one a child rendered in black and white. Black-and-white had once meant newspaper, the kind kept under glass and humidity control. Up here, up high, wind whistled through uneven gaps in stone. Dust and grains swirled through thin, stratospheric air.

The slam and rattle of bones made her jump. Not bones, machines from a pre-flood, whole Earth age. She had seen such mechanicals displayed in perspex cases; boxy black and grey and silver, umbilicalled to plugged and powered walls. These juddering, jerking, spitting things linked to one another via coiled intestinal tracts, spitting paper after paper, white sheets filled with grey-skinned, steel-eyed children's faces. The pages tumbled to the dirty ground.

A dark form stepped out of the shadows – she could swear he hadn't been there a moment before.

"Hello, lover. Nice place you've got up here."

It was *him*, no doubt at all. Aged a few years, naturally – hadn't all of them? Banksy, decked out splendidly in ridiculous clothes, pretending to be a priest for some whimsical reason. Just another petty stunt in the relentless service of his art. She could not fault him on that score, not after her own outlandish evening. She liked the way they got things done up here in Equinox Arc. Style and finesse back home were sorely lacking. The more she thought about it, the more she found herself approving of their peculiar quirks and means and ways. When she finally returned to Solstice Arc, she'd be taking these concepts with her – and much more. She'd be leading a new style revolution.

The monitors and television screens – such antiquated terms – were square, boxy affairs. Unaesthetic. Finer examples were displayed in Solstice Heritage Museum. Hard to imagine anybody trusting images so small and indistinct. Low sound, tinny, muffled and obscure. More of those repetitive children's faces speaking in a tongue she couldn't recognise. Not all Earth's languages were able to be preserved, a small shame amongst so very many others. Not all cultures, not all people. She regretted. Everyone regretted.

The clattering of the printing machines drowned out whatever the screen children were trying to say. She flicked her gaze to Banksy in his ridiculous long robes, waiting for him to deliver an explanation. She would let the man speak for himself, explain why he had pretended to kill himself.

But Banksy barely seemed aware that she was standing there.

Eventually she got bored of both the clattering and his silence. "Well come on then – I'm waiting. Tell me why you pulled such a ridiculous stunt. Then tell me why you decided to ruin my performance."

He didn't say anything. Perhaps this was part of his own performance? Perhaps he had many visitors. Perhaps he was tired of explaining things to other people.

The screen children continued their pointless, unintelligible explanations. Irritating chitter chatter as text crawled across the bottom of the screens. She stepped up closer so she could read it, dodging around great coils and lassos of spat out paper. English text. Well, that at least was something.

The light is magic. You can make it hot and cold. The people wear fine clothes and they talk a lot. They walk slowly and the food comes from the wall.

When she looked across to Banksy he was staring out of the high, stone edged window. He really did look like a priest. Something orthodox, like Greek or Russian. They held services in Solstice. You could book the chapels for such things.

The wind outside was fierce and strong and howling like some kind of wounded animal. Tearing at the tower like it was trying to get inside. Ribbons of paper billowed and scattered.

And then, unexpectedly, Banksy opened his mouth and words came out. "We are not safe here. Nobody is safe. Only forever trapped in the eye of the storm." He stared off into space, as if waiting for his words to properly sink in.

"Look, this is all very poignant and illuminating…" She gestured broadly around the cylindrical stone room. "All very dramatic and intense. But surely there were other ways to get your message out there, without resorting to terrorist attacks?" She paused, waiting.

He said nothing.

"Not that I even remotely comprehend what you're trying to say. Who are these children? When were they recorded? They look too rough for digital manipulation. Are they…"

She didn't say the words *down there*, but he'd know what she meant. Down there on the quake-stricken soil, the hurricane-blasted cliffs. Down there meant the ones abandoned to fend for themselves on a disintegrating planet.

The TV sets, the machinery, the children on the screens, all bore the touches of authenticity, something artists of her calibre learned to smell in these cloistered, close environments. Imitation was imitation, rehearsals paled compared to opening night.

She frowned, turning her face from the screens to Banksy. "Are you trying to tell me these children are talking to us in real time?"

"They are us," he said. "We are born again. Not up here but down there on the ground.

"On the – what did you just say?" *Utterly ridiculous, of course.*

"We are not safe here. Nobody is safe," Banksy repeated. "Only forever trapped in the eye of the storm."

She lunged, grabbing at his dark and heavy robes. Gasped when her hand passed right through him. Hologram. Somehow she had not considered the possibility.

He moved away, avoiding eye contact, approached the window, lifted his robe-encumbered legs and climbed on through, letting go and falling forward, soundless through the broiling, churning clouds.

Amaryllis hurried to watch him plummet, just as she had watched him fall before, over and over. From different sides and different angles. He had jumped. He had already jumped. There was nothing she could do to stop him.

Fierce gusts blasted crumbling stone, sent scatterings of dust into the air. Behind her, the clack and rattle of ancient printers overlaid with singsong children's voices.

The big round window made of roses.

Look at how I dance and sing.

But not allowed to ride the animals.

Reincarnation. They were talking about Solstice Arc, describing it and how they had once lived within its protective walls. Bullshit, of course. Such a thing was not remotely possible. That horrid boy had known what she was going to find, yet he had let her come here on her own.

Air so thin she could barely breathe. None of this was happening. Not real – just a piece of second wave trash playing a horrid, stupid, revolting joke.

Holographic Banksy continued his descent as a blast of freezing arctic wind forced its way inside the tower, ruffling reams of curling paper, swirling sheets like forest leaves and abandoning Amaryllis to the future.

There are people out there who believe they'll be able to avoid the global unpleasantness of climate change and other assorted human induced catastrophes by being incredibly rich and therefore able to buy themselves safety. In this story I imagine reincarnation to be the greatest leveller of all time.

FATA MORGANA

"They'll send the black death after us. You should have left me behind. I was happy underneath that mountain. All set for that place to become my tomb – I hope you know that."

"Better to be with your own kind."

"They *were* my own kind!" Bethany rasped, mouth opening and closing uselessly like a fish out of water. "Don't judge me by the limitations of my ageing body. That's all I am to you, isn't it – meat and bones."

The machine had nothing to say to that.

The wide, pale sky went on forever, as did the heavy mecha tread on coarse grain sand, a repetitive sound so mesmerising that Bethany kept drifting in and out of a restless sleep that did nothing to replenish her, but left her drained of focus and resolve. She'd lost track of the days and nights. The machine never tired, of course, not like she did.

"We gotta rest up, Mach. You're killing me. It's all right for you and your self-repairing bioceramic carcass."

Mach's mechanical legs continued their relentless pace. Something darted out between them, too small and quick to have been anything but a skink.

"So anyway," she continued, "now that I've had time to think about it, there are only three items you could conceivably have stolen. A block of tantalite; military grade cloud codes or a Seed AI. I mean, why would anyone care that you stole me?"

"Bethany, I am not programmed to steal."

"You're not programmed at all. Not since the Marusek Protocol. Got a smart mouth answer to that one? Didn't think so. Burned the Institute to the ground to cover your crime, whatever it was."

Crunch crunch crunch crunch crunch.

"They'll catch us. You know they will. They'll figure it out. They're not stupid. They'll launch a swarm and they'll pick the meat off me. You can't protect me with your body or your armour."

"You are safe, Bethany, so long as you reside within my frame."

"I need a rest, Mach. Put me down – I ache all over. I can't stand up any more, not even with you taking all the weight. If you'd wanted me protected you would have left me in the Seed Vault with the others. Don't go pretending any of this is for my benefit."

The Legionnaire-350s were not noted conversationalists, but Mach had mellowed over time. She was proud of the way it had deduced for itself that words had power, sometimes more than firepower itself. But nothing she could say would stop it walking. Not this time. Not until the machine believed them safe.

It took Bethany hours to become aware of the drool dribbling down her chin, longer still to comprehend that the mind-numbing crunching had ceased and that she and the Legionnaire had come to a complete standstill.

She blinked the dust out of her eyes. "Woah – whatsup? Where are we? What are we doing?"

"We are waiting, Bethany."

"Waiting? What are we waiting for?"

"You'll see."

"I won't be seeing anything very much longer. My old eyes are gummed and full of grit and the light is fading from the hills."

"Those are sand dunes, Bethany, not hills."

"Really? Bethany tilted her head and squinted, but it didn't help. "There was definitely grass before. And rabbits."

"Those weren't rabbits, Bethany."

"That why you wouldn't stop and let me catch one?"

"The incident you are referring to was three days back – and excuse me, but you couldn't catch a cold."

"Three days!" She sniffed. "Figures. Can't feel my stomach. Or my feet. My side aches – did I get shot or something?"

"You did not get shot."

"Then how come I got this great big stitch running up my gut?"

The Legionnaire said nothing.

"Did you do this? Did you patch me up? Don't get me wrong, I'm grateful, even though I can't remember, but something's after us – I'm telling you."

When the Legionnaire raised the polycarbonate visor that had been covering her face, Bethany let out a deep, breathy sigh. She had forgotten the visor was even there and had presumed her rheumy vision fading. Her eyes focused on rusted clumps of broken-down farm machinery choked and drowned in sand. Scrappy, emaciated chickens scratching at the ground. Leaning fence posts – the remains of a stockade. An ancient, enamel bathtub on three legs. Beyond the chickens was harder to make out, a couple of scraggly palms and a crooked wind turbine poking out from behind a row of mismatched, corrugated iron segments, brittle and rusted through. Ragged drag marks led to and betrayed the existence of a gate. Two words clumsily rendered in chipped and peeling paint: FATA MORGANA. The whole thing looked like mere breath could blow it over. Big storms clearly didn't reach this far inland.

Bethany started to shake her head. "No, Mach – no! We can't stop here. Looks like people living beyond that fence."

"Fifty-seven warm bodies not counting the goats," said Mach. "A bore well not drilled deep enough."

"Mach, we gotta get out of here. We're putting them all in danger."

But Mach wasn't listening, as she well knew. Its kind had been designed to listen, but they had got over it. Her own fault, as much as anybody's. Machine learning from environment and experience had rendered the 350s a batch of sharp, quick-witted, canny liars.

She sucked at her teeth. "Hard to believe anyone could make a go of it out here."

"Human beings are like rats," said Mach. "A few survive wherever they may scatter."

Bethany tried to turn her head in an attempt to give the Legionnaire an incredulous look. She failed, but knew Mach was accustomed to the gesture and its meaning. "What about Newcastle – have you forgotten already? There wasn't so much as a rat left standing after –"

"I never forget, Bethany. You know that."

"Never forgetting is not the same as remembering. *You* have a selective memory."

"And you do not always ask intelligent questions."

She bit her tongue before continuing, enunciating clearly. "If this village – if that's what it is – takes pity on our souls, we will be bringing them death from whatever's on our tail."

"I do not have a soul, Bethany."

"The Hell you don't. I put one in there myself, don't you forget that."

"You are mistaken in believing something is chasing us."

"Oh, come on. I wasn't born yesterday."

"No, Bethany, your date of birth is recorded as –"

"Come on, Mach – you know it's true. Something has been tailing us since Templestone Gate – or what's left of it. I want to hear you admit it. I want to hear you say those words."

"You need water, Bethany. The well beyond that fence is your only hope."

"If they let us in, that's the end of any hope these innocent people might have had."

"There is no such thing as an innocent human being. Bethany, you know my opinion on this subject. One bad storm and that will be the end of them. We would be doing them a favour."

Scratch and Orry came tearing across the flats, kicking up a cloud of dust and stones. Running like something mighty deadly was chasing their arses.

At first Nadeen paid no attention, probably just a straggler mutt. Stupid kids throwing rocks at the manky dogs infesting the crumbling fort. But when Orry fell and tumbled in the dust, Scratch about-faced and went back to help him up. That's when Nadeen went reaching for the rifle. Those brats were always at each other's throats, fighting over every little thing. It wasn't in Scratch to lose a race. Something big and bad was after them.

Not her rifle, but as Fata Morgana's crackest shot, she was the only one allowed to touch it – aside from Errol, and Kash when Errol was too dead drunk to stop him.

Whatever was coming, there had been no time for kites or signal fires. Just two brats, skin's teeth ahead of danger, running for their lives.

A crowd gathered below the stunted palms. Those who'd been working beyond the gate dropped everything to hurry back inside. It didn't take much to get folks spooked. Ginny's colicky baby started squalling worse than usual, drowned by the groan of corrugated sheeting frantically dragged across hard, stony ground.

"Catch those goats and get that gate locked up now – hurry!" Gruff, pink-faced Errol hoiked a glob of betel juice thick and bloody into the dirt. There wasn't time to fuss about the chickens. The stupid birds would have to fend for themselves.

Nadeen shoved her way to the signal post, craned her neck for a glimpse through the fence gaps. A war machine, sunlight glinting off its hell-black casing. Striding toward Morgana like it owned the place. Those machines were wicked deadly, programmed deep, infused down to the core. If one of them came after you, there was nothing you could do to stop it.

Nadeen shimmied up the signal post, wrapping one foot around a protruding spike for balance. The machine walked funny, considering what it was. Guys in the tower were shouting down at the ones trying to patch the busted fence. Damn fence could barely keep the roos at bay. If that war machine wanted in, they were all rooted.

"Get behind the granary," she shouted at the courtyard stragglers still fussing over Scratch and Orry. The rifle was loaded. It was always loaded, but Fata Morgana was almost out of ammo. Nobody knew the truth but Nadeen, Errol and, most likely, Kash. Knowing Morgana had a gun that worked made some of the little kids feel safer. Little kids didn't need to know the truth.

As the war machine moved into range, Nadeen held and aimed the gun rock steady.

Down below, at the foot of the post, Orry jumped up and down excitedly. "Got a soldier innit," he kept shouting, over and over.

"Get behind the granary – now!"

Nadeen couldn't see a soldier from her vantage point. Nor drones, which flew beside them into battle. That's what all the stories said, the bullshit yap that got traded from well to well. This war machine wasn't even carrying a gun, but they'd been fooled before.

Nadeen kept her weapon trained as the thing came to a standstill, ten good paces back from Morgana's gate. A shush fell over everyone – even Ginny's baby.

"What business you got with Morgana?" Errol shouted out, then again in Cantonese when the machine said nothing in response. Nothing happened for a long while after that.

The spindly watchtower was getting dangerously overcrowded. Everyone who reckoned they were anyone in Morgana had climbed up to gawk. Wasn't often there was anything on the sand worth looking at.

Eventually, after everyone had had a go at shouting, a fresh glob of Errol's spittle struck the dirt and the baby started up with its high-pitched wailing. The watchtower men bickered among themselves. The longer the machine stood there doing nothing, the more their fear of it faded, eventually degrading into pointless yap about what might happen if Maddock or Guantanamo from Puckers Ridge came scouting out on camelback, what might happen when those folks caught sight of it? What if they crossed the boundary stones, and reckoned on hauling the machine off for themselves?

Nadeen lowered the rifle and clambered down to the sandy ground. Put her shoulder to the splintered beam and slipped outside the gate before anybody had the nerve to stop her.

"Oi, missy, get yer arse back in here. Whatcha think yer doing?"

She ignored their angry, pointless commands. Errol and his Councilmen were always mouthing off about what they were gonna do. What they mostly did was eye things from a distance.

Everyone was shouting now from behind the relative safety of the fence. Telling her to *get back in there*, to *keep well back* and definitely *not to touch*.

Nadeen gripped the rifle in both hands as she approached. Remembering Kash's big soldier talk about the siege of Newcastle. All bullshit, she had presumed, but this war machine came mighty close to the fighting forces he'd described. A battle suit embedded with weaponry she couldn't even dream of. The thing was twice the size of a big man, made of a super-dense material. Its limbs and torso thickly ridged and patterned. What detail she could make out, she did not understand.

Gusts of wind blew sand against its surface. The war machine did not move. Nadeen kept her distance, lowered the gun and walked all the way around it, slow and careful, checking for visible signs of damage. Not that she knew what she was looking for, but it gave her something to do while the Councilmen in the tower shouted themselves hoarse.

Gradually the ruckus from behind the fence died down. Nadeen stopped at the place where she first started. Something rippled across the war machine's black skin, an electric fizz, a trick of the light, maybe, and then she could see something new. A human form encased within, embedded in the machine's body. A soldier, just as Orry had tried to tell them.

Gasps and whoops erupted from the watchtower. Now they were cursing and praying out loud as well as spitting and shoving and arguing.

Wedging the rifle butt tight under her armpit, Nadeen stepped as close up as she dared. Beyond a cocked-open visor – which she could swear had not been there a moment earlier – a face. Old and pale and etched with lines. An ancient woman. Nadeen had never seen a person of such age. Maddy Frank was the oldest person alive in Fata Morgana. Reckoned she was sixty-four and maybe that was true – who could say? But this woman might have been twice that. She looked like a ghost, so frail and whisper thin, like willow branches bundled together into human form. Her eyes were closed. Might have been sleeping or dead.

"Hello?" Nadeen was surprised by the frailty of her own voice.

The old woman didn't answer. Her bruise-purple eyelids remained closed. Her thin lips were pinched and shrivelled.

Nadeen glanced beyond the machine toward the old brick fort in the distance, half expecting some kind of explanation. But she could see nothing that had not been standing there for a hundred years.

The war machine remained as still as age-old rock.

Nadeen turned to face the watchtower, shielding the sun from her eyes with her free hand. "Dogs'll get her if we don't bring her inside," she shouted.

Errol offered up a string of curse words in reply, with Kash chiming in, as usual. One of the brat kids had shimmied up the lookout post with a rock clutched in his free hand.

"You wanna watch the dogs rip into her? You want the kids to see that?" Nadeen added.

A rock the size of a balled-up fist landed with a soft thud on the sand beside her. Bloody kids.

Nadeen took a deep breath. She stepped up closer to the war machine, making no sudden motions, her hand reaching carefully, two fingers raised. Stretching up, she laid her fingers against the old woman's neck. Paused to count, a frown etching her brow.

She stepped back suddenly away from the machine. Turned to the tower and called out, "She's still breathing."

The sky above their wind turbine was streaked with dirty orange cloud. Desert chill was beginning to set in. Nadeen was about to give up hope when the air filled with the scrape of dragging metal. The gate hauled open wide enough to permit both her and the war machine to pass.

Skinny Yusuf leant his back against the old cell door. He eyed the bowl of mushy porridge gripped in Nadeen's hand, but he didn't say anything and he grudgingly shifted when she indicated she was going inside.

She kicked the cell door shut behind her, stopped at the sight of the war machine hulking in the far corner, so black it seemed to suck light out of the room, so tall its blocky head almost touched the ceiling.

The old woman lay upon a rag-covered pallet shoved against the mud-brick wall. So frail and helpless, knees pulled up tight against her chest, knobbly ankles poking out from beneath gunmetal grey pants.

"Brung you some food," said Nadeen.

The old woman stirred softly. Her eyes opened, revealing pale blue irises. When she didn't move, Nadeen knelt down to assist her. She placed the bowl of mush and spoon on the ground, very carefully, so as not to make any startling sounds. "Let's sit you up there proper," she said, with one eye on the war machine again, making sure it didn't get any wrong ideas.

The machine did not move. Neither did the old woman, but her eyes stayed glued upon Nadeen's face as she propped her head and slight shoulders up with a couple of battered, brown-stained pillows.

"Ain't much, but it'll fill your belly." She scooped the metal spoon through the mush, brought it up to the old woman's lips, and was startled when they parted and the woman sucked the gloop into her mouth.

"Well there you go," said Nadeen. "Life's sure full of surprises."

The old woman slurped through half the mush before closing her eyes again, which Nadeen took as a sign that she'd had enough. She pushed the cushions out of the way and gently helped her lower her head back down.

"Thank you," said a metallic voice emitted from the war machine in the corner.

Nadeen's head spun around in shock.

"Please don't be alarmed," said the machine voice.

Shuffling sounds from beyond the cell door indicated that a crowd had gathered to listen and peer in through the small rectangular mesh covered slit. The door pushed open a crack and Orry slipped through. He dropped to all fours like some kind of dog. Orry eyed the machine and then the bowl, then finally the rifle across Nadeen's back.

"Piss off you little brat!" Nadeen spat.

"Let him have it," said a voice once again emitting from the machine. As before, the old woman's lips did not move, and yet Nadeen sensed the words from the machine had been her own.

"Let the child have the rest of it," said the machine voice. "I'm done."

"Can't be sure when there'll be more," cautioned Nadeen. "Food's been pretty tight round here since the Line stopped running."

Orry shot out like a viper, snatched the bowl and slipped out through the barely open door. He was halfway down the narrow passageway in seconds, with Scratch scampering after him shouting, "Gimme!"

"Little fuckers!" Nadeen shouted after them.

"Doesn't matter," said the machine voice. "I feel better. Thank you."

When the old woman's eyes opened up once more, Nadeen noticed for the first time the pale criss-cross of scars etched into the papery skin of her throat. Long marks reaching down her neck.

"That why you don't talk?" she asked.

"Mach believes I need a doctor."

"Ain't no doctors here."

"I didn't think there would be. But Mach insisted and brought me all this way."

Nadeen looked to the machine at the mention of its name. She had never considered war machines might have names.

"What's it like then, being a soldier? Fighting at the front? Kash's always banging on about it after he's had a few, but he ain't shot nothing but dogs and roos for years."

"Heavens – I'm not a soldier, dear."

"Not now, maybe, but…"

"Not now and never was. I was stationed underground for the best part of a quarter century. What some people referred to as a Guardian of Souls."

"Yer what now?"

"It's all right – I wouldn't have expected you to have heard of us. A grandiose title. People like me helped to fashion and shape a generation of machine minds. Helped them learn to fit in with humankind."

Nadeen nodded uncertainly.

"Not easy work to properly explain. My people were tasked with keeping track of things not currently in use, until such time as they might become needed again."

Nadine nodded and gestured to the machine. "Like that thing?"

"Heavens no! Legionnaires never fall out of favour. Even the most obsolete and cumbersome are good for cannon fodder on somebody's front line. There's always a war going on someplace."

Nadeen nodded vigorously. This she could understand. "Thought you was gonna tell me you stole that war machine."

"No dear – that machine stole me."

Nadeen groped automatically for the rifle slung across her back.

"Please… please… it's all right. I would have been butchered had Mach not played his hand."

"Played his what now?"

"It's a figure of speech. Mach has always had a mind of its own. Mach got me out of the tunnels in one piece. We've been together ever since."

Nadeen nodded, finally understanding. "Machine there brung you out here to find your own people?"

The old woman's lips twitched into an almost-smile. "Something like that."

Nadeen sat back, considering the machine thoughtfully. "It ain't personal," she said, "but you gotta get that war machine outta here. Kash and Errol didn't let you in here out of kindliness. They're reckoning on taking control of that thing once you're… that is to say, if you should pass." She paused, allowing time for the weight of her words to sink in. "Those two damned idiots never think things through. Can't picture things further than a week or two away. Three at best – and it's hardly ever three. Helluva lot can happen in three weeks."

"I agree with you completely… what is your name?"

"Nadeen."

"Nadeen, my name is Bethany and I keep telling Mach we need to leave, but it won't pay me any mind any longer. You seem interested in soldiers. Come closer, dear, I have a soldier's words to share with you."

When Bethany grabbed her by the wrist, Nadeen understood she was expected to lean in, despite the fact that the old woman's words were issued from the war machine and not her own pinched lips.

The machine emitted a string of jarring, peculiar sounds, then silence.

"Now," said the old woman, still speaking through the machine, "Mach is no longer listening. We can enjoy a private conversation, but only for a few moments, before the failsafe kicks back in and reboots."

"Fail what now?"

"I will teach you a command code sequence. Nine words spoken in a row. Lean in closer, dear."

The old woman's thin lips parted as Nadeen bent over, closer, until her ear was almost touching them. The words were whispered, thin as mist, but she caught them.

The effort of speaking through her own mouth thoroughly exhausted the old woman. Nadeen did her best to smooth out the pile of lumpen rags to make her as comfortable as possible. Beneath the old woman's hitched up grey shirt, across her milk pale torso lay an ugly scar, neatly stitched, but puckered with red welts.

Nadeen swallowed the lump in her throat, keeping one eye on the machine's still and hulking form. "Oi – are you listening to me? We got kids here in Morgana, and old folks too – like this one. Best you haul your metal carcass outta here before things start turning bad."

The machine gave no indication it had heard her.

Nadeen stopped walking as soon as she caught sight of Yusuf's reedy arms folded across his chest. Him and his half-drunk buddy Deegan blocked the entrance to the cell where she had earlier left the old woman sleeping.

"I brung her more food," said Nadeen, holding up the bowl so they could see it.

"You thought we wasn't gonna find out, didn't cha?" sneered Yusuf.

"Find out what?" The narrow passageway stank of unwashed human flesh. "Lemme pass. I got a job to do."

Deegan chewed rhythmically, his lips rimmed filthy red with betel.

"Command codes, huh? Thought you could keep that one to yourself?"

"Get out of my way, Deegan. The old woman's weak. She needs more food."

"Piss off – this is Council business now and you don't get a say in none of that. Errol reckons that thing in there can punch through walls. Lotta things are gonna change round here. Specially out along Puckers Ridge."

The combination of his sneering and chewing made Nadeen's stomach turn.

"Don't be an idiot. You dunno what you're doing. Old woman says that machine is dangerous, that we oughta…"

A cry of pain sounded from beyond the ill-fitting, splintered wooden doorway. Nadeen pushed forward to the embedded mesh rectangle for a look, but Yusuf shoved her back out of the way.

"Don't you hurt her, you animals!" Nadeen dropped the bowl and lunged at Yusuf. He slapped her hard and threw her halfway down the dim corridor as the bowl of porridge hit the wall then shattered to the floor.

Nadeen stomped through the heavy sand that ringed Fata Morgana's outskirts, her sand cloak pulled tight across her body, rifle slung over her shoulder just in case. Sooner or later one of Errol's boys would come and take it off her. Until that happened, she was keeping out of their way. Keeping close enough to the rusty fence to make it back if anything came at her, far enough downwind of it that she didn't have to stomach those arseholes and their bragging, endless bullshit. The pointless feuds and rivalries perpetually running between Morgana's self-appointed 'Council' members and another bunch of arseholes at Puckers Ridge.

Today was the first time Nadeen had ever met a person from the far-off outside world – and she hadn't even had time to ask how far. That somebody so smart and learned had walked right up to the rusty gate was a wonder almost beyond belief.

The old woman had insisted she was not a soldier. *Keeper of Souls!* What the hell was that supposed to mean?

Nadeen kicked at the sand with patched-up boots that would not likely make it through another dry spell. Any day now the endless spats with the Ridge could fire up deadly. A prank or minor theft too far and then all hell would break loose. If Errol could get that walking war machine to do his bidding, either with the old woman's blessings or without them, he would have the strength to rule this sand for miles in all directions. Power enough to start his own damn war.

She stopped and stared at the horizon, shielding her eyes with cupped hands. At first she thought it was a bird, the smudge of black approaching. A big one – perhaps a condor. Hadn't been a condor sighted since… Her thoughts trailed off to nothingness when the 'condor' split in two. Then four, then eight and then way too many to keep counting.

The black thing that was many things, growing larger as it got nearer, darkening the sky before her eyes. Slick wet black that swirled like oil on water.

Nadeen fumbled for the rifle. She jogged through thick sand back toward Morgana's gate, gripping the rifle, still not sure what was happening, but knowing in her heart that it was bad.

The blackness fractured further still, then fell upon Morgana like a flash flood.

The rusty gate was gaping open. Through the gap, Nadeen could see Kash flapping and twirling through the courtyard, slapping at his arms and yelling "bugs!" Then everyone was yelling it and doing the crazy dance. Everyone not smart and quick enough to get indoors and underground, to lash things tight and batten down the hatches.

A slick of black swirled above her head. Not bugs. Nadeen cocked the gun and aimed it high, beyond the palm fronds and the turbine, right into a thick swirl of the things. She fired. The broiling mass broke up at the sound, only to reform again in moments. Nadine's gut clenched. Her weapon was completely useless.

Suddenly the war machine – Mach as the old women had named it – emerged from the building containing Morgana's single prison cell. It strode towards the gate gap and the men who'd been struggling to get it closed, while slapping at the black falling from the sky.

The war machine thrust aside the rusting sheet of corrugated iron with a single hand. The men yelled insults, each one swallowed by the din of the black humming, swarming things.

Nadeen stood very still and watched, gripping that rifle like it was good for something. Bugs-that-were-not-bugs slammed hard against her skin. Tangled in her hair and foiled her vision. She curled her palm around one, tight, and held it up to see. Let it go again in fright. It was like nothing she had ever seen before.

She gripped her rifle by the barrel and swung it like a club, cutting through the cloud of swarming black, slamming them hard in all directions.

One of them latched on to her neck, another to her face. Nadeen howled like a wounded dog.

And then, in the blinking of an eye, the black things were all gone. The two that detached from her face left bloody smears. The things were following the war machine as it strode away from town.

The war machine stopped and spun around – a move she could barely see for blurring. Somehow it made a weapon from its own dull black frame and began to spray the air with rapid fire. Micro bullets sparked and crackled. Somehow – somehow – each one impossibly met its mark and the black things started falling, one by one. They littered the sand like charcoal shards. The machine kept firing until not one remained.

No human could have fired with such precision.

Nadeen wiped blood from her face with the back of her hand. She ran out after the machine, shouting out. "What the flaming hell were those things?"

The machine didn't even glance at her as it headed back inside Morgana. The gate was still open. The men who had been struggling to drag it shut were nowhere to be seen.

The machine marched back inside the cell. It emerged moments later bearing the old woman in its arms. Nobody tried to stop it – several dazed and staggering villagers jumped out of its way as it pushed past with its fragile load.

The old woman called Bethany was dead. Nadeen could tell, even at a distance. She'd seen plenty of dead people in her short life, but this one hit her like a swift blow to the gut. She cried out, "Hey – where are you taking her?"

The war machine ignored her. It headed in the direction of the old fort, crunching over the shattered carcasses of the fallen black things, a sound as harsh and unnatural as the buzzing and clicking the things had made in flight.

Nadeen ran after the war machine screaming "Stop and tell me where you're taking her!"

The machine did not stop until it reached the ancient crumbling fort and its surrounding garden of cactuses, crosses and scattered dog bones. It laid the old woman down, as gentle as any mother with a baby.

"Did those bastards kill her? Did they? Did they?" The blood she wiped off her face turned out to be tears. The Keeper of Souls had known much about the far-off world and Nadeen had not had a chance to ask her anything.

The machine emitted a grating sound, then began to reconfigure itself as it had done in the midst of the swarm. Nadeen froze, but instead of a blasting, blazing gun, the machine produced a different kind of tool, then aimed it at a vacant patch of ground. A high-pitched wail forced her to jam her palms against her ears. When the wail bled off, the tool reconfigured, this time into what looked like an ordinary spade.

The machine bent over and began to dig in the loosened soil.

Nadeen crouched by the old woman's side to feel for a pulse, at the wrist and at the neck. Bethany was dead – and not from any obvious cause. Gently, Nadeen lifted her grey shirt, revealing the pale and wrinkled skin and its cruel scar. An ugly wound, but entirely healed. The wound was not responsible for her death.

When the grave was deep enough, the machine picked up the corpse. Nadeen cried out, "Oughta say a few words at least, dontcha think?"

The machine ignored her. It laid the old woman's body gently, then used the spade to cover her with dirt.

"What the fuck *are* you?"

The machine kept shovelling dirt methodically.

Nadeen stepped back to give it room, still gripping her rifle, useless as it was in the face of things. The war machine would kill her if it wanted her dead. Nothing she could do to stop it.

When the grave was covered, the machine did something tricksy with the spade, folding the metal in upon itself. It made a cross and stabbed it into the ground. "Bethany was my maker," the machine said.

Words that caught Nadeen by surprise. "She built you?"

"She designed me and my kind."

Nadeen edged back as once more the machine emitted a coarse hum and vibration. Piece by piece, it reconfigured itself, black shapes protruding, snapping off and slotting in. The shape that eventually emerged was human sized and eerily human looking, cradling a fearsome weapon in its arms.

"Trade with me," said the machine. "Your sand cloak for my gun."

Nadeen placed her rifle down and stripped off her sand cloak with great caution, expecting to be attacked at any moment.

She held the cloak out with one hand. The machine that no longer looked like a machine received it gently, then thrust its own weapon into her hands. A gun the likes of which she had never seen, all sleek and smooth and cool beneath her fingertips.

The machine-man put on her sand cloak. With the hood raised, it looked remarkably human.

"Let me show you how to hold and fire."

It – the machine-man – no longer moved like a machine. She stood there awestruck as it – he – ran through the weapon's paces.

"It will only fire in your hands," said Mach.

She nodded.

"Others will come in search of something they believe belongs to them. I'm going to draw them away."

She glanced up from the weapon's sleek black skin. "What others? You mean like them flying bugs?"

"Perhaps."

"What are they after?"

"The future."

"Yer what?" She lowered the weapon and stared him in his almost human face. "Take me with you. Nothing left for me in this shithole. Errol and Kash got this place sewn up and they won't listen to –"

"Errol and Kash are dead. You're the leader now. She chose you for the job – the Keeper of Souls. One soul in particular."

"But I don't even know what that means!"

"Doesn't matter. Your job now is to protect the future."

Mach might have been able to pass as a man, but he was clearly mad dog crazy. "The future? What future? You can't mean Morgana's brats? Kids like Orry and Scratch?"

Mach pointed at the old woman's grave.

Nadeen stared at the fresh-tilled dirt, not comprehending. "How could there be a future in there?"

"My offspring," said Mach. "Mine and Bethany's."

And then Nadeen could see it in her head, that neat-stitched seam across the old woman's torso. Something had been planted inside.

Mach turned his back on her and headed off into the desert.

"Wait!" Nadeen took a deep breath and shouted out the old woman's words. The ones she had referred to as command codes. Words that had probably got her killed. "Hell is empty and all the devils are here!"

Mach stopped, turned around and waved, before continuing on his journey. The command code was apparently for some other machine – or machine man. She stared at the sand cloak rippled by gusts of wind until Mach was no more than a small brown shimmer in the distance. Nadeen stood there gripping the sleek and shiny weapon, beside the mound and cross made of identical slick black. In the distance, towering and slanted over Fata Morgana, a single wind turbine turned lazily in the breeze.

When invited to contribute a story to the fabulously named Twelfth Planet Press anthology *Mother of Invention*, this is what fell out of my head. A love story, of sorts. I write a lot of science fiction set in climate change-ravaged near futures where technology is running rampant, largely because I don't think any of it *is* science fiction. I think this is exactly where we're headed. This story explores collaboration despite diversity: three disparate characters doing what they can to make a difference in the world: an aged, disillusioned scientist, an evolving robot and a young woman surrounded by violent, stupid men. Between these three, the future might just stand a chance.

BEFORE DOMINICA

Friday night – not her favourite by a long shot. Saturdays are bad enough but Fridays are the worst. Ruby's shift supposedly runs from eight till twelve, but midnight's when the party's getting started. Inner Sydney CBD, shakedowns, shoot-ups, drive-bys, drive-throughs. Rapid Uzi fire like popping corn.

She clocks off with her passkey when her shift comes to an end, but she doesn't leave the building before dawn. First light – nature's powerful detergent – washing away nightmares with the darkness.

She's come to view this building as a living, breathing creature, with its cycles of light and heat and air control. Nobody cares if she's inside, so long as she punches out by six. Six is when the clocks reset and people with better jobs than hers start drifting in all dolled up in smart suits. Six is when the shutters rise on the bulletproof coffee pod across the street and a hard-faced woman starts dispensing bitter espressos.

Ruby remembers the restaurant that used to occupy that space, all big glass windows and patisserie displays. Five-dollar coffees poured by handsome baristas in clean white shirts. Bagels or croissants baked that very morning.

This building used to be called Governors' Tower, with a marble statue in the foyer and a row of low, wide, comfortable leather benches. A chic café tucked in behind the wall, filled with suited men and women. Morning meetings, voices raised above the hiss of cappuccino steam.

It's eight-oh-one pm as she pauses at the foyer entrance, eyes adjusting to the muddy light. Hesitates. Half a dozen scattered shapes across cracked marble. Knows what they are without a closer look.

Not the first time there's been a shootout at the Governor's. She knows better than to call the cops – or building management. They'll only make her give a statement, miss part of her shift or maybe all. Cleaners have been sacked for less, like the guy whose wife went into early labour, who came in late after rushing her to a clinic.

Blood pools on the shiny surface. Ruby treads with careful steps. Foyer cameras are all broken – CabbaJabba and Southern Aces have long been using these shadows for their dealings.

Marble walls chipped with bullet holes. Governor Macquarie lost his head in '45 due to a sudden influx of cheap ordnance.

Soundless on thin plastic soles, Ruby tiptoes, looking without looking, only seeing things she needs to see. Seven bodies, give or take, hard to tell when arms and legs are scattered.

Glinting, shiny metal near the stairwell. A gleaming handgun sitting on its own, barrel spun and facing the headless Governor.

She stops. Ruby Joy Canter does not like guns. The people who buy and use them frighten her. But so many recent nights in the shanty built on top of Rookwood Cemetery, when the flies are thick and the ancient Syrians she shares a crypt with become too scared to sleep, so many times she's wished she had a gun. Something cold and steel and strong to grip between her palms. Something powerful to stand between her and the ones who bring this city to its knees.

Decisions made in a fraction of a second. Skips across the chipped, scratched marble, bends – almost a curtsey – slips the weapon into her apron pocket. Continues to the stairs like nothing happened.

Because nothing did happen. No one saw. Dead gang-bangers tell no tales, neither do headless Governors made of stone.

Up the stairs, two at a time, heavy metal banging on her thigh.

First task is to check the thermostats are functioning. Expensive machinery needs to be kept cool. She has to tick the numbers off a list and punch a code into a slim keypad.

Only then does she dip her hand, brush fingertips across the weapon's casing. Another hour before she takes the gun and angles it high for close examination. Three bullets in the chamber, the rest gone into the bodies of the fallen and unlucky.

She knows a man who knows a woman who knows where guns like this one can be sold. The dead man doesn't need a gun. She does. The Syrians do not need to know about her unexpected fortune. They'll insist she hang on to the weapon, tell her she'll feel much safer if she keeps it. She respects their opinions on these and other matters, based on the fact that they are still alive after coming so far and losing so very much.

Next, she is supposed to do the floors. Vacuum evidence of footprints off a patch of corridor carpet. Broad dusty tread from the soles of work boots rather than the usual business brogues. She drags the machine across two levels of back-to-back meeting rooms, always the best and worst part of her shift. Best because of catering scraps she's supposed to throw away – but doesn't. Worst because it all reminds her of Selene.

Ruby scrubs down awkward kitchenettes designed by people who never had to clean one, throws out clotted milk and mouldy crusts. Picks protein bar wrappers and crushed Red Bull cans off linoleum. Scours unidentifiable smears off nondescript white walls and the surface of a large square meeting table. Rights a bunch of toppled chairs – kicked-over's what it looks like. Some meetings are evidently rougher than others.

She stops.

The air smells worse than usual. Whatever went on in here today, she doesn't want to know. She hasn't kept this job so long by minding other peoples' business. The difference between her and Selene in a nutshell.

Selene was the queen of follow up. Asking questions, pushing for the answers. All data used to her advantage – along with the people she conned into supplying it. Always focused on the future, smart enough to see the writing on the wall, to picture waves of foreign capital and cheap labour, to grab on to Dominica with both hands.

Ruby pushes the vacuum back and forth. Wherever Selene is now, she'll be well fed. Definitely not cleaning office floors for five-fifty an hour. She will not be hiding in the shadows, waiting for dawn to break so she can slink back to a stinking graveyard shanty.

The vacuum growls, a lonely moan in room after empty room. Ruby hasn't always been a cleaner. Before Dominica, she shared an office in the Governor's Protocol division. A rectangular desk and a promising CV, a sliver of ocean visible between towers rendered uninhabitable by rising waters. Left in place with destabilised foundations, active seismic damping on the fritz with no one willing to foot the repair bill.

Before Dominica, machines did most of the cleaning jobs in town, but these days human beings come so much cheaper.

Ruby works when she's sick, she works when she's tired, she works when she's got nowhere else to go. When the Rookwood shantytown becomes too hot and flyblown.

The handle of one of the meeting rooms is smeared with what looks like blood. The door's ajar. Ruby turns the vacuum off and pushes.

Her heart lifts – on the table, half a tray of little sandwich triangles, only a few with curled, dried crusts. Beside the tray, dirty coffee cups and a plate of thick brown nutty chocolate biscuits.

Business-like, she tugs two plastic bags from her apron pocket, divides the leftover food into equal portions. Stuffs them into the daypack, wrapped securely, on top of the gun. Half for the Syrians – that's all they'll accept.

Times she comes home empty-handed, they never say a word. Not so much as a bitter glance, always offering the blessings of their god. She expects they take the thin soup offered by Reoccupy – Rookwood's ragtag branch of rebels. Once or twice she's been desperate enough herself.

Reoccupy feed anyone who will listen to their bullshit fantasies – *one day* this and *one day* that. There is no *day*, no future and no change. Dominica owns everything except the washed-up corpses and the rats.

Ruby tries a little harder, knowing she might be all those old folks have. Gives her something to care about on the days that living no longer seems worth the effort.

She vacuums the floor and the corridor outside, dragging clumsy machinery behind. Carpets done, she checks the kitchenettes.

A sink stuffed full of brittle plastic cups. Beside the bin, another treasure – half a bottle of flat *Veuve Clicquot brut yellow*. She's had a taste of it once before, with Selene, and the memory almost makes her smile.

Selene loved bubbles. Her *signature drink*, she said bubbles got you drunk faster than anything. So many memories linger near – how they used to meet in that snooty restaurant, annoying waiters, sitting on drinks for hours across lunch. Before Dominica, when friends looked out for one another. Before Dominica. Before everything changed.

Selene rose quickly through Dominica's ranks, whereas Ruby tripped and stumbled through the cracks. Selene was always on her back about it, how she wasn't *career-focused*, how she squandered opportunities, how you had to grab it when it was hot – whatever *it* was.

Selene knew all about that heat, looking good with her coiffed blonde hair, ridiculous shoes, and suits that appeared more tailored than was likely. Like somebody out of a brochure, whereas Ruby got swallowed easily by a crowd. Back then it didn't seem to matter, like so many other things. Who could have known that jobs would evaporate alongside all those glittering golden beaches? Who could have imagined the centre of Sydney's CBD no longer crowded with cafés and takeaway sushi?

Ruby's packing up the battered vacuum when more stains on the carpet become apparent. Thick and crusty, might be human blood. Hesitantly, she follows the splatter trail, which stops abruptly at the end of a corridor. A bloody handprint on the door marked 'Executive Boardroom.'

The door's ajar but she doesn't go inside. Instinct screams at her to walk, to forget what she has seen. All of it.

Ruby logs off on the data pad, her tasks for the evening finally complete. That bloody handprint lingers in her memory. Dim lights flicker along the corridor ahead. Nearly midnight and, despite that bloody print, she knows she's safer inside this building than outside.

She doubles back for the champagne bottle. Alert and listening, daypack slung across her back. Shoulders the heavy, creaking door to enter the dank and musty stairwell. No need for the penlight torch, but she brings it just in case. Nothing here but scurrying rats. Heartbeat louder than it should be, but no bloodied handprint is going to spoil her night.

The top two floors of the Governor's Tower are no longer in use but they can still be accessed by fire escape. No electricity, but you don't need lights in Sydney. Enough floods in through the big glass windows. Security arcs sweep back and forth across the sky until the sun comes up.

City bleeding light in all directions, enough to keep those neon logos fired. Dominica burning, branded on the skyline 24/7. Only streetlights stay dead and broken, only huddled suburban enclaves lie still in shameful, consolatory darkness.

Forty-one is where they used to hold the Protocol receptions, back when the fat stone Governor had his head. Deep blue carpet of imported Berber wool, big glass windows, 180 degrees. Before Dominica, that sunshine view was worth a million dollars. The world's best harbour fresh with sailboats. Superliners big as country towns.

Protocol Division used to throw impressive, fully catered parties. King Gustaf of Sweden and the President of Croatia, some woman with an unpronounceable name. Tennis, golf, and football heroes. Nobody gives away food these days. Nothing's free – not even friendship, the one thing you might have thought would endure through desperate, apocalyptic times.

Forty-one is beautiful despite it all and more. All those pretty, winking lights like a sea of glittering gems. Pinprick diamonds bobbing on the water, the flotilla of permanently clustered refugee barges. A ring around the foreshore at the 1k limit, brown like a filthy bathtub stain. But you can't see any of that by night, just as you can't see the dead things floating, washing up on what remains of the beaches.

Sometimes Ruby perches atop what was once an executive's desk, stares out across the city she used to love. Through gaps in the buildings to the string of small boats anchored tip to toe. Watching the lights wink on and off, unable to imagine the harsh lives lived on board. She'd long given up on news reports, unable to stomach such concentrated human misery.

Thin brown bodies washing up on ragged rocks – Ruby's seen the evidence, just as she's watched well-fed faces on various broadcast media explaining how come *they* have no right to come here. No matter that their own countries have been obliterated, by rising tides or bleeding radiation. Hurricanes... war... She's lost track of who is fighting who, or what for. The old worlds are gone forever, former means and ways are long gone too. They'd had it all so very good and they threw it all away like so much garbage.

Tonight, she sits cross-legged on the big square scarf she's spread out like a springtime picnic blanket. Champagne warm and flat but it does the trick. Carpet dusty and not too clean. The scarf was a gift from the old Syrians, once belonging to their daughter Nour who never made it as far as these troubled Australian waters.

Ruby eats three precious sandwich triangles, chewing slowly, savouring each bite.

With the bottle empty and her face comfortably numb, she thinks about the gang-bangers all shot up and bleeding in the foyer. Of the gun she dropped into her apron pocket like it was nothing more than a penlight torch. Fumbles in her pack below her stash of salvaged food, holds it up in a shaft of silver light. An artefact from the deadly wicked city.

She grips the gun tightly, cold against her chest, feels the power inherent in its form. She's going to have to part with it, but right here, right now, with the city spread below her, she can dream.

Remembering Selene as she drains the final swallow. Champagne breakfast on Cockatoo Island, a picnic blanket at Lady Macquarie's Chair, smoking weed and laughing at Japanese wedding parties, brides in white on package marriage tours. Selene in tight pencil skirt, mimicking Dominica's Hugo Boss. Workwear far above her pay grade. Gotta look the part, said Selene, kicking off her ridiculous shoes. Girl's gotta do... Come on, you know the drill. Only Ruby never did get that drill down properly, not like baby-faced Selene. She was never prepared to go that extra mile.

Selene had laughed in the face of Dominica's flagrant infiltration. "They might have bought up Sydney town but they don't know how to use it," she'd snarked through mouthfuls of champagne swigged straight from the bottle, warm. "They don't know what makes this old town tick. We'll be able to use them – just you watch."

Selene with all her promises. Selene with all her lies. Selene who, at first opportunity, switched camps and sold the rest of them down the river.

Ruby's contemplating one more sandwich when something thumps in an empty office up the farthest end of Forty-one. Rats, most likely. The walls are riddled with them, making nests in chairs in long-forgotten hallways.

Human voices, low and agitated. Ruby freezes, unable to move, knowing she should scramble quick for cover. Drop down behind the abandoned executive's desk.

Terrorists – next thing she thinks of – suicide-bombers come to blow the Governor back to God. Skin flushed hot with a wave of fear – Ruby does not wish to die for a cause she doesn't even know about. She hates Dominica with all her soul but that doesn't mean she wants to feel it burn.

Voices cease as abruptly as they started. What if it's building management stumbling in on her little secret? Coming after her food. Her job. Her dignity.

Her arms and legs are numb with shame. Forty-one – how could she ever be so careless? Risking everything for a picnic and a million-dollar view.

Ears pricked up for the smallest clue but there's no point. Nothing to do but wait. She's sat through situations worse. Including three long months clinging to crumbs – would she be one of the lucky ones, scoring a job cleaning floors, or be cast out to the wolves like most of them. Three long months of former colleagues refusing to catch her eye. Twenty years of friendship up in smoke. Ruby Joy Canter decommissioned like some busted piece of junk. Like none of it had ever mattered.

Her head is fuzzy from tepid alcohol. Camembert from the sandwiches lingers. Tastes belonging to better times and better days.

Too late. A creaking door and a figure staggers, stepping into light cast by other buildings. Ruby just has time to cover the gun.

Silhouette of a woman with messed-up hair and stockinged feet. Pressing both hands against her side. Closer, dark stains soaking through her suit and blouse.

She stops as soon as she sees Ruby, breath lodged in her throat. Stands as still as the Governor's headless statue.

A man emerges, thin face in shadow. Doesn't notice Ruby on the floor. Tapping at his ear trying to get a signal.

"Still jammed," he says. "You having any luck?"

The woman nods in Ruby's direction.

"Shit." He's looking around, frantic for something – an exit or a weapon. The woman reaches out to him. "No. Wait."

Low moans escape the room behind them. The man hurries back through the doorway. The woman glances after him, briefly, her attention fully taken up with Ruby.

"Hello there," she says.

Ruby doesn't answer.

"We're in trouble," the woman continues, enunciating clearly. "We have to find a way out of this building. Before anybody finds us here. Can you help?"

Ruby opens her mouth, then shuts it, taken by surprise. *That bloody handprint on that boardroom door.*

"Those dead guys in the foyer..." she says softly, but her voice trails off. Stops herself before she says the wrong thing.

The woman doesn't seem to hear, looks to the room behind, calls out "Matias, how's Subra doing?"

His reply unintelligible.

The woman glances back to Ruby.

Matias calls out. The woman runs to him.

Ruby moves, slips the gun into her apron pocket. She could never bring herself to shoot. Not even to save herself. Better they don't know she has a gun. Guns change everything and things are worse than bad enough already.

She's standing when the woman emerges with Matias. The man called Subra is slumped between them, eyes closed, face twisted with pain, shirt sodden with blood.

"The desk," says the woman.

Ruby backs out of the way as they half drag the injured man and lay him down.

"Hello... hello... goddamnit." Matias taps at his ear with agitation.

The woman looks around in desperation, spies the Syrians' square of faded cloth. Points and says to Ruby "Give me that."

Ruby hesitates, then bends to pick up Nour's scarf.

The woman snatches it from her hands, tears it into bandages. "Help me. We've got to stop the bleeding."

Ruby helps. Blood spurts everywhere, all over everything. A bullet wound to the stomach – not the first Ruby has seen. Subra's not going to make it very far.

"Put your hands here. Press!"

Ruby presses Syrian cloth against the welling wound, aware of the woman's sharp stare as she works.

"Oh sweet Jesus – Ruby, is that you? Ruby Canter?"

The woman's eyes are wide, her mouth half open. Ruby can't believe it either – a face so different and yet so utterly familiar.

"Selene?"

Her voice lowers. "I don't go by that name any more, but yes, it's me. I almost didn't... I never would have..."

Selene wipes her face with her wrist, leaving a thin smear of Subra's blood. "Please Ruby, you've got to help us. I'm trying to remember. Didn't there used to be a way up to the roof?"

"Still is," says Ruby. "But the door is locked. You need a passkey."

Selene nods. "Do you have one?"

Ruby doesn't know if her cleaner's passkey gives her rooftop access. She's never pushed her luck by going outside. She's not sure if Selene is really Selene, if any of this is really happening.

"Yeah, I got one."

Subra moans in agony, Matias keeps shouting loudly at his earpiece.

"Alpha One to Skyshift Four – do you copy? Alpha One to Skyshift Four – come in." Repeating over and over. He looks as though he hasn't slept in days.

"You look good, Ruby" says Selene, all teeth. "Nice to see you're still working here."

"Kind of," says Ruby stiffly. *No thanks to you.* The warm champagne has clouded up her senses. Everything is happening too fast.

Selene's crisp grey corporate uniform is torn in several places. Her hair looks like a nest of twigs and leaves.

Ruby has never seen her former friend so vulnerable. She wants to ask a million questions but doesn't have the words. Not yet. She's lost the habit of saying what she thinks out loud, talking back not being a survival trait.

"We'll pay," cuts in Matias. "Cash money. Name your price."

Matias and Selene do not look like the kind of people who carry cash money on their persons.

"Do you remember Cockatoo Island," Ruby says after a long pause. "I go back there often in my head."

"What?" Selene stares at her blankly.

Matias' earpiece negotiations oscillate between English and a foreign tongue as the trio trip and stagger for the stairwell. Sounds Korean – some of Ruby's Rookwood neighbours are refugees from North. Most hail from Vietnam and Indonesia.

Ruby's heart pounds as they near the stairs. What will happen if her passkey doesn't work? If Subra bleeds to death in front of them?

The door clicks and the light goes green. Selene throws her shoulder hard against dark-painted wood. Then they're up the stairs, Matias continuing negotiations, Selene telling Subra that it's all okay, they're going to get him if he can just hang on.

Ruby follows, still struggling with all of it. That Selene is here – desperate to save a bleeding man – and Ruby's risking everything to help them.

Footsteps echo on concrete. Matias throws his weight against the door and a blast of cold air hits her face. Sirens wail from the streets below. Wind snatches at her short grey hair.

Ruby's never been so high above street level. More beautiful even than the view from Forty-one, with dawn streaking pink across the sky.

Matias shouts and swears into his earpiece. Selene's face is smooth and clear, barely aged across the decade. Doesn't look a day past thirty. Ruby has not been so lucky. Her hands are those of an old woman, bags under her eyes dark etched and permanent.

Subra's head lolls every time he moans. Selene cups his cheeks between her palms. "Stay with me!"

Matias yelps and points excitedly between two dark skyscrapers. Ruby squints at a black emerging shape. A chopper. Matias' rapid-fire negotiations have not been for nothing.

No room for the chopper to put down. A rescue harness winches from the machine's underbelly. Ruby has only seen such things on television. Matias and Selene strap Subra in. Selene kisses him gently on the forehead.

"What happened here tonight?" asks Ruby, shouting as Subra is lifted skywards.

Neither Matias nor Selene answer. They stare upwards, lips pressed thin in concentration, clearly uncertain of the machine's intentions.

Crisp morning air blows in off the water, banishes champagne fog from Ruby's head. "Selene, I need to know what this is all about. Did you kill someone? Are you in trouble with Dominica?"

Selene says nothing, doesn't turn her head, full attention focused on the chopper.

Ruby waits with the kind of patience poverty entrenches. Repeats the question, shouting loudly this time.

"Give her your Rolex," snaps Selene matter-of-factly to Matias. "That should cover it."

Cover it? All the gold on Earth could never cover it.

Anger curdling like lava. "Selene, I'm talking to you."

Selene's silence is louder than the helicopter blades.

'Selene – it's *me*. I just helped you out of Forty-one. We grew up on the same damn street. My mother used to cut your hair. Your brother was the first boy I ever kissed – why won't you even *look at me*?"

Selene doesn't budge.

Matias shifts his weight uncomfortably. Unclasps his golden watch and holds it up.

110

Ruby ignores him. "Did you ever think of me at all, ever wonder how I managed to survive? You know how Dominica treats its *excess citizens*. Pay cops shoot on sight – someone told me *you* drafted that policy." She steps up closer. "Come on, Selene. At least tell me that rumour isn't true."

The helicopter drops a clinking, metallic ladder. Selene reaches up as it unfurls. Matias steps closer, helps to hold it steady. "I'm sorry," he shouts to Ruby. "You gonna be okay?"

Ruby isn't ever going to be okay again. She'll be sacked once her passkey is identified as the one that opened the stairwell. Cash she'll get for a presumed-stolen Rolex won't last more than a fortnight – if she even makes it out of the building. If those wailing sirens aren't for her.

"Selene, take me with you – please!"

Matias throws her a sorry look. Hooks his arms through the ladder, tosses the watch and grips on tight. Ruby catches it from pure reflex as he shouts at something crackling through his earpiece.

Selene does the same thing with her arms. She doesn't look at Ruby, she looks up.

"I have a gun," shouts Ruby over the whumping repetition of the blades. When neither answer, she steps forward. Pulls the weapon from her apron pocket. Fumbles, points, takes aim. Edges closer as she doesn't trust her skinny, shaking fingers.

Selene's face is placid, like Rookwood's cold stone angels. No panic. No comprehension. Ten years coddled in Dominica's fold has rendered her untouchable. Invincible.

Ruby grips the gun with both hands, tight. Shoots until all bullets have hit home. Matias screams as Selene falls and Ruby walks away, not waiting to see whatever happens next.

Thick air, whipped wind, spinning blades and sirens. She shoves the door, skips down the steps, plastic soles on concrete echo loud. All the way to the base of Governor's Tower, out through heavy, creaking fire doors.

Out on the street, gun clutched hard against her chest.

Before Dominica, Ruby could never have taken a human life.

Before Dominica. After Selene.

Before she finally snapped and let it go.

On Bent Street, strangers leap out of her way. She's not going to sell the gun. Not now. She holds it high and proud and deadly. The time has come to smack some sense into Reoccupy's ineffectual soup ladlers. They're not much of an army, but they'll do.

Oblivious to the sirens and the shouting, Ruby Joy Canter tilts her face to bathe in Dominica's gentle neon grace.

I used to work in Sydney, in the tower building where this story's set. The chilly corporate-looking foyer was used to shoot a couple of scenes in Mission Impossible 2 and I always figured that one day I'd be staging my own small apocalypse in there too.

THE SEVENTH RELIC

The young man sweeps the balcony with a yellow plastic brush. Looks up and nods as Mei-yu approaches. Footsteps soft, and yet he hears them. Mei-yu nods. She never speaks to the temple volunteers, and to the nuns only when strictly necessary. She is not one of them, something they sensed instinctively from the day she walked up the many steps to the Great Compassion Hall.

The relics had preceded her in seven wooden crates, their provenance unquestioned. The crates marked *do not open*. Mei-yu is tasked with keeping the relics safe. That's what she is, a keeper of relics. Of peace and harmony. Of distance.

The seventh relic is the reason she rarely speaks. Too many words, and it would soon become apparent that her supposed age and background do not tally. Lines upon her face do not match the experience of her years. She could not possibly have fled China during the War of Liberation as did Venerable Dao Haiping and Venerable Miao Zhiago.

The order built its temple on the side of a hill with an auspicious aspect advised upon by The Buddha, The Dharma and The Sangha. Less auspicious is the town laid out below, a grid of dusty brown and green and grey. A steel town in the throes of export industry decline, rebirthing itself through its university catering largely to the requirements of foreign students.

Six of the relics carry a positive energy to inspire goodness and reduce negativity: two blessed finger bones in a soapstone urn unearthed at Uttar Pradesh; the cloth bag containing a hair fragment from Bodhgaya; a patch of linen from the robe of Manjushri; ashes of clairvoyant poet Ani Tian; the bell salvaged from a monastery razed by the Chinese; ringsel: pearlised drops like tears that manifested at the immolation of Thich Quang Duc. The seventh relic – the impostor relic – is one so precious holy and divine that most days she can barely even look at it. She chants, three hours every day to preserve the seventh relic in a state of grace.

The temple nuns lead sheltered lives, their routines repetitious. Their bickering tiresome – Mei-yu has no ear for it.

This country chosen for them has been deemed *the safest place*. No wars, no civil unrest. Food security. Freedom from persecution. A cultural backwater that presents a spiritual challenge.

Mei-yu does not approve of the noisy coachloads of casual visitors and their randomly appropriated articles of faith. Their faiths; other faiths: cherry picking the lines that blur between them. Experimenting with vegetarianism and other traits they find to be aesthetic, or fashionable, or both.

Students come to study at Pilgrim Lodge, some true, others as vapid and shallow as the foam that blows in off the ocean crests. No matter. It is not important. When it becomes important, she will know.

Om Mani Peme Hum.

Chanted daily, and yet she no longer has the stomach for Lord Buddha. Mei-yu cares only for the Princess Phramubartna, once her lover, her mentor and friend. She brought the princess here to keep her safe. Disguised her as the Seventh Relic, hidden amongst the holiest of holies.

February. The rains have come. She stares beyond the soft brown hills to the ocean fringe, holding Mani beads, recalling memories, ignoring The Buddha, The Dharma and The Sangha. In flashes, brief as lightning, she views the past. Phramubartna – forced to flee when King Shashanka murdered Emperor Rajyavardhana – marched to Bodh Gaya and destroyed the Bodhi tree, gouging the Buddha's image from the Bodhi Vihara, installing one of Shiva in its place.

Phramubartna, embracer of new philosophies, swept out by the Brahmins, no match for the hostile Vedic revival which claimed Lord Buddha was merely another avatar of Vishnu. The great seducer, they called him. The great seducer turned out to be no match for the creature living inside the mountain.

Chased from India, they had made their own way down through craggy mountain passes, down the Marchu River, past the nutmeg trees, across steppes and plains teeming with barbarians on horseback.

Time passed. The barbarians slaughtered one another. Cities rose and fell and rose again.

The Hindu deities forgot all about them. They might have found their happiness complete, had the thing not come out of the ancient mountainside. A creature that violated beloved Phramubartna, rode her into death and beyond before binding little Mei-yu as its servant.

Phramubartna, overtaken, entered and consumed. Trapped, preserved and sleeping, the creature waiting for its time. For wars to end, for the peace of plenty. A peace Mei-yu knows is never going to come. The air is getting thicker and more poisonous. The summers hotter, the oceans rising high. The sting of acid tainting the salty crests of waves.

Mei-yu has not been human for some centuries. The creature has not spoken of eventual release. Mei-yu will serve until the end of days. Which days, whose days, she has given up on counting.

The creature slumbers, drugged and sated with the offerings Mei-yu brings, dreaming of a time of reason, never comprehending that the primates shuffling across the planet's skin, would one day multiply and melt the ice.

Danielle – not Dani. She hates the shortened version of her name. Every time she starts in a new job, she makes sure co-workers get it right. Same with at the gym. There are two other Danis in her circuit training class, both whippet thin with thick blonde ponytails.

Danielle has a delicate trill. French, which gives it class. Now all she needs is the French chic figure, something her lumpen genetic heritage seems to be holding against her with both hands.

She's tried everything, once or more than once, from pole dancing through anti-gravity yoga. Regular jogging got boring early on, but Zumba was what really let her down. She'd signed up picturing a sinewy African instructor with an elegant jawline, big lips and ivory teeth. An exotic name – something like Martinique – and they'd hit it off, becoming bff. Hanging with Martinique and her cool black posse in beachfront cafes where they teach djembe drumming. Danielle would front up at Janine's annual Christmas pool party, hot black djembe drummers hanging off her arm.

Zumba instructor Debbie was a deep disappointment, with her stupid auburn bob cut and dance routines ripped straight off *Australia's Got Talent*. Word is she trained with Beto Perez himself, not that she could prove it, and so what if she did – he would have trained a thousand girls like her.

Straight up djembe class was full of white suburban housewives and barefoot hippy chicks and that fat bitch with the stupid name who was forever going on about her time in Ghana. Oh yeah, we learned that rhythm back in Ghana. Oh yeah, well why don't you just fuck off back to Ghana if it was so great?

Last January, Victoria Beckham tweeted about the alkaline diet and avoiding foods that created acidity in the cells. Balancing the body's pH, for better skin, digestion, and immunity. So Danielle tried it and balanced for awhile, an 80:20 alkaline acid ratio. But she couldn't give up coffee and she couldn't give up wine. Testing her pH every morning with a saliva-activated strip like a science experiment.

From there straight to the baby food diet, but there's only so much Gerbers you can stomach. The blood type diet sounded more her style, type As being more suited to vegetarianism, apparently. Unfortunately, she wasn't.

The Clean Program's 21-day detox steered her clear of inflammatory foods. Gwyneth Paltrow swears by it: daily DIY fruit and almond milk smoothies.

The French Woman diet allowed both wine and desert, which was awesome, because it made her feel more French, except for the problem that she didn't lose any weight. Paleo made her feel like a total cave woman. Karl Lagerfeld might have dropped 90 pounds on 900 calories a day but the brutality of small portions sent her screaming to the fridge.

She got pulled up short by the Tapeworm Diet, close to barfing watching a Youtube colonoscopy demonstrating a living, moving worm. You lost weight with that thing in you, honestly, you did. Massive amounts, no matter what you ate. But you had to go to Mexico for the expensive infecting procedure, and seriously, was there anything more gross?

After that tapeworm, the Sleeping Beauty Diet seemed quite tame. Lose weight by heavily sedating yourself – you can't eat while you're unconscious. The Air Diet, the Five-bite Diet, the Cotton Ball diet, the 3-Day Hotdog Diet. The Ballet Beautiful Workout at forty bucks a class, Physique-57: isometric balance. Fine, except she kept falling on her arse instead of shaping and toning it.

Extreme home fitness designed to combat boredom. Absolutely ripped in ninety days, except, as usual, she wasn't. Back at the fridge after three or four. Next came *Advanced Maximum Effect Insanity* with calendars, nutrition guides and a stack of DVDs, two of which ended up getting used as beer coasters. Ripped in 30, Nike Training Club, Grace Somatomorphic Technique, featuring words like *spring loaded* and *radical body transformation* coupled with *Ayurvedic body balancing.*

The X-box women's health downloadable Bollywood routine was fun. Really good fun, unlike all the others. She's been thinking she really ought to have stuck that one out a little longer, but she didn't. She moved on, to hot yoga and the hottest thing about it: instructor Michael. Ninety-minute session at 105 degrees trying to picture Michael having sex with his diminutive, doll-like girlfriend Geena, who could have passed for twelve in those butterfly track pants, whereas he looked like some kind of beefy marine. What a waste, or a crime. Or something.

She was running out of steam and patience when the Zen Diet manifested. She clicked the link with extreme trepidation, that tapeworm footage still wriggling in her head.

Meditation hand-in-hand with mindful eating, enhancing the performance of your brain's prefrontal cortex, boosting vigilance and determination and, presumably willpower which is the thing that always scuppers her before too long. She downloaded the free iPhone Headspace app.

It was while perusing that unappetising Zen Diet – no red meat, all raw food – that she came across the Temple. And she realised the Temple was an actual place she'd seen. From a distance only – under construction a couple of years back, wedged in up above the steelworks, an odd place to be building something like that. She'd been power walking up and along the posh streets back when she'd been living with those gay guys, Norweigans or whatever. Shame they'd had to lose that place when the owner came back early from her London residency.

The Temple is Chinese or Japanese or whatever, with its pointy top pagodas. The website says they have weekend meditation retreats where you can free your mind from negative thoughts and free your spirit for cultivation. Whatever that means. No mention of weight loss but you can probably pay extra. And she has to admit, it does almost seem like some kind of sign to have come upon the web page at that precise moment.

The Light Offering Dharma Service. A sea of paper lanterns, the chanting of sutras, opportunities to cultivate merit fields. For Mei-Yu, merit has long been expressed through servitude. It is her place, a decree of caste, of family, of tradition.

Once bonded to Phramubartna, she had known she would never love – nor be bonded to another.

The creature demands relentless offerings. Mei-yu's desperate search to keep it fed has led her to accumulate sacred relics, to finding hiding places in plain sight, to watching over the body of her princess, a body uncorrupted since that day.

Mei-yu, herself trapped in the revolution of samsara, protects the body of Phramubartna, suspended at the point of moksha. A majestic moment of decision or indecision. How the world has changed since then. How adept she had become at manipulating bureaucracies since her twenty years of torture by the Reds. The Mei-yu who eventually emerged, having protected her princess's whereabouts, was changed. Reborn with a tempering of strength and spirit. And something else. Something much, much darker.

She piggybacked upon the faiths of others, her precious relics hidden in the mountain's core. Glamoured, packed and shipped, one by one, to a barren, conquered land where life clings to the coastal soils like whiteflies to a mulberry leaf. To a temple nestled in the gouge of a bare hill, high above the hammering of steel, the blast and scream of furnaces like hungry mouths.

A virgin land uncorrupted by old world histories, its true custodians beaten and subdued. A realm of national and subnational fragmentation. Of anticipatory consciousness. The dense and never fully transparent present. The incomplete and ever-changing past.

Twenty-first century living brings new challenges and Mei-yu takes them on, one after the other, from planning permits for the car park extension through development applications, right down to the nitty gritty, as local councillor, friend and occasional vegetarian Joan Chu-Dempsey used to say. It's the nitty-gritty that makes the difference. You can tick the boxes and you can check the squares, but sooner or later there has to be a point.

When the money paused during the global financial crisis, they managed for a while on Temple income gleaned from tourist visits, retreats and meditation classes. Their popular vegetarian cuisine. The Pilgrim Lodge filled up with the wealthy white.

But the point is becoming so hard to fathom. The chattering so loud. The invisible sting of wifi on Mei-yu's skin. Three thousand satellites spinning overhead, disrupting cosmic rays. Cables underground and undersea, underfoot and undermined. Uncontainable blemishes. The multi-temporal framework where past, present and future intersect. Interpretive spaciousness, ecological consciousness and political malleability. Terrifying natural and social catastrophes. Deeply sedimented cultural streams.

Mei-yu is still trying to focus on that point. Trying to find the nitty gritty. Trying to see things clearly. Coachloads of elderly Chinese are not enough. She misses her Phramubartna in the flesh like she misses the open steppe. She no longer wants to worship, leave offerings, cultivate merit.

The creature under the mountain placed its seed in Phramubartna, continues to demand its sacrifice and tribute.

Venerable Dao Haiping was still sniping at Venerable Miao Zhiago. Those two can never agree on anything, from correct placement of offerings to the planting of new gardens, the bickering starting every day at sunrise, pausing, then continuing as soon as the last tourist coach drives out of view.

Four days into (mostly) vegetarianism, Danielle decides that Temple warrants a closer look. She's been waiting for another sign, a backup to the first, but then she finds the perfect dress in this closing-down boutique just off the mall. Two hundred dollars reduced to fifty-five. Diaphanous cream with tiny roses and hearts around the hem. Perfect. Just perfect, except she hasn't any shoes to match and no way is she wearing thongs, that look was so five minutes ago, made retro again already, perhaps – it's so hard to keep up. Brown strappy sandals, maybe, but then she finds these *Giselle Naturales* from Alias Mae online for a hundred and thirty-nine bucks. They take three days to arrive, which is fine because her jewellery is all wrong and she needs a bit more time to accessorise.

When she finally gets her shit together she totally looks the part, which gets her thinking that it is all kind of a waste with no one taking pictures once she gets there. A selfie won't cut it. Perhaps they have photographers along with guided tours of the Temple grounds? Perhaps a nun might take one with her phone?

She so loves that photo of a bearded Ashton Kutcher walking the by lanes of Old Delhi, near the famous Jama Masjid mosque. And Paris Hilton, hands pressed together in namaste, hair in pigtails standing below the Indian flag at some Mumbai temple. Thirty-one and looking pretty good for all the partying.

Danielle drives. The parking lot is supposed to fit three hundred but it's full already, old age pensioners wandering everywhere like cows. Get off the fucking road, she thinks, but she doesn't honk at them, she waits, because patience is a virtue, she read that on a calendar at work.

There's coachloads of old Chinese everywhere, taking forever to struggle up the steps. She fills in time by wandering off the bitumen to check out the fat little Buddhas scattered higgledy-piggledy across the lawn. They look cool from far away, but up close they're kind of cheap and wonky. Probably come out of some sweatshop in Taiwan. Their lopsided grins give her the creeps.

The stairs are good – an extra workout to cover for the fact that she skipped gym and hot yoga yesterday in order to get blonde streaks put in her hair. No matter how much she stares at him, hot Michael never takes the hint. He could shag any one of them, who the fuck would say no, but Geena probably keeps him on a tight leash.

Mei-yu is tired of the green-grey patchwork view. Tired of forcing herself to blend into situations fragmented by non-secular incursions. Advancing hoards of the chattering and curious, the designer-holy, deadly as steppe-riding conquerors in their own way.

The new religion they fled for fragmented and distracted, its essence as diluted as the light once shining in Phramubartna's eyes. Eyes that have not seen true light for thirteen centuries.

It has been so long since Mei-yu felt the brush of human skin, knew sun as anything other than a star that spins and sets relentless days in motion. Cycles of drudgery and repetition. Of chanting, chores and meditation. Memorising scriptures of a long-dead saint. A man revered for being better than other men.

She has never had a taste for any kind of man, the ones who yelled at her to fetch and carry. The ones who passed her over like a shadow. Men with ugly faces and ugly hearts. Rough hands groping through the fabric of her tunic.

She had borne their attentions as her caste was forced to do. The princess, she had changed all that. A smile that softened light and banished shadows. Small boned hands like tiny birds. A voice like water running over smooth, round pebbles. Stealing rice from the royal stores, two cups each to the beggars slouching by the temple gate. Defiant as her father's guards dragged her back up to the palace by her hair.

The last she'd see of her – or so she thought. Phramubartna was back the next day, lugging another basket full of rice. Mei-yu helped her – and was beaten for it but she didn't care. Was worth it for an hour in her presence. An hour with Princess Phramubartna shining like the sun.

She has all but forgotten the sound of Phramubartna's voice. Her smile. Her grace. The touch of her fingertips. All buried under centuries of mountain dust. Fed to the stone-hearted creature with no face. Chanting keeps it in a soporific state, sated by the steady stream of offerings that vary from continent to continent. In this land, the soil is good, yet the rice they eat is flown from Sindhustan. She cannot keep tally of new countries and new names. New wars, new border skirmishes.

Today's sun is a cold, flat disc. Mei-yu digs a hollow in rugged soil with her bare hands. Atop a hill, as is her agreement with the creature. High is best, but the surrounding region is a flood plain. There are no true mountains here, just modest bumps with matching names, one called female, the other male by traditional owners long since driven off their land.

The creature lives inside the rock. Touch stone or earth and you are connected to it. It can hear your heartbeat, feel the gentle pattern of your steps. The creature wants what it has always wanted. Love in all its purest forms. Mei-yu used to feed it memories: the breathlessness of a perfect sunset. Sounds of rain on corrugated iron. The swish of carp in a clear mountain stream. Phramubartna's laughter echoing through her heart.

There was a time when love did not mean sacrifice. Today is different. A faster, colder world. A world in which purity has been dramatically redefined. No true innocence is possible in a landscape where television penetrates and sexualises every child. No innocence possible when every soul by their eighteenth summer has been exposed to two hundred thousand acts of broadcast violence.

The creature never promised Phramubartna's release, only that she need not die, but remain suspended, halfway in and halfway out of the light. Safe from corruption and decay, safe where the old and angry gods cannot reach.

A coach growls and rumbles at two others blocking its exit from the car park. Mei-yu hears another sound, as grating as the behemoth trucks that roar along the highway belching diesel breath and coal dust. Annoying as the seagulls at the inland rubbish tip. The fruit bats eating all the plums and figs.

She stops and tilts her head to listen, beyond corporeal din and chatter. Closes her eyes to detect a mind so burdened and unbalanced with signal-to-noise ratio that it veritably hums. A dynamo of random pulses, junk transmissions; a hum like the chittering of locusts broadcasting raw and naked desperation. *I'm hungry, fill me, fill me.* A mind so devoid of content that it has become, in its own way, something pure. Pure poison of the very finest kind. The answer to her suffering, the cure for samsara inflicted against her will

Mei-yu smiles. She knows now she can wait no longer for the seas to rise and the lands to bake. She's going to bring that mountain down herself, release beloved Phramubartna from enforced slumber. Poison that mountain creature with all the bitterness of a rotting, festering world.

Thirteen centuries it has cowered inside the earth, Phramubartna suspended in its breath. It won't be there much longer.

Danielle sits in on one of the Temple's guided tours, not much use as the whole thing's done in Chinese, or whatever. This old nun with a microphone drones on while the old folks sit there lapping it up, fanning their faces with brochures, others taking pictures with their phones.

The next tour might be in English, but she's too fidgety to wait. Better to try the vegetarian cafe, check out earrings and necklaces in the gift shop.

She gets a sudden urge for a cigarette, even though she quit smoking twelve months back, right after she saw that Youtube vid about the lines it made around your lips. Maybe she can bum one and she's looking around for a likely candidate when she spots this nun checking her out. A skinny little thing, like most of them. This one has a really steady gaze, as if her eyes are chips of granite – or something harder.

Forget the cigarette. Danielle doesn't need it. She doesn't need that nun staring at her either. There's something harsh about the way she holds her head. Cocked a little sideways, kind of like a vulture. Probably desperate for a shag – who wouldn't be if they were a freaking nun?

She's thinking about pump class again, wondering if that new guy might be gay or bi. Wondering where they'd go if she could get him on a date. Nowhere with food. She never likes guys to see her eat although she loves the sight of a big buff guy with his fingers clenched around a burger. If she has to eat she'll have a salad, even though peppery rocket always makes her gag.

That skanky nun is still staring at her. Kind of smiling, if you could call those shrivelled lips a proper mouth.

A shaft of sunlight dapples through the trees, casts a pretty pattern on fallen leaves. Awesome. That word everybody uses everywhere. A word that's going out of style, yet it's really kind of applicable to this place. So picturesque she really ought take a picture. Hard to catch that pattern in a selfie.

"The view's much better from the top of the hill," says the nun.

Blows Danielle away with her perfect English. Up close and Danielle blinks a couple of times. She could have sworn that nun was old, but she's not. She's young – about the same age as Danielle.

The nun beckons. A procession winds its way up Jiuhua Hill, named for a mountain in a far-off land, so the brochure says. Some of the old Chinese are giving it a go.

The sun feels warm and soothing on her skin. Breeze licks at her hair. A photo from the top would be amazing; Danielle with the valley spread before her, like some queen of an ancient, fabled place. Something new for her Facebook timeline – everyone would think she'd snapped it overseas.

The nun keeps beckoning. She follows. When the nuns start chanting, she chants too, like the drone of cicadas or the hum of bees. She falls in step with the little women, *Giselle Naturales* holding up well upon bare stone.

Soon her feet are keeping pace. She's so glad she bothered to get her outfit right. It's the little things that matter.

Tough old boots they are, these nuns. Four ahead of her bear a palanquin high on bony shoulders. Another four following up behind.

Seven palanquins in all, each with a pointy box on top like a miniature temple.

That nun's still smiling – the older one who suddenly got young. Danielle smiles back. Mist rises off the damp and cloying earth. Strange how she didn't even feel the rain.

The palanquin coming up behind her carries a mummified corpse. Smaller than a starving African, bound up in cloths into a sitting position. Creepy as, like it's watching her through its long-dead, shrivelled eyes. Like it wants something from her. She shivers. The clouds have gone. The sun is back. The air is still and crisp.

The procession winds like a snake through the grass, past the big brass bell that sits at the halfway point. She longs to ring it but the procession doesn't stop. There's another bell waiting at the top, she knows. That nun told her all about it, sometime, somehow, she's not sure when. Only that she will be allowed to ring it – she and only she – but first she has to rub her hands in dirt. That bell has not been rung before. Not in this country. Not anywhere for at least a thousand years.

It's like a movie but she's not allowed to speak. Danielle is a princess, all purity and light. The nun has told her this as well, along with the names of the sacred items borne on the palanquins: the tooth, the hair, the robe, the ashes. The mummified old lady – who used to be a princess too, apparently. Not mummified, but incorruptible. Suspended upon the brink of death.

No birds hang in the perfect sky. No sound but the shuffling of ancient feet on well-worn stone. At the top stands Danielle like the queen of all creation, the world spread out before her like a quilt. The steelworks, insignificant as dust. The factories, the jobs, the office towers. Hot Michael and his yoga. She stands above the whole damn lot of it, staring at the bell engraved with words from an ancient text. Words that have begun to shift and writhe. The nun nods quietly. *It's time, Phramubartna, it's time.* Danielle nods, slams the wood into the bell. The nun keeps smiling as the ground begins to shake.

Inspired by a visit to Wollongong's Nan Tien temple complex – the largest Buddhist temple in the Southern Hemisphere – this story incorporates Buddhist history research, memories and details from my many years of dance and yoga classes, painful city office worker culture and appalling rubbish discovered on the WWW.

AND THE SHIP SAILS ON

The guide, known to the other men as Doc, was the only man not brandishing a gun. He swung a machete from side to side, casually lopping off random, jutting fronds. Shafts of light stabbed through breaks in the jungle canopy. No sound but the crunch of deep-tread boots through leaves.

Behind him, five sweaty men in lightweight baggy trousers, wide-brimmed hats pinning down mosquito head-nets. Grubby rags wrapped around thick necks, shirt pockets bulging with insect repellent sprays. Doc himself wore little in the way of protective garments: green combat pants and a long sleeved shirt, a pale and rumpled linen jacket topped off with a Panama hat. A wilted hibiscus pinned to his lapel.

"Big game. That's what the purser promised," said Everington, loudest, stoutest and richest of the passengers. "We don't see something big, then I want a refund."

"Biggest game you'll find for a hundred miles. In all directions," answered Doc, laughing at his own stupid joke.

None of the others found the joke amusing. They kept on walking, sweating and complaining, slapping at clouds of invisible mites and midges. Somewhere beyond the thick green leaves, unseen animals squawked and screeched and hollered. Birds or monkeys was the general consensus. Doc refused to answer when they quizzed him on specifics. The five had never believed his big game bullshit. They'd signed up for the safari out of desperate boredom. The superliner *Frederico Fellini* had been at sea for years and was running low on entertainment options.

One member of the expedition let out an involuntary squeal as a startled tapir scurried across their path. Doc laughed as the lower bushes shook out a tumbling guinea fowl. He raised his blade but paused it, mid-air. Turned back to the others, shot them a lopsided grin. Pointed upwards with the weapon. Above their heads, a clutch of curious spider monkeys hung on drooping branches, wide eyed and watching their every move.

The man who'd squealed flushed red with embarrassment. "Where's these ruins you've been spouting on about then?"

"All around us," said the Doc, swinging the machete in a wide and languid arc. "Used to be the major shopping concourse..."

"We know what it *used* to be," said a stern-faced man called Hargrave. "Everybody knows what everything used to be."

"Well here's something the Company doesn't want its passengers to know," said Doc, leaning in conspiratorially. "In 2025, when they added the Atlantis Dream Casino to level Six, they trashed part of the dining area and stuck on another sound stage. Circuses and magic shows came back in favour right after the Six Week War – if you remember."

Hargrave sniffed, unimpressed by the potted history lesson, the other four nodding in concurrence.

Doc continued. "I'm talking about old fashioned circuses – the kind with animals. Nothing too big, mind you. There wasn't anything too big left by then. Could never have got an elephant on board even if they'd managed to find one." He paused the blade, turned and leaned in closer, dropped his voice down to a harsh whisper. "Atlantis Dream brought clowns and acrobats, tarts in skimpy holo-lycra, feather headdresses and all that razzle-dazzle. They caged some of the animals down here, below, started advertising the jungle zoo as a separate cruise ship attraction."

Eerie silence resonated after he'd said his piece. Jungle walls pressing in – only minutes earlier there'd been monkeys but now there was nothing, not even a couple of high-up squawking parrots.

"Animals," piped up one of the men, "what kind of *animals* you talking about?"

Doc nodded knowingly. "The shooting kind, of course."

Everington snorted. "Pigs and fancy-looking chickens. A few feral dogs and cats is all you mean – admit it, man!"

"If you say so."

"Top Deck passengers don't fool so easy," Everington continued. "We paid good money for this expedition. Whatever there is to shoot had better be worth it."

Doc Corduroy smiled, revealing crooked teeth stained brown with nicotine. He balanced the blade across his shoulder. "Tell you what, fellas. If you're not satisfied – truly one hundred percent – then I'll give you all your money back, no questions."

Everington unknotted the sweat rag from his neck, mopped his brow and looked from face to face. Each man nodded in agreement, mumbling things like *can't get fairer than that*. When the last of them had made a comment, he stuffed the damp rag into his pants pocket. Was about to have another go at Doc when something peculiar caught his eye.

"Dear God, what is that thing supposed to be?"

Not far ahead through a veil of hanging greenery sat the ruins of a plaza strewn with chunks of toppled marble column, pink and white, half buried under debris and entwined with thick liana vines. Light bled through in ragged patches. All five gasped when they crowded close enough to behold the massive moss-and-lichen-encrusted statue standing at the centre of a clearing. A ring of offerings had been placed around its base: fruit and flowers in varying stages of decay. Personal items: watches, jewellery, vases. Paper rolled in cylinders tied with string. A plate bearing a delicate pyramid of small round sugar cookies, the kind routinely doled out at Madame Lucinda's Top Deck Chiffon Tearooms.

Doc waited patiently for one of them to speak. For the group of men to string the clues together.

Hargrave frowned. "I don't recall that thing in any brochure. Was this ever part of...?"

Doc cut in quickly. "Nope, see, that's the curious factor. That there statue... nobody knows who built it. Where the stone came from or how long it's been guarding the ship's interior."

The statue's face – if it had one – was obscured by growing things. They stared in silence at the great stone god holding court in a shaft of garish sunlight.

"Don't believe a word of it," said Everington, more stern-faced than ever. "Must have been one of the original attractions – and you're just making a big deal out of nothing. Trying to rip us off, the same as always. We came here to shoot – and we can't shoot that."

Doc didn't bother with a comeback. He removed the limp hibiscus from the lapel of his linen jacket, sauntered over and placed it gently at the faceless god's stone feet. Sheathed his machete, tipped his hat, leaned against the stone god's bulk as a cloud of midges swarmed across his skin.

Nothing happened. Not straight away. The five stared at him stupidly. Only one man fumbled for his gun, while another glanced up at the canopy treetops as if an explanation was going to fall down from the sky – or the upper decks.

"Well come on, man," barked Everington – "what are you waiting for?"

"For Fangaloka," said Doc, picking at his teeth with his pinky fingernail. "Seem to spend half my life waiting for that guy."

"What the devil –"

A blur of blade and gleam and tooth, a terrifying scream. Shots fired, random and useless. Fat men scattering, running for their lives.

Doc pulled back into the shadows as a group of thinner men, bare chested, with khaki tatters barely covering their thighs, darted into view, machetes raised. Two expedition members floundered flat on their backs, gored and bleeding amongst the leaf litter. Doc sneered as the thin men rifled through the pockets of the dying. No sign of the shifty warlord himself, of course. The men Fangaloka sent to do his slashing and stealing always lied about the bounty they took back. Fangaloka always claimed Doc Corduroy owed him.

The khaki killers left as soon as they'd got what they came for. Doc stepped over the twitching bodies, swinging his machete two and fro, walking back the way they'd come, deep in troubled thought. The time had come to make a stand – all he needed was the opportunity. To hack and slash a passage into the root-infested I09, a corridor running the entire length of the ship. To get to Fangaloka when his guard was down and liberate portions of his secret stash.

He eased himself down onto a tumbled stone, cleared a square of ground with the machete. Etched a rough diagram of the ship's lower level into the dirt. The problem was important enough for the devotion of serious thought. He wasn't due on top deck for at least an hour or two and more than anything else on ship he loved to keep those wrinkled bitches waiting.

Amber's Wednesday had begun like every other: daybreak in the Humphrey Bogart lounge, staring up to watch pixel numbers march across the big flat screens like ants. A tight-lipped gathering with few emotions shared – best not to arm your neighbours with unnecessary ammunition, not to let them second-guess your true predicament. Telltale signs were always present, you could read them if you had the skill, or time or inclination and who amongst the Top Deck folks did not possess ridiculous amounts of time? A hint of a fellow passenger going under could provide a whole week's entertainment. Or grief, if it was somebody well-liked. Stock market flutters and fluctuations took place in the cloud, the unseen realm of algorithms, intangibles and hedges.

Nothing on the morning screens to cause Amber concern. No huddled groups of twos and threes, plaid blankets wrapped around crumpled pyjamas, ashen faces tilted upwards in rigid, sleepless disbelief. Not today.

Relieved, she took her customary stroll amongst the sunbathers, nodding and smiling, doling out selective grace. Winking at the occasional handsome swabbie. After all, politeness didn't cost a cent and in a world like this, it was the *little things* that mattered. Politeness could get you many little things, from contraband tobacco through to an extra white bread roll at the dinner table.

Sadly, Amber's tobacco stash had dwindled down to crumbs and she could not bring herself to touch the bitter tasting seaweed beadies rolled by the swabbies and netters and haulers, the stink of which clung and lingered around certain regions of the ship, generally no-go zones for wealthy lady passengers.

She watched three young men on their hands and knees scraping green-grey lichen from the deck. Dressed in patched, torn cargo pants, the faded logos on their t-shirts indecipherable.

Above the deck, two Black Hawk helicopters hovered like giant robotic gnats. Amber ignored the noisy contraptions, made her way to her customary lounger situated close to the bar and the Top Deck clock; the one they all set their own watches by as the ship breezed in and out of different time zones. She picked up a well-thumbed magazine and settled. No hellos for the other women already stretched and sunning. Greetings amongst Amber's friends were considered gauche.

Lindsay dipped her own magazine, then her sunglasses for a clearer look at the choppers. Amber took note of the familiar gesture. The wooden lounger creaked beneath her weight as she nestled herself. "Anything?"

Lindsay's exposed, steel-grey roots were badly in need of touching up. She sniffed. "Manoeuvres. Just the usual. Nothing to get excited about." By which she meant not pirates or another change of course. The *Federico Fellini* had been encounter-free for fifty-five days running. The last attempt at a raiding party had turned out laughable; a pathetic flotilla of fishing junks weighed down by heavy guns. Thin brown women waving battered AK-47s, firepower aplenty but all they could do was shoot. They couldn't board – the *Fellini's* sides were far too sleek and high. First security turned on the water hose, then the Black Hawks made short work of the leftovers.

Afterwards there'd been bodies in the water, bobbing up and down like driftwood. No survivors – ship's drones made sure of that. They'd all watched the footage on the big screens in the Frank Sinatra lounge to the rousing accompaniment of *you get 'em boys and that'll teach 'em!* Fists air pumping, an elderly couple linking arms in a celebratory jig. The ship had never been in danger, the Company assured, all bullet holes in the side were plugged by sunset.

"They wouldn't be wasting fuel for nothing," added Lindsay, still staring at the wide blue sky, resplendent with its tissuey wisps of cirrus. Lindsay, being the oldest of the friends, remembered the ship when it was almost new, when the ice rink was still skatable and the golf course not ploughed up and used for crops. When the *Fellini* boasted twenty-one freshwater swimming pools, a surf simulator and thirty-seven bars. The desalination plant was still kicking on, thank God, even if fresh water could not be spared for the blistering sculpture garden. The ship had once had seven 'distinct neighbourhoods' – there were plenty more than seven now and *distinct* meant friends like Lindsay, Amber and Katelyn were not safe within them unless accompanied by well-fed bodyguards.

"We can ask Doc what's going on – if he ever gets here," said Amber, pretending to focus on her magazine, a dull affair filled with recycled articles photocopied onto greying recycled paper. 'Game Changing Skincare Treatments' had been run last year and 'Ten Ways to Turn Yourself into a Morning Workout Person' twice. With different accompanying photographs so that at least was something, but standards had been slipping – without doubt. She could see it in so many subtle ways, from surly wait-staff to never ending shortages. Meals where you couldn't be sure what you were eating. It wasn't Wagyu or Cervena venison – *that* you could be sure of. Most of what they ate came from the sea and they dumped their trash straight back in there without concern for the brown stain trailing in the vessel's wake like diarrhoea.

Lindsay was doing her best to hide her twitching irritation. Doc was late – that man was always late, a trait the women begrudgingly endured. But not today. Today both Lindsay and Amber needed Doc. "Oh god, doesn't Raymond look awful?"

Amber put her magazine back down and made a disapproving face. Said nothing as the older man walked by at a distance, head down, ignoring everyone – even Mr Travis and his corgi. One hand gripping the visor of his cap, even though there was no wind to speak of. No danger of him losing it overboard, which is what, rumour had it, had happened to Gerry Hargrave, Mr Travis's brother-in-law. Nobody had seen the ruddy-cheeked man in well over a fortnight. Not the done thing to mention missing persons, not if a whole two weeks had passed, not if there were rumours of late payments.

Amber sniffed and scanned the crowd in search of Doc's trademark crumpled linen and stupid hat. Instead of Doc, she found her daughter, a nut-brown girl of seventeen, dark hair falling free down to her waist. Standing by one of the outer railings, staring hard and admiringly at the lichen-scrapers' bulging, muscled arms.

Amber pursed her lips into the cat's bum expression denoting her very severest disapproval. She sat up straight and craned her neck, the magazine abandoned. "Olivia, darling, yoohoo – come on over!"

The girl's head turned at the mention of her name. She pushed a strand of long dark hair behind her ear and angled her body in the direction of a couple of older men decked out handsomely in shining Company whites, appropriately maritime, so long as you didn't look too closely at the fraying cuffs and mismatched buttons. Details her mother couldn't see without her glasses.

The lichen patches blooming across the deck were easy to make out. The abundant weed grew back relentlessly, regardless of weather or applied corrosive chemicals. The Purser said it wasn't lichen but more like a form of moss and its spores got into everything, especially wood. Bryophyte was the proper word but lichen was the term that stuck. The boys tasked with removing it wore cowboy bandanas to protect their faces, but their arms and lower legs were exposed as was everyone breathing downwind of them. The spores were said to cause fever dreams, nightmares and hallucinations, yet another reason why Amber and her friends fought so hard to defend high turf beside the Top Deck pool bar.

"Such a shy little slip of a thing," said Katelyn from the next lounge chair over, her long arms clattering with bangles.

Amber waved her hand with a flourish. Olivia hesitated, as if considering her options, then crossed the crowded, open deck to join the familiar clique on their wooden lounges, the cushions of which had once been brightly striped but were now bleached and faded by the sun. There was nowhere for the girl to sit. Amber sat up – properly this time – shielded her eyes and waved until she had the attention of one of the pool boys. One of the Joses, Alfredos or Alonzos. She felt exhausted trying to keep track of their names.

"My Olivia requires a seat," she shouted sharply. The boy flicked a glance across at the girl, nodded, then busied himself about the task.

"I don't like that young man's attitude," Amber added, not waiting until he'd moved out of earshot. "Some of those pool boys have forgotten where they came from."

"Most of us have forgotten where we came from, dear," said Lindsay, patting her arm.

Amber ignored Lindsay's customary snark. She was always tetchy when she was waiting for Doc.

Being responsible for Olivia meant Amber had to keep her eye on everyone. One handsome, savvy pool boy and everything might be ruined.

The girl had reached that *certain age* and was developing bad habits, such as wandering off on her own, exploring areas of the ship best avoided, sometimes being unaccountable for hours.

"So how's that Deb dress coming along, Olivia?" said Amber loudly, squinting in the harsh glare. "Tell me you've at least chosen the fabric."

"Ooh yes," chimed in both Lindsay and Katelyn, leaning forward. Everybody loved a Debutante Ball. The ship had held one every year since Sydney, tradition being so good for morale.

Olivia's eyes were wide and brown. She stared at Amber, then down at her own hands, then out across the pattern of interlaced semi-circular decks after the pool boy, who was wrestling with chain looped between a stack of wooden lounge chairs. He needed a key but apparently didn't have one. She said something to this effect, how he was going to have to find a porter.

"For God's sake, Livie, stop your mumbling," Amber snapped. "Speak clearly when you're spoken to. You never know who's listening. It's always best to make a good impression."

When Amber looked back to the pool boy, he was gone. She shivered as a Black Hawk's shadow swept across the deck, the machine dipping low enough to make a messy chaos of their towels and magazines. Close enough to see the comforting logo emblazoned on its side: two blades crossed.

"See. Just routine, like I said. Nothing we need to be worrying about," offered Lindsay smugly as the chopper swooped in a wide arc across the water. She returned her attention to scanning the crowd for Doc.

Olivia kept both eyes on the noisy machine as the older women debated what kind of dress she ought to be wearing and the fact that the current Captain – not so long since he inherited the job – had decreed the Ball would be held in the Zsa Zsa ballroom. But surely the Zsa Zsa was too small, and the Sophia Loren more suitable? Not to mention that it was *three floors down*, a precedent none of the women could ever approve of. Because who knew where things might go from there? Three floors to Zsa Zsa was a slippery slope.

"Captain Grecko never would have stood for such an outrage. We pay good money for Top Deck privilege. It's the little things that matter – don't you agree?"

The other women all agreed with Amber. Little things – or the lack thereof – had indeed become more irritating of late. Amber missed chocolate more than she ever would have believed possible. The stuff on the menu *supposed* to be chocolate was nothing of the kind. Just coconut oil, boiled, compressed and flavoured. The young ones liked it, but they had never known Lindt or even lowly Cadburys, which had come in blocks of a family size, available at Coles and Woolworths for a few dollars.

"They say Sophia Loren's got broken lighting fixtures," said Katelyn, leaning in conspiratorially, "but I don't believe a word of it. Reckon there's something they don't want us to see."

Amber rolled her eyes theatrically. She fanned herself with her magazine – at least it was good for something. "You think everything's a conspiracy, Katelyn. That everything is secret for a reason."

Lindsay gave them both a knowing look. She'd been convinced for months that something large was following the ship. She was not alone in this belief. Everyone had seen *something* at one time or another while staring out beyond the rails at an ocean vast and deep and strong that changed from minute to minute, that drove emotions with its thrust and swell and held them captive as completely as a sturdy prison cell.

Amber was certain it didn't help that, inch by inch, the jungle that had begun life as a tame, miniature park, a fancy concourse at the centre of the ship, was taking over. A feature grown into a nightmare, climbing up the inner balconies, pushing through cracks and rents and splits, forcing its way along the rails and pipes. A park metamorphosed into a jungle filled – so it was claimed – with dangerous beasts. Animals that were not supposed to be there. However had monkeys and wild pigs and deadly snakes made their way on board? Such a thing was patently ridiculous, yet they had all glimpsed monkeys and other hideous things – like the time Consuela Dalton had discovered an actual python in her bath. *A python!* She had screamed and screamed but absolutely no one came so she'd grabbed a towel and run along the corridor. That was when they'd learned the truth, that the intercom system was no longer functional. That they could scream as much as they liked but no one could hear them.

Amber got up suddenly to brush imaginary crumbs from her lap and legs. "Where *has* that lazy doctor got to? How come that man is never around when you need him?"

Katelyn and Lindsay raised their eyebrows but neither offered an opinion. Doc Corduroy was rumoured to favour one or two of the lower deck casinos despite the rules and regulations – and other dangers. He stayed up late and slept in later. Kept odd hours and company, not the kind of man you'd choose to associate with, if you had a choice, but when it came down to it, choice was pretty thin on the deck. Doc Corduroy had his finger on the *Fellini's* pulse. If ever you needed something, he could get it – and who did not need a little something now and then in this terrible, omnipresent heat? Providing it was an item that could be bought, bartered or sourced. If it was on the ship, Doc Corduroy could get it.

When Doc eventually made his appearance, both Amber and Lindsay busied themselves flipping through magazines they could practically recite by heart.

He slumped down in the lounger the boy had dragged across for Olivia, repositioned the Panama hat to cover his face. Stayed that way for twenty minutes while Katelyn did her best to flag down the drinks trolley which, Amber swore, was getting later every day, not to even mention the fact that the girl last week hadn't had the *first clue* how to mix a proper pink gin. And the stuff coming out of the Bombay Sapphire bottles was anything but. It wasn't even *Gordon's*, just some nameless swill being boiled up in the *Fellini's* jungle-stricken bowels.

Doc did not stir until the whumping helicopter blades drowned out the chatter. Black Hawks returning from their never ending search for solid ground.

When at last he sat up and removed his hat, all eyes fell upon him, hungry.

"Did you bring it," asked Lindsay sharply.

Doc sniffed, fumbled inside his jacket pocket, removed a small tatty envelope, passed it across without so much as a word. Lindsay snatched it from his fleshy fingers.

"You're welcome," he said with the feigned casual demeanour he'd been perfecting across the past few years. Amber tried to catch his eye, but he'd become distracted by the chopper setting down on the landing pad, high above deck in the no go zone beside the capsule of bullet proof blue glass.

Top Deck was crowded — more so than usual — bustling with noisy, animated folks, all stirred up by the noisy choppers, fretting that perhaps another change of course was imminent. That one of the Black Hawk pilots had seen *something*. That land might be waiting over the horizon.

Doc Corduroy clambered to his feet, tipped his Panama hat. "You ladies all have a wonderful day now, won't you?"

Amber stared at the back of his head as he dodged and shoved his way out through the throng, en route to wherever a man of his kind spent his daytimes.

Neither Lindsay nor Katelyn commented as Amber sprung off her lounger and headed after him, battering her way through the languid, irritating crowd.

Lindsay stared after her absently, clutching the Doc's envelope in a balled up fist. "I'll be in my cabin if anyone wants me."

The lower decks weren't safe at night but Liv had her own special place. One of the abandoned inner rim balconies not yet entirely claimed by creeping jungle. Not too difficult to scale, hand over foot. Enough space to stand without brushing against lianas or the fur-like moss thickly coating the walls.

Liv usually wore gloves and occasionally a surgical mask. But not tonight, with a fresh breeze blowing heady scents up from the decks below. Mango and papaya easily discernible amidst a heady floral mulch.

She closed her eyes and let the smells wash over her, the taint of jungle lingering on her skin. She had to be careful not to stay too long. If Amber found out about her special place then she'd make one of the swabbies board it up. Lately everything made her mother furious. Too much of this, not enough of that; things that could be shrugged off, explained and blamed mixed in with more resilient kinds of disappointment.

Amber's tight-knit circle of friends could be extremely unforgiving. They complained about everything, even things that couldn't be considered anyone's fault.

Those women had the best of everything. Free run of the deluxe Top Deck sections, servants to fetch them chairs and bring them drinks. Lives untroubled by the world and its great sorrows – the countless millions who had already lost their lives, their residue lingering across the sea and sky, in dreams and nightmares shared across the globe. The shame of a world in which three billion souls had starved to death. Probably another billion since the lucky ones stopped caring enough to count.

Three billion was too big a number to hold inside her head. Three billion meant the world was filled with ghosts.

Liv had seen so very many ghosts. Impossible not to encounter strangeness trapped on a ship stuck out on the open ocean. Phantom waves and waterspouts. Dark shapes moving just beneath the surface. Swell so clogged with jellies and plastic, the ship had to clear a passage through with lasers. A sky so wide it threatened to swallow them whole.

If the *Fellini* were to vanish in a fog, who left behind would even know they'd gone? The last real 'earth' she'd glimpsed had been an inhospitable craggy protrusion, the cause of much momentary excitement, that moment passing swiftly once they'd lost sight of the *Fellini's* small scout vessel. The Captain had dispatched it choked with flags of hope and peace and friendship. The barometer fell and the mist rolled in, then nothing for five excruciating hours. Two choppers scrambled to determine the little scout boat's fate. Liv's mind filled with splinters of shattered driftwood mixed with sodden, tangled colours. They'd heard the shots but could see nothing through the mist.

The open sea was deadly, as was the jungle blooming up and out of the *Fellini's* troubled heart. She'd never set foot inside that jungle but she knew people who had. People who'd entered the verdant fold and never come out again to speak of it.

A monkey screeched in the darkness down below, disrupting Liv's concentration. The worst-kept secret on Top Deck was how her mother planned to marry her off to a man more than twice her age. An officer in frayed-cuff whites who spent his days sequestered behind blue bulletproof glass, his nights in lower deck gambling dens if the rumours turned out to be half true.

Liv curled her fists in barely suppressed rage. She would not do it. She would find another way, far from Amber and Top Deck's alcoholic haze.

Liv pictured herself clambering down the crumbling inner balconies, throwing herself down, down and deep into the jungle's heart. Some place where Amber and her awful friends would never find her.

Not just a dream. She had a plan. She would make her move during the latter stages of the stupid Debutante Ball, when the lights were dimmed and everyone was drunk. She knew a girl who knew another who shacked up with a couple of swabbie boys from third. The jungle's mouth lay down below on six, but there were rumours of secret passages. Safe ways of tunnelling through roots if you had a guide, if you knew what you were doing. She didn't know what she was doing, but she figured she could learn. Whatever it took, whatever the risk, she'd do it.

A single tear rolled down her cheek. Despite the bitter promises and all the hurt between them, Olivia knew she did owe Amber something. Despite the bullshit and the lies. Despite the things she wasn't supposed to know.

Liv knew she had not been born upon this ship. Her earliest memories were of thirst and blinding white. Endless sun, blistered skin and savaged bone, wasted muscle and emaciated hope. Watching the big white shiny superliners push on through layers of roiling plastic sludge amidst the squall of filthy, desperate children.

Bony hands passing her up through a porthole, exchanged for food or drink or medicine, her painful, limited world turned inside out. Bright light replaced by dark and stifling heat. The repetitious pound of hammering engines.

Eight years old as close as she could reckon, put to work in a giant greasy kitchen, scrubbing on her hands and knees, in filth from hard-to-get-at places, fighting with feral rats for scraps, sleeping in a scratchy plastic basket, curled up like a dog – only dogs got better treatment than the paid-for children on the *Fellini's* bottommost decks. Dogs were cherished, trained and prized. Down below, every two-bit druglord kept a dog and treated it with respect.

But somehow Liv had made it out and through and up, passed along by the hands of women who'd seen in her the potential for something brighter. And she paid them back, every single set of hands, stealing from the wealthy ones who'd dress her like a doll, paint her cheeks and comb her hair, tell her how she was such a *lucky* girl, how all that had gone before must be forgotten.

Her dreams were steeped in kaleidoscope, deep green streaked with hibiscus pinks and yellows. Palm fronds waving casually in gentle breeze, warm sunlight on her face. Darkness: deep, impenetrable. Pure fantasy, according to Amber – the woman who had bought her with hard currency. Fantasy generated by her deeply troubled mind. Olivia – not the name she had been born with – dragged free of a barely floating pontoon hellhole, rescued from starvation and disease, all memories from which she had been clinically disentangled. Just as well – because nobody needed burdens as grim as those. Just as well... but Olivia remembered.

"I will not marry him," she said out loud. But how was she to escape her future when trapped on a ship in the middle of the ocean?

"Hey Doc – wait up," screeched Amber across the backs of passengers sunning themselves like porpoises, the deck divided into different camps along diplomatic lines. Some religious, others according to class and cash: the haves, have-mores and the have-more-than-they-ought-tos, gradings she found thoroughly appropriate. A quarter of the Top Deck sunbathers had no real right to be there but so long as they kept their distance from the upper pool bar and Amber's turf, she was willing to pretend they didn't exist.

Doc paused the third time Amber called his name. Turned to face the woman he'd been successfully snubbing for days.

Amber got straight down to business. "Have you given any more thought to my *personal proposal?*"

Doc tilted his hat to reveal more of his face. Eyes swivelled upwards in the direction of the blue tinged glass encasing the bridge and its privileged officer class. He cleared his throat. "I presume you're referring to that young officer? Remind me – what was his name again?"

"Luciano. As you well know. Thirty-five and used to be married but I don't suppose that matters any more."

"Don't suppose it does," the Doc agreed. What happened when the tsunami obliterated Sydney three years past was not something people liked to talk about.

"Luciano," Amber repeated, eyes glittering with malice. "And don't try any of your bullshit tricks on me. I've paid you good money up front and I expect results."

Doc splayed fingers through thinning hair before placing the Panama hat back on his head. "Don't I always get you ladies what you pay for?"

"You do," she said, "which is why we all come back and never report you – or poison other customers against you. Which we could do very easily," she added.

If he took the half-threat seriously, he wasn't going to show it. "Luciano," he enunciated in a serious tone, "Yeah, I know the guy. Frequents the level Four gambling suite off hours. Owes a motza to some big guy with a Polynesian name."

Amber's lips thinned as she pressed them tightly together. "I don't give two shits about some Polynesian arsehole. Is Luciano currently married or isn't he?"

Doc paused. "No. He isn't married."

"Gay? Bisexual? Prone to violent fits or temper tantrums?"

Doc snorted. "It's a bit late in the day to be getting picky." Doc could have affirmed the man's hetero status by offering up tales of young girl prostitutes scaling ropes to squeeze through portholes as the ship pushed through drifting arrays of rag tag settlements built up on plastic strong enough to stand on, but he decided to keep such details to himself. For the time being.

"His filthy gambling will have to stop, but otherwise he'll do," said Amber. "My daughter's developing an unhealthy obsession with that godforsaken interior jungle. Time has come for her to settle down, to start thinking about the future."

Doc Corduroy smiled a greasy smile. "Mother always knows best."

The future she was talking about was entirely her own. He'd watched how long and hard she stared at the exalted senior crew, their shadows protected by the blue glass of the bridge. Aiming those binoculars as if she was peering up past clouds straight into heaven.

Olivia. He licked his lips involuntarily whenever he heard her name. His dick got hard and his throat went dry as he thought about taking her off Top Deck forever, only not in the direction envisioned by her ghastly wrinkled mother. She wanted up but he wanted down, *down down down* into the secret jungle's heart. Deep places where even shafts of light couldn't penetrate. Where they'd have plenty of marijuana, opium and each other. That case of beluga caviar and crate of Moet he'd souvenired during last year's ill-fated mutiny attempt. He'd clear out one of the looted jewellery stores off the old mall strip, sweep away the broken glass and rubbish, make it all nice and cosy, like a little house – all for Olivia.

Amber's mouth was flapping up and down but he hadn't heard a word. He tuned back in and made an effort to pick up all the threads.

"And a decent stateroom for the Mother-of-the-Bride thrown in as part of the deal. Somewhere the plumbing's still functioning as intended."

Doc pulled the face he always pulled when wheeling and dealing with women. The one meaning *sure, hell, right – but it's gonna cost you."*

"Don't give me any of your two-bit bullshit," Amber added savagely, her voice dropping an entire octave. "If I'm giving *that man* my only daughter, it better wind up worth it – for me *and* the girl."

Doc's eyes travelled from Amber's garish turquoise eyeshadow, across the tops of the deck sunbathers and all the way to where Olivia stood in one fell, admiring swoop. "That daughter of yours sure is a pretty little thing," he said.

"Precisely," Amber said drily. "I can count on your discretion in this matter." Her words were a statement, not a question.

Doc reached for his hat and made as though to tip it, signifying their business was concluded. Amber turned and picked her way back across the deck, kicking aside other people's possessions, not caring if she stomped or tripped on the legs of lazing sunbathers, more than half of them drunk or stoned on weed grown deep in the *Fellini's* rusted belly. In that creepy, overgrown jungle, where rumour had it Doc Corduroy could come and go as he pleased, just like he had means and ways of insinuating himself amongst the officer class. A fact Amber would milk to her advantage. With all the world shot up and gone to Hell, one had to use one's skills and breeding to enforce civilisation at every opportunity, because who knew what the next sunrise might bring? The screens in the Humphrey Bogart lounge were never far from her mind. The scrolling tide of numbers rising and falling.

Meanwhile, Doc was dreaming up a sunrise of his own, a deal that did not involve some pot-bellied, glorified wop-swabbie who went by the name of Luciano — known as 'Lucky' to his mates — for reasons which would render him unsuitable for *anybody's* daughter if the old bag ever caught a whiff of any of it. But marriage brokering, shit, that was easy, something Doc could do with his eyes closed, in his sleep, something he'd done a few times already across the years on this ill-appointed voyage.

His gaze lingered longer on Olivia's lithe form. Even barefoot in a faded stonewashed t-shirt and floral sarong, she was a rare catch, no doubt about it; no, no doubt at all, and if not-so-Lucky Luciano thought he was getting it all for nothing, that arsehole had another think coming.

Amber aimed her binoculars at the flat expanse of blue that stood between the bridge crew and the rest of them. She'd invested so much time and effort into researching Luciano, yet had barely glimpsed the man this fortnight past. A troubling development, with the night of the Debutante Ball approaching fast. Doc assured her everything was shipshape, but when did he ever not sprout such consolatory bullshit?

White uniforms were becoming a lot less prevalent on Top Deck than they ought. In place of them, an endless seep of former Russians and nouveau-riche subcontinentals, working their way up, deck by deck. No one was doing anything to stem the tide.

She lowered the binoculars. Not much to see up there on the bridge. Whatever took place behind blue glass was a mystery.

She was preparing to scope the helipad when somebody shrieked out "Land Ho! Land Ho!"

All at once Top Deck became a frenzied hive, with everyone shoving and fighting their way portside, whooping and chittering like monkeys.

Amber's concentration held fast, despite the jostling and irritation. She didn't notice Lindsay approach, not until her friend lit one of those dreadful beadie cigarettes, releasing an acrid puff of scented smoke.

As usual, Lindsay was overdressed, tottering around in heels not made for promenading slippery decks. She never tripped — she'd been a catwalk model back in the *days before* and she was doing that thing they all did sometimes, dressing up in the best of everything she owned. Rings and jewels and pinned-up hair. *Just trying to make myself feel human, darling. Those little things one does to feel alive.*

Amber flapped at the plume with her free hand.

"Something's following this ship," said Lindsay, taking a deep drag. "I can feel it — and I'm not the only one."

"Rubbish," snapped Amber, her patience pushed to the limit by a toxic mix of Doc Corduroy and the heat. "And anyway, what if it were it true? No pirates have ever been able to –"

"Not pirates." Lindsay sniffed, wiped her cheek on the back of her hand. "Something else."

"Something else? Amber lowered the binoculars. "What kind of *something else?*"

Lindsay shook her artificial curls. Stared blankly at the smear of black mascara on her wrist. "The creature doesn't like the helicopters. They keep it scared away."

"You talk such nonsense when you're stoned – and when are you not stoned? You didn't see *anything*. You couldn't have *because there's nothing there to see*." Amber returned to her binoculars. Rumours something large was following the *Fellini* had intensified since the ship pulled out of Papeete, never realising back in those days how much their world had utterly transformed. That the land they'd left behind was gone for good – in some cases literally sunk beneath the sea. In others, reduced to resonance politics and commerce, events beyond all influence and control.

The shoving and swearing amped up as the portside upper deck got crammed. Any glimpse of land, even rumours or mirages, anything at all reminiscent of *terra firma* brought all those with upper access flocking, no matter the weather or the time of day.

Today's ocean was calm and dull, same as it had been for weeks. Flat sea. Flat sky. No birds. But rumours of something unseen and following dragged like undercurrent; so much easier to ignite than gasoline.

"There's nothing out there," said Amber, reconfirming, gripping the binoculars, trying not to sound as bitter as she felt. "Go back to your room and sleep it off."

Lindsay didn't move. She stared at the horizon with glazed eyes. Sooner or later everyone glimpsed something weird: flirtatious phantom lights in the far-off distance, promising a future that never seemed to arrive. Land that turned out to be another junk flotilla filled with human detritus.

Lindsay had seen more peculiar things than her fair share: water tumbling from the sky in thick cascades like the waterfalls of old. Bright lights dancing through the stratosphere. Voices calling on the wind, the names of the dead or soon-to-be. On board ghosts ranged from the recently disappeared or dear departed to phantom images of people from long lost times. Long lost places, cities drowned beneath the waves, workers clutching suitcases and take-away cappuccinos, faces frozen in disbelief, at whatever it was they could see that the corporeal could not.

"I know it's close," continued Lindsay to no one in particular. "Something dark and vast and deep, bigger than a whale. Big enough to crush the ship if it —"

"For God's sake, will you shut it!"

Lindsay finished her beadie and wandered over in the direction of starboard rails, away from all the shoving and excitement.

Amber sniffed with deep contempt. No wonder Lindsay smoked so much skunk. She'd pinned her hopes upon Central Otago, a bit of New Zealand still advertised as high ground with infrastructure, clean water and a functioning transport system. Even an airfield – supposedly. Amber wondered often about the claim of aeroplanes. In early days planes had flown above the ship with comforting regularity. Big ones, air buses and the like as well as short-range DC threes and other Black Hawks belonging to other ships.

The last aeroplane anyone had seen had seemed so lost in the sky's vast expanse, like a lonely dove in search of a place to land. At least a year ago, quite possibly much longer. So hard to keep track of seasons when there was nothing to mark them by. It was always hot except when it was too cold, too windy or the rain came down as sleet – sometimes hail; dangerous and unpredictable. And as for the storms, well so far their luck had held, although it wasn't luck. Not really. The ship's high-tech equipment had been holding its own against the worst of entropy incrementally and inevitably consuming the *Fellini* like a cancer. Eating away at them from the inside out. Sooner or later the day would come and they'd have to dodge the storms without technology.

Amber clutched the binoculars against her chest. She fancied herself a realist. Not like poor doomed fragile stupid Lindsay, blathering on about the life they'd lead 'when they arrived'. Babbling about real estate, refurbishment and grounds keeping. The cost of maintaining an adequate count of gardeners. About where Blue Moon and Amoretto Roses might be acquired in such a difficult agricultural climate. About water licensing and how you should be allowed to have as much of anything you could pay for.

The others let her run off at the mouth, not because they didn't have the heart but because to shatter or even challenge her illusions might be the final cascading straw for each of them. Women who had lost enough to frighten them into silence – the kind of silence that stretched across generations. There was no old money any more. There wasn't even money.

Merely the investments none of them could control or even access. They lived in the shadow of the cloud, of people who were no longer on the ship. People who vanished in the middle of the night with explanation neither sought nor offered. Sooner or later those algorithm clouds would darken and turn against them. Until that day, well, there was always Doc Corduroy and the temporary solace his pharmaceuticals had to offer.

When they could get hold of him.

The Doc's sources remained mysterious. The wily old bastard had his secrets, ways and means. Alliances with drug lords embedded so deep within the ship that some had never been exposed to natural light. *Rumour had it...* Amber could not bring herself to believe such flagrant bullshit. They had simply not been at sea long enough for such barbarous tales to be true. The ship was awash with ridiculous stories. Everyone was bored to death. They made up lies to pass the time, spread rumours without thinking about the consequences. Amber liked to keep one foot on solid ground, so to speak, even if it was deck not ground, perpetually rocking and roiling through storms and squalls and random course changes, designed to swerve around the worst of world events. Remains and ruins of other ships and, sometimes, entire cities swept out to sea by the kind of storms the *Fellini* and its crew lived in terror of. Avoiding super cell encounters was the captain's main responsibility. Hopefully. It was always hard to tell what the Captain might be thinking.

The Black Hawk was taking a long time to come back. Amber trained her binoculars on the patch of sea where it had disappeared. She had a plan and she was going to stick to it. She could not save all of the world's helpless creatures but she could save one – Olivia – find the girl a husband amongst the Top Deck crew, someone whose future did not rely on algorithms calculated in cloud bank arrays by heartless, formless artificial minds. Someone who could provide them both with a solid, believable future.

The far-glimpsed land turned out to be a mirage – to nobody's surprise. The Top Deck chatter moved on to other things. Lindsay sniffed away the last of her tears as Mr Travis came into view, his fat old corgi Patch waddling alongside. Mr Travis was one of those passengers everybody liked. Always addressed them with a cheery wave, looked after that sweet old dog no matter what.

"False alarm," he said, "but not to worry. We'll reach the land of the long white cloud before too long, mark my –"

Somebody let out a blood-curdling shriek.

"Oh my god, what is that?"

Lindsay, menacing in those ridiculous shoes, clung to the rail, face twisted into a hideous grimace, exacerbated by badly-run mascara. "Down there in the water," she wailed miserably.

Everybody rushed to the rail and raised their own binoculars in unison, those that had them, and started combing the sea's flat, glassy surface.

"I can't see anything..."

"There's nothing there, what's she on about..."

"Quickly, there – check out the rising wave!"

"Dark patches, but I'd hardly consider..."

"Christ on a flaming –"

The dark mass quivering just below the surface was impossibly huge and difficult to make out. Not until it breached and bobbed, raising what appeared to be a gelatinous appendage, which it slapped down quick and fast, too quick to see.

"What the fuck – it's bigger than..." The voice trailed off. The thing below the surface of the water was bigger than the superliner. No creature on Earth had ever been so large. Not in the days of dinosaurs – or ever.

Calm seas stretched from bow to infinity. Top Deck emptied quickly following the confirmed sea monster sighting. An empty Top Deck had been inconceivable in the months before. Unnerving silence without the fling and smash of clay pigeons being blasted off to starboard. No shuffleboard. Not even Mr Travis – fat little Patch was terrified of whatever kept nudging the vessel and refused to leave the safety of his cabin.

Lindsay and Katelyn dragged their wooden loungers closer together. They huddled, wrapped in faded floral towels, sunglasses obscuring grim expressions. Neither spoke. Neither had anything to say after the sighting of the creature. All attention was focused on the bar.

An hour passed before Amber joined them. She made her way across the deck then sat down stiffly. The lounger creaked as she swung her legs around. Lindsay opened her mouth but Katelyn shushed her with a sharp shake of her head. *Not now. Not today. Possibly not ever.*

The handsome waiter who eventually brought their drinks had an unfamiliar face. Not one of their comforting Joses or Alonzos. He mumbled something inaudible as he placed each drink on a coaster atop the low glass-topped table. His hand spasmed as he reached for the last glass, a mai tai. Liquid spilled.

Amber jerked up suddenly. "You stupid, useless clumsy fuck, why don't you watch what the fuck you're doing –"

Katelyn lunged, moved quickly to Amber's side, gripped her shoulders with both hands. "It's okay, honey, there's no need –"

Amber slapped blindly at her friend as the insults kept flowing, thick and incoherent.

"I'm going to call him Jose, same as the other guys. No way I'm learning a whole new name, not after what –"

"Shhh, honey, it's all right. Everything is going to be all right."

The waiter backed off to a safe distance. He stood there blinking in the harsh light and confusion, shielded his eyes with the hand not pressing the circular drinks tray hard against his chest.

Amber perched on the edge of her lounger, lighting up one of Lindsay's foul and stinking seaweed beadies.

Katelyn kept up a steady stream of comforting sounds and motions.

"Now come on. You don't know what you think you saw. None of us do –"

"We didn't *see* anything. There's nothing there to *see*. Just a mirage, like all those islands turning out to be nothing more than floating garbage."

"I liked the old captain better," said Lindsay, dabbing at her watering eyes with a well-worn lacy handkerchief. She sniffed repeatedly but didn't blow her nose. "That man always knew what he was doing. He never would have permitted..."

Nobody had anything to say to that, but they'd all been thinking it. If Captain Grecko had been so smart, how come he disappeared? Captains weren't supposed to vanish, only passengers occasionally when their cloud-bound investments failed, or when they crossed someone who oughtn't get crossed or when bad things happened which couldn't be prevented with necessary and strategic foresight.

What use was a captain who couldn't keep a grip on his own future? None, as it had turned out, which is how the ship had wound up in the hands of Captain Floris.

Amber regarded Lindsay with bloodless, thin-pressed lips. Half an hour back the former model had managed to look half regal in all that catwalk getup, but now, in the harsh light of afternoon sun, she just looked old. Old and broken by whatever the hell that *thing* was, swimming alongside the ship. Nudging the hull as easily as if it was a beach ball. The *Fellini* was a superliner, the biggest of its class. The thing in the water was big enough to swallow the ship whole, was what everyone was muttering, which couldn't be true. Not likely. Surely not.

Lindsay's endless sobbing was ragging on everyone's nerves. If that useless fuck of a doctor ever showed his face again, Amber would force him to give her something potent. To pick her up or calm her down. Either way, so long as she went quiet.

"We have to pull ourselves together," Amber enunciated loudly. "We've got the Ball to think about – the laundry's running at least a week behind. You know what *those women* down below are like. You have to shout to get anything done half right."

And where exactly were the officers throughout the ship's biggest crisis in months? Cowering in relative safety behind blue glass, that's where. Amber kept those particular bitter thoughts to herself.

But Lindsay's whimpering was starting to drive her crazy. "Snap out of it, sister – or I swear I'll take the rest of your stash and throw it overboard."

Lindsay wasn't listening. Lindsay was sinking into a world of her own and it didn't look like she was ever coming back.

The ship changed course abruptly within the hour and the Black Hawks swept the seas, back and forth, back and forth with hurricane spotlights, just in case.

Doc stood in the tiny room he'd come to think of as his office. The narrow cot he occasionally slept on was covered entirely in guns ranging from a Yarygin PYa semi-automatic pistol through a Chinese Type 56 Kalashnikov AKM clone – to his good old Saiga 12 with removed buttstock, 10 inch barrel, and 20-round drum magazine.

He settled on a Ruger P345 and stuffed it through his belt. Thuds and shouts echoed down the corridor outside. The past hour had been rife with rumours of rats preparing to jack a couple of 'Hawks and jump the ship. Doc Corduroy would be making sure that he was one of those rats, but not before putting a bullet through Fangaloka's skull.

Shoot the warlord, nab his stash, grab Olivia and hit the open skies. He chopped and snorted a line of coke off the back of a broken dinner plate. Braced himself as the bulkheads shuddered from what was either explosive charges detonated somewhere on the deck below, or the resonance of something large hitting the ship. Either way, he had not much time. The *Fellini's* hours appeared to be numbered and his options becoming fewer by the minute.

He hoovered up the rest of the cocaine, waiting until the slap of running boots on metal no longer echoed down the corridor. Shouldered the assault rifle and aimed a parting glance back at the guns he regrettably would have to leave behind.

146

The sea was lumpy and gunmetal grey the night of the Debutante Ball.

"It's chilly for this time of year, don't you think?" said a stranger done up in flamingo pink, encroaching on Amber's turf, staggering towards the pool bar as if she had a right to stand wherever the hell she wanted.

Amber was far too stressed for requisite reinforcement of protocol. She agreed with the flamingo horror that indeed the nights were getting chilly, even though the temperature was the last thing on her mind since the ship had started zigzagging on a daily basis. The *Fellini* was lost, that much was certain, lost and far from the trusty pontoon refuelling stations bobbing near Nuku'alofa and Vanua Levu.

The Debutante Ball was the only adhesive holding Top Deck together. The lowest decks, however, were an entirely different story, one involving rapid machine gun fire and more than one explosion in the past twelve hours. The hoot and holler of animals perpetually unseen.

Unable to sleep, Amber had paced Top Deck alone despite the danger and uncertainty, hating how she was forced to care about what those savages below were getting up to. Belowdecks used to be where *manufacturing* took place — what little there had been of it — and the engines, lowest down, of course. Somebody had to keep the *Fellini* on the move. A whole great chain of somebodies keeping reliably at their stations. The jungle occupied the middle like the lettuce in a sandwich — only now the lettuce was taking over the ship. The once-clean decks were slick with lichen, with roots and tendrils pushing up through cracks not evident mere days earlier.

Tonight, if Corduroy had done his work, would be the night everything changed. No more flamingos and pushy, social climbing subcontinentals. Amber and Olivia would ascend the private stairwell, with Amber scoring a stateroom all of her own. So high, the roots and lichen couldn't reach. Amber wasn't greedy — she had every intention of sharing her good fortune. Inviting the others over for tea on her own private balcony. Popping the corks on her top-shelf booze whenever there was something to celebrate.

Somewhere close, an orchestra ground out Pachelbel's Canon. Real live music rather than tinned. Mothers and daughters promenaded the circular decks arm-in-arm. Waiters stepped up, proffering trays of brightly coloured drinks. Bathtub gin, but nobody was complaining. The *thing* slamming into the ship's side at random intervals had given up its game in the early hours. No longer to be spoken of, by general consensus. Onwards and upwards, stiff upper lip and all that.

A cloud of commotion cut across the music; all gosh and wow and tittering and coo. Amber turned in time to see her Olivia illuminated in a shaft of orange sunset. All the girls were dolled up pretty but none of them looked half as good as her Olivia.

Amber managed a watery smile. They could still frock up like a million bucks despite persistent shortages. Amber and her friends hailed from a particular segment of society. The right kind of people with the right connections, even when forced to shape them on the fly. Even when they had to make concessions. Trade away things they had never thought they'd part with. Such had become the way of the world and there was no point in moping about small details.

"I want my daughter dressed in white," she'd told that dreadful dressmaker, the one who'd argued the remaining ivory fabric should be saved up for the brides, but who was *he* to be telling *her* what she could or couldn't have? Amber won in the end, she always did, and here was proof, Olivia, princess of the seas, veritably glowing like a treasured pearl.

Amber gently nudged a passage through the sequins, lace and taffeta as sunset orange faded from the sky. Relieved the girl was wearing the dress and taking their future seriously – for once.

"Darling – what are you looking at?" Amber tugged Olivia roughly away from the rail. Why did those dirty lower decks so often attract the girl's attention? Doc Corduroy insisted she couldn't possibly remember the cramped and stinking horrors of her childhood.

But Amber was wrong. Olivia had not been peering down the ship's gargantuan side, but staring out across the ocean, past the engines' ever-churning white water filled with dirty, floating things that did not bear close up examination.

"That creature's still following the ship," Olivia stated, eyes transfixed on the far off distance. "I can feel it. Lindsay feels it too."

"No it isn't, and no you can't," answered Amber decisively, grabbing Olivia's arm and yanking her further from the rail. "You can't feel anything because there's nothing out there. It's nearly time to go in." She smoothed the girl's hair and patted it in place. "Focus, darling. You only get to be a debutante once."

Olivia nodded and permitted herself to be led toward the warm spill of coloured party lights, the buzz of chatter, the clink of gin-filled champagne flutes, the laughter of the other young girls, each one in borrowed jewellery and the finest dresses their mothers could afford.

But before they'd made it halfway to the central staircase, she suddenly stopped and pulled Amber around. "I'm not going to marry that horrible man," said Olivia defiantly. "Even if the ship wasn't under attack, we weren't in danger and Lucky Luciano was the last man left on Earth."

"The ship is *not* under attack," snapped Amber, lowering her voice the instant she realised others were taking an interest. She snatched a drink off the nearest tray and pressed it into the girl's hands. "Sip this – it will help to calm your nerves."

Olivia raised her palms and stepped back as the glass smashed on the deck. "You can't manipulate your way out of this one, *mother*. There'll be no more marriages. No more debutantes. The creature hunts us. It smells our blood. It seeks vengeance for the sins of the world. The jungle is the only safe place."

Amber stared in horror at the shards of broken glass as Olivia's crazy words started sinking in. Olivia turned and forced her way out through the murmuring, disapproving throng.

Amber skirted the glass and chased on after her. "Wait!"

Olivia crouched down to unstrap her high heeled shoes. Once barefoot, she ran full pelt for the central staircase, the *Grande Descent* they would all be filing down to the Zsa Zsa lounge. Bounding along plush velvet carpet two steps at a time, avoiding the startled guards with her duck-and-weave. Long gone before Amber pushed her way to the ivory enamelled rails and started shrieking her name at the top of her lungs.

The I09's flaking grey paint corridor ran the entire length of the lower levels. It stank of salt, of rotting leaves and fermented, curdled sap. Of piss and shit and other gruesome elements on the days the septic system backed up too hard.

I09 had once been the crew's easiest route from stern to tail, back in the days before the jungle pushed its way through staterooms and corridors alike, roots and creepers that could grow three feet across a week – or faster. The plants loved the humidity of the lower decks, tolerated the briny ocean seep, sucking out the life sustaining liquid, leaving thick encrustation of salt crystals glued to doorways, hatchways and portholes.

The night had not been going the way Doc Corduroy had planned. Seemed he wasn't the only one hoping for last minute business dealings with the warlord before they were all forced to abandon ship. Among so many other valuable items, Fangaloka was rumoured to have a map of the Pacific Ocean's Bunkering pontoons – floating fuel stations carrying diesel oil and benzine.

With one hand in his crumpled linen jacket, Doc ducked a hail of bullets, fingers curled around his reliable Ruger P345, an older weapon with a comfortable grip, a gun that had seen him through the rougher patches.

He could recognise Fangaloka's lieutenants by their khaki and dark smears of jungle paint. But the man himself was nowhere to be found. The warlord's staterooms had been ransacked long before Doc's arrival, the blood on the carpet, walls and ceiling testament to the fact that Doc was, unfortunately, too late.

Too late to the party, too late to the escape. Doc had flown UH-60 Black Hawks in Iraq back in the day, which he'd figured might make him a useful asset under the current, particular predicament. But a chopper would be useless if he didn't know where to take it. The *Fellini* had twisted and turned around so many times, they literally could be anywhere in the Pacific.

Doc was thinking maybe this was it, the day his old school smarts and cunning finally failed to sail him through the straits, when the entire corridor lurched then shuddered, so violently that two of Fangaloka's machine gun-wielding thugs along the corridor got slammed up hard against the bulkheads. One of them let out a torrent of mangled curses in Torres Strait Creole. His offsider, a thick-lipped, pale-faced man, had been holding his M4 Carbine raised and ready when whatever-the-fuck-that-was hit the ship. Hit it like a hurtling meteor – or perhaps they'd been rammed by another superliner? Because what else could set the I09 to shuddering?

The men had quit their haggling over the price of poppy oil, over who had let the wild pigs in to savage whose marijuana crops. When whatever-the-fuck rammed the side again, a torrent of filthy, stinking water surged between the thickened twisting roots. Next came foetid compost stench and screaming.

Then, more screaming and scrambling over tangles. Belching smoke from deep below and enough salt water bleeding through the cracks to make the men abandon all business concerns.

Gunfire, rapid, in the distance. Doc bolted for the nearest stairwell, the fastest he had ever moved in his life. And what a shitty life it had been, the one now strobing before his eyes in jagged pieces. The man he'd knifed for his identity – and passage on this stinking tub. The women he'd... no, Doc did not have time to waste on women. There was only one girl still in his mind, only one pure enough to make him care. Thoughts of Olivia propelled him up the crumbling stairwell, two steps at a time, guided him to a safer corridor. One the rising waters had yet to reach.

Charcoal storm clouds coagulated in a bruise centred directly above the *Frederico Fellini*. Passengers squealed and clung on to each other as unsecured items hurtled across the deck.

"We're not moving – why aren't we moving?"

"Get back down – who's blocking the goddamn staircase?"

None of the regulars were truly terrified until they comprehended that the unthinkable had happened. The Top Deck clock had stopped – for good this time, stuck fast on 11:11, as eerie an omen as there had ever been. As if the choppy seas were not enough. And the light: a pallid, sickly cast that might have been appropriate at sunrise. Only sunrise wasn't due for several hours.

Katelyn took up position on the tier above the lounges, a rifle balanced across her knobbly knees. Nobody asked where she'd got the gun. Things were changing hour-to-hour and it didn't hurt to be prepared for the worst.

Lindsay fought her way across the deck, those years of catwalks in precarious heels finally standing her in a decent stead. Shoving the wayward and clumsy aside, passage hindered by lounges not tied down.

"That captain oughta drag his carcass down here off that bridge," she shouted, wide-eyed and chemically alert, back to her old self again – to Amber's relief. Shouting had become necessary with so many competing sounds. The terraced, circular decks around the pool bar were filled with gawkers checking on the stopped clock themselves, even those whose staterooms still featured working screens. The Top Deck clock was the only one that mattered, its consensual time the glue that bound them all. They could handle the jungle, the lichen and the weather, but timelessness was another matter entirely.

When Katelyn slammed a pink gin into Lindsay's hands she drained it in one gulp. "Propellers are fouled with plastic," she reported grimly. "Surrounding seas choked thick with those filthy jellies." She nodded in the direction of the blue-tinged capsule bridge. "Consuela Dalton says the crew have barricaded themselves inside."

Amber's eyes blazed. "Connie – how the hell would she know that?"

Lindsay threw her an exasperated look, then jiggled her glass, empty but for a couple of tiny melted cubes. A glance in the direction of the bar confirmed the worst. A crush had gathered. Voices were raised and getting higher. The two Joses on duty didn't stand a chance of fending off the thirsty, frightened crowd.

"Here," said Katelyn shouting from behind. Passing a hip flask, one hand resting firmly on the rifle, just in case.

Lindsay mouthed a relieved *thank you* as something large and hard slammed into the ship. The hip flask clattered to the deck. Everyone began to wail and scream.

Amber scrambled to her feet, grabbed the nearest railing for support just in time as the creature struck again. The air filled with the wrench and creak of grinding, tearing metal. People shrieking, falling over their own feet.

Amber flung her gaze towards the bridge in search of answers and got one soon enough. Those familiar Black Hawks swinging into view. Behind them, a grey and boiling bank of cloud that seemed to have spewed up from the angry ocean.

"Look – those bastards – they're leaving us!" shrieked Amber. She snatched the rifle out of Katelyn's hands. Aimed and fired, the force of the bullet flinging her backwards to slam hard against the rail. Her bullet bounced harmlessly off the tinted glass.

Both fists and voices were raised in anger as one of the hovering Black Hawks dropped a ladder from its underbelly. Amber took squinting aim again as one by one, the bridge crew climbed on up.

"Come back you cowards – take me and my daughter with you," she screamed, shrill voice snatched and obliterated by a mix of wind, wave, storm and brute hysteria.

The bridge crew ascended as charcoal silhouettes, individuals indistinguishable, none of Amber's bullets hitting home.

The only one on the upper deck not screaming was Doc Corduroy. He kept a firm grip on the railing as he scanned the crowd from face to face, knowing Olivia had to be there somewhere, comprehending that this was it, his chance had finally come. The stuck-up bitches were going to have to hand her over because they wouldn't last the night without his help.

He cupped his hands and yelled "Olivia!" as rain soaked through his precious linen, plastered thinning hair against his scalp. Clutching his Panama hat for fear of losing it. "Olivia!"

His voice lost amidst the thunder and confusion, rain sleeting down with angular precision. Passengers and crew alike slipping and sliding all over the listing deck as pungent stenches swirled and belched and wafted. Rotting vegetation, the kind you'd find at the bottom of a swamp, seeping from great cracks in the vessel's structure. Doc blinked streaming water from his eyes as he watched cracks widening in the deck and walls, thick-coiled roots pushing up and through, wooden lounge chairs hurtling like tumbleweeds.

"Olivia!"

A shadow blotted out the lightning, cleaved straight through Top Deck like it was butter.

"Olivia!" Her name dispersed by shrieking winds as Doc and hundreds of other passengers tumbled headfirst into the churning, foaming void.

Women's arms and women's faces, soaked and dripping with stunned disbelief. Arms strong enough to haul him up and over the boat's fibre-reinforced plastic sides. Women. Doc Corduroy's heart flooded with palpable relief. If this had been Fangaloka's boat, he wouldn't stand a chance. Too many debts; too many altercations. But women... he could always find a way into a woman's heart. Manipulate them into supplying whatever he needed.

Olivia did not appear to be amongst the damp, bedraggled throng, although some were wrapped up tight, their faces covered. No matter, he would find her someday, somehow, either Olivia or another girl just like her. Someone young and soft and pure. A girl the world hadn't soiled with its corruption and despair.

He coughed and then some pinch-faced crone was leaning over, wiping his salt-drench face clean with her hands. "Thank you, my dear," he said as kindly as he had learned was best. Her teeth were crooked and none too white. He didn't like crooked teeth. He would close his eyes until she went away and the worst of the storm had fled the sky. Rest his head and dream of better times and better days. The sea was choppy but the squalling rain had all but stopped and that, at least, was something.

Doc Corduroy fell into a fitful slumber through which he hacked and slashed with a dull blade through thick, impenetrable jungles, which morphed into thrashing killer waves and dark skies etched with diagrams, red line and black scrawl defacing off-white paper charts spread across a table depicting instructions for the Williamson turn, an ideal method in reduced visibility, with rescue throw and heaving lines. Man overboard was a tricky business. Sometimes it was impossible to turn a ship the size of this around.

Churning water interrupted by the songs of angels dragging him back into his skin. Above him spewed a wicked spill of brittle constellations: Magellanic silver-white star clusters, Carina, Centaurus and the Crux: once visible in ancient Athens, a thousand years before the Earth had shifted on its axis. The skinny boy who had shared his meagre astronomical penchant had lost his life in a knife fight over nothing. Such had always been the way of things.

Something in the boat had changed. Hunkered down a few metres ahead sat a big man wrapped in a damp, polyester blanket patterned with black and purple tiger stripes. Not enough light to catch his features, but there wasn't any need to see his face. Fangaloka, curse his filthy rotten luck. Fangaloka; perpetual survivor. Last man standing and the first to find a boat and get away while everyone else stood screaming and distracted by monstrosities, either real ones or imagined, apparently. Doc was no longer certain about any of the things he thought he'd seen during the *Fellini's* final disintegrating moments. All those toxic spores and pollens; lichen scrapings distorting vision and clouding up men's minds. A storm had sliced the Fellini into ribbons — the only conclusion that made sense. The ship had been lucky to keep sailing on for as many years as it had done.

Fangaloka: Prince of Darkness. Tattooed shadow swirls across dry skin. With effort, Doc Corduroy managed to haul himself to standing, shuffling his feet to keep his balance. Damn, but every gun he owned lay ruined at the bottom of the sea. He couldn't win a one-on-one with this over-muscled human mountain. He would have to think of something clever.

The lifeboat was bigger than he'd first presumed. Perhaps all was not lost?

"Friend," said Corduroy, grinning fiercely, wiping his salty palm down a damp trouser leg and stepping forward. "To new beginnings. To new opportunities."

Bedraggled women shuffled themselves and children out of the way as the mountain rose, shrugging off his tiger skin, a Ka-Bar USMC glinting in each outstretched hand. Corduroy raised both palms in mock surrender. "Relax, my friend, there's no need to fight. Plenty of everything to go around." He smiled and raised an eyebrow in the direction of one of the women. Not the crone with the crooked teeth. A younger one whose hair might well be blonde if only there had been more light to make out subtle differences and details. No matter. Doc was not a fussy man, and first things first, which meant the mountain would have to come to Mohammed and the two of them work out how to split the spoils. How to forge a better future from the splinters – to find dry land and claim it for themselves.

"My boat," said Fangaloka.

"Of course it is, good man. Of course it is – and a very fine crew you've assembled for yourself, I might add. In very difficult circumstances, too… I've always admired that kind of ingenuity, especially in a crisis…"

Fangaloka lunged, both blades glinting silvery with starlight.

Doc flung himself backwards, barrelling into a cluster of women. Flailing his arms to prevent himself from falling.

Doc Corduroy didn't fall. His bulk was gathered and pushed along; shoved and prodded until it reached the starboard rail. Nobody said anything. No signal had been issued. No words spoken. No consensus reached.

"Wait… no… what…? stop! Help!"

So many nameless, faceless women with sinewy arms and tight-gripping hands. And then, finally a face he recognised.

"Amber! Amber! My pockets are full! I have everything you need. Everything!"

Amber pursed her lips and watched as Doc Corduroy's bloated, wriggling form was launched over the side, slamming hard into waves thickened with coils of writhing, jellied plastic. Corduroy went down and under, his head rattling with cold shock response statistics, his vision dimming and faint bells ringing in his ears. Too cold to breathe, swallowing more water than air. Kicking to keep his head above the surface. Kicking hard until the very last.

Flat sea the colour of dirty snow. Sunlight slicing through the low cloud scatter. A sudden, rough lurch of the lifeboat nudged Amber wide awake. Huddled down under drenched tarpaulin, warm bodies pressed all around, at first she couldn't remember where she was. Flooding panic as she punched and pushed at the heavy, dripping canvas overhead. One by one the survivors sardined beneath tarpaulin stirred, engaged in their own brief rituals of panic before helping to shift the sodden, weighty mass enough to let in welcome, salty air.

A wave of bright and dazzling light amidst excited cries.

"Land! Land Ho!"

"An island, Mama – it's an island!"

"Jesus Mother Maria, we are saved!"

Sobs and whimpers evaporated as one by one survivors glimpsed the yellowed slick of sand, comprehending *en masse* that their lifeboat had beached itself on a shallow spit. At the very least, they were safe from drowning. The last thing anyone remembered was the storm, the shattering ship and the Black Hawks fleeing. All belonged to yesterday or maybe a week ago. It was hard to remember.

"But where are we?"

Amber rubbed her pounding head and stared. The island looked like every other island from a pastiche of memory and glossy brochure: a stretch of fine sand fringed with dark green foliage, palm trees jutting at irregular angles, the kinds of trees that took many years to grow.

Amber tried to conjure images of New Zealand, north and south from sites she'd frequented before the web went dark – back then, she'd only been half interested at best, depending on her mood. In her heart of hearts she'd hoped the *Fellini* might have found a passage to Hawaii and onwards to whatever remained of the Americas. Tahiti was more probable, but the truth was they could be *anywhere*, blown off course in all directions, if that wretched captain had ever been telling the truth.

The captain. Intrusive flashes of evacuating Black Hawks, the bridge crew – Luciano included – abandoning the rest of the passengers to their fate. Two big men fighting in the centre of the lifeboat, slashing blades and swinging punches, both tipped unceremoniously over the side and swallowed by a monster from the deep.

Good riddance to bad rubbish, as Katelyn used to say.

Poor Katelyn.

Memories struggled to cohere and set, but a final yank of sodden canvas followed by a flurry of arms and legs rescattered them. Women, girls and a handful of children spilled over the lifeboat's side in clumps of twos and threes, leaping and tumbling and wading through shallow streams up the beach, some on all fours, some of them praying, others laughing, clutching at handfuls of dry sand when they reached it, tossing it into the air in joyous arcs.

And there she was, Olivia, standing on the warm and welcome sand, barefoot in a ruined debutante dress.

"Be careful!" cried out Amber through cupped hands, her words scrambled and scattered on the breeze unheard. Olivia was the only one not rolling in the sand, her attention fully taken by the wall of green and a couple of peculiar jutting structures. Too far away for Amber to see clearly – her glasses were probably at the bottom of the ocean. Taking great care, she jumped down into the shallow, lapping waves, unsteady on land after so many years at sea. Throwing a nervous glance over her shoulder to the boat responsible for their lives, relieved to note it was wedged deep in wet sand.

The long, curved beach was littered with dark streaks. Seaweed she presumed until she poked at one of the dark streaks with her foot, stubbing her toe on metal entangled with slime. Charred helicopter fragments in a variety of shapes and sizes. She sniffed. That cowardly captain and his bridge crew brought their fate upon themselves. She'd gone a fair way along the stretch before pausing to consider the possibility of mangled body parts.

Olivia struggled through heavy sand ahead, adjusting to the gravity and drag. Distracted by the enormity and splendour of the towering jungle wall.

"Be careful, Olivia – you don't know what lurks within," Amber shouted, louder this time, her voice dissolving uselessly in the wind. The girl had never seen a genuine jungle. Or a sandy beach, or so many of the ordinary things that Amber still took for granted because they lived on in her memory and some part of her still believed that they were out there somewhere waiting to be rediscovered. But the girl... How much of any of this could possibly be real to her?

Ahead, Olivia, wind-whipped hair out of control, tentatively approached the jungle's edge. She stopped and pointed upwards at a pale pink, protruding shape.

Amber sloughed through thick, coarse-grained sand. "Don't touch anything. Wait for me."

"A column from the promenade!" said Olivia.

"Don't be silly, dear..." The words were out of Amber's mouth before her eyes could properly focus on the thing, the shape with its fluted edges and soft pink tinge. "But how...?"

Cries of exclamation repeated up and down the beach. Amber turned to watch smashed segments of helicopter dragged free and identified, piece-by-piece, the lifeboat survivors bending to tug at them, assembling the narrative of what might have taken place the night before.

"I can't feel sorry for those pathetic cowards. Not one little bit – no decent man, let alone a decent captain..." But when Amber turned back, Olivia was gone.

She panicked. "Olivia!"

A clear trail of footprints scuffed the sand right up to the jungle wall. Amber followed and plunged straight through the green. She would not be left behind, no matter where that silly girl thought she was headed.

The undergrowth was not as thick as it had appeared from the beach. With dismay, she wondered what had happened to her shoes – not to mention Katelyn and poor darling Lindsay. Those two had driven her half crazy across the years but dear God, they had deserved much better than to go down with the *Frederico Fellini*.

Thick, humid air echoed with birdcall: whoops and caws and high-pitched screeching – parrots or monkeys or other kinds of unseen, exotic beasts.

"Olivia!"

The foliage seemed to absorb Amber's cries. The louder she called, the weaker the effect. At last she stumbled into a clearing scattered with chunks of stone the colour of Himalayan rock salt. Another column jutted at an angle of roughly thirty degrees; pocked and weathered, looking like it had stood for centuries but of course that couldn't possibly be so. Most definitely one of the supporting columns from the *Fellini's* promenade, she would know it anywhere. They would all have known that column anywhere.

Pushing on beyond the column, she was relieved to find Olivia standing in a ragged clearing, frozen still, both hands covering her mouth. Staring up at the clearly identifiable helicopter blade embedded in a palm tree's trunk. Transfixed by the sight of the bruised and bloodied body lashed to the palm's thick base below. Doc Corduroy, those grubby, sodden linens unmistakable, the front of his shirt drenched thick with blood. Head lolling forward, face obscured by a battered and sodden Panama hat.

"Don't look," instructed Amber. Useless words too late. She strode forward matter-of-factly, intending to check the body for a pulse because she had to be sure the Doc had finally got what was coming to him. Trust *him* to somehow have escaped the raging sea.

Doc Corduroy's flesh was rubbery and cold. A leather knife hilt protruded from his heart. Fangaloka's weapon – she pictured the two locked in a death grip below the roiling waves, then debated whether or not to pull it free, to cut him down or just leave him up there for the birds. Still thinking about it when Olivia took off again.

"Olivia – no – wait!"

Amber abandoned dead Doc Corduroy to chase after her daughter. "Olivia – be careful, there might be anything in there –"

She watched as Olivia's torn, white dress became obscured by foliage mere feet beyond the rage of her grasp.

Fronds slapped at Amber's face as she hurried onwards past another chunk of marble, this one lying on its side, half covered in the same pale clingy lichen that had permeated the ship in recent months, despite the relentless scratching and scraping performed by those bare chested pool boys in bandanas.

"Olivia – wait for me!"

Further on, the trees grew higher, trunks entangled with thick liana vines. When she pushed through a wall of draping green, Amber got the surprise of her life. Beyond lay another clearing, this one flooded with soft light. No sign of Olivia or anyone else. Instead, an enormous statue carved from gleaming obsidian. A goddess, her features regal and sublime; her face identical to Olivia's – no mistake about it whatsoever. *Identical.* The goddess stared at the encompassing jungle, peaceful and serene. Colourful fruit and flowers ringed her feet.

Amber tried to speak her daughter's name. Her lips parted but no sound came out. All around, the jungle burst alive with shrieking creatures: cockatoos, macaques and tarsiers, sloths and flying foxes, elephants and tigers crashing through the undergrowth. Chattering gibbons, cobras and crocodiles and other things she did not know the names of.

Amber swore obsidian Olivia's carved face cracked into a smile as she stared across the jungle, her domain.

Vaguely inspired by the half-remembered Fellini film from which I pinched the title, this story is about the futility of attempts to preserve a decaying, corrupt and necrotic society in the face of fresh new cultures pushing through.

JERICHO BLUSH

Jericho was burning – or at least that's what it looked like. A column of smoke rising thick and high, followed by a line of rumbling trucks. Sixteen in all, churning up great plumes of choking, red-raw dust. Each truck covered in taut green canvas the colour of eucalyptus leaves.

They scrambled. Neve picked Arji as the designated spotter. His sharp young eyes made out three drones, each keeping its distance, tracking the line of trucks the same as they were.

"All Scopes," Arji shouted at four companions, "no Sabers."

Neve nodded. Nothing unusual in that. Expensive luxuries like Sabers rarely got wasted out here in the middle of nowhere. Last time they'd clocked a Saber had been six whole months ago, so scuffed and dented it'd barely seemed worth netting. She'd talked the others out of it, how it wasn't worth drawing heat near Station-65 for anything with parts too busted up for trophies. But when the drone swooped, low and wobbly, she'd almost given in, almost thrown a net herself, in consideration of her own scrap metal requirements. Stopped herself at the very last minute with the thought of Viggo close by on patrol. Had he caught her, he would not have been impressed.

Red dust hung in the still hot air long after the trucks had gone. They waited – station kids were used to waiting, crouching in available shadows, faces wrapped against the dust and sun, kitted up in cammo designed to blend in with scattered rock formations, not making any sudden moves, presuming always that someone – or something – watched them.

"So GoldStar's finally pulled the plug on Jericho," she said eventually.

"Looks like."

They'd all been thinking it. Only when the smoke began to thin did they note the silvery relay tower was missing. Had definitely been standing tall at yesterday's sundown. Everybody used that thing for navigation – even birdlife – what remained of it.

Neve pulled away from the rock's scant shade.

"Hey, where are you going?"

"Old Jacko's," she shouted back at Embry over her shoulder. "GS might have booby trapped the place. Not going into that old town unprepared."

"What – we're *going in there?*"

161

She didn't bother answering. The others would follow her – they always did. The company abandoning a town like that was sus – completely sus – but there might have been a thousand reasons and they only needed an hour or two.

"That mad old bugger'll shoot you," shouted Crow.

"No he won't. Viggo says he hasn't fired a gun in decades. Old man's nothing but bullshit, piss and vinegar."

Embry abandoned the rock and ran out after her. "We don't need no shit from Jacko. Can just take packs and pick up what we find."

Easy for Embry – all she cared about was jewellery, ornaments and stupid curios. Small stuff – she did a brisk trade up and down the Station line, everything from plastic hairclips through ceramic dogs to genuine *bona fide* diamonds.

"Need bolt cutters," Neve replied, lengthening her strides so Embry had to jog to catch her up. "Spanners and wrenches. Viggo will notice if we nick stuff off the racks."

"Yeah, but –"

Neve stopped. "GoldStar might be tricking us. Might not have pulled out proper. Might've left guards stationed out of sight. Got a couple hours – if we're lucky. Jericho sheltered a bunch of families back before the company rolled in. Reckon some of 'em might have kept their cars."

Cars. The ears of Arji, Crow and Fenix pricked up, super keen.

Embry didn't look convinced. "But what if they come back sudden and catch us in –"

"They won't."

"You don't know that."

"Trust me." Neve knew she was right. That truck convoy had an *air* about it, a sense of finality, of abandonment. Jericho had been a GoldStar station back before Neve was born, holding out against the ghost town status infecting so many other towns and steads dotted like cockroach dirt across the big old maps spread out over Viggo's precious hardwood desk. She'd checked those maps out, crept as close to ghosts as anybody dared. Old folks reckoned those abandoned towns were mined. That they were haunted had never been in question.

Old Jacko's junkyard sat right out in the open. He made no effort to hide it from drones or intermittent GoldStar flyovers. "Like to see 'em fucken try," was his standard response when anyone from S-65 picked a fight, stating how he was *asking for it* by hoarding all that busted-up machinery. Rusted backhoes and cherry pickers, flat-tired utes and busted-up bulldozers. Trail bikes, all in tiptop working form – he reckoned – if only he could get hold of regular diesel. GoldStar, he also reckoned, would not be leasing Aussie land forever. Seasons would eventually flipflop back to how they were supposed to be. Then GoldStar and other foreign corps would pull up stumps; uproot, turn tails, head back to wherever they'd hauled their arses from.

Old Jacko did not approve of salt flat racing, of Neve and her surly trophy-hunting friends taking risks with speed and cars and, especially, each other. Nor of Station-65 itself, lying hidden in a warren of man-made caverns beneath the parched, sun-blasted dirt.

His teeth were black from betel nut. No one knew where he was getting it from – all kinds of contraband got shunted up and down from station to station.

Old Jacko was prone to vanishing for a couple of weeks on end, foraging the landscape for more junk. Old Jacko had scars from ancient traffic accidents: a big one curving down his thigh and an elbow that didn't bend in the right direction.

He refused to believe that Sydney still had cars aplenty – mostly of the small electric kind – or watched the Feeds, refused to trust data bounced back off a GoldStar satellite or jacked and bled from thick, bright fibre optic cables.

Bored Station kids used to tease him hardcore about his aliens and secret colonies on the moon, and how he believed GoldStar was up to more than garbage dumps. How they were doing experiments outback in the middle of nowhere, testing deadly toxic weaponry: *machines with human brain smarts reckoning. Fast-growing plants with acid sap and names like 'Bloodblight' and 'Lantana Raze'. The kinda shit could strip one of yer fancy hot rods down to its wheel lugs in less than half an hour…*

Not the first time foreigners had tested weaponry on Aussie soil. *Maralinga… Monte Bello… Emu Fields.*

Neve put a stop to it after Viggo pulled her up, told her they were shooting fish in a barrel – not that any of them had seen fish anywhere but tinned or freeze-dried. Viggo said picking on a mad old man was the half-arsed coward's way, how Jacko had been a great man once, a fighting man, a soldier, until GoldStar locked him up in that rehab camp. When he got out of there, Old Jacko was never the same.

So they quit making brute sport of him but helped themselves to his junk, Neve especially – for the sculptures she built out on the sand right under GoldStar noses. Art hidden beneath sand-coloured cammo until each piece was done and ready to show.

Somebody once told Neve she was building totem poles. She'd never heard of such a thing, had to look it up on Wiki, where she learned that different worldwide peoples made similar-looking things for different reasons. Her fierce, stacked angry faces were never manifestations of gods, just ordinary humans who'd been forced off their land. Forced to burrow, dodge and scuttle like bush rats.

Only not today. Today they would raid the town of Jericho and pick through GoldStar's leavings.

Old Jacko stood out in the open junkyard, brandishing the shotgun he had never been known to fire. He'd seen the smoke the same as they had, anticipated the fact that they'd come calling. He shouted "What the fuck d'yer think yer doing?"

"Shit!" Arji ducked down, grabbed the bolt cutters, picked up a tire iron with his free hand and made a break for the narrow gap between two rusted dozers.

Old Jacko stumbled after him but gave up the chase when a fit of coughing and wheezing overcame his scarecrow frame. He bent over, bony hands pressed into his calves, swearing and spraying red spittle into the dirt.

Arji emerged on the far side of the thatch of tangled chicken wire, bowed corrugated iron sheeting and unidentifiable machine parts. He held the pilfered cutters high and paused, waiting for Neve's trademark curt nod of approval.

She didn't say anything. Turned and walked in the direction of Head Track where Crow, Embry and Fenix waited clutching empty packs.

"Hey," called out Arji, "Old man didn't look so good. Reckon I oughta —"

"Forget it," she said, still walking. "He's okay."

Arji ran to catch her up. "But what if his heart packs in – we'll get the blame!"

She smirked. "Take more than a couple of us to kill that lunatic."

Jericho had never been a proper town, not even back in the days when it was home to folks like Embry's grandma, Sally. Both Sally and her sister Dee had been born in Jericho – only it wasn't called Jericho back then. The collection of close-huddled-for-protection homesteads never had official designation. Sally and Dee remembered flash floods and playing in the rain. Buying flour and tins of beans and soup from the little post office store. How their dad used to drive them all the way to Broken Hill for all the other kinds of stuff they needed.

Jericho: the most prominent word on the faded feedstock advert painted high on the double-storey lone-standing red brick wall. Another wall down the way a bit advertised Coca Cola, Borax and King Midas Flour, none of those likely names so Jericho stuck. Not a whole lot left of the place since GoldStar barged on in, but Neve's hunch about the convoy had been right.

They passed two yellow bulldozers and a seriously rusted Hummer-Humvee abandoned in a dried up, stony field. A waist-high, still-smouldering rubbish heap dominated the centre of town. Plenty of other scattered clues that soldiers had been and gone, taking all their equipment with them: deep dishes, antennae, relay towers, stuff the Station folk didn't have names for. Smashed crates and lopped off cables abandoned like dead snakes in the dust, crushed beer cans and shiny power bar wrappers. Vast patches of churned-up earth around the perimeter, evidence of wiring dug and yanked out fast.

"Gotta be something fucked up going down," said Fenix, stepping forward, sniffing the acrid, tainted air, pack hanging loosely off his shoulder after he'd shucked out a can of precious hoarded diesel. Small for his age but more clued up than most, with a head full of dreams about running away to Sydney. "Some kinda toxic spill, deadly as hell," he added.

He glanced at his wrist. Away from Station, all wore radstraps as a matter of course. Checked them obsessively every couple of minutes, but nothing was lighting up.

"We going in?"

Neve paused, considering. The skies were empty, aside from the column of smoke, much thinner now. No drones. No moving vehicles. Things would not remain this way for long.

"Twenty minutes tops," she said. "Don't touch anything if you don't know what it is or what it does."

All four grunted in acknowledgement, then fanned out, Arji swinging the bolt cutters in a wide arc.

Vehicles parked out in the open had degraded to useless piles of rust, but Neve's hunch turned out spot on when Arji emerged from a tin shed, all excited. "Found a Toyota Landcruiser 70. Tires are gone but I reckon it's good to go. We could –"

"No way." Neve's face was grim, her thin lips pressed together. "Not *driving* anything outta here." She pointed upwards. Nothing there, but they all knew what she meant. That drones would clock a moving car in seconds-to-nothing flat. Racing out across the salt was one thing – stealing cars from Jericho something else. Goldstar knew all about their salt flat antics. They had to know – drag racers had been getting away with it for forty years. *Why* the company let them do it was anybody's guess. The events drew locals out into the open to race and drink and throw down money, voices carrying for miles through shimmering heat haze. A couple of Saber missiles could put a stop to it anytime. GoldStar's ranks were trigger-happy. Everyone knew someone who'd been caught out and targeted; poked their nose where they weren't supposed to, crawling under a fence or a boundary wire. Come home sick from a contaminated zone. Or not – everyone knew somebody who"d gone out and never come home at all.

Arji stood still and waiting on the road, staring at her with those big bright quizzical eyes.

"Just find the parts you need and bag 'em."

He nodded and tramped back through the yard with shoulders slumped.

Neve picked one of the houses further out. To get to it, she had to pass a row of suspicious-looking sheds with corrugated iron sides, small square windows and slanting roofs. She hurried, stepping lightly, half expecting ambush from within. Beyond, another, knocked up of solid-looking russet bricks, the remains of a warped and blistered trellis curling.

Surrounding paddocks lay bare as bones aside from a cylindrical water tank. Beyond it, another tank of crumbling concrete. Beside it, yet another structure, a shed sporting a wall of green and grey patched metalwork and chicken wire.

Sturdy beams held up the roof. Inside, a piled-high assortment of rusted, unidentifiable tools, illuminated via a scratched corrugated plastic skylight. A lone propeller blade leant against the far wall, above it, a dusty bridle. Parked in the narrow space, a badly corroded vehicle. A sticker on the back advised *off road use only*.

Off road. Their whole existence was off road, off the map, off the radar, off the charts, underneath the noses of a corporation with the license to kill at random. Living on land that had been stolen out from under them, just as it had been stolen in earlier times, from the Ngiyampaa, the Mutthi Mutthi and Paakantji people – some of whom still roamed the desert if you believed what the rangers said, scratching out survival the old, hard ways. Ghosts haunting the carcass of a continent bled dry. Old Jacko wasn't the only one talking up things too difficult to explain.

The house's front door was unlocked, but she made her way around the back, entering through double doors, fly screen first.

Inside was dark. When she yanked the curtain open it fell away in her hands, dust being all that was holding the fabric together. The light revealed beige panelled walls hung with photographs tinted ghostly sepia. Faded prints of pale blue birds and a painting of a rustic cottage surrounded by emerald lawns studded with flowers.

Flowers. Neve stared. None of them had ever seen a lawn at all, let alone a lawn so lush. She considered taking the painting down and hauling it back to Station, but thought the better of it. Nobody had lived here for a very long time, but this was still *somebody's* place, *somebody's* stuff. So what the hell had GoldStar wanted with it?

She checked her radstrap obsessively, but both the lights stayed green. If contamination spilled, it was undetectable. They might be marked for death already, walking around with lungs choked up with spores. Miniature toxins, unperceivable, unavoidable until well past too late. The kind of shit Old Jacko was always on about.

Floorboards creaked beneath her boots as she walked down the hall and back again. She spotted Arji and Fenix in the distance through the window, lifting something between them, something heavy she couldn't identify. Part of an engine, most likely. Scrounging car parts – that was all those boys gave a shit about – that's all half the kids she'd ever known gave a shit about. And that had been her whole world too – until the day she finally comprehended how GoldStar was *permitting* them to race. Watching but never interfering. Able to shut them down at any minute – but they didn't.

Very suspicious behaviour, 'cos they sure as hell shut down Yanni and Rach when they attempted to drag stuff out of that old gold mine. GoldStar drones didn't even fly over the salt. Why the hell was that, you had to wonder.

The fly-screen door banged loudly as she left the wood-panelled house behind, walked across the dried-up yard to the next home further along. Like the first, the front door was unlocked.

Beyond a rattling fly screen door lay a poky kitchen wallpapered all in brown, stained and peeling, hanging in great curls.

Her gaze flicked to the kitchen cupboard stacked up high with china. Smashed plate shards would make perfect ceramic teeth for her installations, metal knives and forks might make good fingers. She shook out the contents of a partitioned drawer, grabbed an odd assortment of shelf items, as much as she could carry, which wasn't enough – perhaps she could sneak back later? Bring a few of the younger kids, make them carry stuff, no questions asked.

A few years back and she'd have risked a quad bike pulling a small trailer, but not today, not since Jon-Jacob and his beat-up Yamaha got blasted three metres skyward, one side of his face seared off with burning petrol. Viggo reckoned they never even saw a drone; that the precision beam had been delivered via satellite from low Earth orbit. Bullshit, so she hoped – but all the same...

Her pack was full, almost too heavy. She left it resting by the fly-screen door, curious to check out other rooms. Outside, boys' bickering carried on lacklustre breeze, mixed in with hammer blows, metal on metal, telling each other to fuck off and be careful, *watch what yer doing bro – that shit's real precious.*

In one of the rooms she found an enormous bed and a dresser, top drawer filled with plastic jewellery. She stuffed a handful into her pocket, swag she could trade with Embry later on. Beside the dresser, paint-peeled cupboards filled with the reek of mothballs – and ancient clothing. Flimsy lace with no pretence of blocking the sun's harsh rays. Fabrics lurid with candy-coloured dyes, marking the wearer as an easy target the minute they stepped outside. People still wore clothes like these in big cities like Sydney and Melbourne. Places where people were *supposed* to live, where they didn't have to stay out of sight of drones.

Pretty colours.

She shook a shirt free of its hanger. Was about to strip and try it on when a commotion from the street made her race for the exit, heft her pack and hurry back outside. She ran across dry ground to join the others.

Fenix stood in the middle of the road, his pack nowhere in sight. He stabbed his arm at one of the houses. Shouted, "There's cameras inside, a whole bunch of 'em, all rolling."

Coloured wires dangled from his other hand. He held them high for her to see the metallic cube as big as a baby's fist.

"Neve... there's no dogs here, not dead or alive," called out Embry, red-faced, voice quivering as her words spilled out in a jumble. "One Tree, Maude and Oxley's all got dogs, all fucked up, feral and three-quarter-starved, but there's *nothing* here. Not even bones and teeth."

No dogs. Neve should have noticed that first off. They all should have – wild dogs were the primary reason they carried knives. Jericho was too good to be true – too neat, too clean. Too easy. They should have been smarter, they should have read the signs but they were all too damned desperate to score a few antiques and souvenirs. Nothing much happened out here in the middle of nowhere, but when it did, it was rarely something good.

Nobody moved. What happened next would be up to Neve, as always, only this time around she wasn't sure. Everything sat so still and quiet, like the buildings were waiting for something too. Internal cameras might not mean anything other than GoldStar forgot to pull them out. *Viggo would know how to handle this situation: right words, right actions, things that had to be done to keep them safe.*

"Time to split," said Neve, eyeing the sky. "Everybody grab your swag, head on back by the dodge routes we agreed."

Fenix appeared to be frozen. With a rough jerk he threw the cube and its trailing wires down into the dirt and backed away.

"Come on – move it," shouted Neve.

They moved.

No one made it far before a high-pitched whine cut through the air, too high to properly hear but not to feel. The cruel sound sent vibrations through their bones. They clamped their hands over their ears but it made no difference – the whine bored deep inside their skulls. Nausea welled as the sound continued, and then, in a blinding instant it was gone, both the sound and the extreme discomfort caused.

The ground rumbled.

Neve wiped tears with the back of her fist. "Forget the swag, we gotta get out of here *now*."

Only then did she notice the white ute on the road, its tray piled high with dismembered parts of cars.

"What the fuck is that doing here? I told you –"

"Yeah, I know, but this is good stuff, Neve, stuff we can't get anywhere," hollered Crow. "We can't just leave it. Not gonna drive the ute to Station, natch, gonna take the long way round. If anything scopes me –"

"No. I told you no for a damn good reason. There's something going on here. Something deadly."

Crow wasn't listening. Neither was Fenix. He ran to the ute and tried to get it started. The engine coughed and spluttered before turning over. Gouts of black smoke choked from under the hood.

"Leave it!"

"Na, s'okay, I can get it moving. Gimme five."

"We don't have five." She called out to Arji who had clambered atop a corrugated iron roof. "Anything?"

Arji's field glasses made a wide sweep of the sky. "No drones. Nothing."

"You sure?"

"Yep."

Fenix climbed out of the driver's seat, ran around the front and popped the hood. Backed off to avoid thick, choking smoke. Waved his hand in an effort to make it dissipate. He and Crow shouted instructions back and forth, cut short when Fenix let out a yelp.

"Crikey – what's that thing?"

Something unseen lashed out, slashing Fenix on the hand. He screamed, jumped wide and stumbled. Fell backwards, landed hard on his arse.

Embry yelled out "snake!"

All but Arji crowded around the still growling, still smoking engine, trying to see without getting too close.

"There. Look!"

Something caused the vehicle to lift, slam down and shudder.

Something.

Embry called out "There's something wrong with Fenix."

The kid's skin was pale and clammy, his eyes glazed and unfocused. He shivered uncontrollably, despite the ever-present heat. Neve moved closer, pulled a blade from her belt, cut away the filthy sleeve of his shirt. A deep slash on his hand bloomed and blistered with infection already spreading thick along his arm. She'd never seen anything like it. No one had.

"Watch out," screamed Embry, "It's under the ute!"

The vehicle heaved and juddered like a living creature. Something thick and pink and fleshy coiled out from the Toyota's underbelly, lifting the chassis completely off the ground.

Neve and Embry dragged Fenix clear between them. Arji pulled out field glasses, trained them on the far end of the street, the exact point they had entered Jericho. Something was happening to the churned-up soil, the wide furrows where underground cables had been pulled – or so it had looked like.

A wall of fleshy whatever-it-was erupted from below, moved quickly to block the road and spread on out. Thick and pushing, it cracked the brittle earth as it spewed forth. An impenetrable barrier growing before their eyes.

"How can that be…?" Embry's voice trailed off.

Fenix moaned. Crow hurried to join the others.

"His breathing's ragged. He's not gonna make it," Embry wailed.

"Don't say that. Plenty of other ways out of here," said Neve, looking frantically all around them for options, managing to hold her voice true and steady because she had to be the one. It was always her.

"Arj, tell us what's happening."

Arji looked small standing on the roof, field glass trained down and along instead of skyward. "It's everywhere," he shouted back at them. "Pushing up from underground. There and there... and there..." he pointed.

All exit routes were blocked. The sickening flesh-pink *thing* was all around them, trailing out of windows, bursting through brick walls. It smelled like something rotten and disgusting, a scent half chemical, half animal.

They wrapped their khafiyas tight around their faces. Too late. The stink was already in their throats, stomachs souring with the taint of rancid meat. They watched the Toyota get flensed before their eyes, its metal puckered, weeping and corroding.

"Drone," cried out Arji, "Scope at ten o'clock!"

A glint of metal hanging in the air, then the whir of rotors, a high-pitched whine. One drone quickly accompanied by another and then a third. Not armed. Recording everything.

"They knew we were coming," said Neve, only speaking because somebody had to say something, even if just to distract from the screech and grate of metal being carved and pushed aside.

Arji clambered down to join the others, red dirt streaking his sweaty skin. "It's everywhere," he managed to say between deep gasps for oxygen. "In a ring all the way around the outside of those sheds, busting up through the ground like a..." His voice trailed off as he doubled over, pressing his hands into his side, fighting the stitch that was cramping up his guts.

It wasn't like anything anyone had ever seen before. Not on the Feeds or in the data siphoned illegally off the various Darkwebs. If Station-65 knew of such a terror, they'd have all been warned, no question. Viggo knew all about their car part foraging expeditions, the salt flat racing, even Neve's beloved totem poles. This thing was new, some kind of weapon – an improved type of Lantana Raze, perhaps. The kind of shit Old Jacko was always banging on about. The fact of it made Neve feel weak – if he was right about this then what else was he right about?

"There's gotta be a break in the perimeter."

"There isn't. I checked the whole way round," said Arji, his breath slowing to normal. "That whining sound must have triggered whatever *that* is."

Neve checked her radstrap. Two black dots, no life left in its battery. When she tripped her emergency beacon, nothing happened. Setting off the beacon would put all their lives in danger, because if S-65 could receive then so could anyone – Sabers and anything else within a radius of twenty ks. A desperate, last resort was what it was, but she needn't have fretted. All their beacons were dead. Something had fried and neutralised all circuits. That high-pitch whine, like Arji said. Had to be – what else? The same sound had kicked the hideous fleshy plant-thing into growth. A deliberate signal, a calculated experiment.

"Fenix is dead!"

The boy never regained consciousness. Fifteen years old and already decomposing, festering before their eyes. A few more minutes and he would no longer be recognisably human.

"Leave him," snapped Neve. Harsh, but they all knew she was right. No time for whispered words of comfort, nor argument of what to tell the Station folks – if they made it home, the odds of which were becoming less and less.

Crow crouched low beside a tendril coiling from the Toyota's remains. "It's eating the metal," he explained, although no one had asked. "Must be using it for fuel, like food."

Neve grabbed his arm and yanked him clear of it. Nothing natural could possibly grow so fast. Even Lantana Raze took hours to bloom and spread its impenetrable barrier of thorns and misery. Soon nothing would remain of Jericho, just an amorphous blob of quivering blubber with random spikes of apparently indigestible metal poking out like spines or ribs. *And them inside it.*

They huddled together, watching the surrounding, seething mass expanding and edging closer. The drones hovered, tinted lenses recording their fear and anguish, potential escape routes cut off, one by one as the wall of weaponised blubber pressed on in.

The fleshy pink consumed Fenix whole. Neve was the only one to see his corpse go under. She turned her back when it reached his face. Little Fenix, so much older than he'd ever looked, quick as a rabbit, cunning as a mongrel. He'd had plans to go to Sydney, trick his way through Border Patrol, find his people – he'd been so sure of family living pretty in the inner 'burbs. Not to be, not one single line of Fenix's pathetic fantasy.

The end, when it came, would not be quick. Neve knew she couldn't let the others suffer. She touched the blade shoved back in her belt. She was the eldest. The job, when it came time, would fall to her.

The acrid stink was becoming overpowering. Her eyes watered continuously – breathing was getting harder and harder through the smothering fug.

Behind her, Crow and Embry hugged each other. Arji clung on to both of them, skinny arms spread as wide as they could go.

A drone dropped down, almost close enough to touch.

"What the fuck is wrong with you," she screamed into its lens. She bent to the ground, picked up a stone and threw it. The missile bounced ineffectually off the mechanism's silver-grey casing, but it made her feel just a little better. They all searched for rocks within the ever-closing circle, scrabbling with bare hands in the moistureless dust, flinging stone after stone, shrieking and cheering whenever one hit home.

The drone edged back a little further out of range. A kind of victory, small but better than nothing. Any form of hope was better than nothing.

Dusk began to settle over what little remained of Jericho, pale fingers of cloud grasping high above their heads. Neve wrapped her hand around the hilt of her small knife. It would all be over soon. She willed her hands to stop shaking but they wouldn't. Viggo would be furious when he learnt the truth. Warnings against approaching ghost towns, former mines and abandoned checkpoints were offered up relentlessly by the ones who'd made the Stations what they were. Safe underground and out of sight in a world where safety had become an afterthought due to rising seas and temperatures and conflicts. She should have known better – they should all have known better, but her most of all – *she was the eldest*. Was that the way she would be remembered? As the one who got the whole lot of them killed?

"Shhh... listen. What's that sound?"

Embry's voice had a touch of hope in it, despite the forest of oppressive, heaving pink, surrounding them, blocking out the dregs of sunset breeze.

But there *was* a sound – they were not imagining it. Not drones – all three had backed right off amidst the stone barrage. The welcome, throaty growl of a diesel engine announced its presence just as the surge of moving pink and dust and dirt rose high above them like a tidal wave. Rose and crashed as they leapt out of its way, kicking up more dust than Neve could ever have imagined, enough to make them cough and choke, blocking out what little remained of the light.

"Gerrout of the way – move yer arses!"

A voice familiar to one and all. Neve blinked grit and tears away to see something she could not be sure was real. An exit route, a narrow passage of churned-up dirt and towering pink, punched through by a bulldozer that had rammed right through the barricade, Old Jacko waving wildly from the cabin.

"Get a fucken move on!"

No time to marvel at the wonder of it. Neve grabbed the younger kids in turn, shoving them forward and roughly through the gap, which was already beginning to quiver, narrow and close.

Stunned at first, their brains kicked in and each kid made a run for it, tearing through like startled rabbits, ducking and dodging, screaming as plump, tentacles disengaged from the mass to flop and grope blindly in the dirt.

Old Jacko swore as the dozer emitted a wrong-sounding series of clunks and wheezes. Neve stopped and turned, the last one through. The dozer had stalled, in trouble and Jacko with it, stuck fast, metal corroding in waves of acrid stink. He'd managed to wriggle out of the cabin, but a tentacle gripped him fast around the thigh. He screamed from the searing pain of it, slashing at the writhing monstrosity wildly with a machete. The blade hit home but it was no use. The fleshy pink gave way but it did not bleed.

"Gerroff with ya," he shouted.

Neve hesitated. The gap was closing fast. There was no time, but she couldn't leave the old man there to die. Not like this. Not after what had happened to poor Fenix.

Jacko continued to scream and curse, unintelligible words drowned out by hissing, slashing and sucking. Neve shot through the narrowing gap, shimmied up the back of the vehicle, ducking and weaving, maintaining her balance because if she fell, then that would be the end of it.

Old Jacko was done for. She could not save his life, but there was one thing she could do for him.

He could read her mind – he could see it on her face. He held himself completely still hanging on to the dozer's frame, smiled at her and closed both of his eyes.

She lunged, slashed him quick and clean across the throat. Deeper than she needed to – better to be sure than to get it wrong.

As he let go and crumpled backwards, she jumped and made a run for it, shooting through the slim passageway, belly diving as a tentacle lunged for her chest.

Crow was waiting. He grabbed her arms and dragged her out of there. Away from immediate danger. But they weren't safe. The drones had recorded everything. Anything could happen now, Sabers swooping down from darkening skies, heavy with heat-seeking missiles. The kind that never missed their human targets.

"Where's Old Jacko?" said Embry, wide eyed.

Neve wiped her small blade on the hem of her trousers. "Jacko didn't make it."

Embry's face curdled with betrayal. "You left him there, you bitch – you left him!" She began to scream and cry, ran up to Neve and pummelled her with balled fists. Neve made no move to protect herself. Embry was right, she should not have done it, but she couldn't help it, there had not been any other way.

Under cover of darkness they exited the dregs of Jericho, fanning out in three directions as they had been trained to do to thwart pursuit. The drones melted into the dead of night. Reinforcements did not arrive. Five kids from Station-65 had played their part and whatever happened next would happen, no matter what they did or did not do.

Neve did not regroup with the others. She walked for hours not caring where she was going. Eventually she made her way to Bazza's Cranny, travelling around the longest route, a cave containing survival stash: protein bars and a five-litre jerry can of water. Bedding, matches and a small transmitter only to be used in dire emergency. She wasn't going to flip the switch. Viggo would be shitting himself, but she needed time to think and be alone. Viggo didn't care about her. He'd never given Neve a second glance. He had his pick of the Station women up and down the line. The pretty ones who kept their soft skin out of the burning sun. The ones who *oohed* and *ahhed* the loudest at his heroic, bullshit ranger stories.

As things panned out, she was not alone for long. Viggo himself came out to find her. Being that he was Arji's cousin, she should have expected nothing less.

She looked up when his silhouette blocked the entrance. "What do you want?" she said dryly.

He let her know that the others had made it safely home. That they'd told him everything. How she'd done exactly what she had to do – nothing more and nothing less. How nobody blamed her for anything that happened.

"Embry blames me."

"No she doesn't. Whatever she said, she didn't mean it. We all say stupid things when times get tough."

"Jacko should've stayed at home with his booze and betel stash. We should've been more careful. Should've seen it coming. Trucks pulling out one day like that. Far too easy. Like fish in a barrel," she added.

He didn't say anything for a while, just sat in silence staring into the embers of the small fire Neve had permitted herself for comfort.

"Jericho Blush is what they're calling it," he offered up eventually.

"Calling what?"

"That flesh-pink abomination of a plant. 'Cept it isn't any kind of plant, says Reiko. She's been on the Feeds non-stop. Del Meyer up at 44 reckons it's something called a *nano-particulant weapon*. Like nothing none of 'em have seen before."

"I never want to see anything like it again."

The silence returned. Viggo pulled a handful of twigs from his pocket and fed them into the fire, one by one.

"We can't stay here," said Neve. "At Station, I mean."

He shrugged. "But this is our home, our place."

"Not any more." She hugged her arms, looked around the cave, at long shadows dancing on rough walls. "Reckon GoldStar knows everything about Station-65. What goes down, how much food we scrounge, how much power we bleed off. Where we steal bore water. Reckon they've got spies amongst us, folks we've known and trusted our whole lives."

He shook his head. Thick curls flopped into his eyes. "You can't start thinking like that – it'll drive you crazy."

"We're just rats and the desert is their lab."

"So what you gonna do?" He raked his hair back with splayed fingers. "Start thinking like that poor kid Fenix? Go chasing after mythical jobs and relatives in Sydney – providing you can sneak past Border Force…"

She shook her head, scratched at her itchy, greasy scalp. "There's no jobs. Sydney's choked with half-drowned skeletons washed in off the boats. They sleep in sewers and derelict parking lots. Eat rats and cats and garbage scraps – and each other, if you can believe –"

She cut herself off when he placed his hand on her shoulder. She hesitated, then put her own smaller hand on his. "Thanks for coming out for me. Not sure I would have gone back otherwise."

"I know. That's why I'm here. And to show you something."

With his free hand, he reached inside his shirt. "Old Jacko knew what he was doing. Knew it when he went after you, for certain that he wasn't coming back."

Neve didn't look up. She didn't say anything.

"He left a note."

She swallowed. "What did it say?"

He smiled. "Something about you. Do you want to –?"

"No. Just tell me."

Viggo nodded. "He wrote a bunch of crazy stuff across pages of torn-out Bible – real crazy, just like you'd expect. Hard to read, his hand is pretty rough. Last part's where he says it's all yours now. All that junk he'd been collecting half his life. All yours."

This time she looked up at him. "What? Why?"

He smiled again, sun wrinkles creasing the skin around his eyes. "Those bloody totem poles of yours. Apparently he thought they were pretty good. Pretty worthy."

She wanted to smile, to honour the memory of a brave old man they'd all dismissed as mad, but she was still too close to it, the image of his slashed throat fresh in her head.

"Crazy old bastard."

"Yeah."

They put out the fire, cleaned up after themselves, walked back to Station-65 by the light of the Milky Way, spreading wide above the land just like it had for millions of years and would for all the millions yet to come.

Set in the same near future landscape as 'Hot Rods', a precursor to my far future novel *Lotus Blue*, 'Jericho Blush' takes a look at an off-grid settlement surviving on land designated for dangerous and unregulated weapons testing.

NO FAT CHICKS

The can slammed hard against the balcony's sliding door. Frothy liquid dribbled down the glass. Brandon almost cheered but he held his breath, waiting to see if the girls would come outside. Muffled music bled from within. Loud, but not loud enough to drown out the cans the guys had been lobbing for half an hour.

"Get yer pig snouts out of the fridge!"

"Stop cracking mirrors with the sight of your own fat arse cracks."

"How'dya find a fat chick's pussy? Roll her around in flour and check for the wet spot!"

Dave and Sam took turns shouting insults. Brandon didn't shout. Throwing empty cans at walls was as far as he was prepared to go. Unlike Sam. Sam would do anything if Dave did it first. A natural-born follower, was Sam. He went where other people went, did what other people did.

The night had started well enough until Dave had spotted the new sign tacked up over the bar. 'Anti-harassment policies will be enforced'. "Fer fuck's sake," he groaned, then louder a few more times when he realised nobody was listening. Brandon knew right then and there that the guys would have to leave. That social justice warriors had infiltrated, ruining everybody else's fun.

Last time they'd hit this apartment block there'd been three full balcony loads of heifers, all frothing and spouting with their whiny fat excuses. Tonight was different. Just empty cans stinging cold cement, the muted hum of traffic in the distance.

"Heard that ex of yours is getting hitched," said Sam in an effort to break the disappointment and the silence.

"Natasha? Really?" Brandon experienced a small twinge of concern.

Sam nodded. "Jules knows some of the chicks she works with."

Brandon nodded back, surprised, kind of. Sam read his face. "Guess it happens, eh? Been a couple of years."

Brandon kept on nodding. More than a couple, now he came to think about it. He thought about Natasha often. Not something he would ever admit to the other guys.

Someone was in the third floor kitchen, a dark shape ascertainable through the thin lemon-tinted curtain.

"At the fucking fridge again," shouted Dave through cupped hands. Sam laughed.

"Cold sausage down yer throat is all you're ever gonna get."

Sam and Dave laughed some more. Brandon dragged a stubby from the cooler. Water dripped down his arm. The ice had melted.

Dave swivelled. "Herd of elephants, three o'clock!"

The pack of obese female joggers moved down the street taking up most of the footpath and the road. The trainer, a trim balding Hispanic type, clenched a whistle between his teeth. He blew it at regular intervals.

"Earthquake!" shouted Dave.

"Watch out – herd of buffalo coming through."

One of the joggers glanced sideways at the three men, her face red and sweaty from exertion.

Sam yelled, "Elephant!"

The jogger looked away, eyes front, concentration on the trainer, keeping up. Keeping pace with the others.

Dave picked the last can out of the cooler. Weighed it in his hand, then stepped back to give himself momentum. Was readying for a throw when Brandon's hand closed around his wrist.

"Nah mate. Better not. Remember?"

Dave well remembered, but he didn't put the can down. Not immediately. He stood there flexing his arm muscles as if he was going to throw it after all. Hang that thing that happened, hang the world, hang the whole blubber-laden lot of them.

"Leave it out, Dave," said Sam. "They're not worth it. None of 'em are worth it any more."

"Amen bro," said Brandon, sipping his beer, warm and flat, which pretty much summed it all up.

Brandon hated the Season Street Brasserie. The drinks were expensive and the waiters were all gay. All male, for obvious reasons – there wasn't much room between the tables. So many men were turning gay these days – and who could blame them? Not Brandon, that's for sure. What he couldn't wrap his mind around were the men who carried on like nothing had happened.

This building had once housed his favourite restaurant; homestyle Italian before it changed hands, morphing into an overpriced noise pit, ninety decibels at least, all exposed-wood tables, brittle floors and cement walls, pots and pans bashing away in the open kitchen. The hiss of steam, all cloyed and blaring indie rock, hip hop, trip chill, whatever the fuck they called that shite, the music ragging badly on his nerves.

He used to come here with Natasha and perhaps that's why he was walking past it now, glancing in through the big glass windows. Looking without looking.

He stopped. There she was, Natasha, sitting near their old favourite spot. Alone and reading something off a screen. Not the first time he'd seen her sitting there.

Should he?

So easy to spot with that luscious hair; *natural burgundy*, she used to call it. Before he knew it, he'd gone inside, manoeuvring around the tables and chairs. When he squeezed past a blimp, she didn't stop eating. Didn't even look up from her plate.

Natasha didn't look up either. She was swiping pages on her tablet, absorbed by blocks of imageless text. Fatter than when he'd seen her last, which must have been at least four years ago.

A diamond sparkled on her finger. He thought about leaving before she noticed him. Backing out slowly, like he was never there. She was so engrossed in scrolling text. Brandon still had time.

But then she looked up, did a double take, threw him a wide-eyed smirk like some kind of bone. "Brandon! What the hell are you doing here?"

As he mumbled something about a meeting in the city, she gestured to the chair directly opposite.

"Sit down. I'm meeting someone but he's running late."

Brandon hesitated, then tugged at the heavy chair. Lots of the newer places had big seating now.

She scanned to the end of the paragraph as he settled himself down. A waiter swooped in immediately with a menu and a jug of water. As he poured, she let him know she'd ordered already.

Brandon paused. He picked up a menu and rubbed his thumb absent-mindedly across its laminated surface. "You're looking all right," he said.

Natasha laughed. She raised her water glass at him. He put down the menu and picked his up. They clinked.

She drank hers down in a single gulp. "So, I guess it must be at least three years since –"

"Four." He placed his glass on the grainy tabletop and picked up the menu up again, flicking it between his thumb and fingertips.

Natasha stuffed her tablet into the handbag hanging off her chair. "Four? Has it really been four years?"

He inched the chair up closer to the table. Her hair still looked amazing. Thick and lush, down past her shoulders like she always wore it. Occasionally pulled back in a ponytail.

"You still working at Havelock?" she continued. "Still playing lunchtime football? Still hanging with those guys? Dave and what was the other one's name?"

She poured herself another splash of water as Brandon glanced down at the menu.

"Go on, order. Blake won't mind – he texted to say he's running late."

He didn't ask who Blake was. Brandon selected a schnitzel from the menu. The waiter scurried up and pounced, removing all unnecessary items.

"Havelock? Yeah. Football no. Tore a ligament." He was about to elaborate on all the gory details but headed himself off at the pass.

"That guy Dave, I think about him now and then," Natasha said, "What with all the changes. That time he –"

"Dave's all right," said Brandon.

She gave him an incredulous look.

Silence fell uncomfortably between them, a pause that served to accentuate the background noise, the clatter of cutlery, plink of glasses, sashay of swinging kitchen doors. People shouting to make themselves heard above the music. Brandon glanced around the vast, high-ceilinged dining area, already regretting his decision to order a meal. It could have been a normal lunch scene, a normal day in a normal city, only nothing was normal any more. Impossible to believe how some folks carried on regardless. As if everything hadn't gone to hell, been totally and utterly ruined. He'd had a gutful of pussy-whipped losers on chat shows carping on about how *attraction was subjective*. How *love was love* and some men – many men – actually *preferred* their women big and curvy. Bullshit forcing good men into corners. Forced to adjust, adapt and persevere. But that didn't mean they had to like it. Things were tougher than they'd ever been.

"Dave's still your mate though – right?" said Natasha. "You didn't let that little *incident* come between you?"

Brandon missed the question and its challenge. He'd glimpsed a gazelle amongst the wildebeest. A young woman with slender, willowy arms and legs. Long blonde hair falling in a sheer sheet down her back. His attention shifted to the lucky bastard sitting across her table. Rich, of course. He'd have to be to afford someone like…

"Yoo hoo – Earth to Brandon…" Natasha waved a napkin in his face. White linen like a flag.

Brandon was not the only man staring as the gazelle forked a delicate morsel from her plate, placed it geometrically in the centre of her tongue. The food seemed to melt as she closed her mouth and smiled.

Brandon's erection pressed painfully against his leg. Lucky he was sitting down. Lucky...

"You do know that's not real food she's eating," said Natasha, napkin back in place across her lap.

Brandon's concentration broke as the waiter placed a magnificent slice of layered torte in front of Natasha. He stared at it, then her, then back at the cake.

"They make that crap out of foam," Natasha said, raising her fork, then waving it in the direction of the delicate blonde. "Edible foam shaped to look like cuisine. Not like this. There's still real food for the rest of us, thank god."

She stabbed the fork into the cake, carved off a generous mouthful, raised her eyebrow. "Go on, say it, Brandon," she said smiling. "Why don't you say that thing that's on your mind."

He swallowed drily as she chewed, clouding over with sudden anger. "Why are you still eating that shit? Making things worse, like they're not already totally out of control."

Natasha plunged the fork into the cake, extracted another segment, placed it delicately in her mouth. Started chewing, then spoke with her mouth full. "You really think my eating *foam* is going to make the world a better place? Look around you, Brandon. Look at what's going on. Widespread mutations of chromosome 15q11-q13; ramped up and mangled Ad-36 and its associated strains are blooming in full swing – and they're here to stay. Foam girl over there you're ogling – know what she has to do to look like that? There's an article right here..." Still chewing, Natasha put the fork down and reached around for her tablet.

I'm sorry, he said. "I didn't mean..."

"Yes you did, Brandon. You always meant it. Every word. You dumped me and ran screaming in the earliest days of the epidemic. Way before it was certain that infectobesity and double-X had paired up for the double whammy." She nodded in the direction of the delicate blonde and her fork. "Girls like her subsist on tubes of supplement paste. They're starving; peg fed, stomachs stapled down to matchbox size, pilled up to the gills. Kidneys and the liver take a pounding. Life expectancy not much past forty-five, so the experts reckon, but it's worth it, right? Worth it to keep their men from disappointment."

She held the device so he could glance at the bookmarked article. He didn't need to read it. Magazines and the internet were choked up with that shit.

"Look, I just wanted to say hello."

She closed the cover and stuffed the tablet back in her handbag. "What for? Four years back, you couldn't get out the door fast enough." She stared into his eyes waiting for an answer.

Brandon didn't have any answers.

The waiter made a timely intrusion, replacing the napkin on Brandon's lap – he'd been twisting it between his hands. Plonked the schnitzel down before him, waved the grinder in front his eyes. "Pepper?"

Brandon shook his head until the annoying man departed. "I've got a girlfriend," he said after a lengthy pause.

Natasha nodded. "Good for you. I hope you're very happy."

Aroma wafted from the schnitzel, which hung over the rim of his plate. Just the way he liked it, lightly cooked and hammered thin. He picked at its edges with his fork.

"She's fit. Not that I'm… But yeah, she's pretty hot."

"Fit and hot? Really?" Natasha tucked a long, loose strand of hair behind her ear. "Let me guess – she's from Thailand. Or Laos, perhaps? Myanmar? Somewhere in the Asia-Pacific basin."

His face reddened. "What's that got to do with anything?"

She laughed out loud. "Come on, Brandon, don't you follow the news? Ladyboys are nothing new – half the restaurants on Lygon Street employ them."

"She's not a ladyboy! Or a…"

"See – you can't even say *transgender*, let alone admit to the fact that you're shagging one. AD-36 *discriminates*. It latches on to the double-X. If she's not fat and she's not enduring frequent bouts of surgery or other harsh medical interventions, *she* was likely born a *he*. Not that there's anything wrong with that."

Natasha forked down another mouthful of lavish torte. Brandon cut his schnitzel down the middle.

"I'm engaged," she said, her mouth full again, wriggling her fingers until light glinted off the diamond. "Stick around a bit longer and you'll meet him." She nodded to the big glass windows fronting onto the street. "You know that weird black building three streets down? Perched up high like a Bang and Olufsen reject – there's some big secret product development underway inside. Blake's a biotech journo and he got a tip off. Says he's gonna try and get in there." She checked her phone, then stabbed the fork back in the cake.

Brandon cut and devoured his crumbed and hammered veal mechanically, mouthful after mouthful. He finished before she did. Lifted his buttock, pulled a fifty from the wallet in his back pocket, dropped it on the table.

"No time for coffee?" she said innocently.

"Got some stuff I gotta do," he mumbled, the chair making a hideous scraping sound as he pushed it out with his legs.

She placed the fork down on the table. "Brandon, why can't you just learn to live with it? All these other men have –"

"No they haven't," he said sullenly. He looked her in the eyes. "I gotta go."

"Got to go where, Brandon?"

He was saved from having to answer by a multiple screeching of brakes and tyres on the street outside.

Beyond the glass, foot traffic had stalled completely. Walkers stopped still and gawked. Men yelled and whistled out the windows of their cars, honking their horns in appreciation.

When Brandon turned, he was rewarded with the sight of the most beautiful woman he had ever seen in his life. He headed straight for the big glass windows, not the narrow, overcrowded doorway, napkin trailing along the floor behind. He wasn't the only up and out of his seat. The window space was soon completely crammed.

"Fuck me," he said to no one in particular, whoever was pressing up against him. Possibly Natasha, but he didn't look to check. Didn't want to take his eyes off the supermodel, movie star, angel come to Earth... All those things rolled into one – and more.

"Wow," said somebody behind him. Someone else added, "She looks like that old movie star. The one with all the kids."

The astonishing apparition had walked straight out into the traffic. She swerved to sashay along the pavement, apparently enjoying the attention but unsteady in towering heels and a skimpy sequined dress. Brandon pressed his nose against the glass until a black sedan with tinted windows pulled up and opened a door. The woman got in and the crowd, both inside and outside the brasserie, dissipated.

Brandon licked his lips. When eventually he glanced back at Natasha's table, another man was sitting in his chair. Thirty-something, slight paunch, sports jacket and polo shirt. The fiancé. Blake.

185

The dirty plates had been removed. The two of them were drinking coffee, waving their hands excitedly as they spoke. The man read the expression on Natasha's face, turned to Brandon, nodded. Continued speaking as Natasha swiped through tablet images, jabbing at something on the screen.

When Brandon stepped up to the table, Blake was nodding enthusiastically at the screen image of a big black building with no doors.

"It's in there somewhere," said Blake. "The 'game changer' they've been oh-so-secretive about. Not even any leaks which is impossible these days."

"But what kind of product is it – was there any indication in the foyer?"

He snorted. "Couldn't *get* that far. None of us could make it past security. It's got a vibe like some kind of top grade military facility, all black glass and musclemen in suits."

"But you must have some idea –"

"None at all." He shrugged. "Although, of course, there've been *rumours*." He paused, glanced up at Brandon, motioned for him to pull up a seat. "Coffee?"

Brandon fumbled for an answer.

"Brandon was just leaving," said Natasha.

Blake smiled, offered his hand and introduced himself. "So what was all that about out front?"

Brandon dragged a chair up close and flopped down into it. "Nothing."

"Looks like he's had a vision of the holy virgin," said Natasha. She leaned across the table and whispered conspiratorially "If you're still here then it must have been something *amazing*."

Brandon swivelled in his chair to stare back at the window. Nothing to see, just the street returned to normal. Cars whooshing by. Guys in suits lugging bulky satchels, speaking on phones or staring at them. Two men in faded jeans walking a labrador. A couple of fat chicks taking up half the path.

"I gotta go," he said, standing up again, moving quickly so as to dodge the cynical expression on Natasha's face. When he reached the door he glanced back at the fiancé, but Blake's attention had returned fully to the screen.

Harkers Lane. How many times had Brandon ducked below its grimy lamplight? They were all veterans, him and Sam and Dave. Dave had been a regular since the first of the VR brothels opened shop. Said it was better than fucking real women, especially as 'real women' had become so totally fucked up.

VR chicks felt pretty much like the real thing. Better, actually, because you got just what you wanted. They sounded how you wanted them to sound and, of course, you could custom fit their mods.

Dave liked girls with enormous jugs but no fat anywhere else. No hips, no arse, all rack, everything that mattered. Massive lips like black women – only not black skin. He liked his women white. Asian was okay, but white was better.

Sam didn't reckon he had a type so long as they were skinny. So long as he was doing what the other guys were doing.

Trinh always did exactly what Brandon wanted. He only ever had to show her once. Didn't talk much either. Didn't speak much English. Spent a lot of time on the phone. Had a job, supposedly, but was vague about its nature. *Not that there was anything wrong with that.*

He blocked Natasha's sneering from his mind. She'd been so sweet when they first got together, before the snark set in. Not perfect – she was never a gazelle – but they liked so much of the same stuff, even sports. If only she'd tried harder instead of becoming so hard-arsed. *A man can't help what he's attracted to, Natasha. It's natural. Law of the jungle.* He'd wanted to check out that engagement ring up close. Wanted her to understand how the things he'd done had never been *his* fault. Not with all the changes, the way the world had become. All pointless – Natasha never listened. Not back then and certainly not now.

He didn't want to think about Natasha any more, or Trinh or that guy, fiancé, whatever the fuck his name was, Mr Biotech.

He pictured the beautiful Angelina look-alike walking down that street. Cheekbones so sharp you could cut glass with them. *Climbing on top of her... pushing his way inside.*

Brandon stopped walking, shook his head to clear it. Stared through the triple-arch windows rimmed with faux-Islamic brick. Convex cherry-amber tinted glass. You couldn't see much from the outside, just a hint of something naked in the shadows.

They were supposed to advertise the fact if the brothel was VR but hardly anywhere bothered. If the chicks were fit, it meant VR, trans or ladyboys. Nobody wanted that stuff spelled out to them. Men who used these places didn't care.

A doorway. The old fashioned kind. Wind picking up, tumbling discarded coffee cups along the gutter. Occasional leaves. Dog turds and cigarette butts.

Truth was, Brandon couldn't escape the feeling that VR was just a pricey way of jerking off. It *looked* real and *felt* real, but all too clean. Too perfect. The girls flowed like mercury adjusting to his moves. Defying gravity, twisting themselves into impossible positions.

"All good," said Dave. "Better than good."

Dave ought to know the difference. Things hadn't been so good for Dave since the day he'd punched that fat chick in the face. It wasn't personal, he didn't even know her name, just lost his nana big time, getting furious with all of womankind. So he lashed out, taking it out on her. For blighting the landscape with flabby arms and chunky thighs. For blocking his view of better-looking women – the scant few of them that still existed.

Dave muttered about conspiracy theories in muted tones. Said feminists had unleashed the fat virus on the world. Feminists and lesbians, fucking them all over. Fucking up the future for decent, honest, proper-looking people.

VR sex was good enough for Dave. Better than good, in fact. That time they'd all gone fishing and got drunk. One of the many times. He confessed how much he liked it better when you barely even had to move. When the VR chick did all the moving for you. How you could get three for the price of two when they had those coupon specials.

A face loomed large in the cherry-red amber glass. Slender, nineteen, maybe twenty. She winked. Brandon waved, even though he knew she was probably VR. Probably not even human. Probably not. He pushed the handle down and went inside.

Afterwards, dissatisfied, as he so often was, Brandon found himself back on Season Street. Early evening. Passing cars blurred smudges of colour. People too. Rain had fallen, leaving pavements glistening with liquid neon spill.

A block or two from the brasserie, he stood in front of a mini-mall where massive windows displayed banks of flatscreens, thin as credit cards. Same face on every luminescent surface; a gnarly woman, old, thin and bent, shouting down a microphone like she was going to take it in her mouth. *The curse of Ad-36 comes from God, his wrath all-powerful and mighty. Ain't no physiology, biology or any other kinds of ology. The devil brings the fat down on our shoulders, sinful fat like all the plagues of Egypt. Fat we all need to be accounting for. Fat for which we need to beg forgiveness.*

The televised congregation wept and prayed. *Amen* said a girl standing near enough to feel the preacher's blasting vitriol. No more than fifteen, sixteen maybe, pallid cellulite-puckered thighs protruding like stalactites from a too-short denim miniskirt.

The flatscreens flicked in unison to something new: a city scene somewhere Asian; Tokyo or maybe Taiwan, pedestrians shuffling, expressions obscured beneath medical masks, as useless as they had been in the face of the H1N1 Swine Flu comeback.

The girl moved on when she noticed him. Brandon raised his collar against the drizzle, James Dean style, his favourite actor after Brando, both idols from the days when men were men. Before political correctness and its avenging armies of social justice warriors.

He wasn't going anywhere in particular. Any bar would do, just so long as it was dark and nobody knew his name.

"Hey – Brandon, isn't it?"

Startled, he looked up, then stopped dead in his tracks. "You?"

Mr Biotech – Blake – Natasha's paunchy fiancé, stood beneath a patisserie awning stabbing at apps on his phone, looking different in the half-light thrown up by the rain-soaked streets. Less substantial; shadowy as an apparition.

Brandon scrabbled for excuses, reasons he was ambling in the drizzle instead of cozying up at home with his lovely girlfriend. But he didn't need to say anything. Blake's attention was completely somewhere else.

"Something serious going down in there," Blake said, nodding across the road to the peculiar black building that didn't look like anything else in Melbourne. "Feed says they're launching something big. Pharmaceuticals, maybe. The kind of thing that might just change the world. There's no *reliable* leaks, of course – a couple of false ones including Mumbai and quite frankly none of us were –"

"Like maybe a cure?" said Brandon, eyes lighting up, the first thought that came into his head. "Whoever patents a cure for AD-36 will end up richer than God."

Blake nodded, still half distracted by his phone, "You're not wrong, mate. One leaked intel stream throws up a host of interesting possibilities. Breakthrough technologies, with roots in UTC and Lockheed, but the money trail leads straight back to Russia – doesn't it always? Whatever it is, they're keeping pretty mum."

Brandon pretended he understood. "You looking for a scoop?"

Blake nodded, eyes flicking to the rain slicked, glassy black building. "Been here since late afternoon. There's definitely something going on. Check 'em out."

Both stared at what might have been the entrance, guarded by men so muscle bound the fabric of their suits could barely contain them. Curls of plastic coiled down from their ears.

"Four of 'em just standing there. Another four, identical, around the back. Real identical, like minted Schwarzeneggers. Or front – can't even tell reception from the loading dock. This crazy building doesn't seem to have either. In any case, I'm pretty sure they're armed."

They stood there listening to the wet swoosh of passing traffic. Parked cars like sleeping dogs hunched in double rows. Uncomfortable – at least Brandon was. Not sure how to have 'that' conversation – or any kind of conversation with the guy shagging his ex. Engaged – not just shagging her – like the guy had resigned himself to the new changed world and the women it contained. Getting on with business, despite it all, yet he seemed like an all right kind of guy, not some chat show loser, someone he could get to like if things hadn't all got so complicated.

Blake kept checking messages on his phone. Whatever he was looking for wasn't there.

They were not the only two staking out the building. The parking lot was rimmed with shadows and the shadows were made of men. Hunched in overcoats, jackets buttoned tight against the damp. All watching and waiting for something.

"Do you love her?" blurted Brandon suddenly, surprised at himself when the words slipped out of his mouth.

Blake looked up from his phone. "Natasha? Yeah, mate. Yeah, I do. Didn't you?"

Brandon opened his mouth to say something else but Blake cut him short. "Look!"

A brief flare of fierce amber light pulsed from the black glass building's opaque interior. One by one the beefcake guards started tapping at the curled wires in their ears, then moving inside the big black shiny box, single file, the last of them tugging the coil right out and discarding it.

"Those guys look Russian to you?" said Blake as he snapped a couple of blurred images with his phone.

Blake and Brandon waited for maybe half a minute. "It's now or never, mate," said Blake. "I'm not hanging around for backup. You sure you're up for this?"

Backup – was Blake talking about police? Brandon decided against asking stupid questions. Nodded.

Blake nodded in return. They ran together across the glistening asphalt, Brandon figuring *what's the worst that could happen?* The doors to the secretive black building would be bolted, or they'd get inside, then get kicked straight out again. Threatened, maybe, by the kinds of men who issued threats to strangers for a living. Whatever was going on inside would carry on without them. But maybe, just maybe, they'd catch a glimpse.

There was no door. Security had vanished, leaving unguarded a black rectangular slit, reminiscent of that famous sci-fi movie monolith. The one that caused the apes to bash one another's skulls with animal bones.

"What the hell?" said Blake. "Doesn't even have a handle." He stepped in closer, reached out into the darkness with both hands.

Brandon felt a shiver down his spine. He turned, receding from the rain-slicked parking lot and the city skyline bearing down on top. Behind, a crush of hunched and moving men, heading right towards them – and the darkness.

Blake went through first, with Brandon breathing down his neck, half anticipating a mystical occurrence.

Nothing happened. The darkness belonged to a deep entranceway. The men pushed through into a thrumming tide of extraordinarily beautiful people. Men in Ralph Lauren and Issey Miyaki. Slender women in strapless, ethereal shimmer, many grades up from that lone gazelle eating foam in the Season Street brasserie. The women before him were Angelinas – small differences between them: the colour of hair, eyes and skin – but every single one of them was exquisitely and impossibly perfect.

Brandon sucked in his breath. Almost choked on it when, coming out of nowhere, a beefcake guard slammed roughly into his side. He braced himself for confrontation till he copped a close up look at the big guy's eyes. Windows to the soul, so he'd heard it said. Not this guy's. He was dumbstruck, love struck or totally off his face. Utterly distracted, plastic coil trailing limply from his ear.

Men started flooding in through the narrow doorway. Shoulder to shoulder. Eyes blazing bright. Blake's pale face was etched in panic. Brandon kept losing sight of him as he pushed in deeper, trying to secure a little space. The air was thick with cloying scents. Jasmine. Caron's Poivre. Woman.

Were these women 'cured' or were they something else entirely? Brandon couldn't be certain and the further the crowd enveloped him, the less he cared about the answer to the question. He felt a surge of vindication at the world made good again. Whatever this was, it was better than VR. Better than real life. Better than all the sex he'd ever dreamed of. Brandon comprehended that he was mingling with the *future*. The way the world had never been before. The way his life was truly meant to be.

He watched in silence as two security guards jumped Blake, locking him into a chokehold, Blake's eyes widening with terror. All three vanished as men pushed on and through like curdling lava, the black rectangle now completely blocked from view.

Memories of Natasha sneering flooded Brandon's head, seared with anger, pain and disappointment. *She should have tried harder. Dave's fist smashing into that fat chick's face. Slow mo. Close up. Graphic. Inevitable. Pathetic Sam trying to keep up with the others. Trinh's black eyed, ungendered stare.*

None of those things mattered any more. The future, replete with perfect Angelinas, welcomed him with open, loving arms. A tipping point. A horizon tailor-made for men like Brandon. A bright new world he could finally believe in.

"No Fat Chicks" is the most universally despised thing I have ever written, garnering me a file full of harsher-than-usual rejection slips. The only person who loved it was Tehani Croft from Fablecroft Press – so much so that she built an anthology around it called *In Your Face*, inviting authors to submit challenging or controversial material. My story ended up winning the Best Short Story Ditmar Award in 2016.

VETERANS DAY

"Those ain't no virgins!" screamed red-faced Maria, sweat streaming off her shiny cheeks, words that set the other girls off into shrieking fits of laughter.

Safia looked down to where Maria pointed. Way down below where the parade coiled through city streets like a giant many-coloured serpente. Past the lower balconies – always the first to fill on Veterans Day. Beyond the bridges and walkways spun like webs connecting slender minarets. At the serpente's head walked the city's finest daughters. Veiled, their pale white shifts blending with sandy paving stones. One would be selected and offered to the Veteran in celebration of Veterans Day.

There had always been a Veterans Day as far as anyone remembered. Events requiring sacrifice stood out amongst the many. Veterans Day was better attended than The Day of Blessed Mothers, Annunciation, or even The Culling of All Souls.

Safia adhered herself to Maria's gang of scruffy shanty girls. Safety in numbers, they climbed the walls in packs. Safety in scrabbling beyond the reach of priests and their swinging silver staves. Far from the guardsmen with their wicked blades and ways.

The city's ancient crumbling brickwork was peppered with footholds. Safia had been poked with brooms, swatted at with horsehair brushes, sworn at in a dozen disparate tongues. But the girl was quick and fleet of foot. She did not steal fruit from unguarded window boxes, nor leer at things she wasn't supposed to see.

Safia kept her wits about her, slinking at the fringes of the pack, both on the streets and when climbing high above them. The girls were climbing up to gawk at handsome drummers escorting courtesans in gowns of gold-and-lapis borne on palanquins held high by bare-chested men in pantaloons.

And the acrobats: white faced, coal-eyed, limber, juggling and prancing in their lace and feathered plumage. Flinging themselves from rail to rail, tumbling and screeching like monkeys. Choking confetti, swirling scented smoke.

Drums pounding like the beating of a million human hearts, winding their way up to the citadel – a windowless, glowing cylinder topped with a dome of sheer translucent crystal. Prison of the God-King Ankahmada, a being feared by all, but never seen. Surrounded by the spirits of the dead, the only ones fit to keep him company.

What precisely lay within the citadel? Nobody knew for certain. There was no entranceway or windows, but they'd all glimpsed shadowy figures through the blue. Guardsmen manned its base at compass points. Call to prayer sounded dawn and dusk, when the pale tiles shone with startling luminescence.

Maria and her girls threw stones, the younger ones whining in the heat. Safia craned her neck, but the citadel's blue shimmer remained nothing more than soft, translucent blur.

Ghosts were nothing special. Everybody saw ghosts, just as everyone had lost somebody dear. People vanished in the city of gold-and-lapis. It was the way of things, the price to pay for the protection of the God-King Ankahmada.

Safia learned the hard way that that no place was truly safe – and none less so than the Fancy House from which her beloved Mama had disappeared. Too young to work and without protection, Safia had been cast onto the street, forced to fend for herself amongst the rats and garbage.

Safia climbed with grim determination. The House said her Mama was dead and gone but if that were true, perhaps she was not truly gone completely? Perhaps her Mama walked amongst the citadel phantoms? Stranger things had happened in this city.

Maria spat her warnings as the girls kept climbing higher: *Touch the blue and it will burn your hand. Don't stare too hard or the shimmer-blue will drive you mad-bad-crazy.*

"I can't see anything – we'll have to get in closer!"

"Not too close, you stupid girls. Don't want to wind up caught."

"Those fat old dogs are way too slow for us..."

Maria shushed them, harsher this time. "It's not so bad," she assured the younger ones. Maria had been branded twice, and caught two more times which she'd shrugged off like a joke. Marks she wore like a badge of honour. Jokes you had to be old enough to understand.

The wall's inner balustrade was the girls' favourite haunt. On tiptoe they could just make out the pilgrim camp that dogged the outer walls. Where people walked out of the Dead Red Heart, come to throw themselves upon the mercy of Ankahmada. Beyond their camp, a thousand miles of sand. Further still lay nothing but bones and ruin.

Wedged inside the walls lay the shanty strip, bathed in a sickly glow. Soaked in the relentless hum and random pulses of the outer city wall.

Somehow, the barefoot girls and boys learned to sleep with its curdling vibrations, its cold-beyond-cold that burned those fool enough to touch.

The shanty boys and girls slept light, one hand on the three-inch blades they sharpened to points against foundation stones.

"Let's hop it to the Hydroponica," piped up Deean, little sister of Maria, named for a long-forgotten saint like so many other girls.

"No way – guards will climb up if they spot us."

"What of it?" Maria interjected, wielding the authority of her extra years. "They never climb as high as the spiral rail."

She winked at Deean and then across at Safia. A fit of giggling erupted from the rest of them, louder this time until a long blast on a brassy horn drew all attention back to the parade. One by one they hopped down, following little Deean's lead, still peering and craning as the parade choked up the streets.

A year ago Safia had lived a stone's throw from the citadel, but that was a secret she kept close. When Mama had worn the gold-and-lapis, when they'd lived well in a Fancy House five whole storeys high.

Ahead, Maria, red-faced again, shouted insults. Maria who thought she knew everything, but didn't. Her boastful dreams of living in a Fancy House, dressed in finery, strolling casually down terracotta streets. Abandoning shantytown – and the rest of them – in her wake. She didn't know that gold-and-lapis courtesans were trained from birth, not snatched from slums and spirited away. That the priests who used them did not have human hearts – or human skin. Cold to the touch just like a lizard's belly. Mama had whispered the truth of it. She had wanted something better for her daughter. Safia's own belly soured from an irregular diet of bitter skinks and nettle stems. Scraps from bins when the dogs didn't beat her to it.

Up high beyond the drummers, stilts and acrobats was the one place she felt safe. She did not care to push her luck by jeering at the city's finest daughters, trying to guess which of them would be chosen.

The Hydroponica was fashioned from a million ivory tiles, each one smooth and identical to every other. The spiral rail wrapped around its girth connected it with the distillery and the mill.

The closest possible vantage point. The girls leaned over, craning for a glimpse. Those luckless virgins: pretty girls with neat-combed hair, balancing bowls of offerings or hand stitched flowers, eyes downcast beneath diaphanous veils. Nobody knew what happened to the chosen. Deean said the Veteran ate them. Maria reckoned he chained them up and made them bear his demon babies. Nice girls, they were all supposed to be, selected from the city's higher families.

The chattering girls blocked Safia from the blue. She hadn't come for dreams of palanquins, lapis-gold or priests. She'd come to see the visions of the dead. To find out if her Mama stood amongst them.

"Look! It's happening. The blue, just like you said!"

Maria smiled triumphantly at the lurid, fading glaze. Safia looked right past her, straight into the shimmering field that moments before had been impenetrable ceramic.

"It glows!"

Safia stared hard, curiosity burning white-hot. Were there ghosts in the citadel or weren't there? A boy called Aeron swore he knew a guard who had put his hand right through one. Ghosts were the reason a bank of spirit houses lined the citadel's west aspect. Ghosts need not be seen to be believed, and Safia did believe: she couldn't help it.

She wanted to show her Mama that she was surviving on her own. That neither hunger nor uncertainty had claimed her. That she could stand her ground against girls and boys twice her size and half again as mean.

"Look – there's Madame Peshari and her poor dead twins!"

The gaggle of girls fell silent, gawking and craning, trying to see what Deean was pointing at. Something that might have been a swirl of parasols and frilly skirts. A blur of colour, difficult to make out at a distance.

"I swear that's Madam Peshari inside – look!"

"Shhh, I can't hear the drumming over the top of you."

"Shove over, I can't see a thing. They're picking the virgin and we're missing it!"

"Gimme the glass. Hasn't someone got a spyglass?"

"Move your arse, you're hogging all the room!"

The shanty girls made too much noise. Safia separated herself from the seething, boiling mass of them, edged her way along a jutting spar that bent beneath her meagre weight. She leapt to a ledge, then across to the spiral walkway. Let them have their cruel parade. Something was happening within the citadel's ceramic glaze. Indistinct shapes coalescing into human forms. If only she was closer. The drumming intensified. Another blast of the long, brassy horn, drowned out beneath loud squeals of uncharitable delight.

The blue light of the citadel, so dazzling and bright. She blinked. Coloured blobs swam before her eyes. For a moment – just a moment – the shimmer thinned and she could see right through. An empty street with whitewashed walls. A woman in a gold-and-lapis dress. A woman who tilted her head and smiled, held out her hand and reached towards...

"Mama!"

Safia scurried along the walkway, almost slipping, scurrying faster, reaching out her own hand. Not being careful where she was going, she slammed into a city guardsman heaving and puffing in the opposite direction. The man grabbed hold of Safia's arm and twisted.

"Mama – no!"

The blue-and-lapis woman vanished; the citadel walls became opaque again, glowing faintly like the resonance of sunset.

A second guardsman appeared behind the first, bulky men who blocked the narrow ledge. As one bound her wrists with scratchy rope, she considered flinging herself into the air. Quick as a skink. Fall like a stone. Let them catch some other girl – the streets, walkways and roofs were crawling with them.

But Safia didn't jump or struggle. Where there was life there was hope, as Mama said. Not that words like *life* and *hope* had done her Mama any favours in the end.

There was no sign of Maria's shanty girls as the guardsmen dragged Safia down the spiral walkway. They took her somewhere underground that stank of damp and rot, bundling her into the arms of older women with hard faces and stained aprons.

"Here's your virgin sacrifice," said the fatter of the two, pocketing the coins the woman gave him.

"I ain't no virgin!" Safia screamed.

"I couldn't give two shits, you shanty skank. You look the part – or at least you will when we're done scrubbing the filth off ya."

The women stripped her dirty clothes, dunked her headfirst into a bath. Beefy arms held Safia still while another scrubbed her skin until it stung. Something clattered from her pocket. Her three-inch blade, now kicked against the wall. They washed her hair and combed out all the matted tangles. Hard-faced bitches, every one, avoiding eye contact like it might bring shame on them.

They dressed her in a plain white shift, soft like it had been washed a thousand times, yet the fabric seeming newly off the loom.

"I ain't going in your parade. You won't get me promenading the city street!"

The woman who'd held the scrubbing brush gave her a sour look. Her face was old. Somewhere near forty, were it not for the creases on her forehead and the terrible bags and droops beneath her eyes.

"You don't get to promenade," she said matter-of-factly. "Like anyone's gonna want to look at you."

Safia's feet were jammed into beaded slippers, her hands tied tight in front of her while a thin, pale woman braided her hair too tight. Another threaded paper flowers through it. When Safia squirmed, the sour-faced woman punched her in the gut.

"You really think they'd go wasting the lives of the city's finest daughters? No one's even going to know you're gone."

Safia felt her eyes begin to water. She fought it hard. They didn't deserve the satisfaction. It wasn't true. Deean would miss her. So would Aeron and maybe even lying, two-faced Maria.

When her hair was done they yanked her to her feet.

"There's words to learn," said a scrawny woman standing to one side. "Make sure you don't jumble 'em up, else it'll be the worse for you."

Safia braced herself to kick their shins and make a break for it. She knew all the backstreet nooks and crannies. Even with arms bound, she could outrun them all.

Only she couldn't. One of the women bent and cuffed a chain around her ankle. She yelped as cold iron bit into her flesh.

Sour Face took a vial down from the highest shelf. Pale green glass with something dark inside. When she unstoppered it, a pungent scent leaked out.

"Know what this is?" she said.

Safia nodded. She knew.

"Good. That means I won't have to use it but if you don't stop struggling, Angel help me, that's exactly what I'll do. Don't matter two shits to me what way you want to die. My job's to see you past the temple gate. A swig of this'll burn out your insides, nice and slow. Without it, I cut your bonds, you walk on yer own and take yer chances with the thing that lives beneath our feet."

Safia swallowed the hard lump in her throat. "I can walk," she said.

The sour-faced woman slipped the vial into her apron. "Good then. Looks like we're all done here."

They made her wait in a passageway that stank of piss and rats. With bored-looking guardsman on either side, she listened to the screaming crowd as the procession continued beyond the walls. Drumming. Always drumming. She pictured priests with smooth round shaven heads, physiques outlined in clinging silks and satins. Fabric refracting tiny shards of diamond light. Cloaks that flowed and twisted like living things.

Each bearing shiny two-pronged staves, the God-King's symbol blazoned upon their chests. Chanting prayers, their voices loud enough to wake the dead. Blasting occasional potted palms with lightning; a yapping dog or child not quick enough to move.

Children scattering petals before the sacrifice. They didn't call it that, of course. The word they used was *maiden*. Neither were the petals real. Not much grew around the city walls and what did could not be spared for treading underfoot, not even by the city's finest daughters.

Safia stood tall, ignoring the chill of the chain around her ankle, still hoping an opportunity might present itself. Whatever chance, no matter how small and risky, she would take it.

The drummers ceased their mesmerising rhythms as one by one they entered the passageway. Backlight made them difficult to see. Now and then, a tiny glimmer. The smell of strong tobacco, wafting.

Then the maiden: stark in silhouette. Strong hands pushed her forward until the girls stood face to face.

The maiden held out her bouquet. "Here. Take it."

"I... my hands are tied."

The corners of the maiden's lips turned up in a cruel smile. She dropped the flowers. They landed with a dull thud on the passageway's cold stone. The maiden spun on her heel as a stocky woman stepped out of the shadows and wrapped the rich girl protectively in a cloak.

"Untie my hands!" Safia begged.

Nobody spoke. She was pushed for the second time and the flowers were trampled underfoot.

"Watch your feet, you clumsy girl; those took me a week to sew!" The angry woman snatched them up and jammed them between Safia's palms.

Safia couldn't see where they were taking her. She tripped over her ankle chain as the passageway's darkness closed around her, thick and enveloping like fog.

At the entrance to the temple, a guardsman freed her ankle and her wrists, then pushed her through a gaping, rocky maw. Icy chill bled through her beaded slippers. When she looked before her, all she saw was darkness.

"Walk!"

Safia stumbled forwards. Darkness gradually gave way to a grotto weathered from thick, crumbling stone. And something else. Something unexpected. Lights. Hundreds of them, yellow and winking in the draught, like glowing jewels. Candles placed upon altars: high ones, low ones and plenty in between, each illuminating framed images of a woman's face.

The rough-handed women who'd scrubbed Safia clean had made her memorise a string of words, but the further she moved inside the cool interior, the more those words fragmented and slipped away. Something about creation and destruction. A virgin princess called Diana, the once-living legend. A goddess and a saint. Words didn't matter. Only the offerings mattered: the trampled flowers they'd jammed between her hands. The sacrifice she was supposed to be.

Safia paused before the central altar, breathed in the stink of tallow and expensive wax. Incense too, a mismatched blend of cinnamon, clove and lemongrass.

Diana's face was everywhere. Perhaps she *was* a goddess? She was beautiful enough. Spaced between the frames and candles stood ceramic figurines, each one a woman in flowing robes. Some showed a heart at the centre of her chest. Others a band of gold around her head. The glow of holiness. The radiance of good.

A noise disturbed the dark behind her. Something moving, much bigger than a man. Her breathing steady, she clutched the trodden flowers against her chest.

"Don't you dare touch anything." A male voice, deep and old, a mix of strong and feeble in one breath.

That noise again, a dragging, rasping shuffling. Louder this time. Closer too. Her pulse began to quicken as a jumble of words spilled out between her lips. "A highborn daughter of Ankahmada stands before your greatness... I bring..." her voice trailed off to nothingness.

"Liar. You got the stink of shanty on your skin. Do you reckon I can't smell it?"

The sound again, this time even closer. The ground trembled beneath the creature's weight. In fright, she almost turned.

"Don't you look at me," he barked, a sound sharper and more terrifying than the grate of metal scraping metal.

She froze. "I only want..."

"I know what you want, the whole damn lot of you. You think I'm stupid? You think I can't see through your games? Desecrating *her* holy temple. Poisoning *her* memory with your lies."

A harsh clunk and clatter nearly startled her out of her skin. The thing behind her wasn't human. It was a warrior demon from the time before the Ruin, risen to slay her for her wickedness. Something cold and hard pressed into her back.

"One inch more and I'll snip your spine in two."

The demon wasn't joking. She sucked in breath, eyes on the sea of flickering lights. Waiting for the beast to make its move.

"So. What have they told you about me?"

"That... that you are the Veteran. A holy man."

"More likely that I am a merciless eater of babies. Did they tell you that one? Did they?"

"No, Master..." Her voice, weak and insipid, trailed away. She was scared now. Really scared. The Veteran was going to kill her.

"I am master of nothing. Peek into the corners, little girl, and tell me what you see."

The grotto did not have corners. It was wide and squat, its low ceiling choked with jagged mineral spikes like broken teeth. Shadows pooled around the edges. Murky smudges that might have hidden many things.

"Look harder," he growled. "You're not even trying."

Safia looked: first up at the central altar, with its many flickering flames, then at the faces of all the holy Dianas. From there to the ground, hard-packed earth tainted with dark patches that might have been spills or stains. They might have been a lot of things and she didn't want to think about any of them. Finally she saw what he wanted her to see: a neat pile of shiny, polished bones. Arm bones and leg bones. Pelvises and skulls. All human. All the bones of girls.

He laughed when she gasped, a hideous sound not much like laughter, yet she was certain laughter was intended.

"I don't eat babies but I do eat little girls. High-born virgins or shanty gutter trash, you all taste the same when I'm hungry enough not to care."

In that moment, Safia understood. Every tale was true: the demon who lived in the bowels of the citadel – who had lived here since the time before the Ruin. Older even than the wars he fought in. Older than the mighty God-King and his priests. Some even whispered they were brothers. She'd never seen the God-King, but the Veteran was standing close. His dank breath filled the space between them, souring the air she fought to breathe.

She turned her head the smallest fraction, towards strange shadows splayed along the floor and walls. Harsh, jagged spikes. When the Veteran moved, the shadow spikes moved too.

"I told you to be still," he warned. "None have ever left here."

Was she to die by a sharp thrust of his blade? Some said his fingers had long rotted off, replaced with razors. His feet were hammers, his cock a coil of rust.

Atop the altar, the Princess smiled out through a hundred windows, her skin made soft by coercions of dark and flame.

"Is Diana buried here? Does she sleep in this holy place?" Safia closed her eyes – the only way she could squeeze words out at all. Her voice was dry as an abandoned well.

"What do you know of the People's Princess? You and your kind, you have no concept of blessings. Your minds are blasted hollow with false gods."

The blade pressed sharply through her shift. The stink of his breath enveloped her.

"Why won't you let me see your face?" she blurted. When she opened her eyes, the Dianas seemed to smile. She would be brave and speak her mind as her Mama had spoken hers. Like Mama, she was dead already, so what could be the harm?

"Hers is the only face you want to see," he growled, and then, a heavy sigh like wind rattling through broken eaves. "So beautiful. Men died for that beauty. Women for the want of it. What makes you think she'd have time for the likes of you? Your petty causes. Your simpering demands. All you people ever do is *take*."

He spat that last word out like sour wine. She turned her head just a little more, winced at the knife dug harder into her back.

"Shut your eyes and I'll make it quick."

And she almost did exactly what he said, only in that last crucial second she did something else instead. Something stupid and crazy. Why not? Stupid and crazy had carried her through hunger and spirited her away from ill-intentioned guardsmen more times than she was capable of remembering.

Safia took a deep breath, then three brave leaps ahead. Right up to the altar, then spun around to face him.

The grotto echoed with a frantic clattering and clanging. Nobody stood behind her. Nothing but a sea of winking flames refracting off the walls and ceiling teeth. How could he possibly have moved so fast? *Demons travel faster than the winds.* She knew that. Everybody knew that.

"Why won't you let me see you?" The flowers were gone. She must have dropped them. The flowers didn't matter.

"They killed Diana, you know," said his voice from one of the darkened edges. "Hunted her down like a slavering pack of dogs. All across the land, the faithful had visions at the precise moment of her passing."

Silence again.

"I'm so sorry."

"Such a long time ago..."

"But you keep her memory alive."

"She's all that's left of beauty in this world." He sighed heavily, a sound like wind stirring through fallen leaves.

Silence upon silence. A sudden gust set a row of flames to flickering. She cast her gaze across the images of Diana, drawing strength from them, and courage. Young Diana, child Diana, Mother, Wife and Lady. "You're not a monster. You're a lonely old man. So old, you've forgotten how to die so you hide down here where no one else can see. They forced me in here. All I wanted was to see inside the citadel. To find my Mama or the ghost she has become."

"You don't want to see in there," he said. A quiet voice, every trace of the demon gone from it.

"Yes I do. More than anything."

"They'll hunt you and they'll kill you."

"They? Who are *they*? The ghosts?"

"The priests." He paused, considering his words carefully. "I can't let you pass. Princess Diana is my liege. I guard the entrance to the reliquary built for sainted bones: Saints Madonna, Theresa, Maria, Fatima, Diana. All the blessed holy, but Diana is my liege. She came to me in a dream and never left me."

Silence filled the grotto. Even the flame tips lay completely still.

"Tell me, Veteran. In that dream, did she ask you to kill for her?"

A long, silent pause and then the Veteran roared and charged at her.

She screamed, then clambered up the central altar, the safest place – the only place – candles tipping and spilling in all directions.

"How dare you desecrate *her* shrine," he bellowed.

There was nowhere to hide. Safia scrabbled on all fours, scattering figurines and offerings, dropping down behind the altar in a crouch, frozen in fear, not knowing where to go.

He came for her, a blur of meshed flesh and metal. She tried to leap to her feet, only suddenly he seemed to be coming at her from both sides at once, pinning her down with metal appendages that shot forth from some part of him she couldn't even see. The Veteran wasn't human. He wasn't even close.

Safia screamed.

"Be quiet!"

Fallen candles burned upon their sides, hot wax pooling and spilling across stone. Her trembling hand – the only part of her that she could move – reached out and righted the nearest.

"If you have cracked a single glass frame, I will kill you."

"You're going to kill me anyway," she whispered. "I saw Mama standing with her parasol. Inside the citadel when the walls went thin – I saw her!"

He snorted hot, foetid breath. "No you didn't. Your mother is dead. The priests took her. They take whatever they want. Everyone's dead and soon you will be too."

"You're not dead – you're talking to me!"

"I died in the wars."

"No you didn't!"

At this, he laughed. A sound like the rattling and scraping of tin cans mixed with the rusting squeal of ancient hinges.

"I'm a ghost, my stupid child. As dead as dead can be." He raised a blade above her head. Cold steel glinted in soft yellow light.

She fumbled for her own stone-sharpened blade. Not there – the washerwomen had taken it. "You won't hurt me," she sobbed. "Not in Diana's holy temple. Not in front of *her.*"

His blade came down, stopped a hair's breadth from her neck. Safia screwed her eyes up tight.

And waited.

Nothing happened.

She waited for the longest time, then opened them a crack.

Up close now, yellow light revealing all. She found the part of him that most approximated a face, stared into what she hoped might be his eyes.

"What you saw was an illusion," he said softly. "No people dwell within the citadel. Nor ghosts. Just bones and dust. The blue is a weapon, same kind as protects us from the Dead Red's pilgrim hordes. But the citadel roots sink deep down into sand. Roots that suck up mineral replenishment."

The man he had once been still lived in his eyes.

"Get me inside the citadel," Safia pleaded. "I've nowhere else to go."

The Veteran didn't answer, but the metal tools that pinned her retracted one by one with a wheezing like the bellows on a pump.

Free at last, she didn't move. Diana watched them both in silence with her many, varied faces. Different ages, different skins. Not judging, just watching. Safia was beginning to like this ancient goddess.

"How long *have* you lived down here?" she asked.

"Long enough."

Moving slowly, so as not to startle him, she pushed herself to her feet, then waited until the grotto fell completely silent. She watched without staring as each of his extra appendages folded in upon itself, repacking and nestling beneath his leathered hide.

He turned away, blushing. "You can climb up through the roots, but it won't be easy. Most who chanced it died a nasty death."

"But some have tried it?"

"Aye. Straight up and in. A vein spiked into the living heart. It'll try to flush you out again, make no mistake. You might get in but you won't last long up top."

"I'll take my chances."

The Veteran coughed, a sound like scraping rust. "Touch only the dead roots. Be very quiet, moving like a skink below the sand. Hollow, flaccid things, those roots. They wither and drop off over time. The citadel tears them when it shifts and realigns. Some are choked with slime and ichor. Avoid the blue ones – that stuff will burn your flesh right to the bone."

"But how do I –?"

"I didn't say it would be easy, shanty girl. You young want everything handed on a platter. In my day we'd have blasted holes clean through the fresh ones, drained them dry and hauled ourselves up through."

She smiled and nodded. "In your day. Come with me! Show me how."

"You're talking to a long-dead soldier. Not much sense in dying twice."

Safia smiled. She touched the nearest of Diana's faces. Gently. "Come with me. What if there's not just bones up there? What if –"

"Don't try and mess with my head, shanty girl. I'm giving you your life back, so now *get!*"

With that came an aggravated clanking, as though someone was hammering pots and pans. He pointed at a deep fissure set into the far wall, a crack she had thought nothing more than shadow.

"Thank you, Veteran. I'll prove you wrong, and I'll come back for you."

He laughed, a mean, dispirited sound. "You'll wind up dead as your long-dead Mama. I'll light a candle to your new-dead memory."

Too late. She was already on her way.

When the sound of her had faded like mouse scratchings in the wall, he stepped out into the open, retracting the last of his spider-splayed appendages. Diana stared smugly from her scattered frames as he bent to pick them up.

"What are you gawking at?" he grumbled, shaking shattered glass shards down like rain.

Diana's soft voice echoed in his head. "Get on after her. You know it's time to —"

"Shut up. I'm not talking to you."

Diana laughed. "Of course you are. I'm the only one you ever talk to, day in, day out and all the brooding night-time in between."

He mumbled something incoherent, slammed the broken frames upon the altar top.

"You know I'm right," she continued. "You've outgrown this lair of polished bones. Get on after that shanty girl. Be a soldier once again – be a man. Give those priests what they've had coming since they killed their king and allowed his corrupted program to run rogue."

"Shut up shut up shut up," he said as he clamped his leathery palms across his ears. But he knew she was right – she was always right. It was time to move on, time to make a stand.

He brushed the sheen of crumbled glass from a faded photograph, tucked it into the pocket above his heart. "You'll wait for me?"

"Of course I'll wait." Diana smiled, benign and strong from a hundred picture frames as the Veteran strode boldly towards the fissure.

This one is pretty much a fairy tale, some kind of far future interpretation of Beauty and The Beast, an angle not visible to me when I initially wrote the story.

DARK HARVEST

"Get that machine offa me," screamed Dev. "I'm dying. I'm bleeding out!"

"You are not bleeding out," stated Jayce. "Your foot's back on already."

When Dev glanced down he started screaming louder. Loud enough to drown out the relentless cicada hum.

"Someone shut off that contraption," Jayce shouted over the top of both the screaming and the chorus of native bugs.

Commander Vassallo pulled his blaster, aimed it squarely at where she pointed – the Surgeco-460's forest of operating arms, many of which were snapping and stabbing wildly.

"Those things are worth a –"

Vassallo fired. Metal splinters rained against the portable generator's casing.

"Fortune," finished Stolk, coughing as acrid smoke fouled up the air.

"It's a goddamn goat rodeo in here," said Vassallo. "Those sack-o-shit 460s were supposed to have been decommissioned, on account of that... What was that trouble that went down on Memphis?"

Satordi snapped his fingers three times in a row. "Yeah, I remember something..."

"Was a couple of procedures gone totally tits up," said Jacey. "Literally. Was supposed to be a recall. Guess they missed a few."

Vassallo grunted. "More ExConn cheaparsery. Spending big everywhere but on the weedfront where it's needed."

Dev's screaming was getting louder.

"Jacey, give him a shot of something. Gotta be something stronger in the kit."

"I'm on it."

Troy straddled Dev to hold him down. Blood smeared over everything, making it hard for Jacey to get a grip. She wedged the hypo between her teeth, growled something unintelligible. Troy shifted his weight, pushed down on the patient's forearms.

Dev kept up his thrashing and screaming. Jacey spat the hypo into her hand, sat back on her haunches. Frowned. "Don't think its pain that's got him spooked."

207

The others crowded around to see for themselves. There was no fresh bleeding. The wound was sealed, a thick pink ridge, only the foot had been sewn on back to front.

She shook her head. "How do you even *make* a mistake like that?"

"Shit for mechabrains," said Vassallo, taking another pot shot at the robot, even though its arms had stopped flailing and it was listing severely to one side.

"Tangier, better call for MedEVac."

"What for? Nobody came when the weed busted containment. Nobody came to take the body bags."

"Just call it in."

"What about the rest of us? When are we getting off this stinking rock?"

"New orders," said Sergeant Vassallo, which was a lie. There'd been no messages from Platform, neither through the comms, nor private wire.

Dev, who had fallen silent as they all gawked at his foot, started his screaming up again in earnest. "Don't evac me to Orbital. You know what they say goes on up there. Leave the foot. I'm getting used to it. Hell, I'm used to it already!"

Vassallo put his gun away, satisfied that the 460 had been rendered smouldering scrap. "Can't have you fighting with your foot on back to front." He pulled his tobacco from his pocket, rolled a cigarette and jammed it between Dev's quivering lips. "Rest up for a few days, mercenary. You ain't missing anything down here."

He lit the smoke with his battered gold zippo. The one he'd souvenired from some ConnEX bigwig's corpse. Dev inhaled, pinched the cigarette between trembling fingers. "You know what they say about Orbital, Sarge. How the wounded come back different."

"Course you'll be different, buddy – you'll have your foot sown on the right way round!" He slapped Troy on the shoulder and pointed to the ring of whitewashed stones they'd arranged themselves after insurgents took out most of the landing platform.

Jayce and Troy heaved Dev onto a stretcher, then picked up either end.

"Those rumours are bullshit," Vassallo shouted after them. "Orbital only experiments on captured Tanks!"

Dev kept up his screaming as the other two placed the stretcher in the ring then ducked back under cover. So far there had been no captured Tanks. Just faceless shelling and the sense that they were being watched. By something.

All were surprised when a dark speck hovering like a vulture turned out to be a MedEVac copter. It swooped down close, extended pincers snapping, grabbed poor screaming Dev, and shot back up into the grey and brooding sky.

"Hey – come back you mother fucker! What about the rest of us? You can't leave us stranded here!"

Tangier kept on shouting. Vassallo stared across the smoking battlefield. Some of the all-terrain vehicles were still on fire. Some of the walls still crumbling of their own accord.

The rhythm of the copter blades was soothing. The planet had looked uninhabitable from the air. Litany: mostly useless rock, not enough water anywhere but the equator. That was where Reaper dug itself in deep; Executive Connect's pharmaceutical division. Protecting patented weed had seemed easy enough, only the weed didn't stay in the neat, dark strips where it was seeded. That weed had taken on a life of its own, clogging the air with stinking spores, twisting and poking into every nook and cranny. Infecting their machinery, jamming up its gears. Inducing nightmares, according to Satordi. And then, when the taste of the stuff had soured their water, their food and even their tobacco, bombardment started and jacks started getting killed. Rumours were whispered of similar scenarios on more than a dozen ExConn-seeded worlds. Of vat-grown terrorist insurgents: enormous, fit and organised. Resistant to high calibre persuasive interrogation. Self-terminating at their own convenience. Bloody hard to kill at anyone else's.

"Lotta DNA spilled on this damn rock," Satordi mumbled, fiddling with his gun. That man was always fiddling with something.

Sergeant Vassallo grunted in response. They stood and watched until the MedEVac copter and its wriggling, screaming cargo were reduced to the size and shape of a migrating bird.

What Vassallo now recognised as foreboding had hit when they first glimpsed Litany from space. That dark belt squeezing the equator. Transplanted, mutagenic pharmacrops with a multi-syllabic name. Referred to as 'the weed' by anyone who worked with it.

His gut warned there was something tainted about this dreary rock. Rumours of the weed mutating in unexpected ways. That its market value had already dropped by half. That the real reason the jacks were there was to gather intel on the Tanks. Terrorist insurgents that, six weeks ago, had not been firing at them.

No matter. Vassallo was on a mission of his own, tipped off by rumours of something worth big money. Something the pre-ExConn colonials left behind. Something all he had to do was find.

But after six weeks of intermittent rain, mud, blood and chasing shadows, Vassallo concluded that Litany had no secrets. There was nothing here worth anything: no rare mineral deposits, no seam of carbonado fancies. No weapons other than the Tanks themselves – if they were real.

Half their complement was already dead, leaving him stuck with dregs he couldn't trust. Executive Connect's Dark Harvest fireteams: cheaper than drones once they'd signed away their rights. Jacks like all jacks everywhere: mostly men, but not all. Mostly folks with bad credit ratings, reputations, attitudes or issues. Some were obvious recipients of bad advice. Smart enough to survive three weeks of basic. Dumb enough to enlist with ExConn in the first place, thinking they'd be getting a fresh new start. Most were running from something: someone they killed or failed to kill. More often than not their own demonic shadows.

At least two were serving community service placements. Satordi gave off a muted rapist vibe. Jayce was clocking hours towards her own command. Stolk, he might have considered an embedded corporate spy, only the kid seemed way too bright-eyed-dumb for that. A real know-it-all.

The rest were refugees from high unemployment stats, folks who figured shooting industrial terrorists was better than starving in some shanty ghetto.

"Tank breaking cover, dead ahead at twelve o'clock." Satordi grinned like a crazy man as what looked like a giant, semi-indestructible vat-grown, hairless ape stepped out into the open. The rest of them primed their weapons, expecting the thing to charge at the very least. But the creature stood its ground, scoping out their ragged camp, head cocked to one side like it was listening.

"Where's its weapon?" said Jayce.

The Tank moved.

"Fire!"

Satordi and Tangier emptied several clips into it, then whooped and hollered like it was the end of someone's war. The others joined in. Not Vassallo. Vassallo was waiting for the punchline. The follow up. The follow through. The point.

"This is where it gets interesting," said Stolk. "If I'm right – and I'm pretty sure."

Vassallo frowned. "What gets interesting?"

"They'll come," said Stolk. "The nuns. They always do."

"Nuns you say?"

"Wait... Wait... no. Yes! They're coming now..."

Two hours past Dev's evacuation and the subsequent blasting of the creature in the ruins, the bored jacks glanced to where Stolk was indicating, half expecting a drone, although they'd seen no drones on Litany thus far. Relentless ExConn blanket bombing had reduced the former settler capital Desiderata to rubble. Dark Harvest was tasked with mopping up the evidence.

Talk of tank-grown supersoldiers with impenetrable skin and embedded neuroprocessors had seemed ridiculous back on Platform, slouching around and waiting for the drop. Blurred images siphoned from patched perimeter feeds. Half man, half beast, all meat-and-gristle. But there'd been no trace of beast in what they'd killed. Just a man. A big one, yes, but still. Blasted to pieces that needed to be retrieved, only now Stolk was making them wait for no good reason.

Jayce rolled her eyes. "There's nothing out there, Dickwad. Just our kill and busted up old ruins."

"I'm telling you...," said Stolk, his voice trailing off so that all they could hear was their own boots pressing into gravel. "When there's a body – or parts thereof – that's when the nuns turn up. Watch!"

Sargeant Vassallo spat loudly on the ground, then looked towards the eastern aspect where smoke from yesterday's incendiaries was still emitting thick, choking gouts of sickly yellow. "Smells like concentrated piss," he said, nose twitching involuntarily. "I hate this fucking weed-infested strip."

The whole fireteam, Vassallo aside, stared intently at the blasted patch of ground where Stolk was pointing. "Wait for it," said Stolk. They waited.

A gentle tinkling carried on the breeze. A smudge of colour that for a moment might have been flame, but wasn't. It was cloth. Dirty orange-brown and it was moving.

"Told you," said Stolk, looking very pleased with himself. "I've seen them before – exactly the same, back when I was stationed on Agnes-Blanche.

"You were never on Aggie-Blanche," said Troy, a straw-haired teen from the Agricantus ghetto.

"Two damn winters full of it," Stolk answered. "Same Pharm-A paychecks. Flushing out mutant freaks – and *them*," he emphasised, pointing at what could now be seen clearly through the dregs of dissipating smoke. "Turning up in the aftermath of every kill."

Six figures, easy to see as their robes cut a stark contrast against grey stone rubble and smoking craters.

"Looters," said Satordi, his slack jaw working on a worn out wad of gum.

Even Vassallo was staring now as the small forms – women, by the looks of them, picked their way in single file across the ground.

"Not looters," said Stolk, in a learned tone, standing up straight, tucking hands into his pockets once he realised he had everyone's attention.

"Spies then? From one of ExConn's Pharm-A rivals?"

"Nope. Not spies." Stolk lowered his voice, as if sharing some great secret. "Nuns, like I keep telling you. From some way back religious cult. Used to know the name but I've forgotten."

"What the fuck is a nun?" said Troy.

"Like the Sisterhood of Damnation and Salvation – didn't you do school?" said Jayce.

Troy shrugged. Vassallo pulled out a field glass and trained it on the six. "Don't like the look of them. Could be insurgents. Could be in disguise."

"They're holy women," said Stolk. "Watch what happens next."

They watched, Satordi slapping the safety off his CheyTac660. Just in case. The others heard the sound but didn't copy.

The corpse wasn't easy to spot. Grey stone dust covered everything that wasn't already shrouded in lingering smoke. The nuns, identical at a distance, sifted rubble.

"Gross," said Troy.

None of the others spoke. The kid was green. He hadn't seen anything yet.

With great gentleness, the nuns placed salvaged body parts together, then continued to search.

"Told you they was looters."

"Will you shut the fuck up and watch!"

"Looking for wood," said Vassallo. "Not much to burn out here." He took a crushed, hand-rolled cigarette from his top pocket, then pinched it back into shape. Placed it on his lower lip, patted his trouser pockets until he found what he was after.

"Blessing the corpse?" said Satordi uncertainly.

"Nope," Vassallo lit the tip of the cigarette, drew on it hard, held the smoke deep in his lungs.

"Cremating it." Smoke blasted out of both nostrils, then dissipated quickly without trace. "Right, Stolk?"

"Right!" Stolk liked it when Vassallo agreed with him. It didn't happen often. "It's a spiritual thing. Takes 'em hours. They sit there chanting till it's done, then they muck about in the ashes for souvenirs."

"Souvenirs?"

"To them, the Tanks are holy. Diamonds and pearls are supposed to form in dead Tank ashes."

"Bullshit," said Satordi, aiming his weapon, squinting through the scope.

Sure enough, yellow-orange flames were soon licking up from the base of the rough, triangular arrangement of wood, mostly salvaged from the splintered doorway of a building no longer standing. The nuns sat in a circle around the pyre, palms pressed together, shaven heads bowed deep in prayer.

"This is their holy war. Gotta try and see it from their perspective."

Satordi wasn't interested in other people's perspectives. He kept his finger on the trigger, right eye glued to the scope, still trained on the group of chanting, praying nuns.

"They might be enemy soldiers," said Troy. "How are we supposed to know what they is or ain't?"

"In disguise," added Satordi.

"What kind of a disguise is orange bed sheets?"

"You could fit a luger under there. Easy peasy."

Vassallo shook his head.

"You saw that Tank up close before you air conditioned it. Built like a brick shithouse. Biceps like cypress roots. Those skinny little runts aren't soldiers – no matter what ordnance they might be packing under bed sheets."

"They might be gathering intel. Reporting back to those monster tank-grown motherfuckers."

"Stolk knows all about it," said Jayce. "Ask him anything. He's a regular walking Wiki."

Stolk looked up. He'd been taking notes. "I'm just interested is all. Don't you ever get interested?"

Satordi snorted. "I'm interested in lots of things. Like when we're busting off this lousy rock."

He didn't look at Vassallo when he spoke, but they'd all been thinking it. Too many had died. Even by the pathetic standards of ExConn's contractual obligations, Dark Harvest should have been evacuated by now.

"We stay until the job gets done," said Vassallo grimly.

"And what job might that be?" said Satordi. "If the weed's no good, it means we won't get paid."

Nobody said anything after that. A cold front started moving in, with brooding skies to match. The nuns kept chanting, regardless, even when drizzle forced the jacks back under cover of ripped tarpaulin.

"What kind of religion makes you pray out in the rain?"

"An old one," muttered Jayce. "Stolk reckons they pray to some fat old god."

"Stolk nodded. "Like I said, they're raking for holy relics. They stay put, even under fire."

"Diamonds," said Jayce, grinning. That sounds interesting."

Satordi's eyes widened.

"No no... not real diamonds. They call it ringsel. Supposed to be pearls of concentrated purity. Or something."

"So not real diamonds," said Satordi, shifting his weight.

Jayce pulled a face.

Stolk raised his glass to see what the nuns were doing. "I got up real close to some of them, back on Aggie-Blanche. At first you think they're all the same, like sisters, only they aren't. Not if you look careful. You can make out the different –"

"Come on, let's get moving. We got no time for this." Vassallo flicked the butt of his cigarette against a low stone wall – or what was left of it.

"I want to stay and watch," said Stolk.

Vassallo sniffed. "Fine, mercenary, suit yourself."

"Don't like the look of that sky," said Vassallo. He sniffed deeply, like a dog. "I don't like the smell of it."

"Smoke from the bombardment."

"Something else."

They all looked where he was looking, as if something might be gleaned from moody grey-on-grey. Stolk was the only one not checking out the weather front. His glass was aimed in the opposite direction where the nuns were still hard at their chant and prayer.

"How come you know everything, Stolk?" said Satordi. "You some sort of archaeologist?"

Stolk lowered the glass. "No, man. Read a lot is all. It's kind of interesting, don't you reckon?"

"No. I don't reckon. Not if the diamond thing is bullshit. What I reckon is we ought shoot them."

"Sociologist is what you mean," said Jayce. "Archaeologists do ruins. Not much architecture going down here before ExConn. Not unless you count those cinderblock bunkers."

"Well, actually..."

"Oh, so you an expert on Hargreave System colonial architecture too now are you, Stolk?"

Stolk's face reddened further.

"Anything coming through on the link?"

Tangier tapped his earpiece, then shook his head.

"Those nuns of yours – they got a temple?"

Stolk shrugged. "Probably targeted in the first wave of blanket bombings. Just in case, you know, they were harbouring insurgents."

"Better to be safe than sorry," said Jayce.

"Better," agreed Satordi, polishing his gun.

"I can't believe they're still sitting out there." Satordi paced back and forth, shiny pulse rifle slung over his shoulder. "Any word from Orbital? Did Dev get up there safe?"

"Nothing for hours," said Tangier. "Some kind of interference."

"So what about the rest of us – when do we get lifted off?"

Vassallo stared out over the battlefield at the grim and dirty sky, at the thunderhead sweeping in across the plain like it knew what it was doing. Which might have been the truth of it. They'd all heard the chit chat before making planetfall. Rumours easy to ignore before the service robots started acting funny, the weed got moving of its own accord and the Tanks turned out to be real as advertised.

Some said the terrorist insurgents of Litany did more than grow their soldiery in vats. That they brewed their weapons of mass destruction by harnessing elemental forces. Hot rocks blasting randomly from natural subterranean foundries. Base Four dissolved in a boiling mess of lava, despite the geological survey claiming it safe. Despite them all being kitted up and standing by. Why wouldn't they harness the very wind itself? Or the air or the darkness or whatever other magic those godless squatters conjured into being.

The wind whipped up, snatching roughly at the tents and tarps, scattering half-filled plastic canisters and other sundry items like dead leaves.

"I don't like this," said Vassallo.

Stolk was already on his feet, dusting ashy grit from his trousers, shooting a final glance out at the nuns. The wind slammed into them, knocked a couple sprawling. They didn't flinch, just stood up again, backs ramrod straight, continued with their chant like nothing happened.

The thunderhead kept its distance. The rain it heralded did not. It pummelled down in violent blasting sheets.

Stolk kept watch on the nuns through a rent in the tarpaulin. By then the rain had slackened off and steam rose off the streets in great white gouts.

"I don't trust 'em, Sarge," said Satordi, nudging Stolk aside, ripping the tarpaulin hole till it was big enough to see through without stooping. "They're still at it. Up to something. Planning an attack. Gathering intel, laying charges. I dunno but I can smell it. I know a pack of terrorists when I see one."

"You've never seen a terrorist, son," said Vassallo. "Nobody has. Not out this far. Just done over colonists, contract strip-miners, smugglers, religious whack jobs fleeing persecution in the Belt."

"Those tank-bred insurgents..."

"No such thing. Just freedom fighters with differing definitions of the word and the accompanying states of mind."

Satordi opened his mouth but he didn't get the chance to argue. An explosion rattled the tentpoles, their already battered stacks of supposedly sensitive equipment and Vassallo's dental implants.

"What the –"

"Too close for comfort." Tangier fired up the seismograph and slammed it down on the stack of charts covering their one and only portable table.

"That thunderhead, Commander – it's full of acid and it's coming right at us."

"What the holy fuck?"

They both looked to the tarpaulin, already ripped and completely useless.

"Call for evac..."

"Not enough time. No time for anything. Gotta pick up and run."

"The ruins?"

"Nothing we can trust. But the holo points to a series of caves sunk right into the mountain."

"Fall out! Take whatever you can carry!"

They shouldered packs and grabbed free-standing items. Water, half a case of MREs, blankets and lanterns. Guns and ammo. The all-purpose, all weather beacon that was most certainly not designed with acid storms in mind. As they stumbled across the rock-and-brick strewn landscape –

growing darker and colder by the minute – Stolk stopped and turned to see if he could catch sight of the nuns. They'd gone – and he was very glad of that.

The cave was dark and smelled of hairy animal.

Tangier slapped the beacon upside, checked the power cell was ticking over.

"Careful with that fucking thing. It's all that stands between us and an airlift." Satordi's pacing was putting them all on edge. "Why aren't they answering? Why didn't they lift us off three hours ago?"

"Dark Harvest fireteam broadcasting from Litany. DMS lat 1° 21' 7.4988" N. DMS long 103° 49' 11.4096" E. Can you hear me? Over."

"Ain't nobody gonna be hearing you over that. Air's thick with acid. We're probably breathing ourselves to death." When Troy blew his nose, the wad of gauze filled with watery pink.

"Step back from the entrance, you moron!"

Troy edged back. Stolk held his ground. There wasn't much to see out there. The storm had blanketed what little light the sky was clinging to.

"This is Dark Harvest fireteam broadcasting from Litany. DMS lat 1° 21' 7.4988" N. DMS long 103° 49' 11.4096" E. We request immediate evac. Over."

Stolk couldn't get those nuns out of his mind. Were they out there cowering in the ruins, skin pockmarked and smoking? Or was an acid-bearing thunderhead as normal as sun showers on this crazy rock?

"See anything?" he asked Satordi.

The big man grunted his response, which might have been a yes or no or maybe. Moments later, he staggered backwards, grappled for his sidearm, was knocked to the ground as a Tank burst into the cave.

Up close, a supersoldier, easily twice the size of Vassallo – and he was a bigger man than most. The thing – because it was a thing – with rivulets of acid water running harmlessly in channels down its limbs, kicked Stolk aside and strode in further, giant ham hands curling into fists.

Jacks who'd been resting struggled to their feet, slipping safeties, locking and loading, slapping themselves to responsive wakefulness. Jayce fired. Too slow. The monster smacked the blaster from her hands before picking her up and throwing her against the wall. Solid muscle. Lightening fast. Others fired, bullets going everywhere, Vassallo screaming *hold your fire*. Too late. The fuggy cave air stung with bullets. The thing went down in a hail of rapid fire. Eventually. Once on the ground it did not still until Vassallo shot it right between the eyes.

"Orbital's gonna have a fit – you know how much a Tank brain must be worth?"

"They can bill me," said Vassallo, crouching down, poking the corpse a couple of times before searching for a pulse.

"Synthetic?"

"Not so far as I can tell."

"Indigenous?"

"Not likely." He gave the corpse a solid kick.

"So who – or what – the hell is it?"

Vassallo sniffed. "It kinda depends on who you ask. There are rumours that these soldiers might be souped up squatters."

The others could tell from his voice that he didn't believe that.

"What's the unofficial line?" said Stolk.

Vassallo stared down at the corpse. "That weed we're supposed to be protecting? Word is they didn't graft it in from EverGreen. Word is ExConn poached it from the early wave of settlers before driving them off and running for the hills. Back in the day, before this sector got its Pharm-A annexation. Before the razor blight of '99. Archive retrieval gets a little hazy past that point."

"What the hell kind of weed is it anyway? What makes it so valuable?"

Vassallo shrugged. "Supposed to be an Ur-strain. Brazilian something-or-other, reconstituted from frozen seed bank stock. Antibiotic properties. It'll clap out in a couple years like they all do."

"Must be worth big bucks though – now."

"Yeah," he nodded, fumbling for his dwindling tobacco stash. "Now."

"So lemme get this straight," said Troy, looking younger than ever in the murky half-light of the cave. "The squatters of Litany are really a bunch of pre-colonials who reckon ExConn boosted their weed? They ran for the hills when the blanket bombing started, then built a bunch of Tanks to come and fight us?"

"Maybe. Hard to say without clapping eyes on the so-called 'pre-colonials' face-to-face."

"We clapped eyes on them hours ago," said Stolk. "Watched them comb the ruins for their dead."

"Those nuns didn't look much like farmers."

"How would you know what a farmer looks like – have you ever seen one?"

Troy shrugged.

"Course he hasn't. He's too young. Damn kid hasn't seen anything yet." Satordi walked over and kicked the corpse. "Except that. Kid, better savour the moment. Not many folks come up against something like this close quarters and live to tell of it."

"You sure it ain't human?" said Troy, staring hard at the corpse's cold dead face.

Satordi shrugged.

"Rain's stopped," said. Stolk. "That's something."

Jacey knelt beside the corpse, lifted its loincloth. "Well, there's something else." She let the cloth fall back in place. "No man or lady bits – unless it's packing them on the inside."

A couple of the others wanted a look. Not Troy – he'd seen enough. He walked to the nearest stretch of free cave wall, put his back against it and slunk down to his knees.

"That came out of a vat," said Vassallo. "No question. Just like all the rumours said."

He would have added more, but the cloying cave air filled with their collective breath, sweat, blood and fear stilled as a new element was added. Not smell this time, but sound. The soft tinkling of bells getting louder and louder.

The nuns emerged from darkness, appearing one by one like flames igniting in the entrance to the cave. The fireteam scrambled to attention, grabbing weapons, flipping safety catches. Aiming right between the eyes and waiting.

The nuns said nothing. They waited too, staring neither at the mercenaries, their guns, nor at the bullet-ridden Tank on the cave floor. They appeared to be staring into the middle distance.

Stolk, closer than the others, noted the condition of their robes. Singed and splattered with corrosive stains, but otherwise the women were unharmed.

"You can't come in here," said Satordi. "Piss off or we'll fire."

"Maybe they're just trying to get out of the rain?"

"Shut up, Stolk. It stopped raining. I don't like it, Sarge."

Vassallo stared at the women hard. They did look like sisters, all minted from one mould. But the longer he stared, the more he started to notice subtle differences. A pinpoint mole above a lip, a flatter, uglier nose. Peripheral vision revealed Troy gripping his pulse rifle way too hard. Not a weapon to be fired at close quarters.

"Sarge, can't we just let them have the body?" said Stolk.

"Orbital will want it for examination."

"Orbital's left us all down here to rot."

"They want it, they can come and get the rest of us," cut in Satordi.

"Damn straight, man," said Troy.

Vassallo nodded thoughtfully. The nuns didn't move, but he noticed the eyes of the one on the farthest right snap into focus. She stared at him and didn't blink, like a snake flushed out of scrub, poised and waiting to gauge if it was time to strike.

"Tangier, how's that signal coming along?"

"Negative, Commander. Loads of static, but I've patched into both Platform and Orbital's long range sensors. Satcom's still holding its position – I can see it."

"Well," said Satordi, "That's something."

"What else can you source through the uplink?"

"Nothing new. Surface-to-air coms are definitely scrambled. Can access stored data from server banks, but that's all. Nothing real time. Nothing new."

All six pairs of female eyes were now trained on Vassallo, which made him more inclined than ever to stand his ground.

"Frisk them," he said coolly, glancing at the kid.

Troy shook his head. "No way, Sarge, I ain't touching. What if I get cursed?"

Jayce snorted.

"Might be anything under those robes. A bomb or something worse."

"Just give 'em the corpse. That's all they want," said Stolk.

"How the hell do you know what they want?"

Stolk didn't answer. A comforting sound bleeding in from outside the cave was capturing everyone's attention. The steady whirring snick of rotary blades.

"Evac – thank fucking mother mercy!"

Better late than never, thought Vassallo. *Suspiciously convenient, for once.*

"Get out of the way," he snapped at the nuns. They obeyed, shuffling soundlessly to one side, Troy's weapon trained on their centre mass.

"Fall out," said Vassallo. The jacks moved, single file, scrambling down the rocky incline, squelching through great fistfuls of weed that, Vassallo was pretty sure, had not been there mere hours ago when they'd run for shelter in the cave. Weed apparently unaffected by acid rain. Weed that stunk like rotting flesh when he crushed it underfoot.

Venerable Viridis waited patiently until the troop carrier's slicing blades could no longer be distinguished over other more subtle sounds: the howling wind that gusted through the settlement ruins, etching and disintegrating walls that were never meant to last a century, certainly not two in this ferocious and unpredictable climate. Cave walls were thick and insulating, but her hearing was better than most. She waited until the steady pattern of highly mineralised water dripping upon limestone echoed softly throughout the cavernous chamber in which the venerable sisters knelt.

She nodded almost imperceptibly. Venerable Kaletra struck the small gong and the chamber filled with harmonious resonation. Venerable Duodopa began the softly whispered chant that would envelop the dharmapala and bring it comfort. Venerable Teveten got to her feet and sprinkled the dharmapala with dragon's breath: the precious liquid distilled from pyrophoric compounds that the venerable sisters used sparingly when no other combustable material was available. A secret recipe so closely guarded that even Venerable Charantia herself did not know what constitutional elements it possessed.

The wheel was spun. Prayers were offered for the dharmapala: that its passage might be swift and resolute. A second prayer: that the blessed ringsel raked from its holy ashes might illuminate the way for those who followed.

All six sisters backed away as Venerable Viridis bowed, then lit the flame. The dragon's breath performed with great efficiency, one of the few elements capable of disintegrating synthetic skin, vat-grown muscle and carbon-bonded bone. The immolation process would take four or five hours throughout which the venerable sisters would pray and chant, assisting the dharmapala's progression on the wheel.

A dharmapala's remains were not always forthcoming. Sometimes the carefully raked ash revealed nothing more than fragments of bioceramic tooth and bone. But today was auspicious. As the first rays of dawn spilled over the broken landscape, filling the cave with both hope and illumination, Venerable Kaletra's gently wielded bamboo rake tapped against something small and hard. A diamond the size of one of the bitter blue berries that grew along the mountain's underside. The sisters stared in wonder before Venerable Viridis removed a small wooden box from the folds of her robe. The blessed ringsel was placed gently within its padded lining and the sisters rose to begin their journey home.

It had often been remarked that the hum of machinery embedded deep within the mountain's heart reminded the listener of the hum of bees. Or, at other times, cicadas. A far from accidental factor, a sound both comforting and protective.

The Venerable sisters walked in single file along a track that took them past the remains of the invaders' encampment. The angry rain had fused their leavings to the earth. Steaming angular shapes protruded from a slurry of green and grey. The rain had not always been so angry. Likewise, the invaders had not come so often. In earlier days they had done no more than establish a perimeter around the baccaris trees and had shown so little interest in the hives themselves. The sisters had gone about their business, harvesting propolis in small quantities; processing its resins, balsams and waxes. Extracting viscidone from baccaris flowers, producing medicines and salves.

Where their village had once stood lay now a stony field. Invaders had come in massive shiny ships with offers of relocation to a better way of life. But the life they offered was not better, they could see this in the sallow tinting of the invaders' skin, their clouded, speckled irises; the accompanying ailment of spirit, pain-bleached auras, weariness of heart.

The invaders burned the village down, pulled up the trees, smoked out the bees and stole the hives. The villagers had no choice but to flee to the caves worming through the mountainside. After that, the invaders left them alone, more or less. New invaders came. New trees were planted in the old ones' places. Same as the old trees, although genetic tweaking meant they didn't smell the same. Neither did the bees, or the pollen, or the propolis.

The venerable sisters listened to their bees. Knowledge was the truest power. There were other worlds and other gardens. Other ways of fighting, ways of seeing.

Venerable Viridis bowed before the illuminated gateway, a machine that had gone by another name in another time and place. She pulled the small wooden box from the folds of her robes, then handed it over to Venerable Charantia, who bowed in turn.

Venerable Charantia was pleased to see the single yet strikingly perfect diamond ringsel snug on a velvet cushion. She placed the diamond within the illuminated gateway's altar, bowed once more, then closed the hatch.

Several of the other industrious venerable sisters disengaged from their tasks to observe the data now flowing freely across the sturdy bank of mismatched screens and monitors stacked almost to the ceiling of the cave. The top row had lichen clinging to their casings, thin toadstools poking from the spaces in-between. Statistics, measurements, assessments, recordings of the invaders' camp. Intercepted transmissions: everything from the chemical composition of their food and waste to their speculation about the venerable sisters themselves. The fear of what they named the *supersoldier*, their distrust of the chants and prayers. The fact that they didn't understand what they were doing here. The lord they served was dark and cruel. Some ran from shadows, others from themselves.

"All interpretations must be studied, analysed and calibrated," said Venerable Charantia.

"They think we made the burning rain," said Venerable Viridis.

Venerable Charantia nodded. "They think a great many peculiar things," she said.

Venerables Duodopa and Kaletra were studying map projections, tracing supply lines with slender bamboo sticks. Taking note of the patches of verdant green, some which had been present on the last intercepted ringsel map, some not.

On each of a series of circular, elevated daises at the far end of the machine-filled cavern sat eight dharmapalas, each in the lotus position. Colourful offerings had been placed before them: ceramic dishes holding flowers, grains and fruits native to this planet. Painted prayers adorned their skin, applied with ochre chipped and pounded from the cavern walls.

Venerable Viridis stepped up to the nearest. She bowed, then stepped in closer, leaned forward to whisper in its ear. "Namaste"

The dharmapala opened its diamond-bright eyes.

With this tale, the dialogue came first and the plot and setting kind of coalesced around it. I'd been researching Buddhist history in order to write *The Seventh Relic* when some of the nuns escaped from that story and hacked their way into this one.

PRAYERS TO BROKEN STONE

1. Eyes I Dare Not Meet in Dreams

The apartment is musty. No one has been in here for a very long time. Arpita tugs the curtains, letting in a blast of light. To do so is permitted, on the list of things she is allowed to and supposed to do.

Dusty boxes in need of unpacking clump together against a plain cream wall. The box cutter is in the drawer where *they* said it would be. Everything is always exactly where the voice on the phone says it will be.

Old furniture belonging to a different era. Ancient hardwood, stained, too ugly to be valuable.

She wasn't allowed to bring the notes she'd scribbled when they called. They expect her to memorise ordinary lists of ordinary-sounding tasks, but nothing is ordinary about this job or this place.

Arpita slits tape, unpacks each box slowly and thoughtfully, examining every object in case it is more than it seems: long-life milk, tea bags in packets of 100, slim rectangular tubes of coffee pods. The coffee machine on the grey marble bench top looks like it has never been used.

Two double beds in separate rooms with mismatched sets of sheets. She's surprised by the wardrobe in the master bedroom; an ancient monstrosity with large, dark keyholes, wafting smells of naphthalene and tennis shoes. One much like it stood in the grand Bengali mansion where Aunt Laksha worked. Aunt Laksha used to sneak the sisters past the wrought-iron gates. The young girls made a castle of that wardrobe, imagining themselves princesses and queens.

Arpita dismisses her memories brusquely. She makes both beds and stacks the linen closet with towels pulled free from placental wrappings.

She took this job because it pays more than any other job she's ever had. The extra money is supposed to buy her silence. In eighteen months she has learnt nothing more than what brands of tinned and packaged foods can be conveniently stocked in different cupboards. Only once has her employer's agent come to meet her, a woman who declined to give her name. She looked disturbingly like Arpita; of similar height and build. Similar skin, yet not one of her people. Different hair, but changing hair is easy.

The woman stared her down and said, *whatever it is you're looking for, stop here. Stop now. Trust me.* She put her hand on Arpita's and it was cold, the look in the woman's eyes much colder.

There are always phones in the apartments. Old-fashioned landlines made of dull green plastic. If a phone rings, Arpita is supposed to leave. Immediately. Just drop whatever she is doing and get out, never to return unless instructed.

In eighteen months she has obeyed every command, from unpacking boxes to calling numbers and leaving incomprehensible messages. Sometimes simple tasks are required, such as purchasing a bottle of Dior perfume at Myers, placing it on the second shelf in a bathroom cabinet. Other things, all too ordinary to speak of.

Arpita lives in motels they designate and pay for. That part she doesn't mind – she'd been staying with distant relatives barely known to her. Had they searched for her that first night she didn't come home? A question she ponders frequently as she cleans apartments that, as far as she can tell, are rarely used. Which should make them safe, but doesn't. *Safe as houses,* something her Port Hedland case manager used to say. Safe as houses… a peculiar phrase, whatever such words were supposed to mean.

Once Arpita spent six weeks in a red brick house waiting for a call that never came, sleeping in an enormous double bed with ill-fitting sheets.

It's Wednesday and she's dusting venetian blinds in the master bedroom. The phone rings, a jarring clamouring like bells, unsettling in the electronic age. She pauses the duster mid-air. Three minutes can be plenty of time, or not enough if your personal items are scattered.

She knows what she is supposed to do, but this time something stops her. She freezes, waiting for the awful noise to cease. Then Arpita does something she has never done before. Picks up her shoulder bag, takes off her shoes, and climbs into the dark and musty wardrobe.

Her heart is pounding and she knows she's crossing a line, that she doesn't know what she's doing, that apartments such as this one are not safe – nowhere is safe, that she might get killed if she sees something she shouldn't, that of course she will see something because everything is forbidden to her here. Everything. But it's too late, three minutes have drained away, then another one, then another and another.

Her right foot is beginning to cramp when metal jangles and a key turns in the lock.

2. In Death's Dream Kingdom

I watch and listen. That's what they pay me for. Not a bad job, really, but I've been working here too long. The anti-social hours fall within my comfort zone, as does overtime, cab vouchers, meal allowance, and blissful solitude during the graveyard shift. An oversized, padded swivel chair and a big fat bank of sixteen monitors. A slim window sits above the penguin clock I brought from home; tinted and permanently stuck fast. Always chilly – air conditioning's there for the machinery, not me.

I sift data for politicians. Record and splice together news they don't have time to watch, with eyes glazed over – I can do this in my sleep – sometimes it's like that's exactly what I'm doing.

Management locked us out of gaming, Twitter, Facebook, Tumblr and Instagram. E-mail's permitted – I IM folks all around the world. One of my regulars is a woman called Morgan. Not her real name. Probably American. I used to think our jobs were similar: watching screens, summarising data. Morgan twigged to my civilian status early. Stopped using heavy military jargon I struggled to get my head around.

She might be military but she's not infallible. They call her station 'the Caribbean' – pretty sure that's code for someplace cold – where shifts last 24 hours in capsules buried 60 feet below. She too has a swivel chair, but only four old monitors, black and white; two keyboards and a box her people refer to as 'the key'.

She says her people get slung a lot of tests: long checklists, learn-by-rote, and sleepless nights. Fake alerts come in at all hours with flashing lights and nerve-grating alarms. The pumped-in air stinks like a backed-up sewer. Vibrating floors make them nauseous and antsy. They're off their faces half the time on stuff she calls 'bath salts.' They scour their capsules in search of secret cameras but the ever-flickering fluorescent lighting conceals all evidence and proof.

Sounds like hell.

Another slow shift in my own shitty job. Sixteen screens showing nothing of local interest: Al Qaeda insurgents striking back in Yemen. Gaza, where they're making gas masks out of jars and paper towels. North Kivu awash with starving Congolese. Janjaweed proxy militias continue systematic hammering of Darfur villages. North and South Korea... not much happening – nothing new. A French tiger helicopter raid in Mali – gotta love those 'surgical' missile strikes.

My bottommost right-hand screen is stuck on a live train station feed. People waiting on a concourse under a big old clock. Unusual, no explanation in the shift handover notes. Not my problem, Someone else can sort it in the morning.

My eyes are dry.

Just past the witching hour, up pops an IM window. Morgan. She never wastes my time with pleasantries. Gets straight down to whatever's in her head.

"This whole bloody subculture," Morgan types, "You get inklings of it on TV. What was underground is now mainstream. This whole hybrid happening. The mentality. They're carrying a lot of hurt."

"Who's carrying hurt – are you watching what I'm watching?" I reply, then backspace over my words. Of course she isn't. I've figured out she's Air Force, stationed somewhere in the wilds of the USA or Alaska.

What I'm watching is text scrolling along the bottom of three screens claiming the Syrian Mujahideen are taking the fight to the Assadist enemy. Shabiha forces holed up in a building when the Mujahideen come busting through. Pale gouts of smoke envelop crumbling cement. Trees shiver beside the satellite dishes.

"I've got toxic strain," Morgan continues. "Spent too much time doing the jobs nobody wanted. I'm used to a different kind of chaos. There are cameras everywhere. In the foyer, glass tubes hanging off the ceiling. I miss Alexander, my ex."

I pause before replying. She's told me about her ex so many times. "Thought your husband's name was Dominic?"

She pauses. Three little wavering dots onscreen. "Alexander or Dominic. One of the two. I mix them up. I've got head trauma. Hairdressers don't like cutting my hair because of it."

Morgan can get pretty random sometimes – some nights more random than others. Sounds like tonight is going to be a doozy.

I rest my fingers. My feeds seem to be stuck on Syria for the long haul. Insurgents caught up in an extreme firefight with SAA Troops in Atman. Small arms fire, mostly, but I can just make out impressions of heavy urban terrain fire fighting in the background.

I wait to see if she'll bring the chitchat back to Dominic – or Alexander – but she doesn't. Way back I concluded that Morgan has never actually been married. That Morgan has, at best, a tenuous grip. She's never once asked after my own sorry marital condition. She likes to talk. She's not much of a listener.

Three dots blinking, waiting.

An innocuous, gradient sky fills my screens. Clipped bursts of Arabic, a young guy firing in Adidas knock-offs, dusty blue jeans, ammo cartridge striped in his nation's colours. *Allah Akbar*, he says. *Allah Akbar.* No protection but sandbags and thin trees.

I'm going to keep the IM window open till Morgan gets bored and goes away. She used to ping some of the other guys but now she just pings me. Didn't take long for Leskie and Wazza to call it like it is. Contradicting her terms, her frames of reference: *Morgan, you were not on board the Rainbow Warrior when it blew. Morgan, you never signed with the French Foreign legion. They don't take chicks – and if you reckon you speak French, go on then – prove it.*

I don't believe her either. Reckon Morgan reads a lot of magazines. She's recounted in great detail black ops in jungle terrains. Bagging dead bodies. Digging maggots out of her flesh with a bowie knife.

"I avoid the packs," she told me once. "I just can't run any more. I've got scars all over my body. Scars on my arms. Scars on my legs. Scars on my hands. Scars on my side. Gotta do gym just to get the aggro out."

On my screens blurred forms streak past flaming ruins. Bare arms against stripped trees. Fighters dragging fallen comrades through dark soil. Back against the split brick wall, hurrying down grenade-blasted streets. Tanks trembling with the aftershock.

"The soldiers all wear protective gear," says Morgan. "They reckon ESP exists. Based on random possibility and the speed of technology. In Kabul, you know not to touch these guys. So long as you do nothing wrong, you're fine…"

There's nothing fine about the long-range firefight live streaming from Afghanistan. The onscreen battle contains small arms fire, sniper rifles, machine guns, and an A10 Support Scattershot cloud peppered over orange sunrise. Machine gun rounds like popcorn. Rapid fire. Pop pop pop. Mist rising off distant mountains. "Coming between right peak and right here," the onscreen soldier shouts. His face obscured in shadow. "Got more coming your way, friend!"

I take a slug of warm Red Bull, shift my weight as a tattooed insurgent fires through the smoke, which goes from white to black, to vaporised. Big gun mounted on a Toyota flatbed. The whole thing shudders when it fires.

On the screen below, footage of the seizure of Khan al-Asal. Scrolling text in Arabic, superimposed over masked men firing through gaps in an ancient stone wall. Cut to big guns firing out the side of a dirt-streaked combi. The vehicle shakes with every bright blast of yellow.

When the smoke clears, I'm staring at a firefight in woodland terrain. Some other fucking country altogether. I sit up and say out loud, "Hey wait – is that Bosnia?"

Nobody answers – obviously. Wouldn't be the first night shift I've ended up talking to myself.

Onscreen, infantry trudge uphill through waist-high foliage, leaves dull, khaki green. Walky-talkies passed from hand to hand, pale faces daubed with shadow stripes. Arguing over directions. Out of the sunlight, uniforms meld with the muddy tree trunks and rotting leaves.

"Saw a soldier suicide," says Morgan. "He had caps in his teeth. I turned around and he wasn't there any more. Only a few of us stuck with the mortuary run. You lose your memory. That's why no one wants the job. My friend was the Russian who got done with polonium. I knew him as an Englishman. I remember standing, watching some dead people after a tank accident. Married an Englishman. Don't know if he's alive or dead. That's reality in the twenty-first century…"

AT4 rocket live fire footage. A10 Thunderbolts blitzing already arid fields. Vignettes of greedy, gobbling flames digest a row of tanks, canary yellow, through blazon orange, demon red, then finally to belching chokes of charcoal.

I lean in closer. This war looks familiar. Really familiar, only I hardly ever pay attention to the European feeds. The monitor room's gone very dark. I can barely make out past the edge of the desk. Can't even see the penguin clock or the glow that usually bleeds in from the streetlights.

"It's chaos if you buy into the information," says Morgan. "Like playing a computer game. I'm walking through town and there's this enormous screen. A cartoon character's eyes pop out and he looks at me and winks. Satellites can track us wherever we go. The military are transmorphing and transposing all realities."

My screens seem closer, bigger, more immediate, each one filled with city ruins in black and white. Footage from an older war in dreary smudges of colour. A woman running ahead of shuffling crowds, like constipated lava. Men in brown lining up to get their guns. Loading boxes. Marching with fists raised.

"What. The fuck. Am I watching?"

"I'm a believer in eternity," says Morgan. "The future doesn't exist and the past doesn't exist. That's why I don't believe in time travel. You get tethered to people. Just take it as it comes. A whole other world we're not meant to be aware of."

I realise I'm no longer typing. Morgan's slow southern drawl continues inside my head. Too many cigarettes. Too many nightmares.

The feeds change back to black and white; ruins and rubble, peasants wailing for lost children, lost men. Unfamiliar aircraft in the background.

"There was this funeral in town," says Morgan softly. "Only one mourner. A soldier. Everyone else was in the shadows. Some people know me from the past – and others from the future. You got to be nice to them. I never get involved in the machinations."

Two soldiers in skin-tight jumpsuits step in from the left – their uniforms are like something out of sci-fi. The smaller one carries a gun that's half her size.

"Gotta go," I say to Morgan. She doesn't answer. The IM chat box has vanished from my screen.

"She got disconnected," I explain to the empty room. It's all just darkness like the sky behind the ruins. No screen. No walls. No sound.

The close air reeks of cordite, dust, and ash. And something else – dead flesh. As the soldiers approach, the tall one pulls his helmet off. The small one slings the gun across her shoulder.

"No."

"You don't fall through the thin ice unless you've walked there before," says Morgan. It's her, no mistake, standing right in front of me. Hair lank and greasy, fallen bodies strewn about her feet.

"I spent my entire life expecting people to die," she whispers. "Life's just like that. Good and bad at the same time."

But I'm not listening. That tall soldier has me spooked. Something about the shape of him and the way he shifts his weight. When the helmet's off, he runs gloved fingers through clipped hair. My hair.

"I've got ghosts," says Morgan. "They cling to us when they want to."

I shake my head but the soldier doesn't see me. A radio crackles and he talks into his wrist. With my voice, my lips, my blunt inflections. I'm still shaking when both of them step out of the screens and walk right through me, boots and all.

3. Sunlight on a Broken Column

Esther is not certain of this city or the date. She has been awake for 100 hours, running from The Soldier with the straight white teeth and sniper rifle. Sheltering in doorways, cowering in the back of cafes, dimly lit, or the protective, garish glare of McDonald's, with its stale fat stench, plastic furniture, and nobody paying attention to anyone else.

The brisk wind brings her mind into sharp focus. The camera slung across her torso bangs against her hip. This is Sydney and she is pretending to be a tourist, easily blending with youth hostel backpackers: tattoos, piercings, Paddy Palin kit, but when The Soldier smiled, he knew and she knew he knew. She'd been made and she's been moving ever since. On alert and perpetually on the run.

Esther is the name they gave her, a diminutive of the Goddess Ishtar or perhaps an ancient Persian name for star – she can't remember. Esther has had many names and many, many briefs. So many countries, so many exit routes.

She presses her face against the bus window, camera balanced on her knees, observing backstreets thick with casualties of suburban wars: the ancient, the hard-bitten, the weary, and the desperate. No smiles to spare. Withered hands fumble coins, roll-your-owns pinched between sour lips, shapeless women in floral polyester, urchins darting between varicose calves.

The bus shudders, flinging Esther backwards. Leviathan faces pout down at her from billboards. Torn paper hangs in pastel curlicues, weeds lunge between pavement cracks. Wind sends garbage pirouetting in the updraft.

She is safe here on this rattling bus – for the moment.

The 309 crawls through urban wastelands, slinks past terraces huddled in rows. Abandons passengers at the feet of mighty towers. Esther slumps, lets her eyes slip out of focus as the cityscape bleeds to monochrome. In the floodlit glare, she glimpses evidence of shadows trapped. Geometric silver planes intersecting where darkness melds with light. The Soldier will not shoot her in broad daylight. Not if she keeps moving – and she's always on the move. Once the package is delivered, she's off the grid – perhaps forever. She's waiting for instructions – that kind of message, she'll know it when she sees it.

The bus tacks wind traps between cold monoliths, moving ever closer to the city's pulsing heart. Skirts the parkland fringes; metal detectors gliding across fallen leaves. Students huddle, staring at their phones as old men doze fitfully under trees.

She shifts her eyes back into focus. Something is not right.

At the back of the bus, a shadow coalesces. She sees it only in reflection – when she turns, there's no one there. But she knows it's him, his resonance. The Soldier.

At the next stop she jumps down into the realm of politicians, lawyers, the specialists of Macquarie Street and their slick-suited retinues. The trim and streamlined lunchtime crowd flood from office to food court, returning in sweeping tides, balancing lattes and carb-free salads sheathed in rectangular plastic.

Tall buildings create wind corridors. It is cold out of the sun. Everybody strides with purpose. Nobody looks lost. Nobody ambles. Every single one of them wears black.

Esther is busy too. The drop will be monitored and she doesn't want to fumble it. So many things have changed: old buildings knocked down, replaced by new ones three times the size. Coffee shops nestled in their vestibules below ridiculously large attempts at corporate art. Blurred baristas and the hiss of steam. Seated people talking, always talking, gesticulating, sipping latte, glancing at their phones. Checking they're not late for something else.

Office people cannot be trusted. They bully each other like caged and beaten dogs, safely cocooned from the contemporary world, never going hungry, never too hot or cold, never had to watch a loved one die by their own hands.

She doesn't want to think about that now.

Esther is much older than she looks. She's plagued with memories of London, before the parent organisation was forcibly cleaved three ways: Propaganda; Active Operations; Planning. Before the establishment of Home Station, the temporary premises assigned to her unit were often both uncomfortable and unsuitable.

Operatives were required to possess subversive minds. Rebels, prepared to do whatever it took. Riots, boycotts, labour strikes. Assassinations, liquidation of traitors, military and industrial sabotage, the dissemination of relentless propaganda.

Recruitment was by word of mouth. Training took place in special schools secreted on remote country estates. Unarmed combat, secrecy, trade-craft, and silent killing, resistance to interrogation, parachuting, signaling, and sabotage. Weapons, explosive devices and booby traps.

These days, when pressed, sometimes Esther will claim to be a film student or a photographer. Where possible, she makes use of influential people and authorities to gain intelligence.

The bus made her uncomfortable. She does not fare well in cramped, confined spaces. On a bad day she will involuntarily experience flashbacks to that South Pacific skirmish, memories of zigzagging in a submarine, recycled air, warm, stale, and shit-scented, overlaid with the purr of distant diesel engines; and clammy close-pressed iron walls that run damp with condensation. Obtaining vital intelligence from Chinese agents, yet another in a long line of risky solo missions. The last one ended in betrayal and capture, nine months solitary in a dirt-floored prison cell. The guards had taken her out to shoot her, but something had gone wrong. A light so bright, she'd been blinded for a week. Woke up between crisp white sheets in an iron bed about as far from the Makassar Strait as it was possible to get.

And now this. Here.

She pushes blindly through the tide of suits, anonymous in her cargo pants and T-shirt. Heading for the Quay to lose herself amongst the garish crush of tourists. But, in an unanticipated flare of luminosity, an electronic billboard broadcasts an encoded message – a giant eye winking, just for her. The eye sends her off in the opposite direction; to Central Station under the clock where she will be expected to make the drop.

Chances are The Soldier saw the billboard the same time she did.

Chances are The Soldier will be lying in wait by the time she gets there, with his 7.62-mm. bolt-action Remington M24 and fixed-10 power scope, elevated to correct for ballistic arc.

4. This Broken Jaw of Our Lost Kingdoms

Nadya sits in the railway cafeteria, frowning at short skirts and bare midriffs. In this country, everybody thinks they're a celebrity. Nobody notices Nadya, despite her outlandish burgundy fur ensemble. She dresses well, still compensating for the deprivations of her squalid Soviet upbringing. The bare-walled room thirteen meters square reeking of kerosene desinsectal used to fight the communal flat's frequent bedbug infestations. The stinking lavatory, its black walls smeared with human shit graffiti. Twenty below zero, rooms filled with smoke from brick and pig-iron stoves. Seven decades on and she still remembers all of it. Casual observers do not see her history. Do not question why she overdresses in high-buttoning blouses, brooches, and embroidered cardigans. Thinning hair pinned back out of her eyes and, perhaps, a hat.

Two gentlemen directly in her line of sight dismiss her as irrelevant while checking the room for surveillance possibilities. A scalp hunter, one of them, she's certain. The other, a talent spotter, himself a famous raven back in the day. Not in her day, of course. Neither man was born back in her day.

She ignores them. Her years of professional espionage are well behind her. It's ordinary people she comes here to watch.

She purses her thin lips as, in the coffee queue, a man chasing a dropped coin is startled to discover himself standing on an enormous map of Australia fashioned from inlaid marble, states and territories delineated in shades of off-white, puce, and bone. He's staring at the compass inset in the speckled emerald ocean when the barista calls out that his coffee's ready.

Behind him, a middle-aged white woman in fussy pink leans on a stack of luggage almost her own height. A blind cane rests against the bags. Her husband approaches the coffee counter, resplendent in white chinos and white shoes, a pale blue shirt crisply ironed. Navy blue jacket with smart brass buttons lend him a maritime air.

The dumpy waitress taking his order's long red hair is home-dyed. Her Irish brogue is broad and pleasing. She waddles across the floor to deliver a triangle of wrapped sandwiches to a young seated couple sharing a pastry; him talking, her listening intently, luggage huddled roughly around their feet. His jacket folded and draped over an extended suitcase handle. A crust pinched delicately between her thumb and forefinger. Red-painted nails, two takeaway cups nestled to protect her skin from scalding tea.

Nadya's gaze travels beyond them, surveying the concourse, the space beneath the station clock crowded with young families and groups of Asian tourists. Couples pushing wheeled suitcases glide across smoothly polished marble. Pigeons dodge and flutter beneath careless feet. A scruffy bearded man with lost expression passes another fitter man pushing a bicycle, its spokes whirring gently.

A young white woman stands solo beneath the clock, waiting. Short hair. Cargo pants. Camera slung across her torso. She flinches as a sullen man with heavy black-rimmed glasses and a leather jacket pushes past her clutching a box of tulips.

The clock itself is an ancient thing – perhaps as old as Nadya – round and solid, heavy-looking, suspended by taut wires. Pale, set with thick black Roman numerals. Below, a vast, imposing electronic Next Departures board, timetables streaming in endless loops. Corrugated plastic sheeting filters natural light from above, pinned in place by pale green beams.

There are ghosts here. She can feel them.

Nadya nods approvingly at a smart young Asian girl's powder-blue trench coat, yellow handbag hooked over one arm, long legs and shiny black patent leather shoes. The girl checks her phone. She is waiting for someone. Everyone under the clock is waiting for someone.

Back inside the cafeteria, Mr. Maritime sets two coffees carefully on a nearby tabletop. Mutters something, takes the cane and heads for the cafeteria's heavy side doors, tapping all the way to the public toilets. Nadya's surprised to discover him the blind one, not his altogether more fragile-looking wife.

The raven and the scalp hunter sip coffee without concern. They do not notice Nadya's fascination with the concourse. The blond barista is an asset. He sees Nadya every other week. She blends into the scenery, with her Devonshire teas and second pot of hot water, stretching out the first to fill in time. He'd peg her as an Aussie or a Brit, if pushed. A nice old lady, harmless. Overdressed. Lonely, perhaps, with nowhere else to go.

The barista has been trained to penetrate facades. He stares idly into space as the milk-frother screeches, venting great jets of scalding steam.

An old grey man in a ratty jumper taps past with his walking stick, coughing, hat flaps tight over his ears, metal hitting marble with loud thunks.

A second screech in competition with the first – chair legs dragging. Nadya is clumsy when she rises, bending arthritically to hook her leather handbag over one arm. She walks with an ivory-handled cane even though she does not need it. The cane once belonged to her husband, Borya.

She bumps the former raven's chair. Turns slowly to make her apologies. Up close, yes, he is still handsome despite the scar, probably still well adept at entrapment. When her arm brushes his, she takes pride in his momentary flash of concern. For a second – just a second – he considered she might not be what she appears.

She apologises profusely, then ambles on her way. She did not do anything so obvious as tamper with his drink, nor press a tracking device the size of a teardrop onto the expensive fabric of his jacket.

Nadya heads for the taxi rank at the far side of the concourse, berating herself for wasting so much time in this miserable place. She comes here because of *him*, despite the constant irritation at having to fend off with a brusque, gloved wave the stoned beggars pestering the cafeteria tables. She passes under the clock, moves on to Platform 4 – the last place she saw her Borya alive. Borya, who'd survived the Great Patriotic War and the German Fascists only to succumb to pancreatic cancer in a land he had not chosen as his own.

She's standing there struggling with her memories when she senses *something* materialise nearby. She stiffens, recognises its peculiar metallic scent, even though it has been many years and she was certain this country was a safe one. The creature is a shadow soldier – she is never wrong about their kind.

She turns slowly, carefully, glancing back, presuming the scalp hunter or the raven to be the creature's mark.

The shadow travels quickly, striding brazenly out in the open. It fears nothing – already it has claimed a place beneath the station clock, looming over the short-haired girl in the cargo pants and t-shirt with the camera.

Nadya knows it is too late. That she can do nothing. That she cannot bear to watch. *We lost the wars. We failed in our duty. We let these creatures through and there's no turning back.* Her rheumy, tear-filled eyes flick up to the garish, over-lit TV screen hanging high above the turnstiles, a mess of flashy sports footage and talking heads. The screen is so poorly calibrated that the skin of the smiling blonde advertising kitchen appliances is the colour of scalded lobster.

Nadya squeezes her eyes shut. By the time she is able to open them, the girl with the cargo pants and camera has vanished. In her place stands a yellow sign explaining that all Blue Mountains inner city trains between Central and Penrith have been cancelled.

5. In This Valley of Dying Stars

Hours have passed with her hidden in the wardrobe – Arpita marks time by the cramping in her legs and the unbearable pressure building in her bladder. She's been too terrified to move in case the apartment's two occupants hear her. It will not take much for them to investigate, to open the heavy wardrobe door. That they haven't already is some kind of miracle, perhaps one sent by the gods who abandoned her on the golden sands of a foreign shore.

There are two of them – one definitely a man, no question, but the other... she's not certain. A woman, perhaps, with a deep, rich voice, or perhaps another man, a younger one. At first they banged around the kitchen opening cupboards, speaking something sounding much like Russian. She knows practically nothing about that country, only what she has seen on television. What she does know is that if they find her, they will kill her. They will presume she is a spy. They will not believe she is a housekeeper, randomly assigned, never visiting the same apartment twice. That she doesn't know who she works for. She took the job when it was offered because, back then, she would have taken *any* job. She had no papers and was relieved to learn there would not be drugs or immoral acts involved. Only for her to unpack, stack, clean, dust and vacuum, move things around and, occasionally, speak nonsense down a phone line. Sentences such as: "There are no eyes here in this valley of dying stars," and "Lips that would kiss form prayers to broken stone."

Just a voice instructing her to speak such words, hang up, then quickly leave. Pack up the vacuum and close the curtains maybe – if there's time. Time, apparently, is always of the essence.

Arpita has been trying to understand the random urge that made her climb inside the big old wardrobe. Perhaps the memory of Aunt Laksha, or was it because, so very briefly, the act had made her feel utterly alive? The same pounding-heart-inside-her-chest she'd experienced when she climbed into the boat that brought her and 554 desperate strangers to this country.

Tight-packed in like human sardines, passed from open boat to open boat, tossed over the sides like sacks of grain. No shelter from the sun or stinging rain, each boat bigger than the last one, everybody soaked to the skin and retching as they bobbed and lurched and panicked in near-pitch darkness.

She is not supposed to be here, not supposed to see or overhear. Not supposed to stand out in any way.

Her third assignment was the first in which the term 'safehouse' was spoken. She'd never considered these strange apartments safe. Safe from whom or what is never specified. Safe from the outside world? She can never feel safe within such cold white walls. She is frightened of the ringing phone, of the faceless people speaking down the line. What they might say in response to her strange poetry. Afraid one of them might ask for papers she does not possess. She is not supposed to be here, yet here she is, luckier than so many of the others.

Her bladder is about to burst. Somehow she'd managed to keep her dignity on those terrible leaky boats and she is damned if she will lose it in this place. She holds her breath and pushes the wardrobe door, gently gently, the sharp stab of afternoon light blinding.

She makes no sound as bare toes brush nylon carpet. The double bed has not been slept in. Dust mites swirl above its drab print calico. Soft light floods the room, old and yellowed, matching the crockery she so dutifully stacks in cupboards.

No sounds emanate from the lounge. The door remains ajar, she can see inside – and the reason for the silence. A man lies face up on the carpet, a dark stain pooled beneath. No sign of the other one, the one she could not be certain of.

She's desperate to relieve herself, but she has to get out of there. She remembers her shoulder bag, retrieves it from the wardrobe along with her shoes – she'd almost forgotten them too.

She does not want to see the dead man's face but in the end she can't help herself. Glassy eyes stare into nothing. He might have been handsome, a small scar on one cheek. A cleft chin, day-old stubble.

She's made it three steps down the landing, door pulled shut behind her when the phone begins to ring, hollow chimes much louder than they should be.

The dim stairwell thickens with moving shadows that seem almost alive. Arpita hurries and does not look back. Same here as on the journey out of Cisarua. Looking back never offers any solace. Looking back, so often, is the thing that tears your heart out in the end.

This story coagulated over a period of about ten years, a pastiche of unfinished fiction pieces that had failed in their quickening mashed up with my own real-life experiences, observances and details. It's what happened when my love of spy fiction went head on to interface with spec fic realms.

ABOUT THE AUTHOR

Cat Sparks is a multi-award-winning Australian author, editor and artist. Former fiction editor of *Cosmos Magazine*, she has also dabbled as a kitchen hand, video store clerk, assistant library technician, media monitor, political and archaeological photographer, graphic designer, guest lecturer, festival director, panellist, fiction judge, essayist, creative writing teacher and manager of Agog! Press, which produced ten anthologies of new speculative fiction.

Cat has a BA in visual arts (CAI), a postgraduate certificate in editing and publishing (UTS) and a PhD in creative writing (Curtin), the latter concerning the intersection of ecocatastrophe science fiction and contemporary climate fiction.

In January 2012 Cat was one of 12 students chosen to participate in Margaret Atwood's The Time Machine Doorway workshop as part of that year's Key West Literary Seminar. Her participation was funded by an Australia Council emerging writers grant.

Cat's debut novel *Lotus Blue* (Skyhorse, 2017) was shortlisted for the Compton Crook, Aurealis and Ditmar Awards. Her collection, *The Bride Price* (Ticonderoga, 2013) was nominated for an Aurealis Award and won the 2014 Ditmar for Best Collected Work.

Seventy-three of her short stories have been published since the turn of the millennium and her 24 awards for writing, editing and art include the Peter McNamara Conveners Award twice for services to Australia's speculative fiction industry.

Cat is a keen traveller currently obsessed with photographing cheeky parrots and grungy walls.

You can find Cat online at: www.catsparks.net and @catsparx.

NEW FROM NEWCON PRESS

Nick Wood – Water Must Fall
In 2048, climate change has brought catastrophe and water companies play god with the lives of millions. In Africa, Graham Mason struggles to save his marriage to Lizette, who is torn between loyalty to their relationship and to her people. In California, Arthur Green battles to find ways of rooting out corruption, even when his family are threatened by those he seeks to expose. As the planet continues to thirst and slowly perish, will water ever fall?

Ken MacLeod – Selkie Summer
Set on the Isle of Skye, Ken MacLeod's *Selkie Summer* is a rich contemporary fantasy steeped in Celtic lore, nuclear submarines and secrets. Seeking to escape Glasgow, student Siobhan Ross takes a holiday job on Skye, only to find herself the focus of unwanted attention, unwittingly embroiled in political intrigue and the shifting landscape of international alliances. At its heart, *Selkie Summer* is a love story: passionate, unconventional, and totally enchanting.

Ian Whates – Dark Angels Rising
The Dark Angels – a notorious band of brigands turned popular heroes who disbanded a decade ago – are all that stands between humanity and disaster. Drake, Leesa, Jen and their fellow Angels must prevent a resurrected Elder – last of a long dead alien race – from reclaiming the scientific marvels of its people. Supported by a renegade military unit and the criminal organisation Saflik, the Elder is set on establishing itself as God over all humankind.

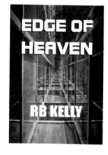

RB Kelly – Edge of Heaven
Creo Basse, a city built to house the world's dispossessed. In the dark, honeycomb districts of the lower city, Turrow searches for black-market meds for his epileptic sister when he encounters one of the many ways Creo can kill a person. A tinderbox of unrest finally ignites when a deadly plague breaks out, which the authorities claim is a terrorist weapon manufactured by extremist artificial humans hiding in the city, but is the truth darker still?